## INTERNATIONAL ACCLAIM FOR A

"Unflinching and compassionate ... ie
Man Booker Prize finalist *Cloud*

"Excellent: smart, funny and authentic." —Joe Dunthorne

"Gavron is one of the most original and powerful writers on the Israeli scene. His clear and honest writing blasts right through the clichés and the politically correct surface to touch the chaotic and ambiguous core of the Israeli identity." —Etgar Keret

"Gavron offers an unusual perspective on Palestinian suicide bombings in this offbeat, often satirical political thriller. . . . Gavron sheds light on the region's intractable conflict by allowing readers to relate to Fahmi as well as to Croc." —*Publishers Weekly*

"This tragi-comedy is to be recommended to everyone who has an interest in the special Israeli view of the current state of affairs." —*Amnesty Journal*

"Shrewdly, rhythmically and provocatively, Gavron connects the life stories of two men who share a fate: Israel, the land where one must choose a side, whether one will or not." —*Stern* (Germany)

"It is the two main characters who bring readers closer to the Middle East conflict than ever the nightly news could. . . . Read it." —*Hamburger Morgenpost* (Germany)

"Sparkling refractions of the everyday insanity in the Middle East." —*Badischen Neuesten Nachrichten* (The Netherlands)

"The best modern novel to come out of Israel in the last years." —Radio Gong

"This novel is cleverly constructed, very contemporary in its subject matter and, because of Gavron's critically equitable narrative posture, exceptionally interesting." —Sigrid Löffler

## ALSO BY ASSAF GAVRON

FICTION

*Hydromania*
*Moving*
*Sex in the Cemetery*
*Ice*

NONFICTION

*Eating Standing Up*

# ALMOST DEAD

## A NOVEL

ASSAF GAVRON

HARPER PERENNIAL

NEW YORK • LONDON • TORONTO • SYDNEY • NEW DELHI • AUCKLAND

Published by HarperCollins Publishers Ltd.

First Canadian edition

Originally published under the title *Tanin Pigua* in Israel in 2006
by Kinneret-Zmora-Bitan.



HarperCollins Publishers Ltd
2 Bloor Street East, 20th Floor
Toronto, Ontario, Canada
M4W 1A8

*www.harpercollins.ca*

Library and Archives Canada Cataloguing in Publication
information is available upon request.

ISBN 978-1-55468-679-7

Printed in the United States of America
RRD 9 8 7 6 5 4 3 2 1

*For Mum and Dad*

'Lost ground can be regained – lost time never.'

Franklin Delano Roosevelt

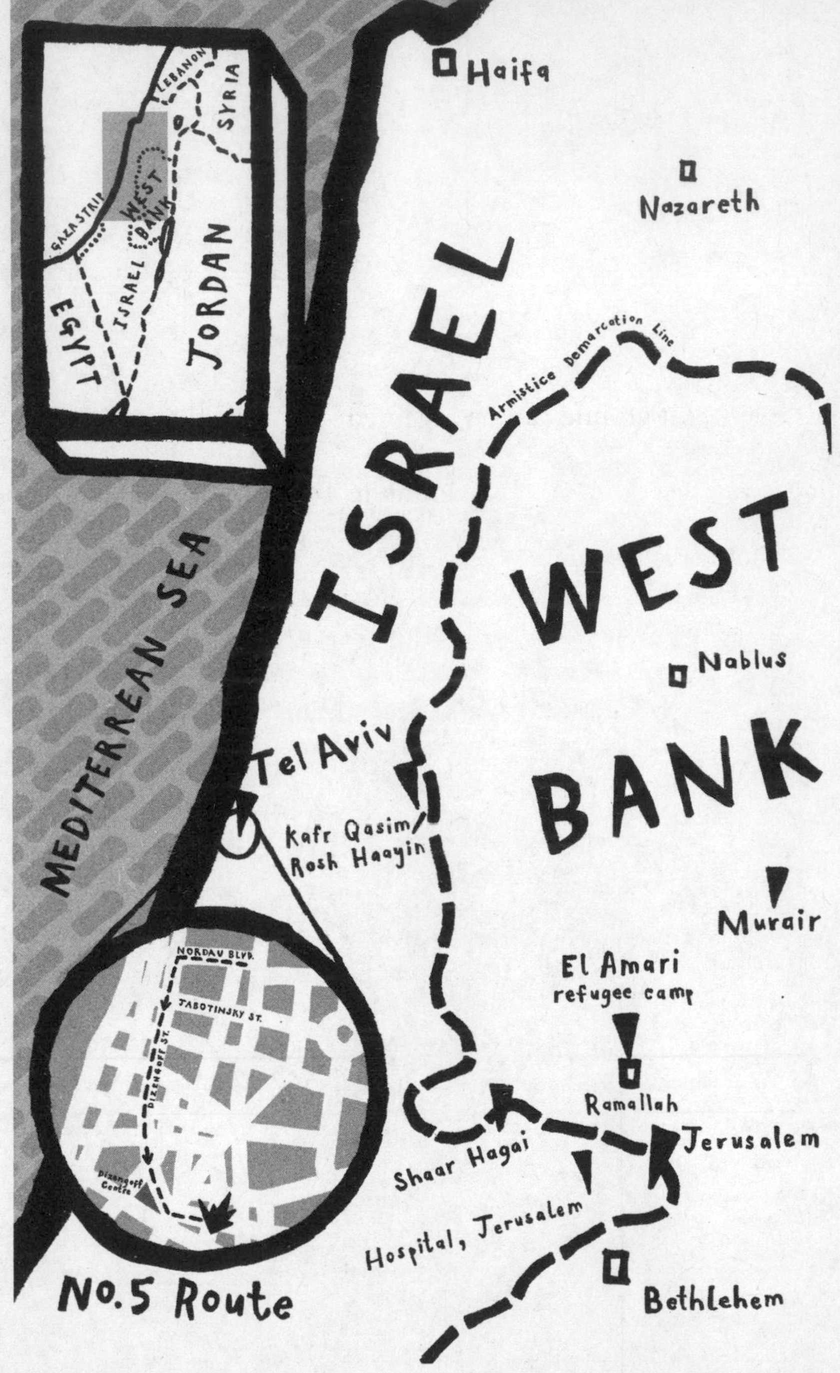

LEBANON
SYRIA
GAZA STRIP
WEST BANK
ISRAEL
JORDAN
EGYPT
Haifa
Nazareth
ISRAEL
Armistice Demarcation Line
MEDITERREAN SEA
WEST BANK
Nablus
Tel Aviv
Kafr Qasim/
Rosh Haayin
Murair
El Amari
refugee camp
Ramallah
Jerusalem
Shaar Hagai
Hospital, Jerusalem
Bethlehem
NORDAU BLVD.
JABOTINSKY ST.
DIZENGOFF ST.
Dizengoff Centre
No.5 Route

# 1

I climbed aboard the Little No. 5 as I did every morning on my way to work. 'Little No. 5' is what I call the minibus-sized cab which follows the route of the No. 5 bus. It's actually a cross between a bus and a cab. You get the best of both worlds – the familiar route and the cheapness of the bus, but they've got the speed of a cab and you can hail them and get off where you like.

And since there were bombs all the time, I only ever took Little No. 5s to work and back. Even if a real No. 5 arrived at my stop before a Little No. 5 I let it pass. A bus was too easy a target for a terrorist – especially the No. 5, which was almost always full and had already been bombed. I wasn't really all that sure about doing this, but Duchi made me swear never to take the bus. And they were never going to bomb a Little No. 5. For one thing, they can only take ten people, eleven with the driver. Plus there's only the one door, at the front, so the driver can see exactly who gets on board.

That day I got on at the usual place. The time was around nine in the morning. A pale midwinter sun was hanging in a translucent sky; wet leaves covered the boulevard.

The driver was Ziona. She was the only woman driver

in the Little No. 5 fleet but she was no pushover. She was always yelling down the radio at the dispatcher in the office, complaining about some guy who'd dared to overtake her or cut her up, or wondering how the hell that Jumbo had gotten so far ahead of her. A Jumbo's a bus, in the Little No. 5 drivers' dialect. The dispatcher was always telling her to shut up and stop hogging the frequency. Maybe she ought to chill out? Maybe she ought to stop drilling a hole in everybody's head, including the heads of the passengers?

And Ziona would take a drag from the cigarette she liked to hang outside her window and whisper to herself as she exhaled, 'Oh, ffffuuuckk your fucking hole in the head!'

We were heading down Dizengoff Street when an elderly lady turned to me. Quietly she said: 'Doesn't that man look suspicious?'

With her eyes she indicated a dark guy at the front. We were sitting at the back. He was wearing a grey wool hat and holding a suit in a suit bag.

'Come on, don't exaggerate,' I said. 'He looks fine to me.'

But I kept looking at him. I thought about the fact that explosive belts were the latest thing – the flavour of the month. Explosive belts must be pretty flat if you can strap them round your body. Just possibly there was one in his suit bag.

'Don't you worry about it,' I told the old lady. 'It'll be fine.'

She gave me a sour look and tried another guy who was sitting at the back with us. She whispered something in the other guy's ear, and he looked towards her suspect and a second later shook his head and flapped his hand. Now I was certain. Just paranoid. Why is everyone so paranoid in this country? Can't dark guys get on buses with suit bags any more?

The old lady called over to Ziona.

'Can I get off at the next corner?'

Ziona looked in the mirror with her big eyes. 'Of course you can, honey,' she said. Ziona was a nice woman. She had short hair and wide shoulders. She's dead now, of course. 'You talking to me, Yossi?' she jabbered into the radio. 'Hey, who's that? You got a driver called Morris next to you? Morris, the driver of Seventy?' Yossi didn't answer. Another driver was saying, 'Hey, what is this, the cemetery? We got no passengers today? Ten minutes and nobody gets on.' Someone else was saying, 'At least you get to see some of these chicks' bellies . . .' and Yossi cut across them: 'Will you cut this crap out! Ziona, you're doing it again, and everyone else piles in after you with their chatter.' Ziona swore to herself. The radio was tuned to a news show. They were talking about a bomb in Wadi Ara. The passengers were listening quietly. Then there was a song.

The old lady got off at Jabotinsky Street. She didn't trust our judgement. On her way out she gave the dark guy a long look. He looked back at her. I didn't think at that moment that his look meant anything. If I did have a sneaking suspicion that she might have a point, that I ought to get off too, just to be on the safe side, I blotted it out immediately. I didn't have time for the safe side. Who has?

'Everyone's under pressure, eh?' the other guy at the back said. He had a little goatee and big aviator sunglasses with mirrored lenses. His hair was the colour of honey, held back with plenty of gel, darkening into curls at the back. Cool, at least in his own eyes. Pleasant smile. Giora, I know now. Giora Guetta, from Jerusalem. I know plenty of things now.

'This paranoia . . .' I said. 'People are completely crazy.'

'He looks OK to you, right?'

I looked once more towards the dark guy. I wasn't sure. Who could be sure?

'Yeah, no problem with him,' I said.

Each of us looked through his window. Winter, but the sun was out. I watched the tree-lined canyon of Dizengoff slide by, the parade of designer clothing shops, an ad for the movie *Monsters Inc.*, a small Gad Dairy truck passing. A builder got on and started shouting at Ziona.

'Why didn't the last two stop for me?' The builder was the father of two girls. I read it later on Ynet.

'Don't get mad, honey,' Ziona said. 'They were probably full.'

'Come on, people, my time is precious,' the builder said.

'Everybody's time is precious, honey.'

If there's one thing I like about the Little No. 5s, it's their efficiency with time. I know something about this: I work in the business of time. For example, all the handling of money and change is done during the ride, not like on the bus, where everyone's got to finish paying while it's still standing at the stop. You give someone sitting in front of you some money and they pass it down, from passenger to passenger to the driver, and your change comes back up, from hand to hand back into your palm. Money circulating efficiently from stranger to stranger, like the bus's blood. Or the way the drivers change money with other drivers: they arrange it over the radio, and when they pass each other they'll stop for a couple of seconds and, one-two, it's done. Or their skill on the road – the way they improvise, overtaking cars and Jumbos by driving on the other side of the road, stealing valuable seconds at traffic lights, avoiding traffic jams by cutting through narrow streets off their usual routes: decisive actions. It's a pleasure to watch them.

Somebody touched my shoulder. I looked up in alarm

and saw it was only the guy in the mirrored shades, with a PalmPilot in his hand. I thought to myself: what are you showing off for? I've got a Palm too. Actually, that wasn't entirely true. My Palm had stopped working a couple of months before.

'Listen,' he said, 'if something happens to me, I want you to tell my girlfriend in Jerusalem, Shuli – I want you to tell her . . .' He was thinking, but he couldn't seem to find the right words. I chuckled. What was he talking about, if something happened to him? Him too? The old lady, OK, she'd probably been paranoid since the Holocaust, but him?

'If something happens,' I said, 'I'm hardly going to be the one left to pass on messages, am I? Don't worry, man, nothing's going to happen.'

'I *know* nothing's going to happen,' he said, 'but if it does . . . If you want, I can also send a message to someone, like, if I . . . you know.'

'No,' I said reflexively. Then I thought: maybe I *should* send a message to someone? Maybe I should get my will written? You never know. I thought that if there was anyone I would leave anything to, it would have to be Duchi. Despite everything.

And then I thought again. Damn – what the hell am I doing, on a bus, on the way to work, worrying about my will? How did I get here? On the back of the bus in front there was a picture of one of those red-jacketed guardsmen in London. It said: 'Going abroad? Take your mobile!' On the radio, a man who was driving behind the bus that was blown up in Wadi Ara told Rafi Reshef, 'I'm optimistic, optimistic, optimistic, optimistic.' We were getting to the busier part of Dizengoff Street, where the towers of the Centre loom and the city crush grows denser. A phone rang and someone answered. I got my little notebook out – since my Palm stopped working I'm back in the Middle Ages – and wrote: *Check again how much rent house New Zealand. Talk w/ Duchi about it.*

'You from Jerusalem?' I said to the guy. 'Me too, originally.' But I saw he was thinking about other things. His expression was serious. Later I'd think about how people sometimes have premonitions. How we found all kinds of clues and hints that Danny Lam left before he was killed, like the poem he wrote a month before, and how soldiers who die are always supposed to say goodbye in a special way in their last phone call. How people always said things in the final days; how they'd had a feeling that *something was going to happen*. On the other hand, everybody says these things all the time. You just pay attention to the ones who actually die. I myself had a sign that I was about to die. One time I saw these birds flying in the dark. I thought: birds flying in the dark, weird, it must be a sign . . . and yet I'm still alive. Even now. Even after the Little No. 5, after Shaar Hagai, after Emek Refa'im.

After Fahmi.

'Stop being a fool,' I said to Giora Guetta. 'Don't think about it.'

He smiled. I stood up, waved goodbye to him and got off the Little No. 5 without a word. On my way out I didn't look at the dark guy, the suicide bomber, again. I think I didn't look at him because I didn't believe he was a terrorist, but maybe I didn't look at him because I didn't want to embarrass him.

I walked into the mall at the base of the Dizengoff Centre through Gate 3. With all the bombs and precautions, the entrance to the Centre looks like the gate to an army camp: barriers, guards and metal detectors that always, always beep. The guards never check the source of the beep so why do they run the detector over us? Just to send magnetic waves through our bones?

Every day I'm treated differently entering the mall. Sometimes they might ask me to show my wallet or phone, other times they just pass the detector over me, or let me through and only then stop me, as if I'd somehow gone through too quickly, or looked suspiciously relieved. One time, immediately after a big bomb, they started asking for ID cards and added another guard near the elevators to the offices. This checkpoint was about seven metres past the first one. Two days later they got rid of the second guard. Another day passed and the ID card wasn't necessary. After the next big bomb you needed it again.

So even when they let me pass and then stopped and groped me seven metres after someone else had; even when I had to take my bag off my back, unzip it, take my wallet out, take the ID card out, open it in front of them and watch them not even glance at it – I might as well have stuck a picture of Arafat in there: they'd have waved me through anyway – I decided to let them get on with their job. Not because I think there's no alternative, but because I no longer have the strength to object. What good would it do if I complained or refused to show my ID? I see people arguing and I can understand, but it never helps them. It just slows them down. It's like footballers arguing with the referee after he gives a penalty – was there ever a player in the history of football who changed a ref's mind?

That day, there was a blood donation unit at the gate. It's important to donate. They say there's not enough blood in the hospitals because of all the bombs. But I didn't have time. I went up to the office. I didn't hear the explosion. Everybody else did, people down at street level, people up in our office on the twenty-third floor. Bombs are something you hear. They're loud. But I was in the elevator and didn't hear it. Not that the boom made such an impression at first. There are booms all the time: sonic aircraft booms, building-site booms, all the accidents and bangs and crashes of a city. So everyone in the office was looking calm. I popped my head into all the rooms on the way to my own room and said hello, as I did every morning, and people smiled and said good morning, as they did every morning. In my room I said hello to Ron and Ronen, and Ron said, 'You hear the boom?'

'What boom?'

It took a few minutes until we realised that there had been a suicide bomb and that it had happened in the centre of Tel Aviv. We turned on the TV in the kitchen and saw the map with the little flame-thing that shows the location of the bomb, and saw it was up the road, at the south end of Dizengoff Street, near the Habima Theatre, and they were saying it was probably a bus.

Everyone in the office was watching the TV. Those who hadn't arrived yet wouldn't arrive for a while because the roads were blocked. According to Ynet there were ten Israelis killed and one suicide bomber. The result: 10–1. The Jews lose again, or at any rate it's a scoreline that's going to need quite a bit of a positive gloss.

Soon I was busy answering the phone and telling everyone I was alive. 'No, they didn't get me yet,' I told the callers. After a few calls, I started answering the phone with, 'This is Croc and I'm alive, who wants to know?' I talked to people I hadn't talked to for years.

'Lucky there are bombs once in a while,' I told them, 'at least we get to talk.'

I started work: I had to talk to our Swiss client, Ivan, work out what he required; I made calls and wrote emails and documents, and at some point Ron said, 'No. 5 minibus – you use that thing, don't you?' I lifted my eyes from the screen.

'What?'

'No. 5 minibus?'

'I call it the Little No. 5. What about it?'

'The bomb. It was a No. 5 minibus that was bombed. Your bus, isn't it?'

'Really?'

My first thought was: fuck, how will I get to work from now on? Those fuckers hit every possible means of transportation. Am I going to have to take cabs now? Buy another car? Too expensive . . .

I entered Ynet again and read the update. Every passenger on the minibus killed. But still it didn't seem like mine. Somehow it seemed it couldn't be the right time or place. There were dozens of minibuses en route at any given time. 'Yeah, I go on one every day,' I was telling everyone nonchalantly. 'Unbelievable. The bomber could have been on the same No. 5 I was on. Who knows?'

Only then did I remember the dark guy and his suit bag, and the old lady who suspected him, whom I'd told not to worry. And the other guy who asked me to send some unspecified message to his girlfriend. This is crazy, I thought, I have to get hold of this guy, and then the phone rang.

'Croc, I'm alive,' I answered.

'Uh huh,' said Jimmy. 'Why alive?'

'Why not?'

'Listen, next week there's a meeting in Brussels, it's important, it's with . . .' Here he mentioned the name of a large Belgian telecoms company. His accent was terrible. 'You coming with me?'

'Do I have a choice?'

'No. I'm telling Gili to book us flights and hotel rooms. Get ultra-prepared. Make sure you're ready with all the presentations. And don't forget tomorrow's company meeting.' Jimmy ended the conversation without waiting for an answer. He does it all the time. He explained once that he didn't have the luxury of waiting for an answer. Jimmy's real name, by the way, is Rafi. Rafi Rafael, or Rafraf, as he's known in our room. When he was an officer in the air force he ran their time management unit. Now he's the CEO of Time's Arrow.

I called Duchi and left her a message: 'Hi. I wasn't killed in the suicide attack in case you're interested. I'm in Brussels next week. Bye.'

And then they started talking about the female driver of the minibus involved in the bomb attack, and it was only then that I understood. Ziona was the only woman driver in the Little No. 5 fleet. I knew it because she was always bringing it up. She was proud of it. My heart stopped beating and my breath got stuck in my throat. And then they started up again, because that's what the heart and lungs always do, when you're alive.

I jogged back to the kitchen. The TV was still on though everyone was back in their rooms. Danny Ronen, the military correspondent on Channel 2, mentioned the name Ziona Levi. A nervous little chuckle escaped my mouth. I went to the bathroom and put my hands, clenched tightly into fists, on the marble. I felt a wave of pain and nausea washing over me, tried to breathe deeply, looked at the mirror, and laughed again. This laughing face: whose was it? It didn't look familiar. Didn't look like mine. The blood was hammering in my temples. I felt very close to passing out. I had to get out, to breathe fresh air. I threw water on my face and made it down to the street and walked towards the site of the bombing, up Dizengoff Street, past the shoemaker's and up the hill, under the tunnel formed by the canopy of branches, and turned right past the gallery. I stopped opposite the museum and concert hall, just before the Habima Theatre, on the side where the post office is. In the time that had passed they'd reopened the road to traffic. Everything had been cleaned up and the wreckage of the minibus had been towed away. The deceased had been removed: all that belonged to them, all that had been them. There weren't even police barriers up any more.

Miraculously – they always use that word, miraculously – not one of the passers-by or drivers near by had been injured. Only a single car parked on the side of the road was totalled (the owner was a guy named Amir who'd just popped into the post office to pay a parking fine – and it turned out he never got any insurance money or compensation: because he was parked in a no-parking zone). A bus passed, groaning and spitting black smoke like an old man hawking phlegm. I looked at the wet patches on the road where the blood had been washed away. The pale sun was gloomy and silent. The traffic was running normally. Two and a half hours since the bomb went off, and it was as if nothing had happened, or almost. Some drivers were slowing down to peer at the wet patches before driving on. On the pavement beside me kids were lighting candles and people were shouting or crying. They had their solutions. They announced their solutions. They said: kill, retaliate, blast them to bits, withdraw . . .

I turned my head away from them towards a gap between two buildings. I wasn't looking for anything. I've no idea why my eyes were drawn there. Maybe it was the tree standing there, an old olive tree that looked out of place among the palms, that didn't seem to belong in the little alley. I looked at the olive tree and moved as if compelled towards it, and that's when I saw, a little above where the trunk fissured, cradled in the crook of one of the bigger branches, the PalmPilot of the guy who'd been sitting next to me.

# 2

*'Good morning, Fahmi.'*

If I am dreaming, this dream is never-ending . . .

*'How are we doing today? Let's have a peek at those pupils . . .'*

Hate this light. Hate the wash. Why can't she leave me alone?

*'Time for your wash, Fahmi. Your favourite part of the morning, ha ha . . .'*

Go away, Svetlana. Fuck you.

*'We are mad today, aren't we? What a face you're making! Let's have a look at what you've got on later. Oh – you've got a deep massage this morning. What fun!'*

I'm floating in the sea. I can see the shore but I can't reach it. The tide keeps me away. I see Bilahl on the beach.

*'Here. That's better. Come on now.'*

I'm not here, I am . . . where was I before she came to disturb me?

*'And visitors in the afternoon! So who's coming to visit you? Who's he going to be? Or she?'*

Where was I? I'm floating in the sea. Where's Mother? Lulu? Rana? Where was I before she disturbed me? With

Bilahl . . . with Croc . . . somewhere . . . in the village? In the camp? In Tel Aviv?

In Tel Aviv.

Shafiq started everything, in Tel Aviv. He wanted to smoke a cigarette with the driver. That's what the driver said afterwards. He took off the belt, locked it in the trunk, they smoked the cigarette and then he put on the belt in the back seat. That all happened when they were still in Jaffa. Then he took a cab to Tel Aviv . . . Bilahl had found someone who knew the Jews, knew Tel Aviv well. He told Shafiq to go to a crossroads near Rabin Square, where they have their demonstrations and crowds gather. Explained to him where he should stand, which corner and what time – a place where there was always a gridlock at rush hour. But then we saw the news, on Channel 2 and Al-Jazeera: he'd got on a bus. No square. No crossroads . . .

What the hell are you – Svetlana . . .?

*'Good boy, Fahmi. Don't make a face, it's only water. Don't you want to look pretty for your visitors today? So just let me get behind your ears . . .'*

Stop it, you fucking whore! What visitors? Where am I? Where was I? Floating among my fragments of memory . . . and you're mixing them up. Getting my wires crossed. Crossroads. Shafiq . . .

Shafiq. He didn't do what the guy who knew Tel Aviv told him. Went with the shaved cheeks and the haircut and the clothes Bilahl gave him, and then got on a bus. Only a little bus, they explained on TV. Danny Ronen, the clown with the eyebrows. How did he get there? How had it been, getting on, paying, waiting? And how must he have felt, a moment before heaven? He must have felt whole. A moment away from heaven. The best feeling he'd ever had, better than anything he had imagined. The moment of his life. And me, with Croc and the green grenade in Tel Aviv, how did *I* feel?

Shafiq would have been sure at the end. Not like me. The light turned green and the driver of the little bus would have pushed the pedal and turned the wheel. Shafiq, and everybody around him, had all lived their lives to get to this moment. Everything heading towards this moment. Every drag on a cigarette, every blink, every swallow of saliva, every emotion, every motion, every breath, every thought, every word anyone on the little bus had ever said had been headed towards the moment when Shafiq stood up and turned his back to the passengers and pushed the button, and his body blossomed with the fullness of his power; his clean, his warm, his Babylonian power . . .

*'That's better. Nice and clean. You can hardly even see the scratch on your forehead. I've got patients here who are totally deformed. Damaged for ever. But you're whole, Fahmi. Perfect for your visits. So, then. Who's coming to see you today? Who would you like? Your dad? Your little sister? Your cute girlfriend?'*

Oh, shut up, you goddamned Jewish whore! Losing my thread . . .

Father. A good man. A sad man, since Mother . . .

'Fahmi, I will not put up with this. Not you.'

'I'm not doing anything, Father.' He was standing right in front of me, obscuring the TV, with his solid grey mane like a lion's. His brown eyes were angry.

'Father, please don't stand there. Let me see, please.'

'I know what you're doing. I know about Bilahl. He's a lost cause, but you? You promised me. You promised to go to Bir Zeit University – you're going to give me a heart attack . . .'

'I will go. I'll fulfil my promise. Please don't worry.'

Later, Bilahl would attack me: Why do you apologise? Why do you grovel in front of him? He's let them humiliate him and walk all over him his whole life. That's what's the matter with him . . .

Oh no. No! Don't touch me there! Oh, fuck you, you filthy Jewish whore!

*'Well done, Fahmi. Now try not to get excited, OK? I'm just going to wipe here. Slowly, very slowly, ever so softly . . . Just going to get you all clean and pretty and smelling good for your massage and your guests. You like that, don't you?'*

# 3

My name is Eitan Enoch but everyone calls me Croc. Because: Eitan Enoch = 'Hey, Taninoch!' That got shortened to 'Hey, Tanin!' And in Hebrew, Tanin means a crocodile. That's the evolution of my name. Enoch itself, it turns out, evolved from Chanoch, the father of Methuselah, the oldest guy in the Bible. A settler told me that once.

I grew up in Jerusalem but moved to Tel Aviv, where I work for Time's Arrow, or *Taimaro!,* as our Japanese customers like to pronounce it. A year and a half ago my older brother left Israel with his wife and three boys because of the bombs. We've got a rich grandmother in Maryland who invited us all to come and live there. My younger sister Dafdaf wants to go too, with her husband. All of us have American citizenship because our parents are from there: my father grew up in Maryland – so green and pleasant, so relaxed and comfortable – and Mom's from Denver. They came to Israel before I was born. God knows what they were thinking of. Every time I visit Maryland, I ask myself that question. Maybe they were excited by the young Jewish state. Maybe it seemed exotic. Or maybe it was that Dad had big ideas: he wanted to teach the young country how to spread peanut butter on its bread. Efraim Enoch from America: the capitalist, the entrepreneur, the great peanut butter importer. But the land of the Jews didn't have time for peanut butter, or, at any rate, not for the one he imported.

When I see them now, it's as if every bomb blows another brick out of the wall of the decision to emigrate. Their mistake. They can't blame us for running away, but their hearts are breaking. It's difficult, what they did: leaving the comfortable life in America while they were still young, travelling to a new, hot, primitive country and trying to build something from nothing: a family, a business, a state. They called it Zionism. And then they had to watch everything get blown to smithereens, their children and grandchildren leaving, going back to America. I'm not going to leave. Or not yet. It's not so simple. Because I'm not sure whether I want to, or where to go – and things with Duchi are uncertain enough . . .

So, I stood there with the PalmPilot in my hand while people went in and out of the post office. Hanging from the façade of the Tel Aviv Museum for the Arts was a banner which read 'Of Life and Death – A Retrospective of the Artist Oli Shauli-Negbi'. The word 'Retrospective' reeled my gaze in. I left. I walked. I walked through the drifts of sodden dead leaves and tried to think whether there was anything I could have done to prevent it. Should I have told the passengers that the dark guy was a suspect? Should I have said something to the driver? Would she have listened to me? The truth is that those drivers aren't scared of anything. Ziona would have pulled over and started interrogating him.

But if she'd done that, he would have pressed the button, or pulled the string, or . . .

Why had he waited until I got off? What kept me alive?

Why had God stretched out one of his long fingers and miraculously tapped *my* forehead? When I got off at the Dizengoff Centre, some people got on and I heard Ziona tell one of them, 'I'm sorry, honey, I'm full. There's another one behind me.' The terrorist had waited until the cab filled up and only then . . .

If I'd told Ziona and she'd talked to him, he would have blown himself up. If I'd shouted to everybody to be careful, he would have blown himself up. If I'd phoned the police, or told the security guards at the mall, nobody would have had time to do anything. All in all, I told myself, walking through the slow grey drops of rain that had started to fall, I was clean. I couldn't have done anything, because the dark guy had come here to blow himself up and he would have gone ahead and done it whatever the hell I'd done. All I could have done was what I did – save myself. And even that I'd done unintentionally.

But then I thought some more and saw I was letting myself off too lightly. There was another thing I could have done. I could have been less certain that the dark guy wasn't a terrorist. I could have saved the guy I talked to. The guy who I know now as Giora Guetta. I could have saved him because he spoke to me after the old lady got off and before I did. I remembered every word – his voice and the way he said it, the look in his eyes, the half-smile of his perfect white teeth, the way he'd swivelled his head towards the terrorist and said, 'He looks OK to you, right?' And how I'd said: 'Yeah, no problem with him.'

Why had I said that?

Because I'd had enough of paranoid and hysterical people like Duchi.

And that's why I go to the opposite extreme: *no problem, everything's fine, stop worrying and crying and moaning about everything!* It was Duchi's fault. Her responsibility. She'd damaged my sense of judgement. Without her destructive influence, without years of living in the shadow of her hysteria, without those years of her continuous premonitions of imminent catastrophe, perhaps I'd have thought more clearly and said, 'You know what? I'm not sure. Perhaps he is a terrorist.' And then maybe Giora would have got off with me. Who knows? If it hadn't been for my girlfriend maybe I'd have saved a man's life.

I found I was hungry for meat. I stopped at Bar BaraBush and ordered a hamburger called 'The Cannibal Is Hungry Tonight'. I waited at the bar and watched the small TV on it showing Channel 2: Danny Ronen talking with his usual serious face, utilising his thick eyebrows, shooting them up and down as he always does. I didn't hear what he said but it doesn't really matter. He always says the same thing: enforce, ease off, close, encircle, shoot the eyebrows, go out on a mission, attack, lock and siege, and the cabinet convened and the cabinet decided and these guys took responsibility and those guys showed courage . . .

I went to wash my hands – I think perhaps I thought I had blood on them – and on my way back I took a postcard on which GET OUT! was written in large black lettering. GET OUT? I didn't have a clue who wanted me out or why. Outside, through the big window, the skies were opening and closing their wet mouths. I went out into them with The Cannibal Is Hungry Tonight in a bag in my hand and GET OUT! in my pocket.

I put the Cannibal and the chips I found next to it on a plate and prepared to have my way with them. Whatever was happening to my mind, my body still seemed to be functioning with amazing efficiency. My eyes sent a snapshot of the hamburger to my brain, which gave out its directives to flood my mouth with saliva and release stomach acids to welcome our new guest – and then the door buzzed.

I looked at the wall and at the Cannibal and decided not to answer. I started eating. A minute later: a key in the front door, the handle turning, somebody entering.

'Why didn't you open up?'

'Hey, Dooch, sorry,' I said. My mouth, which I'd filled with Cannibal a moment before, spoke for itself. I gestured with my shoulders towards the plate. She looked at it and her eyes immediately went into her 'rage mode'.

'Why don't you answer the mobile? And what are you doing at home in the middle of the afternoon? You know there was a bomb?'

'Yes.' I was searching for the mobile in my bag – I must have left it at work.

'You realise how worried I was? You couldn't call?'

'I'm sorry, Dooch, I was sure you were busy and . . . hang on a second, I *did* call! Didn't you get my message?'

'I got one message saying you were alive *two hours* after the bomb! Thanks very much indeed.' I looked at her, surprised. I didn't know what to say. 'It was in a Little No. 5, Croc. At nine-fifteen! Did you think I wasn't going to worry?'

'You know I get off at the Dizengoff Centre! It was after that, near the theatre. Didn't you see the little flame-thing on TV? Here, look.' I found the remote and pushed the button. Danny Ronen and his eyebrows were still talking. 'I left you a message saying I was alive. I don't get it . . .'

'I heard the message, but . . .' Here tears intervened. 'But how could I be sure?' She wiped them away and stood there, fragile and unhappy. 'I wasn't sure if everything was all right. You could have called again. I was so scared! You don't know how scared I was. I spent the whole day waiting for an adjournment, trying to get away to see you . . .'

I swallowed another mouthful – damn, the Cannibal was good! – and went over to hug her. 'It's all right, honey. I'm sorry. Come on. Stop it. I just thought you saw where it happened, you got the message so *obviously* I was alive, and . . . whatever . . . what do I know?'

Duchi disengaged herself from the embrace. 'You're saying I didn't need to worry? I'm just hysterical? And paranoid?' Her tone had changed: the tears weren't there any more.

'I didn't say . . .'

'How could you be so insensitive? Not to call just once more? You did it on purpose, didn't you? To show me I'm just hysterical.' Now there was anger, maturing like a good wine. 'What do you expect me to think? It's the bus you take every morning at that time! And I'm supposed to look at the little flame-thing on TV? What fucking flame-thing?'

'You know, the, you know, the graphic of the map showing the bomb . . . Duchi, I didn't do anything on purpose, I swear, I just . . . You know it was the same minibus that I was on? I actually talked to . . .'

'Oh, you *son of a bitch*!' She was whining now and wiped her big brown eyes with her forearm. She sat down next to the table and absent-mindedly grabbed a handful of chips.

'Hey, go easy on the chips!' I told her. 'How was your day?'

'What do you fucking think?'

We sat in silence for a few moments. I took a bite of the Cannibal and she stole chips and stared at the corner of the table and eventually lifted her eyes to me.

'Tell me what I'm going to do with you, Croc?' she said.

And then suddenly a thought struck me – until that

morning I hadn't known anyone who even knew anyone who'd been in a terrorist attack. A few weeks earlier the water-heater guy had come to do some work, and he said a cousin of a friend of his had been injured in a bomb in Petach Tikvah the week before. He was the closest, until Giora Guetta. But I didn't really know Giora Guetta either. What does 'knowing' someone mean? Knowing the name? Saying hello when you meet? The person knowing you? The number of words you exchanged? I was still trying to puzzle it out when she got into bed.

'Duchi?'

'What?'

'The Cannibal Is Hungry Tonight,' I said.

'Idiot,' she said, and I climbed on top of her. She was satisfied. Then she climbed on top of me in return.

In the morning she made me swear to take a taxi, though I've yet to hear of two bomb attacks happening in exactly the same place on following days. Somehow, despite this clear and logical statistical data, people are convinced that the terrorists tell themselves: 'Ahmed, hey, it worked, let's try again tomorrow in *exactly the same place* since there are bound to be loads of people there and no security.' In practice, the army and police upgrade their security to maximum in the place that was hit, people avoid going to that area and family members become hysterical. I told Duchi all of this and she said, 'But what about the No. 18 bus on Jaffa Street in Jerusalem in '96?'

'Those were a week apart,' I said. But it was a pretty feeble point. So I ended up taking a taxi. A Little No. 5 didn't blow up that morning. But so what? A real No. 5 didn't blow up either, the whole time I worked for Time's Arrow, miraculously. On none of the days I took Little No. 5s to the Dizengoff Centre did a real No. 5 get bombed. So: what? I mean: so *what,* exactly, Duchki?

# 4

Amr Diab is singing *'Amarein'*. It's about two moons. He means the girl's two eyes or her two . . .

Someone's playing this music for me, the two moons of Amr Diab, and I want to move my head but my head doesn't move. If I'm dreaming, the dream is never-ending. But I'm not dreaming, I'm hearing the song; I can smell this smell, I can feel the fingers tearing into my muscles, the heels of the hands kneading my flesh. But my body doesn't move and my eyes don't open.

After the two moons Amr Diab sings *'Nour el Ein'* – The Light in Your Eyes – and 'Always with You' and then Nawal Zuabi starts singing. It reminds me of the show *Ya Leil Ya Ein* on Future TV, the Lebanese TV station, with the dancing and the girls. Who's playing this music for me? I can smell this good smell. Not Svetlana – Svetlana would never have been able to keep her mouth shut. Is the good smell you, Rana? Why are you quiet? Why is nobody talking? I listen, but all I can hear is the music . . .

Where am I? If I'm in heaven, then where is Mother? Where is Grandfather Fahmi?

If they're not here, then I'm not in heaven.
So where am I exactly?

My grandfather, Fahmi Sabich, arrived in Al-Amari in 1949. Most of the inhabitants of Beit Machsir who were driven out that year settled in the East Bank. But Grandfather wanted to stay close to his village. Close to the house he built. He was sure he would return to live in his home. He never did. Never saw his home or his friends or his cousins again. In Al-Amari there wasn't room enough even to raise chickens, but he met Grandmother Samira there. She came from Dir Ayub, a village that doesn't exist any more. The Jews didn't even build a settlement where it had been. They just destroyed it and built a road.

'*Bidak turkusi birasi . . .*' Inside my head I want to dance . . .

I can feel how loose my muscles are now and the oil on my skin and the cool air from the ventilator drying it off. I piss . . . oh, that's good.

'Wow,' the idiot bitch of a nurse says, 'look how much you've made!'

One tube for piss, another for air; one tube for piss, another for air; one tube for piss, another for air . . .

Father was the third of six brothers and sisters. Mother was the third of six sisters and brothers. She was born in Murair, the most beautiful place in the world. Grandfather Fahmi said that Beit Machsir was more beautiful still. Looking west, you could see the Mediterranean from it and on a clear day the houses of Jaffa. When I was ten I told him that from Murair you could see the River Jordan and the valley and the Edom mountains, and on a clear day the houses of Amman, if you were looking east. He laughed at that.

Mother and Father met at Bir Zeit University, and after they got married they moved to Murair. Even in 1977 it wasn't common for a village girl to marry a refugee with no property; or for the man to move into the house of the woman or for a father to leave land to his daughter. My mother and father didn't care. Nor did my mother's father. Dignity wasn't all that important. Life was more important. But Grandfather Fahmi was more conservative. He believed refugees had to remain in the camps, even if they were crowded and uncomfortable, and he stayed in Al-Amari until he died. He said that leaving the camp would be giving up, would be accepting the situation. It would be an admission that we would never return to the homes which the Jews had stolen from us. My older brother Bilahl thinks like Grandfather Fahmi. My younger sister Lulu loves life more than an idea of dignity, like Father. I'm not quite sure whose genes I got.

Grandfather Fahmi had a horse. On Saturday afternoons I used to go to the entrance to the village and wait for him: a distant dot turning slowly into a white dust cloud moving along the horizon. Soon I'd hear the horseshoes clattering on the road, and suddenly he'd be next to me on the grey horse, extending the strongest arm I have ever known and picking me up, and we'd ride home together, me hugging his broad back and breathing in the dust and the sweet sweat, both his and the horse's. Once we were home he'd wash his face and go out to the terrace to drink the coffee that Mother made for him. From inside the house I'd listen to his laughter and smile.

Grandfather Fahmi died ten years ago. Mother died last year. Bilahl moved from Murair to Ramallah five years ago. He was eighteen, and went to study at Kuliyat al-Iman, the faith school in A-Ram – Father and Mother weren't too thrilled about it. He lived in the student dorms for a while and then he moved to Al-Amari, where there was a room in one of our uncles' flats, because Bilahl believed, as his grandfather had, that refugees and the sons of refugees and the grandsons of refugees should always remain in the camps. Father and Mother did not agree . . . I was sixteen. They looked to me; they didn't want to lose another son to the camp. But last year I moved in with Bilahl and Uncle Jalahl. I promised Father I would start studying in Bir Zeit University. I told him that I was just saving on the rent, that I wasn't in the camp as my brother was, for ideological reasons. That's not what I told my brother. I didn't really know what I thought, in my heart of hearts.

Bir Zeit is still waiting for me . . .

Someone switches the music off.

*'How is he doing?'*

Faint voices. It's my father. I can smell his familiar old smoky smell. But why is he whispering?

*'Hello, son. How are you feeling today?'*

Not now, come on, I'm trying to remember something. Maybe you could come back tomorrow? Because I'm not here anyway. I'm floating in the sea. The stars are out and I can see the beach, but I can't . . .

The army erected a dirt ramp around Murair and blocked the entrance to the village. No explanations. The water tankers from Ramallah couldn't get through to fill the main well, and cars couldn't leave the village to go to the second well, on the other side of the ramp. The well dried up. Before it dried up, the water at its bottom got dirty. A virus developed in it. Many people from the village were infected by it, but they recovered. Mother did not. The doctor said she needed clean water to flush out her system and to compensate for all the liquid she was losing through sweat and diarrhoea.

Bilahl and I travelled to the village through the mountains, bypassing all the roadblocks, but it wasn't enough. You could only get over the ramp on foot, and how much water could you carry on foot? Lulu was with her all the time, and Mother's sisters, holding her hand and praying. But everybody was thirsty and the water we'd brought was finished immediately. I told the soldiers guarding the entrance to the village that my mother was dying and she needed water. They tried to contact their commanders. Time passed, and they got no response. They told us to stop nagging them and go home. An hour later they'd still not received an answer – 'It's Saturday, there's nobody to talk to.' 'My mother's dying, why do you need to talk to someone? She needs water.' 'It's very complicated. There are roadblocks on the way. It's not in our power to authorise a trip.' 'Who has the power?' 'We don't know. We're trying to get hold of our commander to ask.' One of the soldiers gave me a bottle of water. The next morning I asked if we could take Mother to hospital. She was in a bad way. The soldiers were angry, told us we weren't the only ones, everybody was thirsty. The soldiers were talking on their mobiles and shouting at villagers who were begging them for help. They shot out the tyres of a tractor and arrested the driver.

The soldier who had given me water the previous day did not remember me.

'What d'you want from me? I'm on the phone to headquarters at my own personal expense! I'm trying to find out what happened to the tanker, OK? I know you're thirsty. I know you want water. We're trying to sort it out and whining at us isn't going to help the situation. So go home and a tanker will come and fill up the . . . Hello!' he shouted into his phone. But I wasn't asking for water by that stage; I was asking for an ambulance.

* * *

*'All these troubles, my son. They're all standing outside. Shouting. "The Croc, the Croc . . ." Something about the Croc. "Switch the machines off!" What have you done? Do you want me to have a heart attack?'*

What are they saying about the Croc? I know him.

Where was I? You interrupted right in the middle of . . . I was right in the middle of something, Father. Come on . . .

An ambulance arrived to take Mother away. Lulu and I got into the ambulance but at the entrance to the village they told us to get out. Only the driver, the paramedics and the patient could stay. Mother said it would be all right. She was on a drip and feeling much better. We hugged her and she blessed us, but when the ambulance started moving I broke down and cried uncontrollably, unstoppably, for minutes, while Lulu tried to soothe me. She was only thirteen and I was over twenty, but it was me who was crying and her doing the comforting. The soldiers, still on their mobiles, stared at us. The ramp that encircled the village lay like a ligature of dirt across the yellow fields. Mother died in hospital. She was forty-two. A week later they got rid of the ramp.

# 5

Jimmy Rafael in the meeting room. Five foot four of solid muscle. His shaved dome gleaming as if it had been massaged with olive oil. Maybe he *did* massage it with olive oil.

'Morning, everyone! I don't need to tell you we have no extra time so let's get right to the point. I've known Dmitry for many years; we've shared a few important seconds in the Time Management Unit in the air force and in time engineering studies in the US. He's going to talk about what he's doing. About how saving a couple of seconds can change everything.' I glanced at Ron. His eyes were making no comment, but to me they were saying, 'Jimmy's time talks: what a waste of time . . .' I smiled to myself.

'I am a certified time engineer and a senior traffic-light technician,' Dmitry began. He was very tall and was wearing a cheesecloth shirt of the kind you never saw at Time's Arrow. 'I work for a private consulting firm in Hadera. My role is to find dead seconds. This story is about how I have found seven superfluous seconds in Rabin Square.

'I don't need to describe the spot: a square surrounded by four roads from two to four lanes wide. Between one and four thousand cars use the square pretty much every hour of the day. My goal was to leave it as empty as possible, and specifically to relieve a permanent congestion at the corner of Ibn-Gvirol and Zeitlin streets.'

He made a sketch of the intersection on the drawing board, wrote the street names, and marked the point of the jam. 'A traffic-light cycle, meaning the time between one green light and the next, is between twenty-four and a hundred and twenty seconds. The seconds are divided meticulously between pedestrians, traffic in all directions and the gaps between. But, as every driver knows, not every direction receives the same time. Traffic-light technicians divide the time at every location according to need. Short greens in city centres are ten seconds long. The longer ones, in less stressed locations, usually take around eighty seconds out of a cycle of a hundred and twenty. In Rabin Square I discovered that the south-eastern corner had traffic lights which were simply throwing time away.' Ron's eyes were keeping up a constant commentary. 'Must have been a programmer's mistake. One of the phases in the process took ten seconds when it needed only three!'

Jimmy tossed his smile around the table. 'Seven seconds!' He beamed delightedly.

'Yes. I had seven seconds available in various different locations around the square, meaning that if I could clear one side, I'd be able to unblock the rest. Perhaps you remember that until a few months ago the whole square was blocked during the morning rush hour? At *this* zebra crossing,' he made some marks in one of the corners, 'scores of pedestrians would accumulate.'

'Yes, I remember!' I said, into a tableful of surprised faces. Dmitry looked at me silently for two point five to three seconds.

'I retimed the whole day – pressure periods, post-pressure periods, after an accident, after a demonstration.

I made an appointment with a municipal technician, we opened the control box and he logged in with his laptop and uploaded my new definitions. The traffic was pretty heavy at the time. Yet minutes after we'd run the program everything started flowing with perfect smoothness. The technician went back to his office and I celebrated on my own with a well-earned glass of wine at a bar.'

'Which bar?' asked Talia Tenne. Talia Tenne likes bars.

Dmitry didn't remember.

After the lecture, Bar sent his numerological reading of Dmitry. It said: 'Dmitry = kind bollocks scrambler'. It's an old Hebrew habit or superstition, doing numerologies, but Bar uses a piece of software he wrote while he was supposed to be working on programming for Time's Arrow to calculate his. Among his favourite numerologies are 'Rafi Rafael = bald for no reason', 'Rafi Rafael = tough midget manager' and 'Time's Arrow = a total waste of time'.

Our business in Time's Arrow is saving time. Not seven seconds – for us seven seconds are an eternity. We work for years in order to save a second or two. Not from traffic lights on a square but from the conversation time of each and every call made to directory enquiries: 144 in Israel, 411 in America, 118118 and so on in the UK, 104 in Japan . . . And why do we need to save a second from conversations to a call centre? Take, for instance, these clients of ours who provide the service in Manhattan. They've got a couple of thousand operators in New York answering calls coming in non-stop – 5.5 million phone calls a day in search of telephone numbers. If we can save one second from each call we save 5.5 million seconds a day, which is 63 days, or almost three working months of an employee. Our software can save a company like that around $10,000 a day.

These numbers were my job. I was the Croc of Numbers! The Belgian company whose representatives Jimmy and

I were going to meet takes 44 million calls a year, or more than 120,000 a day, with 300 operators working at any given time. I worked in sales, selling the product to national or private phone companies, landline or mobile, or companies providing directory assistance, DA for short. Recently phone companies have been springing up, or being privatised, all over the place. And every one of these companies needs DA. The market's worth $145 million this year: next year it's projected to be $200 million.

Pearls from Jimmy's tireless mind: 'Time's Arrow is the Fed-Ex of the twenty-first century. Fed-Ex saved days, we save seconds.' Or: 'We're not only living in a world where every second is worth money, but every *hundredth* of a second.' How do we save this time? Software and consulting. Our software replaces the operator for certain parts of the conversation: it replies, asks for name and location, auto-completes names, searches and finds results in optimal time, reads out the number and dials it. Theoretically, it's also got voice recognition, but that's not perfect (yet), and conversations are still shared between software and operators.

Besides the software we consult: we supply guidance to operators on the software, on how to decrease talk time, on posture and voice; solutions for companies relating to shift construction (work/rest ratio, number of workers per shift, optimum shift lengths), ergonomic call-centre design, HR management, marketing strategies, pricing and distribution. All this, with periodic software upgrades thrown in, is yours for a million dollars on the table and a yearly licence costing half a million, more or less, in truth somewhat less than more – especially lately when everyone seems to be in crisis.

Interested?

I read the names of the dead on Ynet. Some of the photos I recognised. The manager of the minibus company said of the 'driver, 36': 'Ziona was irreplaceable; everybody at the station loved her.' There was Gabriel Algrably, 41, a widower builder who left behind two girls, ages 11 and 13. Two Hungarians, short-contract workers. Mali, a young woman, a student in the Vital College of Design: 'a flower plucked in full bloom'. Shlomo Yarkoni, 29. 'The most wonderful husband in the world,' said his widow Yael, 'four months pregnant and biting back her tears'. The suicide bomber, Shafiq Omar, 19 years old.

I met some of the families. After everything else happened, after they heard about me, they wanted to get in touch. Shlomo Yarkoni's widow Yael called to ask whether I remembered him, but I didn't. I hadn't recognised the photo on Ynet. He probably got on at the Centre. A week after Yael, a woman named Smadar called me, also about Shlomo. He had visited her a few minutes before the bomb. He had left his phone in her flat. The phone rang endlessly all morning, and she didn't answer. She didn't turn it off either. She just stared at it and knew. She'd heard the boom. It was a beautiful winter morning. She sat and looked at the ringing phone all day, his sperm still warm inside her.

There was one unidentifiable body. It had to be him. I took out his Palm and stared at it. Should I hand it to the police? Or his family? But Giora had made me a request, the last request of his life. I turned the Palm on and watched the black letters flicker in the grey liquid crystal. Yesterday, the last day of his life, he'd had a meeting in Tel Aviv at eight in the morning and then nothing until the evening, where he'd written: 'Shuli?' The name he'd told me. The one I was going to look for.

I synchronised – I transferred all the information from Giora Guetta's PalmPilot to my computer for back-up. I saved it just for the hell of it. Much later I thought: I did it instinctively, as if I knew there was information in there that I was going to need . . .

The offices of Time's Arrow are located on the twenty-third floor of the Dizengoff Centre, with views over the Mediterranean and the dense houses of Tel Aviv, ugly when seen from above. I checked the Belgian company's website and then called Switzerland.

'Ivan!'

'Eitan. How are you? I heard you've just had a bomb in Tel Aviv.'

'Oh yeah, yeah: nothing to worry about.' This is company policy – to play down any whiff of terrorist activity in the Middle East in general and the Tel Aviv area specifically. If anything should happen and, with the help of the negative and sensationalising global media, reach the ears of our overseas clients and potential investors, it should be treated with at most the interest an elephant might display at a fly landing on its forehead – not even a passing annoyance.

'Near you, though, wasn't it? Central Tel Aviv?'

'Nooo, not really. Didn't even hear it, actually.' (That's right: I was in the elevator.) 'And you? Anything blown up in Zurich lately?'

He roared. The Swiss are important customers. The system's enjoying great success there. But Ivan is continually asking for changes and new features. He has good ideas, but who has the time? Making changes to the software is like trying to storm the Great Wall of China with the Chinese army ranged along it with machine guns: you have to talk to the people from Product, Marketing, R&D, Quality Assurance (QA), Installations . . . every one of whom is working full time on something else. Jimmy says that, as a small company, we can provide solutions and services with 'a speed and flexibility that bigger companies can only dream of'. This is complete bullshit, of course: we're infinitely less agile or flexible than some giant mega-corporation like Koor.

Ivan made lots of suggestions. I told him they were all excellent. My head was aching.

A few minutes after noon, the inboxes of the thirty or so employees of Time's Arrow all receive a message from Talia Tenne that says, 'Food?' Today she'd ordered from Salsalat but I didn't fancy a salad and went for a schnitzel from the Coffee Bar along with Bar, Ron, Shoko from IT Support and Yoash Green, who works with me in Sales and whose wife left him. Our food arrived with the salads, and we sat with Talia Tenne and the girls in the dining area, where Bar browsed through *Yediot Achronot*, the main paper out here. 'Shulamit Penigstein, seventy-two,' read Bar, 'who disembarked only a few stops before the explosion, had serious doubts about the suicide bomber: "I tried to draw the attention of my fellow passengers to him," she said, "but they just sneered at me."'

'So, Croc,' Talia Tenne said, 'what's this about you being in the attack yesterday?'

'That's right, I'm dead.'

'No, like . . . weren't you near it or something?'

'Pretty damn close. Dizengoff Centre. Big building, not far from the attack?'

'Stop being a pain.'

I like Talia Tenne. She's naive and funny and cares for the nutrition of most of the company's workers, which is nice. And pretty, very pretty. Her skin is as white and smooth as silk.

'Unbelievable how this intifada's getting closer . . . it's going to be here soon.'

Occasionally I looked eastwards out of the dining area's

windows, waiting for a plane to appear and crash into our tower.

'If the mountain doesn't come to Muhammad,' said Shoko, chewing chicken, 'Muhammad will come to the mountain.'

The week the intifada broke out, Time's Arrow had a day of massages organised in the Sea View Hotel in the north. But there were riots on the way north and the roads were blocked. So we went to Sde Dov, the little airstrip in North Tel Aviv, and flew to Mahanayim and took a taxi from there to the Sea View. From the plane we thought we saw smoke from tyres burning on the roads. We sat at the Sea View in white towelling robes, sipped herbal tea and submitted to our oily Swedish massages.

'Don't laugh – they'll take this tower down one day.'

'A booby-trapped car goes to the upper car park, drives straight through that laughable little stick that calls itself a barrier and sits itself directly underneath the building: boom!'

'Shoko, I'm eating, stop it already!'

Twenty-seven minutes is the average time I spend on lunch – I worked it out once.

I didn't feel at all like working. A report on Ynet said the last body from the Little No. 5 had finally been identified. Giora Guetta, 23 years old, from Jerusalem. My man. I can't stay here any longer, I thought, I've got to find his girlfriend. I stood up and said, as I said every day, 'One small step for a man, and an even smaller step for mankind.'

'A half-day, then?' asked Ron. It was a running joke: I always said the same thing and he always gave the same answer even if it was eight in the evening, which it usually was. But today it really was going to be a half-day.

'Yeah. A half-day.'

# 6

Grandfather Fahmi got angry whenever people talked about the war of 1948 as the *Nakba*; the Disaster. People didn't like talking about it at all, but he did. Because he and his friends did things. They resisted. He told me how they used to hit convoys of Jews going up to Jerusalem. They'd descend from the village to the ridges above the road to Jerusalem and shoot at the buses. The road would close and the Jews wouldn't be able to go through to Jerusalem – they managed to cut Jerusalem off for weeks like this. The Jews themselves admit it. They've left the wrecks of some of the buses there as memorials. That was Grandfather Fahmi. He hit the convoys. His name is written on those buses in bullet holes. Later they put armour on the buses and trucks, but Grandfather and his friends still found ways to attack, still managed to stop them getting through. The road was littered with the skeletons of cars – what the Jews have preserved there is no more than a souvenir. Grandfather would make his way down the slope from the ridge to shoot at a bus, and then come back up home to the village. Eight months their heroics went on. And this is why he felt hurt when people talked about a defeat: because they fought like lions. One time a plane crashed near Beit Machsir and six Jewish soldiers were killed in it and Grandfather Fahmi took a souvenir of his own: one of the clocks from the dashboard of the cockpit.

*'Your father seems like a good man, Fahmi. A very sad man. He really doesn't deserve all this trouble. And your girlfriend's very cute, isn't she? How she comes and plays the tapes? I used to hate the songs but, you know, I'm really starting to like them.* Amarein, amarein . . . amarehehehein . . .'

Oh no, please! Don't start with the singing now . . .

*'Now don't get all upset, Fahmi. What are these noises? No need to get cross. I'm here to take care of you. You like the deep massages, right?'*

Svetlana, can't you please just shut up . . .? Grandfather Fahmi . . . I'm . . .

*'We'll get your senses back, don't you worry. The taste and the smell and the sight and the touch and the hearing and the movement . . . Now let's have a peek at how these pipes and tubes are doing! A tube for your piss, another for your air . . .'*

'What are you doing, Fahmi?'

The Croc's talking; he's suspicious.

He looks sideways. 'What've you got there?'

Where was I? The Croc? Grandfather Fahmi?

*'Dr Hartom's coming in a minute, so we want you on your best behaviour, don't we?'*

Dr Hartom's a bitch and you're a stupid little Jewish whore and I'm cold. Can't you stop talking for a second? Can't you see that I'm cold . . .?

The flat was cold. An old spiral heater giving a little orange heat. Tea in glasses. Bilahl with Halil Abu-Zeid: a large, impressive man with huge arms and chest, a shaved head and a beard. A silver ring on his fat middle finger. Intelligent pale brown eyes. Older. In 1990 they deported him to southern Lebanon, and when he came back they stuck him in jail in Ramallah . . .

'My dream,' said Bilahl, 'is to see, on the slope beside the remains of the old buses that my grandfather shot in '48, a Mitsubishi and a Peugeot and a Toyota made in 2000. You understand what I'm talking about?'

Abu-Zeid looked at Bilahl and my brother looked back.

'How were you thinking of doing it?'

Bilahl drew a map on a page from a notebook, with a number of arrows on it. He explained. Abu-Zeid smoked a whole cigarette before he said anything. The smoke coming out of his mouth mingled with the breath coming out of Bilahl's. Bilahl knelt on the floor and warmed his hands by the electric bars. He said, 'It's about time. What did Ramallah do apart from a handful of attacks by Fatah on Route 443 and a couple more on the Settlements? What did Al-Amari contribute? Wafa Idris?'

'We did something big this week.'

'Remember the village of Silwad. Wadi Haramiya. The guy found a spot on the ridge with a Karabin and took out ten soldiers one after the other, and got away without being caught. The road to Jerusalem – it's the busiest road. It's a symbol. It will shock them. They'll think they're back in '48. And the conditions there . . . it's no coincidence that my grandfather sniped at convoys from there. The wadi there's just like the one in Silwad.'

'It's not Silwad,' said Abu-Zeid. 'In Silwad there's a village. Fifteen minutes later the sniper was in safe hands.'

Abu-Zeid took the drawing and touched it to the bare orange spirals of the heater. He stood up with the burning page in his hand, opened a window, looked out into the rain, and threw it out. He closed the window and sat back down in his plastic chair, rubbing the ash from his hands.

'There are problems with this plan. It takes too much time. And the evacuation plan isn't good. Again, there'll be no time. In five minutes the area will be full of road-blocks and helicopters. It's not '48 any more.'

Bilahl looked at him quizzically. 'Is there another way?'

Halil Abu-Zeid said, 'Who will do it?'

*'Svetlana. How is he?'*

What . . .? What now?

*'Normal. A little irritated this morning.'*

*'You checked his pupils today?'*

Oh no.

*'Not yet, Dr Hartom.'*

*'Let's have a look . . .'*

Yaagghh!! Fuck you! You're killing me with that torch . . .!

*'Hmmm . . . fine. Did we have a bowel movement? How's the urine?'*

*'No B.M. Urine's in order.'*

Go to hell, Hartom, I was in the middle of . . . oh, where was I?

If this is a dream, then it's never-ending and never-changing . . . If this is a dream then it's a dream of hell.

*'OK, Fahmi, no reason to be distressed, Svetlana here's taking good care of you. In the afternoon we're going to do an MRI and show you some familiar images and play familiar sounds – test your reactions to stimuli. Svetlana, we have the photographs? Music?'*

*'Yes, Dr Hartom. Everything's ready.'*

Children were playing football in the rain. They shouted and kicked the ball against a wall covered in slogans and posters. Bilahl would send the kids out at night . . . There was a new poster up, of the shahid Shafiq. Shafiq the martyr with the Temple Mount in the background, and puddles, and mud from the dust that the tanks and bulldozers made the last time they were here, and other children playing marbles under a thatch. The rain didn't let up. You could hear the sound of applause coming from TVs in the houses along the way. The wind was trying to blow the sheets of corrugated tin off the roofs, rattling the breeze blocks that held them down. My phone was ringing. Grandfather Fahmi lived in a tent for eight years before he built a house out of scavenged concrete, rocks and tin.

'So you think you're happy now, eh?'

'Father?'

'What will they accomplish, these virtuoso operations of yours?'

'What operations?'

'I'm not a fool, Fahmi.'

'Don't forget what Grandfather did in '48,' I said. 'He scared them, he didn't give up, and he brought pride to our people.'

'Yes. And where exactly did it bring us? To Al-Amari?'

I didn't answer. I watched the kids in the rain: children born here.

'Don't ignore me. Fahmi. You promised me something. Don't forget. You promised me you would not get into trouble. You promised your father. Fahmi. You gave your word of honour to me.'

# 7

In 1935, two weeks after British police had violently broken up Arab protests in Jerusalem, Izz ad-Din al-Qassam gathered his people and announced a jihad. He told them to prepare to leave that same evening, said goodbye to his wife and children and went with his followers to the mountains around Jenin.

Every one of his men carried a small Koran in his pocket. During the days, they studied the Koran. At night they were soldiers. One of those nights, a guard named Mahmoud Salam al-Mahmuzi ran into a Jewish patrol. He shot the commander of the patrol and killed him. Another policeman in the patrol ran to report the incident and, having done so, he ran home, to his wife.

The British retaliated fiercely. A large force was mobilised from all round Palestine and sent to Haifa. The next day five hundred British soldiers set out to catch Izz ad-Din al-Qassam. After a bloody battle which lasted all night, Sheikh al-Qassam was killed and became one of the first of the great martyrs, the *shuhada*, in the long struggle. He planted the seeds of revolution against Zionism and imperialism and inspired a generation to follow him.

The policeman who ran to report the incident was Duchi's grandfather. Her mother was born nine months later. My father was born in the same year, 1935, in Maryland, USA.

I took a Little No. 5 home. As far as I was concerned, the cooling-off period was over after one morning. The journey was quieter than usual; the drivers swore less over the radio and committed fewer traffic violations. Even the Jumbos seemed to drive with respect for the sorrow of the minibus drivers.

'How did you get home?' asked Duchi.

'Taxi,' I said offhandedly.

'Liar,' she said.

'Liar? What reason do I have to lie?' I said, and really, what reason did I have?

'Honestly in a taxi?' She came and gave me a kiss. I opened the refrigerator, looking for something quick. No, not really in a taxi, Duchi, in a Little No. 5. But do you think I'm going to tell you the truth? You think I fancy an argument now?

'Word of honour.'

Nothing is as it was before September 11th. Everything changed that day, and yet, life went on. The summary: Duchi and I live together for four years, we decide to get married, the date we set is 11 September 2001. Duchi's mother gets a heart attack and snuffs it a day before the wedding, the wedding is cancelled, and since then this word – 'wedding' – is never heard in our vicinity. It's as if there are blockades and checkpoints that this word can't penetrate, as if there's a lock-and-siege on it. As if they'd sent a whole army to hunt it down and it had vanished and holed up in some abysmal cave, not even bothering to send us a 'what's up' from time to time. It seems that we're treating the whole thing as if it were a sign from God – or worse, from Duchi's mother – that we shouldn't have decided to marry. She sacrificed her life on the altar of this message. The medium was her message. I guess that's the reason we don't talk about it. I'm only guessing, though, because we haven't talked about it. She keeled over and it was as if a valve holding back an immense pressure had blown and all the attention leaked away from the wedding to the funeral. And it's not as if any of that other stuff helped.

Duchi's first reaction was to laugh. 'No way,' she told the phone. 'Come on, Dad, you're putting me on.' And then she said, 'OK . . . OK . . . OK,' and hung up and said, 'My mother died of a heart attack,' and only then did her eyes well up with tears.

Duchi's younger brother, Voovi, didn't look too broken up about it. Her dad certainly wasn't sorry. Before all of this happened Duchi once made me swear that whatever occurred between us – even if it didn't work out eventually – we would never end up with the hate-hate relationship her parents had.

Duchi's father is called Noam Neeman. That's 'Pleasant Loyal' in Hebrew, by the way: two gags for the price of one. He left Duchi's mother after two kids and six years of marriage and went to Nicaragua with his second wife, whom he dumped after a few more years, kids and arms deals. He returned to Israel at the age of forty-six and married a girl half his age. Duchi was three years younger than her when they got married. She and her brother didn't make it to the wedding. But I like Noam Neeman. A man with balls. Does what he feels like doing. Half the time he succeeds, half the time he tanks completely. Recently, for instance, he failed miserably with a start-up in which he invested a million dollars. He asked me, 'If you had a million bucks in the bank, what sort of investment would you put it in?' I said, 'I'd put it in the bank.' His seen-it-all eyes looked me over with bottomless disdain and he drew on his cigar till it crackled.

'Duchi!' he shouted. 'Couldn't you have found yourself someone a bit more serious than this?' He punched my shoulder with his large suntanned hand. In the end he stuck his million into a new mobile phone company called Wa-Wa. A year later his million was in the sewer.

In truth, Duchi's parents did not share a hate-hate relationship. Ever since Noam Neeman left her, Duchi's mother had been lost. She loved him in secret until the day she died. Loved? She worshipped the ground he walked on. She was completely obsessed with him, but she didn't have him: all she had instead were his two children. And whatever move they made, whatever direction they set off in, they could be sure that Leah Neeman would be standing there, feet planted, wagging a warning index finger. Because Leah was a fountain of bitterness. She just *didn't like life*. There was nothing she wasn't suspicious of; there wasn't a decision Duchi or Voovi could make, or even think about making, that Leah wouldn't respond to with gloomy prophecy, biblical wrath, stricken horror; not a step they ever took without having to hurdle the leg she would stretch out to trip them up.

I thought – and I believe many others thought the same – that there was something fitting in her pulling a heart attack on the eve of her daughter's marriage. She deployed the ultimate weapon in her arsenal, her Judgement Day weapon. And it worked, God knows how or why. The ring I bought ('Diamonds are for ever,' said Duchi, 'so don't buy me one') is still hunkered down at the back of some drawer, waiting.

Anyway, I was standing there with my head in the refrigerator, lying it off. I tried to move the conversation on.

'So how was your day, Duchki?'

Her gesture said, leave it, don't even go there. Another crazy day. In the last few months she'd been coming back home whacked from a case of insider dealing and fraud that was dragging on and on. She would curse the other lawyer, the fool Gvirzman, and the ill-tempered and exhausted judge and her salary and her boss Boaz, who after years of her working her soul out for him was still ignoring her hints about being made a partner.

I ate cold pasta salad for a few minutes without speaking while she watched TV from the sofa. 'Well?' I pressed. She made a face and muttered, 'That son of a bitch.' 'Who, Boaz? Gvirzman? The judge? Who now?' She shrugged. 'Yes. No. All three of them are huge sons of bitches, for sure. I don't know; I don't know what I'm *doing*. Why am I killing myself like this? Gvirzman asked to postpone again without consulting me and when I tell him out of court that it's out of order, the son of a bitch tells me I'm an overgrown baby.'

'Oh, come on.' Sometimes I think Gvirzman's right, but I don't say so.

'What does that mean, "oh, come on"?' She was sharpening her claws for combat. I like her instincts.

'You're in a good company, on a good salary, you work with prestigious clients, handle big cases . . .'

'That's not the point, Croc. I've been stuck in the same place for a year. Even if *you* think it's a good place – and it isn't – I still haven't made any progress for a year. This case . . .'

I shook my head. How much can you moan? How much can you be unhappy with what you have when you have so much?

'Don't make that face. You're not going to convince me I'm having a wonderful time at work – though you're making this great effort to convince yourself. You could just be a tiny bit understanding and supportive, couldn't you? I deserve a little support from my boyfriend after a day like this.'

A day like this. Wow. They asked to postpone without consulting her and called her an overgrown baby. Dear oh dear oh dear. She deserves support. She always deserves it. She's so pitiable sometimes her tone can really flip my switch.

'You know, I did take the Little No. 5, not a taxi.'

Why did I say that? Maybe I needed to have a row.

'Liar.'

'Liar? What reason do I have to lie?' Apart from the obvious.

'Croc.'

'What?'

'You're having me on, right?'

This was the point of no return. I could have hushed it all up and lied my way out of it, or remained loyal to the truth – not something I insist on day to day – and start the world war that was dying to be declared between us.

I gave her a heavy-lidded look (my crocodilian look) and said: 'Not right. I am not having you on. I went on a Little No. 5.'

Duchi's hair is brown and her skin is a colour I used to call caffè latte in the days when we still found the time to lie side by side, stroking each other for hours. The coffee is from her Yemeni grandmother – the one from the night of the incident in '35. The milk comes from her grandfather and father. When Duchi is on the brink of explosion, the skin on her face grows visibly darker and her luminous eyes cloud over, but it's not the colour so much as her expression, like a child's in the second before it cries – only with her it's not tears but fury.

'Why the hell didn't you take a taxi like I asked you to?'

'Because I had this weird premonition that I wasn't going

to get blown up. And you know something? I wasn't blown up! And you know something else? I didn't hear on the news that any other Little No. 5 was blown up today either.'

'Not the point.'

'So what is? You wanted me to ride in a taxi for a specific reason. I thought you were wrong. I was proved correct. And now I don't understand what we're arguing about.'

'I don't believe what I'm hearing. You really, truly, honestly travelled on a Little No. 5?'

'Of course! Why take a taxi?'

'Maybe because *I asked*? That's not a reason?'

'Not if there's no sense behind it.'

'I don't believe this.'

I took a chair from the dining table and sat in front of her. She lowered the volume on the TV, which was on Channel 2: Danny Ronen rambling on and on, his eyebrows conspiring together like a couple of sidekicks pretending to be shrewd.

'What reason do I have to lie?'

'I don't believe this,' she repeated. 'Tell me, is there nothing left between us? Not a little appreciation? A little consideration? A little trust?'

'What's that got to do with it?'

'What it's got to do with it?' She shook her head and covered her face with her hands. She said, 'I should have listened to Uri a long time ago.'

Oh, here we go: Uri. I was beginning to wonder when his name would crop up. Her therapist. Duchi told me a long time ago that he thought she shouldn't stay in our relationship, although he would never come out and say it directly. I argued with her then. She quit therapy and we decided to get married. A few weeks after the wedding that never happened, though, she went back to him. And now he's telling her the same thing once again.

'Uri doesn't know anything.'

'He knows more than you think he does.'

'How could he know anything on the basis of your stories alone?'

'But what's important is the way *I* see and experience things.'

How many times have we had this conversation?

'But he's talking about your relations with *me*. The experience belongs to both of us, no? How could he say anything truthful about it after hearing only your side? I know how you distort things sometimes. The version he gets depends on the way your mood swings on the day you tell him. And your mood's about as reliable as Danny fucking Ronen! You . . . I can't . . . How can you believe a single word of it?'

After that neither of us said a word for several minutes. She turned up the volume. Danny Ronen was saying that the security forces had some leads pointing in the direction of Nablus. Terror cells in Nablus had targeted Tel Aviv in the past and they were the only ones with the capability to stage such a destructive attack. That was what a senior military source had told Danny Ronen. The explosive belt used by the suicide bomber, Shafiq somebody from Nablus, weighed 25 kilograms. The IDF was preparing an operation in Nablus in response.

'Look,' she said, pointing at the TV. 'Ten people died.' 'Eleven!' 'Eleven. And you were on that bus.' 'Not a bus.' 'I don't care what it is! It could have been you! So I was worried, OK? I got scared. My whole body was shaking. So I had a simple request to make. You think it was irrational? You think it was stupid? Fine. But I asked you. Your partner asked you to do something which in your opinion is irrational – to travel, for one day of your life, in taxis. So why do you do the opposite on purpose? What is it in me that makes you want to fight? That makes you incapable of respecting me? Do you hate me? This is hatred. I ask for something and you piss on it. What is that if it's not hatred? So the question is: if you hate me so much what are you doing here at all? Why do you stay?'

Good question. Arguing's a matter of wanting. You can argue about almost anything and you can not argue about almost anything. In my American family we never rowed at all. With Duchi, it's the opposite; we have rows all the time. About anything. It's a permanent row. Perhaps it's compensation after suffering years of row deprivation with my family. Or merely something in her that gets on my nerves. She complains about my family, I do about hers. She's stressed, I'm relaxed. She thinks that if there was a terrorist attack on a Little No. 5, there's going to be another one soon; I disagree. But I don't enjoy the arguments. I don't know why they happen. I assume it has to be her. It *must* be her. She's a lawyer, after all: their life's work is arguing. The difference between me and Duchi, in one sentence, is this: I say, things will be all right, and if they aren't, that's all right too. Duchi says, things will not be all right, and if they are, that's not all right either. OK, two sentences.

'I don't respect you?' I said. 'Sorry, I think *you* don't respect *me*. You don't respect my reasoning – *which has been proved to be correct!* – in selecting the particular mode of public transport vehicle in which I travel home.'

'Don't shout.'

'I'm not shouting!' I mean, it doesn't bother me at all that there are differences between us. Everybody has differences, every couple; everybody should. What bothers me is the way living together turns nice people into mini-dictators. Criticism of the partner's conduct becomes the basis of all communication. Improving the partner's conduct becomes the primary goal. Intimacy is the policing of the other's conduct.

'You are! You always end up shouting! You—'

'Wait, Dooch, wait . . . shut up! Turn it up! Turn it up!'

On the screen there was a photograph of a familiar face.

'Giora Guetta, twenty-three, has been identified as the last victim of the Tel Aviv suicide attack. In Guetta's parents' house in Hapalmach Street in Jerusalem, there were calls for the government to retaliate with maximum force.' A man was saying, '. . . They must do something! This government is abandoning our sons. We're letting them turn our lives into a circus . . .'

Hapalmach Street in Jerusalem. That was where I needed to go. Duchi looked at me, seeing that my attention was elsewhere now. 'What's happening?'

'I have to go there. To Hapalmach Street in Jerusalem.'

'You're not going to any Jerusalem. Are you crazy?'

'I have to,' I said. I kissed her forehead; I was already gathering my bag and phone and jacket. 'I have to go. He talked to me before the . . . he asked me to deliver a message. I have to.' I was all ready to go. 'Don't worry, Dooch. I'll be in touch,' I said, and in my heart I added – maybe.

I was taking the steps two at a time and already a floor down before I heard her voice so I couldn't hear what Duchi said, only her tone; only her anger and despair echoing down the stairwell behind me.

# 8

*'Fahmi . . .'*

Lulu? Lulu. Oh, Lulu, how I love your voice . . .

*'How are you, Fahmi? I've missed you. You . . . you look well. You . . .'*

What, Lulu? Why did you stop talking? Keep talking, Lulu.

*'I saw Bilahl. Dad and I went to the trial. In the end they delayed it. He'll probably get about four hundred years, but he doesn't care. Fahmi, when are you going to come back to me? I rode the horse I was telling you about.'*

With the guy. I told you to be careful of him. You're too young for that sort of thing.

*'You probably would have said I'm too young for it. Uhh . . . yesterday I saw* Noah's Ark *on TV. It was great. You'd have loved it.'*

*Noah's Ark* on Channel 2. I know it – I'm always *on* it. Again and again . . .

'Israel's number-one programme, with television's brightest star, Tommy Musari!' booms the announcer, and Tommy Musari says, 'Fahmi Omar Al-Sabich?' and I say, 'Yes, good evening.' 'Good evening, Fahmi. You decided to follow in the footsteps of your grandfather and shoot Israeli cars in Bab al-Wad.' 'Right.' 'And you' (my partner in the Ark is a Jew) 'you shot and killed a twelve-year-old boy in the Al-Amari refugee camp in Ramallah for making an indecent gesture at you.' 'Right,' says the Jew. The audience applaud and we both smile and Tommy Musari smiles too, with his one non-glass eye. 'Fahmi,' he says, 'tell us why you decided to follow in your grandfather's footsteps.' 'I always admired Grandpa,' I say, 'and he loved me. His name was Fahmi too. He used to tell us how he hit the Jewish convoys going to Jerusalem in '48.' The audience applaud. 'Well, I wanted my life to be worth something too.'

*'Come back to us, Fahmi. I'll come again next week. Goodbye, brother.'*

No, Lulu, don't go . . . don't leave me here! I want to talk to you but this fucking body won't move. Lulu! I can't open my eyes . . .

*'Fahmi? What is it? Fahmi! Nurse! Nurse! Fahmi, can you see me?'*

No, don't call that fucking little fool. Stay here . . .

*'What happened? Oh, he opened his eyes? OK. No, no, it does happen from time to time. It doesn't mean he regained consciousness. I'm very sorry. Were you alarmed at all?'*

*'Not really. I was hoping . . .'*

*'I'm sorry. Perhaps it's time to end today's visit. Maybe it's a bit of a burden on him.'*

Oh no, you whore, no, don't send her away . . . Please! Don't leave me floating out here, with these fragments of memory . . .

*'Goodbye Fahmi. You hold on in there for me . . .'*

Lulu . . .

The early morning news on Channel 2 with Danny Ronen the clown. The security forces think the attack came from Nablus. Who's more of a clown, Danny Ronen or Shaul Mofaz? Not an easy question.

A smoky smell of winter and a hard morning frost on the mud in the alleyways. Now that the rain had stopped, women were hanging out washing, and the muezzin was calling. Bilahl would have made me go to the mosque if he'd been there. He was pushing me to study in his college, Kuliat Al-Iman, the faith school in A-Ram. Not a chance: Dad would have gone nuts. And I still meant to go to Bir Zeit. Uncle Jalahl recommended electrical engineering at the Hebron Polytechnic, but how could I ever have got there? So in the meantime, I was waiting. Helping Jalahl with his electrician's jobs when he needed it. Watching TV. Al-Manar. Future TV. Al-Jazeera. Channel 2. Egypt, Lebanon, Dubai. The world at my fingertips. In *The Mission* on Al-Manar, Ehab Abu-Nasif asked contestants to name the Palestinian village in the Ramle region which was destroyed in 1949 in order to make way for the town of Yavne. Yibne. I got it right off. The shahid Amar Hamud was nicknamed . . . Too easy: Sword of the *Shuhada*. For which organisation did the shahida Wafa Idris volunteer? You're kidding – the Red Crescent. The Jordanian contestant only won four million liras. *The Weakest Link* on Future TV: which painting was stolen from the Louvre in 1911? The Mona Lisa. *Who Wants to Be a Millionaire?* from Egypt: where is Martin Luther King's birthplace? Tough one. Charleston. Atlanta. New Orleans. Little Rock. Atlanta. Yes. After *The Mission*, Al-Manar started showing *Terrorists* and there it all was again, the children bleeding to death in Jenin and Gaza, the bodies ripped to pieces by missiles, the shattered houses in Chan Yunes. I zapped to a rerun of *Ya Leil Ya Ein* – music and pretty girls on Future TV. Music and girls on Future TV . . .

Bilahl and I went on our way that evening after the prayer at the setting of the sun.

We met near a shed at the back of an old house we

used as a hiding place. The two rifles were there, and spare clips which we divided between our backpacks. Bilahl made a phone call and we waited, leaning against the wall. Five minutes later a yellow taxi arrived. I put the rifles in the boot while Bilahl spoke to the driver. We drove to Bidu. The driver was listening to the news. The Jews had attacked Nablus and destroyed Shafiq's family home. The driver said, 'Why can't these Nablus pricks get it into their heads that they're only causing trouble? Every time it happens we all get fucked! Every time there's a bomb I know I'm not going to have any work tomorrow. Nobody wants to poke his nose out. They're all waiting for the retaliation.'

We didn't say anything. Eventually Bilahl said, 'Why don't you stick some music on?' The driver switched stations.

We got out in Bidu, sent the taxi on its way. Bilahl was angry because of Nablus getting the credit. I said that if the Jews thought the operation came from Nablus, at least they weren't going to be coming after us. 'You always see the glass half full, don't you, kid?' he snapped. We walked in the mountains, following the goat trails through the terraces, through the sweet scent of the sage and *zaatar*. The night was dry and cool. Clouds covered the moon.

We hardly talked. I thought of Rana. And of Shirin Abu-Akla from Al-Jazeera. And the beautiful Osnat Dekel from Channel 2. I didn't think it worth bothering Bilahl with these thoughts.

When my brother was ten he threw stones in a demonstration in Murair. Because he was underage they just gave him a fine, and Dad had to pay it. Bilahl told Dad not to. Dad paid, and screamed at him: 'The Jews have the power! The Jews have the power and they will keep hurting us . . .' A couple of years later, he is stopped by three soldiers in one of the alleys in the village in the middle of a downpour. The rain is so hard it hurts; the drops are cold and as sharp as knives. The soldiers stand under a shaky corrugated tin shed and tell Bilahl to stand in front of them, outside the shed, and to take off his keffiyeh. They ask him questions in broken Arabic and laugh at him. The rain is so loud he has to shout. One of them, in the middle, is smoking a cigarette. He stands in front of them in the cloudburst, his hair stuck to his head like a mop, his face twisted from the cold and wet, and what is he thinking about? What is the kid in the rain thinking about . . .? They took him for a ride in their jeep, asked him to show them the *Shabab*, the kids who sprayed the walls and threw the stones, wanted to know who was sending them out, as if anyone needed to . . . At the end of the first intifada, when he was sixteen, they arrested him again for setting fire to the army watchtower at the entrance to the village: a month in 'administrative detention', a month during which he learned a lot about 'the only democracy in the Middle East'. He made a friend there who invited him to the faith school in A-Ram. He moved to Uncle Jalahl's apartment in Al-Amari. Stopped shaving and always went to the mosque for prayers. He talked to me a lot, even before I moved to live in Al-Amari.

'Dad told us not to get into trouble,' I pleaded.

'Dad lives in another time. In another world.'

And Bilahl was right. The world had turned on its head. The peace our father had longed for had turned out to be a monstrous Israeli deception. But he kept insisting that to struggle against it was even worse. Me, I preferred to think about something else. Until the army erected a dirt ramp around Murair for a week and I moved to Al-Amari, where a quarter of the families managed to stay alive only thanks to the rations of rice, flour, powdered milk, sugar and oil from UNRWA. How long could I sit around on my arse watching TV, or boiling the same potatoes and eggs to mix with tuna in a pita, or walking the same streets and alleys between grey breeze blocks and open sewers, hoping that the wind would cover the stench with the smell of cooking or cumin? How long could I sit watching the camp's football team scuff around their dirt pitch? How long for? Even if they are the best team in the West Bank, how long can you do that for?

*'Hoo, what a day I've had! I'm dying to get my head on a pillow. Let's just check everything's in its place . . . one tube for your piss, another one for your air. Lovely. Good boy. Goodnight, now.'*

Yeah, yeah, Svetlana, now go away, I'm busy . . .

*'And Dr Hartom says your scans were very good: your brain responded to the music. And tremendous responses to the photos of your brother and sister.'*

Didn't you already say goodnight?

*'OK, that's it. I'm off. Goodnight,* lyubimyi moi . . .'

On the left we saw the lights of Har-Adar, and on the right the lights of Katana. We skirted around Maale-Hachamisha and Neve-Ilan. We walked for almost four hours. Bilahl whispered prayers. For several minutes we heard the murmuring of traffic on the road like a constant distant rain. A sharp ascent.

'After this hill I think we'll see the road,' said Bilahl.

I was tired, and soaking with sweat, and my heart was going like crazy, but I almost ran all the way to the top. We started descending through the pines. And then I saw the white and red snake of lights, the cars heading in opposite directions, and Bilahl came up to my shoulder and said, 'Yes.'

We descended a little farther until we were at a point not too high above the road with a good view in both directions. The whole ravine was steep – a dangerous place, a place of ancient ambushes. Bab al-Wad: 'The Gate of the Valley'. Not far below us, in a scrubby little central island which the two streams of cars flowed round, one of Grandpa's metal skeletons was resting quietly.

'This is the point,' said Bilahl. He checked the time. 'The getaway car will arrive right beneath this bus's skeleton in a little over an hour. We will open fire together for a few minutes just before eleven and then go down to the ditch beside the road to wait. Let's get the rifle-rests ready.'

We made comfortable rests for the rifles out of soil and stones, a few metres apart, with room enough to lie and aim across a wide field of fire. Bilahl gave me earplugs. I felt sick to the stomach. 'We've got fifty minutes. We will pray. Remember, we are only shooting at the other side, at the white lights. Wait for my sign, and shoot at the windows. From the moment we start, shoot as much as you can. If your weapon is blocked, do the checks I showed you, change the magazine and cock the rifle again. If it doesn't work we will exchange rifles and I will try. The whole operation will not take more than three minutes and then we'll go down to the road with the rifles. Remember Silwad. Be quiet. Composed. Brave. Do as I do. Don't think too much.'

# 9

A soldier was standing by the slip road on to the Ayalon highway with a hitchhiking finger out waiting for a bite. I stopped and lowered the window. 'Jerusalem?' 'Jerusalem.' 'Thanks very much.' 'You're welcome,' I said, and he slung his huge bag into the back and got into the passenger seat still holding his rifle. 'Just don't point that thing in my direction.'

'Don't worry,' he said. 'What does "Every Second Counts" mean?'

'What?'

'The sticker. On the car.'

It took me a moment to clear my head. We were in the green Polo I got from work. I mean, I say 'got', but I paid for it every month out of my salary. I hardly ever drove it because the Little No. 5 took me to work. Duchi was the one who took the Polo to work every day.

'Oh yeah.'

'Yeah what?'

'Sorry, what did you ask?'

'What does "Every Second Counts" mean?'

'Uh, well, let's see.' We got on the highway. It was chilly but I opened the window a crack to feel the fresh night air. 'You know when you buy some new gadget but you can't be bothered to read the instructions?'

'What?'

'Or the bags of pre-washed salad you get in the supermarket? The jeans you buy already worn out and patched?'

'Sure, I've got a pair, waste of time!'

'Exactly! A waste of time. People don't like wasting time. Every second counts. Get it?'

'You make bagged salad and pre-worn jeans?'

I guess that people who don't themselves physically embody the phrase 'Every Second Counts' might be slow to grasp it. When I went up for my job at Time's Arrow, Jimmy Rafael asked me at the end of the interview whether I was a time victim. 'A time victim?' 'Does the question of how to do things more quickly, or do as many things as possible in as little time as possible, ever cross your mind?' 'All the time.' 'Do you ever find yourself consciously accelerating your own thoughts, movements and speech and trying to accelerate them in those around you?' I nodded. 'Planes simply *have to* take off on time? Slow drivers make you want to murder them? Do queues in the bank or in the cinema drive you mad? Do you absolutely hate having to wait for your food in a restaurant?' 'Of course.' 'Every second of wasted time, time in which you could have done something else, makes you furious?' 'Yes! Yes!' 'Welcome to Time's Arrow.' Jimmy smiled, and shook my hand. I felt at home. Later he told me that he tried to pick all his employees according to these criteria, and in fact I liked the way I was always surrounded by people of my own type at work. Some people look down at us or feel sorry for us, wonder why we rush around breathlessly from place to place; what do we get out of it, out of managing to do more things? You can always manage more, they say, but you can never manage everything. So why, they say, don't you find the balance that will let you relax a little and enjoy life? What they don't understand is that, ultimately, that *is* the way we relax a little and enjoy life. The beauty of this way of life is all in the word 'complete' – completing tasks, and feeling complete. I'm jealous of people like Jimmy Rafael who have done and are doing so much. Their lives fascinate me; I want to be like them: a busy week filled with completed tasks is a satisfying week, a hell of a lot more than lying on the beach and incompletely staring at the sun. My hitcher wasn't the sort of guy who would get this. I tried to attack it from a different angle.

'You know Federal Express or McDonald's?'

'Yeah. You work for them?'

'Multinational empires built on the principle of saving time. Before Federal Express, an international delivery would take about a week. Fed-Ex takes a day. Same with McDonald's and food. One-hour photo development. Twenty-minute pizza delivery.'

'Last time I went to McDonald's it took less than a day,' he chortled.

The best test for a good salesman is a tough customer. If I could sell Time's Arrow to this dunce I could sell it to anyone. I liked these challenges. 'We shorten the length of phone calls to directory assistance,' I said: if you can't summarise what your product can do in one sentence, you won't sell it.

'Uh . . .'

'People can't stand to waste even a moment: they spend a lot of time on the phone and they need their numbers right away. We give them the numbers more quickly and therefore more cheaply.'

'So you work for 144. Why didn't you say so? News,' he added, leaning towards the radio and nudging the volume up. Of course, *news* . . . News above everything, above basic good manners, above unimportant small talk about time, above life. Silenced by news, we listened to the headlines.

'Fucking cunts. They ought to wipe out the whole of Nablus.'

'Would that help?'

'The only way to teach them. They came from Nablus? Tomorrow there's no Nablus. Day after that the guy from Hebron will think twice before going on his mission, because he knows that if he goes on Monday, there won't *be* any Hebron on Tuesday. Understand?'

Another genius with his genius solutions. I wanted to say: and what happens if the guy from Hebron thinks twice and still goes? What have we accomplished then? Or if he doesn't think at all and goes? But I didn't rise to him. I didn't have the energy for that stuff. The newsreader mentioned Giora Guetta's name.

'Know what I'm saying?' the soldier was saying. 'It's not rocket science.'

We drove for a few minutes in silence. The news ceded to a phone-in show. Callers sharing their problems with the world. I sighed and changed station. 'It Must Be Love'. I turned up and dived into the song. I sang. How many times had I heard this song fifteen, sixteen years ago, when I was in love? Was I in love now? I didn't know. Maybe not. Otherwise, why did I behave as I did with Duchi? Slapping her down, not supporting her when she asked me to, treating her requests with contempt. Running out of the house in the middle of an argument. If this song is a measure, I thought, I am not feeling now what I felt once. *Nothing more, nothing less, love is the best*. But maybe I can't feel that any more. Maybe, at my age, a song can't measure anything much. I know Duchi is dear to me. Very much so. I know I always regret fights, as now. Hell, what was so damn wrong with taking a taxi after work? She told me once that Uri claimed I lacked confidence, that all my behaviour was a demonstration of power to compensate for the inferiority I felt towards her, because she was so strong and successful. He said I behaved like this out of fear that I wasn't good enough for her, out of fear of being dumped. When she told me this, I refuted this proposition with the following counter-argument: 'Pfahhhh . . .' Once I asked Bar to do us a numerology to see whether Duchi and I were compatible. He fed the data into his software and got 'Croc and Duchi = perfect match from heaven'. But after another huge row I asked him to check it again. He got 'Croc and Duchi = scary future'.

We passed the airport; another plane leaving the country. 'It Must Be Love' finished. The soldier said, 'Hey, could you get me the number of Michal Yannay?' I looked over at him. His face was big, round, pink, shiny. You could say he was chubby. His hair was strange; hair that hadn't quite worked out its place in the world yet, in the taxonomy of hairdos. Whether or not there was a skullcap on top of it I don't remember. Spots round the mouth and a smell of sour glands. I didn't know his name until I heard it on the morning news later. He wanted a kids' TV presenter's phone number. I turned my gaze back to the road.

When I was a soldier, hitchhiking was the thing I liked best. You hang your finger out at the angle you'd hold a fishing rod and you never know what you're going to pull up. A businessman in a magisterial Merc which purrs you at 200 kph to the very gates of your base? Or a political science student from Jerusalem with a rusty Citroën and a smile worth 300 kph? And how far would you get – five, twenty, a hundred and twenty kilometres? I loved talking to the people, hearing about their worlds, their work, their kids, the countries they'd known – any place far away from the loathed routine of army life or the brief leaves at home. And I always loved this road, Highway No. 1. A short transition between two worlds. Between the mountains and the sea, between history and now, between sacred stones and sand. The first sign that you were crossing from one territory into another would always be the hissing and chirping of the radio, the strange music of the cross-purposed airwaves. To our right, the soldier and I saw the Ramle cement factory, a weary but unceasing behemoth exhaling huge plumes of smoke into the huge floodlights which marked its huge perimeter.

He told me he was from Petach Tikva. His friends had dropped him off at the train station in Tel Aviv, where he knew he'd be able to hitch a ride to Jerusalem. He was serving in Bethlehem. What was going on there was a real shitstorm, but at least we were showing them who was in charge. Thank God his platoon commander didn't have any time for all these rules, which anyway they were always changing every week – don't open fire here, don't open fire there, yes this, no that, those are the guys you can shoot, those are the guys you can't . . . His platoon commander said that if a single hair fell from the head of one of his soldiers then the whole of Bethlehem would go up in flames, because you don't mess with the Golani. Not the Golani. They don't piss around, the Golani. One time their patrol came under fire from a sniper but no one was hurt. This other time someone chucked stones at them from a rooftop and a mate of his got this gash over his eyebrow and the platoon commander went wild and they went through all the houses in the street one by one, and pulled out all the men and covered their eyes with flannel blindfolds and tied their hands behind their backs with plastic cuffs.

'But your friend got a stone in his eyebrow, didn't he?' I said.

'Yeah . . .'

'Did any of his hair fall out while this was happening?'

'No.'

'So why punish all the men in the street? The platoon commander said he'd freak out if a hair fell from anyone's head. By the way, what do you do if it falls out naturally? Cheap conditioner? Or one of those really tough combs? Or natural shedding?'

'Pulling a few Arabs out of their homes with handcuffs isn't burning Bethlehem, man.'

Latrun now passing on the right. He didn't have a girlfriend. His parents were divorced. His conversation was peppered with religious expressions like 'with God's help' and 'God willing', but that might have been the influence of religious friends in his unit, not necessarily his upbringing. When a Zohar Argov song came on the radio he wanted me to turn it up, which was kind of weird for such a white kid, liking a guy like Zohar – another late influence, maybe. Everything he mentioned that he liked or was cool was a 'waste of time'. Oh yeah, waste of time, man. And true enough, I was wasting my time, in several respects, though there was no way on earth he'd know that. No, he hadn't ever killed anyone, but his platoon commander, praise be to God, had: waste of time. There was this one time it had happened on a patrol he'd actually been on himself. A bullet in the head! The son of a bitch ordered it. Like you order up pizza, said the platoon commander. Only instead of picking up the phone and saying I want pepperoni, I want onion, I want olives and mushrooms, this son of a bitch held up his hand and made gestures and everybody saw he had a gun in his hand, though by the time they'd run and reached him, no more than, like, forty metres, maybe fifteen seconds, someone had made the gun disappear, which meant another night of blindfolds and plastic cuffs. Fun. That was how the soldier summed up his tour of duty in Bethlehem. Fun: waste of time.

We passed Shaar Hagai with a bus in front of us, a No. 480. 'How's the Polo?' the soldier asked.

'A pleasure to drive.'

'What's the engine size?'

'Thirteen hundred, I think.'

'Mm. And it's an automatic. We'll see how it does on the hill in a minute.'

Don't count on it burning up the road with a fatty like you in it, I said to myself. The radio started crackling and whistling, meaning we were beginning the climb into the mountains. I stepped on the gas. 'Not bad, not bad,' said the soldier and then I saw the flashes, and heard the rear window shatter and something move very close to me and the soldier screamed 'Aiiiiii!!! FUCKING *CUNT*!' and I hit the brakes with everything I had.

# 10

Three minutes.

The skeleton of the bus below me. Grandfather Fahmi's bus. My heart was beating very fast. Blood was surging through me: my fingertips were tingling. I was breathing as if I'd been sprinting, even though I'd been lying motionless for nearly an hour. A line ran dead straight from my eyes down the sight to the white lights below. The earplugs gave me the feeling that I was watching everything from somewhere to the side of myself. I waited for Bilahl to say the word.

The sniper who opened fire on the road at Wadi Haramiya had the advantage of daylight. No flashes of gunfire could be seen. Because of the light and the acoustics of the wadi nobody knew where he was shooting from and he kept it up for a long time. We didn't have that luxury – we had to cause as much damage in as little time as possible. Three minutes.

Bilahl checked his watch. When he saw a bus climbing up the road he said, 'The bus is mine. You take the cars around it. Aim only at the white lights. Now fire.'

* * *

Oh, Svetlana, what's this now? Another wash already? You only did one five minutes ag . . .

*'You know, sweetie, you don't look half as bad as those people make you out to be. Every time I go in or out of the hospital they're there with their signs . . . here, let me just, slowly, let me soap, OK . . . But they can't get in here,* lyubimyi, *don't worry about that . . .'*

I'm floating at sea. I can see the shore but I can't get to it.

The bus immediately skewed round on its axis and skidded to a halt: it seemed that the driver had been hit and wrenched the wheel over. An eruption of horns and then quiet, except for our gunfire. Windscreens shattered in several cars behind the bus. To the left, in front of the bus, rear windscreens shattered. The rifles fired continuously without jamming. We changed magazines. The smoke and the gunpowder scent were choking me. Bilahl's hand was on my shooting hand. 'That's it, let's go.' I started as if he had woken me from a deep dream. The road below us was illuminated by the mess of cars. The bus had blocked both lanes. Shattered glass and smoke. A few cars were stopped in front of the bus, more behind it. Mayhem.

We climbed down to the roadside and crouched in the ditch. I noticed how I was sweating and panting and how strange it was that the time had passed: something you'd been anticipating so much, suddenly behind you. Squad cars and screams on the far side of the road. Some cars on the near side had also pulled up. People were jumping out of them and vaulting the central reservation to the other side, to help. Others stood and watched but most kept driving. One squad car even came over and kept the traffic on our side flowing. Funny, a squad car whose job was to help get us out of there. It had been Abu-Zeid's idea to escape by car but, counter-intuitively, into the west.

He knew it would be the last thing they would think of. There would be no police barriers in that direction, he'd said. And he was right.

The car arrived. This was the most dangerous moment of all: getting into the car with the rifles in the middle of the road, among the cars that had pulled over and the crowd looking on at the chaos. But darkness helped. Clouds concealed the moon and stars, and the hysteria on the ground had no focus or direction. We climbed into the back seat and the car accelerated away.

Nobody said a word. The car had yellow number plates, of course, and the driver had the blue ID card of a Jerusalem resident and an Israeli driving licence. I tried to look at her. I saw long black hair and, from time to time, her eyes in the mirror, examining me. You could see the eastbound traffic backed up for miles on the other side. We saw the last cars braking and joining the end of the tailback. She turned right off the highway and we drove for a few minutes in the dark with hardly any other traffic on the road. Blue lights flashed ahead of us, but it was only an old Civil Guard jeep. Those old boys just pottered around Latrun Park looking for cars with couples fucking in them to leer at. Or that's what Murad, the guy we stayed with in Beit Likya, told me later.

This was Grandmother Samira's area. Murad said that the ruins of her village, Dir Ayub, still existed, and promised to take me there. We ate at his place, and only then did I realise how hungry I'd been. The pitas with *zaatar*, cheese and olive oil were wonderful, and so were the apples and coffee: after intense physical effort the taste buds grow sharper – you've become a predator and the body wants its due. We showered and put on the clean clothes Murad supplied us with. The female driver left with a nervous smile and we switched on Channel 2.

There they were. The bus. The cars. Shattered windows.

Ambulances. Police cars. Danny Ronen was talking over a map of the region. A military source had informed him that the sniper probably came out of the Bethlehem area. Or Hebron. 'We can speculate,' said Danny Ronen, 'that probably the sniper made his way by foot from Bethlehem or from the area around Husan village, crossed the green line near the Israeli villages of Zur Hadasa and Mavo Betar, descending the steep and rocky paths from there to the slopes below the village of Beit Meir, above the Jerusalem–Tel Aviv road.'

'Beit Meir? Oh, you fucking cunt. *Beit Meir?'* said Bilahl.

According to information Danny Ronen had received, the sniper was still at large and the hunt for him was concentrating on the area between the attack and Bethlehem. 'It is mountainous terrain and very difficult to search,' Ronen said. 'Helicopters are floodlighting the area and search teams with tracker dogs are already on the ground, but the hunt could well continue for days.'

'Clowns,' said Bilahl.

Witnesses described how the gunfire had come from the right-hand side of the road; somebody said he'd seen flashes from the sniper's rifle, and then watched him getting up and running up the hill. Danny Ronen sketched escape routes on his map and explained where the military forces thought the sniper was right now. Murad brought a couple of mattresses into his living room and went to sleep. Bilahl and I were full of energy. My heart was still pounding. We drank more coffee. And the shots kept ringing in my ears, and the streams of white continued to flow across the ceiling of the strange room like the lighted windows of an infinite train.

It was only the following morning that the official statements admitted that it was uncertain where the gunfire had come from, and that the origin of the sniper, or snipers, was unknown.

# 11

People always wonder what the last thing going through a person's mind before he died was. Who did they think about – their kids, their parents, their partner, their first love? Did they ever think about love in general? Did their whole life replay itself like a movie? In the case of the soldier who rode with me that night from Tel Aviv to Jerusalem, I'm pretty sure I know the answer. The last thought running through his mind before dying, which he expressed with great conviction, was: 'My finger! Fucking cunt, I can't feel it!'

The Polo was one of the three or four cars in front of the bus which were hit. There were several cars behind it that also got shot up and others damaged in the subsequent crashes, but the bus, the No. 480, was the main target and took most of the bullets. The next day I saw the diagram in the papers. They got the colour of the Polo wrong, of course. And the direction it was facing when it stopped. And the location of the gunmen. But never mind. This is what happened: since we were ahead of the snipers, they were shooting at us from behind. The first bullet shattered the rear windscreen and hit my mobile phone, which was resting in its holder. The second bullet came through the empty frame and hit the middle finger of the left hand of the soldier, Menachem something, nicknamed Humi by his family and friends. That was when I stamped on the brake and Humi screamed. Apparently a smashed finger is immensely painful. I couldn't see much. He was holding his left hand with his right and there was a lot of blood. He screamed with a powerful voice, a huge voice I'd never have guessed he possessed during the previous half an hour: '*Aaaiii!! Fucking* CUNT! *AAAIII!! MY FINGER!!*' In great pain, he said, 'I've got a field dressing in the small pocket of my combat trousers. Get it out.' Field dressing – the kind of hateful phrase you forget exists until you give a soldier a lift. I fished the bandage out but I was too late: he had got out of the car. In retrospect it was a mistake, but he couldn't have been thinking clearly. The snipers kept firing. I don't think they were aiming. Humi was standing on the road beside the Polo. I didn't get out. Call it instinct. I stayed in the car and kept my head down. Humi kept screaming, 'HELP ME! HELP ME! MY FINGER!! FUCKING CUNT, I CAN'T FEEL IT!' and then he was whimpering and then there was a little 'ai' and no more. I didn't hear the shot or hear him fall: what I did hear was a sudden silence. That was the surprising thing. I crawled out of my side of the car and round the front until I got to him. He didn't look too good. His left hand held a palmful of blood and as far as I could see the middle finger – the finger that gestures 'fuck you' – wasn't there. No wonder he couldn't feel it. His throat was a bloody pool.

It was the first body I had ever seen. Until that moment, in the thirty-three and a third years I'd spent on Planet Earth, I had never encountered a body, not in the army nor on the roads nor in hospitals; not Grandma or Grandpa. Humi was my first, and though you might have hoped he was only unconscious, even

I could tell he was indisputably dead. The next day I read that the bullet had hit the third vertebra of the spine. He would have died within a couple of minutes. It is an injury you cannot survive.

I crouched next to him. I didn't touch him or look at him again: I shut my eyes and breathed in deeply. The shooting had ceased when I was crawling around the car and hadn't been renewed. There were shouts from the direction of the bus behind me, and the wounded moaning, begging for help which I couldn't give: I only wanted to get the hell away from there. I ran to the side of the road and blundered into the forest. I didn't know what I was doing: I might have been running towards the terrorists. Maybe I'd have run straight into them and . . . but I didn't think. I had to get into the cool and dark forest and breathe some real air. Not perhaps because it was the first body I had ever seen, or because this body belonged to a guy who'd spent the last half-hour of his life beside me. Nor even because of the responsibility I bore for his death – because it was me who had brought him to the point in time and space where it happened, and the speed at which I drove, the cars I overtook or didn't, the lane I chose, the moment I hit the brake were all *my* decisions.

But I wasn't thinking of anything when I ran from the road to the forest. I fell on to the damp thorns and breathed the air, smelling the moist earth, and then I opened my eyes and saw patches of cloudy sky between the branches and saw myself flying up, above the trees, above the clouds and the sky, looking down and seeing Earth quickly diminishing, zooming out from Shaar Hagai, from Israel, from the Middle East, from Africa, Europe, Asia, zooming out from Planet Earth, from the halo of light surrounding it, from the darkness surrounding the light, past the sun and other stars . . .

and I was in space. I saw aliens fighting among themselves, creatures from different galaxies, and then I stopped. And looked down.

Why does it matter who is where, and which people, on which piece of land?

Zoom in to Planet Earth. Continents fighting continents – black against white against brown against yellow. World wars. Zoom in towards the countries, the neighbours hunkered down in their hatreds; zoom in towards the related nations, the brother- or the cousin-nations of the old Yugoslavia, Ethiopia, the subcontinent, the Middle East.

Zoom in – Palestinians and Israelis.

Zoom in – Orientals and Ashkenazis, right and left. Keep zooming in, to the cities, the quarters, the neighbourhoods, street against street, house against house, flat against flat, husband against wife, brother against brother. Now zoom out, flying fast, with the cacophony speeded up into twittering gibberish, and do it all over again.

I opened my eyes. Another thought fluttered down from the trees and settled in my head. Here is where Tel Aviv ends and Jerusalem begins. This is what I thought. I told myself, again and again. Here is where Tel Aviv ends and Jerusalem begins.

I don't know how long it took before I returned to the car. Humi still lay on the ground. I heard ambulances arriving. I didn't know what I should do. Part of me wanted to get into the car and drive away. It was over, and there was nothing I could do to help anyone. The road ahead was clear, except for squad cars and ambulances arriving against the direction of the traffic. Either my ears or phone were ringing. But as I approached the driver's side, somebody blocked me.

'Yes, sir?'

'What "yes, sir?" My phone's ringing.'

'You just came from the forest out there, didn't you?'

I looked back to where I'd come from.

'What were you doing there?'

I lay on my back and flew out of the atmosphere. What did he want from me? Who was he?

'Who the hell are you? What . . .'

'The question is who are you and what were you doing there?'

I hadn't even registered that he was a cop. I had to fish out my ID card. He went to his car and confirmed that the car was mine and only then did he let me enter it. I stretched my hand out to the phone and then I saw that its display had been shattered: perhaps I'd heard its final dying cry. Could a telephone be considered a victim of hostilities?

Hostilities – what a word. Did the snipers feel any hostility? I guess they did.

I stood around for several minutes, near more people who were standing around for several minutes. The paramedics did their jobs, and we stood around them and looked bewildered. Many people were on the phone, in the talking-on-the-mobile-after-a-terrorist-attack posture: the phone is pressed against the ear more tightly than usual, than necessary, as if the words coming in are more important on such an occasion, and mustn't be allowed to escape. A slight bending of the back and the neck thrust forward as if setting oneself to attack an enemy or climb a mountain. The eyebrows frown, the forehead is creased, and the other hand – this is strange – the other hand is always held to the other temple, thumb to ear, fingers over the forehead. Perhaps it's to listen better, or perhaps it's a way to cover the eyes in a gesture of 'Oy vey'. A whole roadful of people gesturing 'Oy vey'.

The policeman wrote down my details. The ID card was

fished out again. I was told I would be invited to give evidence. I signed something. I checked the car. Apart from the shattered rear window and the shards of glass in the back, nothing had happened. Not a bullet, not a scratch, nor even a bloodstain. Even the phone holder hadn't got a scratch. Only the smell of Humi the soldier, sour sweat mixed with gun oil, lingered in the car. And his gun was still there, too.

I took it out and laid it gently next to Humi's body. I was beginning to feel the adrenalin of the survivor, the euphoria of the saved. Everybody there was, I think. We were alive! The bodies spread around us, the groans of the wounded, the medics working, the smell of cordite, the ringing in our ears – and we were alive! More alive than we'd ever been. Our bodies were trembling with life, our hearts greedily beating, the blood pumping double speed in our veins. My body was working and warmed up and craving motion. I had to get out of there. I got into the car and drove away at a speed I could scarcely contain, and the radio came on with the engine and took me straight back to the moment before it all started. When was it, an hour ago? The sound of the radio, the way the reception faded and the soldier had said something and then started screaming. I changed to a station from Jerusalem and there it was, of course, the old song of mourning: *Bab al-Wad, remember our names for ever, Bab al-Wad, on the way to town*. How many times was I going to hear it in the coming days? It occurred to me that every time I heard it from now on, I'd remember Humi.

Either Humi or Giora Guetta. And if them, why not me? If people shoot at each other, blow each other up? You feel your turn waiting for you round the next corner. Yours, or someone you love. It is embodied in the geography. It is encoded in the national genes. With every attack the feeling gets stronger: that the death of someone close to you is getting nearer by the moment: next week, the next street, tomorrow, today, and then suddenly it's right there. You imagine the mourning, the funeral, the pain, the request to say a few words. What are you going to say? How much better than you with words the deceased always was, how eloquent and funny and unafraid of public speaking? Maybe just stick to that, and not too heavy on the clichés, please. And after the funeral – the rehabilitation, the getting-over-the-pain, the guilt after spending a whole day not thinking about them, the guilt after you laugh again without restraint; the guilt when you're enjoying wild sex or daydreaming or just returning to life. But who was this person I was thinking of? I couldn't make out their face. *Bab al-Wad, on the way to town.*

I opened the door to my parents' house and silently eased myself in. I ate everything in the refrigerator. I didn't realise how hungry I was. Or how tired. In my childhood room, wrapped in sheets smelling of my childhood, my stomach filled with the food of my childhood, I finally slept, and the last thing I thought before I lost consciousness was: I'm still alive.

# 12

*'Is the ice ready, Svetlana?'*

*'Yes, Dr Hartom.'*

Ice?

*'We're going to do an EVM test today. Torch, please.'*

Oh, please, not the torch! Not the . . . aaiiii!

*'Good. Verbalism? Talking? Any of that in the last days? Clap your hand next to his ear, please. Thanks. And the other one. Thanks. Hold this card in front of his eyes. Yes. And this one.'*

*'Sometimes, when he's angry, he makes these gurgling sounds and twists his face . . .'*

Goddam you, you Jewish bitches. Can you not shut up for one second?

*'Here! Exactly like this, Doctor!'*

*'I see. Mmm . . . impressive reactions to loud sounds. And these movements too? Bending the shoulders, converging?'*

*'Converg . . . what? Sorry, I don't understand . . .'*

*'Ice, please.'*

Fuck this ice. Fuck this . . . aaaiiiiii!!

*'Nice. Very nice. His EVM is up a bit. Maybe we're seeing a little improvement. Continue with the therapy as before. Deep massaging, muscle movements . . .'*

*'Yes, yes, of course.'*

Oh, you gang of whores . . .

If this dream is never-ending then I'm in hell. But I'm not here. I'm floating in the sea. I'm riding a white horse. I'm in a car with the Croc, holding an apple.

Bilahl wanted more. He wanted bigger. Halil Abu-Zeid, on the other hand, was careful. He was worried. He knew the Israelis were furious. The smallest error and they would attack with all their claws unsheathed. The night's events revolved endlessly through my mind, trapped in there perhaps because I couldn't share them: the walk, the smells, our eyrie on the ridge, the waiting, the bus climbing up the slope in the far lane, the three minutes when it seemed as if my body was one huge shuddering heartbeat. I thought of Grandfather Fahmi, and of Mother. Abu-Zeid told us to keep our heads down for a week. But Bilahl wanted to get going.

Safi Bari was the bomb expert. Bilahl wanted me to work with him. Because I'd studied and worked a little in electricity with Uncle Jalahl – and still intended, somewhere, some time, to study electrical engineering – it wasn't difficult. I had the basics: a light touch, steady hands, cautiousness and patience. Safi has a degree in chemistry from a Bulgarian university. No one would have guessed he was the number-one bomb guy in the Izz ad-Din al-Qassam Brigades. He was short and thin, with a beard as sparse as a sixteen-year-old's and small mousy almond eyes. He spoke in a clear quiet voice and wore a little black cap and a rather elegant jacket which made him look like a French painter in a cartoon or a movie.

The essential component in most bombs is a molecule named triacetone triperoxide, or TATP, or the 'mother of the devil'. It's easy to manufacture, but unstable and evaporates easily. Dozens have been killed while preparing it. You can prepare it from hydrogen peroxide – the stuff used to lighten hair, which you can pick up in the pharmacy. Or from acetone – the paint thinner you can get in a hardware store, with a small addition of hydrochloric acid. RDX is an explosive based on the same triacetone triperoxide molecule, but its force is greater. It's also more dangerous, both to prepare and to carry. The ingredients of RDX are ammonia, from the packs of dry ice stocked by large supermarkets or from agricultural fertiliser, concentrated nitric acid, which can be produced by melting and filtering black gunpowder from bullets, distilled sulphuric acid from a car's battery and distilled water, from the pharmacy in Ramall . . .

*'Habibi, habibi, habibi, ya nur el-ein, Habibi, Habibi . . .'*

Oh, Svetlana, please don't try to sing. I'm in the middle of something, I'm . . . where was I?

*'I'm really getting into these tapes, Fahmi. She always comes and she never talks. She just plays you the music. Always on her own, never with the family. She's cute. Is she your girlfriend, Fahmi?'*

I don't know who . . . Rana? Rana comes? I haven't talked to her since she . . . she comes here? Svetlana, why can't you shut your mouth? I was doing something important. I was . . .

Sixty-eight milliletres of concentrated sulphuric acid in a flask. Thirty-two grams of potassium nitrate. With a stirring rod help the components blend into each other. Very gently, warm the flask on the cooker. Fill a bucket with ice and a thermometer. Lay a glass in the bucket and pour in the concentrated nitric acid. When the temperature in the bucket goes below 30 degrees, add hexamine – crushed fuel tablets from the Home Centre. Mix. Add ice and salt to the bucket until the temperature goes down to zero. Add ammonia. Mix and keep the temperature below zero for five minutes. Pour the mixture on to a litre of crushed ice and let it melt. Filter the crystals and pour away excess liquid. Lay the crystals in half a litre of distilled water that has been boiled. Filter them and test with litmus paper. Continue mixing in crushed ice and filtering until the litmus paper turns blue and the crystals are stable and safe.

*'Habibi, habibi, habibi, ya nur el-ein . . .'*

God help you, Svetlana. Are you a demon? Have you been sent here to torture me?

*'And what's he singing anyway? I'll ask your sister. Maybe she'll teach me a little Arabic so I could talk to you?'*

God forbid.

Safi is from Bani Naim, near Hebron. His grandfather made explosives from old ammunition shipped by Haj Amin Al-Husseini from Cairo to Hebron at the end of the Second World War. Husseini spent most of the war sitting in Berlin, and after the German surrender he turned up in Cairo, from where he would send over weapons and ammunition that had survived the war. The weapons were rusty or broken or ruined by sand – Italian or Czech or Russian, not as good as the British or German weapons, left lying in the desert for months. But Ali Bari had golden hands. He dismantled the bullets, grenades and rifles and reassembled them. Sometimes he reassembled them differently from the way they were originally made, and occasionally he assembled something completely new. Safi's grandfather lost two fingers and an eye over the years, but the British and the Jews lost much more than that. He was eventually killed in '49 while preparing explosives to be used in Jerusalem. His wife was eight months pregnant and she called the baby Ali, after his father. At the age of sixteen Ali Junior started working in the Hebron quarries as an explosives expert. He had eight sons. 'My father started teaching me at the age of four,' Safi told me. 'My brothers moved into other fields of chemistry. One of them is a professor in Boston. Two work in pharmaceutical factories in Jordan. But Father always continued manufacturing bombs, even after he retired from the quarry. He loved the profession.'

*'Lulu! How are you?'*

*'Me, I'm fine. But how is he? Is he smiling? Or am I just imagining it?'*

*'He's good. We had a successful check-up. Didn't we, Fahmi? Lulu, I wanted to ask you, because he can't tell me—'*

*'What? The people outside?'*

*'No, no, I'm just curious: what is "*yanur aline*"?'*

'Ya nur el-ein. *The light in your eyes. It's Amr Diab. You like it?'*

*'Very much. The light in your eyes. It's Fahmi's song. Every morning I put a light to his eyes with the torch . . .'*

*'I don't know this tape. Who brought it?'*

*'Ah. The girl who comes and sits next to him and never says a word and goes after an hour. A pretty girl. Who is she?'*

*'Don't know. Maybe Rana? Rana, I think.'*

Rana? Truly? Then why doesn't she speak?

Dad called. The calls with him were difficult. He asked about my studies. And about life, what I was doing with my days. About Rana. And I couldn't . . . I hated lying to him. So I tried not talking to him, not answering when I saw where the call was coming from. But it could have been Lulu calling so sometimes I did answer. And sometimes he would call his brother in the flat and then ask to talk to me. I knew he sensed something. I felt he had made the connection. He knew how proud Grandfather Fahmi was of the shooting at Beit-Machsir in '48 and I was sure he didn't want to believe it, but part of him suspected . . .

Sweat on Safi's forehead. From time to time he laid the material to rest and retreated into the corner to breathe air, opened the window, breathed in, and then shut it and went back to work. The blue crystals were drying on kitchen paper.

C-1 compound – the bomb you make from RDX – is made of a mixture of 54.6 per cent RDX crystals, 28.4 per cent mineral oil from the supermarket, and 17 per cent lecithin, from the vitamin section in the pharmacy. Mix the three in a plastic bag. Pour the mixture into plastic tubes and place the tubes into an explosive belt sewn specially with straps for the shoulders and pockets around the body for the tubes and the pieces of metal – the nails, ball-bearings and shrapnel that will fly from the force of the explosion and cause more damage than the explosive itself.

What? What's funny? I love your laughter, Lulu.

*'Was it him, Svetlana? Are you sure?'*

*'Ha ha . . .! Of course! He does it all the time . . .'*

Oh, merciful God. Take this whore away from me . . .

Electricity. Two precautions prevent the explosive from blowing up prematurely. The battery – usually from a mobile phone – should be connected at the last minute. Keep it apart. Besides the battery you need to prepare the actual detonator, which can be found in many places, like missile games from toy shops or military flares. Connect the detonator to some of the RDX tubes, make a safety catch – a nail held across the activation button of the detonator – and then close the electric circuit with the battery. Don't connect it all the way. Now the bomb is ready.

The bomb was ready. Safi said, 'Make another cup of tea,' in his quiet voice, pushing the buttons of his mobile phone.

# 13

I immediately knew who she was. She was on her own.

The broken mother, the shocked father, sisters or friends crying bitterly, the minister the government had felt obliged to send, and whose name I forget, bespectacled, too European for this crowd, chubby, a Likudnik's look in his soft eyes – and there she was on her own, in the corner of the congregation, with her straight black hair and her black eyes, her black coat, her black bag.

The close-packed crowd raised the temperature around the grave by a degree or two. Breath, body heat, traces of hot air blown through plastic car heaters still clinging to the mourners. You could see the steam rising up from them into a rain that fell without pause. I hadn't brought a coat because it's not cold in Tel Aviv. She looked up into the rain, stared straight into the drops while they landed on her face and eyes and mixed with her own tears and dissolving make-up.

'Shuli?'

She looked at me, didn't recognise me, and lowered her eyes. 'Not now,' she murmured, and I stepped back. The father's voice had been crushed into gravel. And then the rabbi, with his clear loud voice, sang songs that he was convinced with all his heart reached the ears of God, whom he was convinced with all his heart existed, and whom he was convinced with all his heart belonged to him alone, who had chosen his people from all other nations, who had chosen from everything only him. 'Ya, right', as Duchi would have said.

Earlier, breakfast with my parents in Rehavia: toast and peanut butter and jam. Unsatisfactory filter coffee. Or maybe I was the unsatisfactory one. At home I drink decaffeinated filter. I went off caffeine as part of the time management and relaxation workshop I attended. I don't remember how it's related but it's the only thing I took home from that workshop, apart from the group leader and time management expert Miriam's mantra: 'Each and every day we all get the same number of minutes' – and, Duchi of course, whom I met there.

Freshly squeezed orange juice and curious parental stares. Yochanan (Jonny) and Leah (Lili) Enoch. The peanut butter importer and the English teacher. She's been teaching English in the same high school for thirty years, and I never stop asking myself, how can you do the same thing for thirty years – and will I need to as well? Mind you, maybe a permanent and secure job is better than convincing yourself that you're going to introduce peanut butter to the natives of the Levant and monopolise the market. But, what can you do, the natives decided to do it on their own, and they even called it 'Egozan', which just means 'nut spread', a linguistic error which almost broke his heart. He turned to exporting, and then back to importing when it looked as if the market was opening up to American products at the end of the seventies. Eventually, when Dafdaf was born and it dawned on him that he had three children to provide for, and his mother in America had threatened to fly over and physically drag him back to Maryland if he didn't get a proper job, Yochanan Enoch compromised and found work as a sales agent for the food giant Elite and thus found himself selling, among the other products he was responsible for getting on to the shelves of the supermarkets and groceries around Jerusalem, thousands upon thousands of jars of Egozan, the paste that broke his heart.

They read about the attack in *Haaretz*. The headline was: 'On The Way To The City'. Twelve dead. It was thought that the terrorists, probably from Bethlehem or Hebron, had walked all night to escape. The radio was on, turned up very loud, voices talking about the victims and their funerals and about the funerals of the victims of the previous attacks.

'Hold on.' I stopped Dad, who was halfway through saying something. '*Giora Guetta's funeral will leave the cemetery in Givat Shaul at ten.*' I looked at my watch and apologised: 'I've got to make a move.' Their curious and worried looks followed me. Some other time, I thought; some other time I'll tell them about being there last night and about the attack in Tel Aviv. And why I suddenly turned up out of the blue. And of course, I owed them an explanation for why Duchi and I hadn't set a new date for a wedding. But I couldn't deal with it now. There was no point, and it was hard enough for them anyway. They'd come to this hole in the desert to give themselves and their children an identity and a good life, and in return all they'd got was destruction.

At funerals you have the prayers, and then the silence, and then the sniffs. At first you don't notice them; your ears filter them out. But once you become aware of them you realise they're almost as loud as the rain. Hundreds of sniffs from all around you. It's infectious. I sniffed too, though I scarcely knew Giora Guetta.

The minister spoke. He said something about the long arm (of the IDF) and the extended hand (of forgiveness). Outreach. That was the word. He said something about wretched creatures. He said something about forces beyond our understanding, and the sniffs said: Come on, shut up.

Giora's younger brother talked about the light in his eyes, about innocence and kindness. About his modesty. I thought about the Giora I had met, with the showy honey-coloured hair and shades. I hadn't seen any modesty there, but who knew, people have their untypical moments. Giora Guetta and I had known each other for about eight minutes and he'd said about thirty words to me. He'd said 'He looks OK to you, right?' and 'Listen, if something happens to me, I want you to tell my girlfriend in Jerusalem, Shuli, I want you to tell her . . .' and 'I know nothing's going to happen, but if it does . . .' I hadn't taken any of it seriously. It was an uncorrectable mistake.

The crowd started to disperse, though some remained for long minutes by the graveside. I stood a good way apart from everyone and watched Shuli out of the corner of my eye. She stood in the corner, separate, on her own. I decided I liked the high arches of her cheekbones. At last she turned and began to walk away. She had long legs and an upright way of walking. Self-assured, but not at the expense of tenderness, I thought. As she passed the fresh dirt of the grave, on which a wreath and a small sign with an image of a candelabrum and Giora's name handwritten on it were laid, she halted for a few seconds and then went on, nodding to one or two friends but not speaking to the parents. At the heart of the little group that was left by the grave there was a girl who couldn't stop crying. Guetta's mother had her enfolded in a long hug. I assumed the sobbing girl was Guetta's long-time girlfriend, possibly an ex, but still loved by his parents, thought of as a family member and recognised by friends as Giora's girl. Shuli, I continued with my theory, was a recent addition. Hardly knew his parents, if at all. Giora had been too nervous to introduce her, because of the sobbing girl. But my script turned out to be wrong: so completely and utterly wrong it ended up breaking the ice with Shuli, because when she heard it she laughed for the first time in two days.

I caught up with her as she was walking from the grave to the car park, measuring her steps carefully on the steep gradient, her eyes on the path.

'Are you Shuli?'

I fell into step beside her and she looked at me. Pretty eyes.

'Who are you?'

'I saw Giora just before . . .'

'He's dead.'

'I know.'

Silence. A pretty voice, too. She kept her eyes lowered. I was panting a little with the incline. The Mountain of Rest, they call the cemetery in Jerusalem, and it really is a mountain: a whole hill of the dead.

'What was he doing in Tel Aviv?'

'What? I don't know.'

'He never went to Tel Aviv. Why on earth Tel Aviv? Wherever he went, he always told me. I never even had to ask. Was he visiting you?'

'No. I was on the bus. The taxi. The minibus. I got off before the . . .'

It didn't seem to be of any interest to her. She kept walking, silently.

'You don't want to know what he told me?'

'Will it change anything?'

'Maybe.'

She didn't answer.

'I found his PalmPilot. Afterwards.'

She stopped and turned and looked towards the mountains, towards Bet Zayit, up at the sodden sky.

'I don't need the PalmPilot. Give it to the police.'

'No, they don't nee . . .'

'So give it to his mother. Or keep it. I don't know. What do you want?'

'I want to know who he was.'

'Why?'

Good question. I passed my hand through my wet hair. 'I don't know, I was the last person who talked to him.'

'So what?'

'Don't move!' She froze. A single step in front of us, on the slippery path, a not-so-big scorpion was watching her. She hadn't seen it yet, and it hadn't seen me yet. Moving carefully, I picked up a fist-sized stone from the top of a gravestone and approached it very slowly, lifted my hand back and crashed it down on the scorpion's head. Shuli jumped and let out a shout. 'What's that?'

'A scorpion. Sometimes they come out in the rain, when it floods their holes. And that's when they're angry, too. I don't know if he would have done anything, but it's best to be safe.'

She didn't move, looking at the crushed scorpion, trembling a little, perhaps from the cold.

'Listen. All I wanted to say is that I talked to him a little. And he said, "If something happens to me, tell Shuli . . ."'

She looked as if she were debating whether to believe me or not.

'Tell Shuli what?'

'He didn't say what. He said it like that. "Tell Shuli . . ." and then he never finished the sentence.'

'Then came the explosion?'

'No. He just stopped, and thought. A moment later we reached my stop and I got off.'

She thought about that for a moment and looked at me. 'That was what he said?'

'I think it was the last thing he said in his life.'

She started to cry.

She needed a lift to the Guetta family home on Hapalmach Street where they were sitting shiva, and I asked her whether she minded joining me for a couple of errands on the way. I showed her my mobile in its holder, with its shattered display, and gestured behind us, and she turned and saw the missing rear window and the glass on the back seat.

'Oh. What happened?'

'You heard about the shooting last night?'

'Bab al-Wad?'

I turned on the radio. *Forever remember our names.* Humi. That was his name.

'What's your name?'

'Eitan. Actually, it's Croc.'

She lifted her trouser leg. On the inside of her right ankle, just above the bone, there was a tattoo of a small green crocodile. It was giving me a little red sharp-toothed grin. I stared back at it, blinked, and looked up at Shuli, who smiled at me too, a warm and beautiful smile. Her deep black eyes, enchanting eyes that held mountains and valleys and seas of mist, smiled too.

We drove to the Orange service centre in Givat Shaul, a short trip from the cemetery. We took a number and sat next to a guy reading *Yediot Achronot.* The headline was 'Like Sitting Ducks In A Shooting Gallery'. 'Bit of a tongue-twister, that,' Shuli said. The guy shifted his paper and flicked his gaze from us back to the headline.

'These dogs. When are we going to get it? How long are they going to let them make mincemeat out of us?'

'Get what?'

'What "get what"?' Another voice joined in: an older man. 'Get that you can never trust these dogs.' He had a copy of *Maariv* in his hand. The headline was 'Like Sitting Ducks In A Shooting Gallery'.

'And if someone gets that, what's he going to do?'

'Go in there and raise hell. Scare the shit out of their mothers and grandmothers. So they'll get it once and for all.'

'They're turning us into a circus,' said the first guy. 'They're doing "Bab al-Wad" again. What is this? A history lesson they're giving us?'

The service centre's queue-routing system gave its demure little modern ping, and the woman at the desk called, 'Avi!' She was brandishing my phone.

'Come and have a look at something. The insurance includes hostile actions, right?'

'What's that?' Avi said.

'Hostile actions?'

She explained to him and he lifted his eyes to mine with respect. 'Really, you were there?' 'Me and him both,' I replied, pointing at my phone. He extended his hand for a handshake and I shook it limply.

'Don't worry, brother, we'll sort you out.'

'The interesting thing,' I told Shuli on our way to Talpiot, 'is that in a shooting gallery you don't have ducks, as far as I know. The last time I was in a shooting gallery was maybe thirteen years ago. But if there weren't ducks then, I find it hard to believe they've got them now. There are cardboard figures of Arabs with keffiyehs. But they could hardly write "Like Cardboard Figures Of Arabs With Keffiyehs In A Shooting Gallery".'

I could kind of hear her smiling.

The third time "Bab al-Wad" came on I switched the

radio off. Shuli said she'd heard about the bomb but hadn't thought she'd know any of the victims. When there was a bomb in Jerusalem, she got worried and checked the names but there was no reason to with Tel Aviv. And that was just the way we reacted to bombs at Time's Arrow. A bomb in Haifa would have our two and a half ex-Haifa residents making the phone calls and waiting for the names to make the TV. With the Jerusalem bombs it fell to me and Ron to take on the role of those in the know. We knew the street names with the little flame-things on the TV that made us the potentially bereaved.

Giora hadn't told her he was going to Tel Aviv. No one knew what he was doing there. He never went there. When she got home from work in the evening she'd called him, but after two hours he still hadn't called back. It wasn't like him. She cracked and called his father, who told her, 'Be strong.' That night they drove to Abu-Kabir in Jaffa to identify the body. They didn't recognise what they were shown. Only in the morning, after Giora's father obtained X-rays of his son's teeth from the dentist in Metudela Street, did they have a definite identification.

The Talpiot Glass and Window Co. was our next stop. After the experience at Orange I had prepared rather a moving speech about hostile actions, but they couldn't have been less interested. They just told me where to park and an Arab guy wrote down my details and told me to come back in half an hour.

'There's a stall that does a great omelette in pita round the corner. You want some?'

'Sure.' She was all right. How many girls these days agree to join a stranger for an omelette in pita less than an hour after their boyfriend's funeral? Later on I learned that she was a chef and may have had a professional interest in the omelette, which doesn't mean she wasn't all right, of course. She was much more than that. She agreed with me about the omelettes: tahini, parsley, tomatoes, omelette, pita, salt, pepper, perfect. 'Waste of time,' she said, and I suddenly realised I hadn't told anyone at work that I wasn't going to be in that day.

The rear windowpane was gleaming. All the fragments and dust of glass on the back seat and the shelf behind it had been vacuumed away. Who would have believed that this beautiful clean Polo had been a victim of hostilities yesterday? Only the smell of the rifle still bothered me. So I bought a cardboard air-freshener to hang on the mirror – it smelled of coconut and called itself *Hawaii!*

'Where to now?'

'Hapalmach Street,' Shuli said.

I connected the new handset to the speaker and it came alive with a sequence of bleeps and chirps that lasted a whole minute: the little device was bursting with eagerness. I would listen to the messages later (Duchi twice, Mom, Jimmy, Jimmy's secretary Gili about a flight to Brussels, something ready to pick up), but with Shuli beside me in the car I merely turned it off and drove where the girl told me to drive.

# 14

The last time I saw Halil Abu-Zeid was when he came to Uncle Jalahl's apartment. He and Bilahl talked while I watched Al-Jazeera. From the little I heard, I realised Bilahl was talking about the next attack. Abu-Zeid laughed and said something I didn't understand. I also saw him taking a roll of notes out and giving some to Bilahl and Bilahl saying, 'No. We need to hit now. We're like a boxer in the ring. When a boxer's got his opponent on the ropes, does he let him recover or does he finish him off?'

'I knew you would say that.' Abu-Zeid turned his big head to one side and shrugged his broad shoulders. 'But we need to stay alive now.'

'He goes in for the kill. He KO's him,' Bilahl was saying.

Next day the shahid Halil Abu-Zeid died and went to heaven and to Allah by way of the offices of the Islamic Charity Society in Al-Birah. He sat and talked there with Dr Hillel, a Hebrew University researcher, and another shahid I hadn't heard of. Dr Hillel said the subject of the conversation was 'life'. He left the building a few minutes before a Jewish helicopter of American manufacture arrived at the scene, hovered in the air above the building, and destroyed it with a Hellfire missile.

*'Who put these things into the heads of my sons? And especially you . . . you promised me!'*

Father, please don't start with the tears now. I had enough with Mother's sisters coming in here and wailing . . .

*'Look at him! My good son lying here like a vegetable. The other one's going to get four hundred years in jail . . .'*

*'Stop talking like this, Father. Positive things, remember? That's the way he stands more chance of getting better.'*

*'What are you talking about? Getting better?* Look *at him! Two sons I had! Two sons!'*

*'Stop it, Father. You promised you'd be positive with him.'*

*'How could anyone be positive looking at this?'*

*'The nurse says he had a good check-up.'*

The body won't move, and the eyes won't open. I'm floating at sea. I can see Bilahl on the beach, and Croc, but I can't get there.

*'Look at his eyes! Fahmi? Fahmi! My son!'*

'Blood. That's what they understand. They're playing a game. They sign peace treaties but you know they've no intention of sticking to them. The Palestinian delegations go there and the Jews sit and laugh in their faces. I don't want to see anyone's children die, but when I see a child on my street killed by a tank shell, or a house with a child in it destroyed by a missile, I have to retaliate. Watch Al-Manar and see what they're doing to us! Killing children is part of their *policy*. With us, if a child gets hurt, it's a mistake.

'I'm not a murderer. I kill whoever comes to kill me. I do God's will. My organisation tell the *Istishadin* to go to places where there's at least one soldier. But *every* Jew is a soldier. Every Jew voted Sharon. Every Jew was in the army, or will be, or their sons or their uncles. Doesn't matter if the Jew works in a bank, a bus, a shop, for the council, *they're all soldiers*. They came to settle in my country from Russia, from Ethiopia, from America, talking about the Nazis. But the Nazis ended in 1945. Where exactly is Hitler? Every year they get a hundred thousand immigrants from Russia. So please tell me where exactly Hitler is in Russia right now, and then maybe I'll listen to the immigrant who comes here at my expense to drive me out of my land with the excuse that Adolf Hitler made him do it. *They* are teaching *us* what is right and wrong? They talk about the Muslims, but who dropped two bombs on Japan and killed three hundred thousand?

'And we – we have two options. Death or death. Which one am I going to choose? I choose the less painful option. To die killing the soldiers who murder my children instead of dying from starvation.'

This was one of the high points of my appearance on *Noah's Ark* with Tommy Musari on Channel 2. I spent hours imagining myself giving this speech, over and over, improving it bit by bit, polishing it to perfection. The Tommy Musari in my head would nod away, fascinated, holding up his hand to stop the settler on the other side who'd be trying to interrupt. Eventually the settler would intervene to tell me that Moses had been here three thousand years ago. But we have nothing, I protested. Our life is worthless. It has no value. Curfew. No food. No work. No university. They kill us and all we do is try to stop them, and the settler said it was our fault and I said Israel bombed Gaza with an F-16 and killed the baby Iman Al-Hiju and what did she do, what was her crime, what was the crime of baby Fares Uda? The settler said that Moses was here three thousand years ago. Tommy Musari smiled and said, 'Don't you go away during these messages!'

After the break he began: 'What does your mother say?'

I swivelled my chair to observe the audience, all of whom I had brought with me from the village. The whole of Murair was there. 'My mother is dead, Tommy. But I know she's proud of me and my brother. Of course she is: she's like Alchnasa, the mother who sacrificed four sons in one day and then thanked God for giving her the honour of the *shuhada*.'

It never ends . . .

I'm hot, Svetlana. Where are you when I need you?

Svetlana. Come to me. Is there anybody here?

You could shine a torch in my eye, if you wanted to. Or give me a deep massage. Even do the ice. Come on and torment me.

Where are you?

I spent all morning soaking the sheets of the bed with my sweat. Bilahl told me about Abu-Zeid and ordered me to come to the mosque. But all my bones ached and I couldn't stop shivering. The phone rang. 'Fahmi? You OK?' Rana: how I loved her voice. 'I don't know . . . a little sick, I think.' 'You're not coming to Murair? You said you'd come back.' 'I said . . . I will come. Some time. You know how tough it is to get through.'

I could hear, just from the way she was breathing, that she wanted to say more. To tell me that these people who called themselves my brothers were only fools. That they wanted to take us all back to the dark ages. But she didn't say it this time. And Bilahl really *was* my brother. I reflected her silence with one of my own. In the end I said, 'I'm not feeling too well, Rana,' and she said, 'OK,' and Tommy Musari asked me if I had anything to say to the Jews.

'Let me say this, Tommy. Islam is the religion of mercy; the religion of peace, love, brotherhood and mercy. The root of its name is *salam*, meaning "peace". Now, your religion also says "Thou shall not kill" but every day you do. Every hour! Everything in this country must be yours; nothing can be ours! All my people are looking for is peace and freedom, that's all. But when you blow up my house and kill my children, when you take five hundred men from their homes and make them stand all night in the street, or arrest them without giving a reason, you leave me no choice but to defend myself! You terrorise us with fire and steel and we cannot allow it. We're not fighting because of money, or even religion, or for the sake of committing a crime. We're not the Mafia. We have a better cause to live for, and to die for – and to kill for.' I finished my speech and the audience rose to their feet and cheered me at length, and my imaginary Tommy Musari said, 'What does your father say?'

My eyes filled with tears. My father would have killed me with his bare hands, but violence was never his way. My father is profoundly disappointed. I promised him I wouldn't get into trouble. He only wanted to live peacefully. He thought Bilahl and his friends were throwbacks to the Middle Ages. He thought we were going to give him a heart attack. But I wanted my life to be worth something. I hadn't done what he asked me. Tommy sat there waiting and I began to cry, and my head spun with thoughts of my disappointed father, my dead mother, my raging brother, and Rana's soft, clear voice. I got up and shouted and threw the pillow at the wall, because all I saw, every day, all day long, was walls. Walls and the grey glass of the TV and blood: whole days went by without my seeing anything else.

I looked around the filthy little apartment, went to the bathroom, put my head in the sink and turned on the cold water tap. I badly needed to wake up.

# 15

Despite breakfast and the omelette in pita, I headed straight to the dining table in the Guetta house. It felt like the natural place to gravitate to. I filled a blue plastic plate from the bowls of salad that I was told Giora's aunts had worked all morning to make: tabouleh, tomatoes with hot chillies, goat's cheese with sun-dried tomatoes.

The house was thrumming with activity. Dozens of people were entering or leaving or milling about and talking. Outside, rain was pouring down the windows. It seemed as if the shiva was drawing life into the house, charging the building with life in order to compensate for its loss. Mr Guetta was holding Shuli's hand and whispering in her ear, tears on his cheeks. Since the only person I knew in the room was occupied, I found myself a chair and concentrated on my salads.

The next time I raised my eyes, Shuli was embracing Mrs Guetta and Mr Guetta was staring at me. I returned the look and he gave a sad smile. I realised I ought to go to him and stood up, in my hand a half-empty plastic plate. He encouraged me with his smile. I looked for a place to lay my plate but the flat was too crammed, so I just headed towards him, shifting my plate to my left hand

and extending my right. 'Mr Guetta, it's a pleasure. I'm Eitan.' He looked me up and down, eyes pausing momentarily on the plastic plate. Who knew what Shuli had told him?

'You're a friend of Giora's from Tel Aviv?' So that was what I was meant to be.

'Ah . . . not exactly. I just saw him on the Little Number . . . on the bus. I got off before . . . I talked a little to Giora before I got off.'

'Yes, that's what Shuli said. Have you any idea what he was doing in Tel Aviv?'

'Uh . . . look, Mr Guetta, I . . . no. I haven't. Not a clue.' I looked in hope towards Shuli but she was still in the arms of Mrs Guetta, both of them in tears, Shuli's mascara running for the second time that morning. I probed my plate with a fork and speared a cherry tomato, which I hurriedly shovelled into my mouth. Someone came over to hug Mr Guetta: my saviour, I thought. But as I turned to go he reached out to touch my shoulder.

'Hold on, Eitan.'

'Sure, Mr Guetta, I'm sorry. I thought you needed to talk to other . . .'

'No, no. I just want to know why he came to you. Why he was in Tel Aviv. That's all. Because he didn't tell us he was going there. We didn't think he had any reason to go there. I just need to understand.'

'But I really can't tell you anything, Mr Guetta. I just saw him on the bus. I exchanged a couple of words with him. He didn't say what he was doing there.'

'What did he say, exactly?'

Should I tell him the truth? He only wanted to know what his son's last words were. He was clinging to the last day of Giora's life. The need to decipher his actions or his motives was holding him together. As if that would change or explain anything. Should I tell him that his son asked me what I thought about the terrorist? *He looks OK to you, right?*

'Nothing,' I said, gesturing with my plate. 'I don't remember exactly. Not anything important. We were laughing about something on the radio maybe . . . The driver, the driver was saying something on her intercom and someone in the office shouted at her . . . I . . .'

'The driver?' Mr Guetta paused to receive a kiss on his cheek and someone said, 'You see what these barbarians have done now? Bab al-Wad, as if nothing has changed! This government's going to pay the price, Guetta, you wait and see.' I saw an empty section of table to lay my plate on, took advantage of the window of opportunity, and a hand grasped my arm and a good smell engulfed me.

'Let's get out of here, Croc.'

There was a giant panda in front of me. I looked in her eyes and I felt as if I was beginning to drown. She said, 'Stop staring at me.' I said, 'OK.' She smiled.

In the car – she gave directions and I drove – we passed roundabouts, large buildings, ascended a slope and descended again, went through a traffic light and down an alley where she told me to park. 'Where are we going?' 'To Montefiore.' 'Moses Joel Montefiore?' We walked down the alley. It was freezing. The wind in a few exposed spots in Jerusalem can be cruel. The only people visible on the streets were the security guards at the entrances to restaurants – the only reminders that there was anybody still living in the city at all. We made our way across the terraces, past the replica of the old Zionist's famous carriage, to the viewpoints looking east over the valley. She vaulted up on to a low stone wall, her hair flying in the wind, and said, 'Look at the desert! Have you got anything like that in Tel Aviv?' I looked at the grey hills and the treeless ravines and shivered. 'Come on, then,' she said.

In the café she cleaned the streams of mascara from her eyes.

Ordered hot chocolate.

Clasped her hands around it.

A security guard (an additional shekel on the bill), a barman, and what looked like a dog curled up at the foot of the bar. Outside the window, Jerusalem seemed to radiate an intense cold, as if it were the city itself that had mobilised the clouds and the winds to scour the humans from its streets.

I found her crying when I returned from the toilet.

I told her my theory about the Guetta family, the much-loved mythical ex and Shuli's comparatively low status. She laughed. There was no ex. Shuli got along fine with his family and friends.

'I'm still angry with him,' she said. 'I don't understand what he was doing there.'

I glanced at the paper on the table between us: 'Like Sitting Ducks', etc. Here too the drawing had my car's colour, model and direction wrong. At least they had Humi the soldier lying in the right place.

'Well, would you like to find out?'

'How?'

I got Giora's PalmPilot out, opened the diary and moved to sit next to her. On the date of his death a meeting had been scheduled at 8 a.m. It said: *B-MW. Coffee Bean, Yehuda Maccabi* and gave a phone number. I called. No answer, so I left a message: please call back urgently, it's to do with the meeting with Giora Guetta. 'You see?' I said. 'We're already a step ahead.' 'Ahead? We're not ahead of anything. What does BMW mean?' 'Relax,' I said in my most authoritative voice. 'Maybe he was buying a car?' 'What did he need a car for?' 'You'll see. The phone's going to ring now.'

It did, but it turned out to be Jimmy.

'Where the hell are you, Croc? What's going on, disappearing like this without any notice?'

'I'm in Jerusalem, Jimmy. Long story. I couldn't get in touch because my phone was involved in this shooting in Shaar Hagai . . .'

'Your *phone* was involved?'

'Jimmy, I'll explain everything, promise. I'll be in tomorrow, OK?'

'You remember we've a meeting in Brussels next week to prepare for.'

'I remember.' He hung up. No time for a goodbye, of course.

In my other hand I still held Giora's PalmPilot. My arm was touching Shuli's, enjoying the warmth of it, clinging to that warmth. I could scarcely believe this girl, who stood on walls marvelling at the desert on the day of her boyfriend's funeral. I told myself not to take advantage. She laid her head on my shoulder and said, 'I need a drink.'

We stayed for three hours. She never stopped talking, and I never stopped listening. She drank wine. Finished a whole bottle by herself. I drank coffee and felt the caffeine boring a tunnel through my brain. The more the wine warmed her up, reddened her cheeks, opened her heart and soul to me, the more the caffeine made everything seem vaguely surreal. She talked, and cried. She said much more than I can remember, a raging river of words, overflowing and then subsiding, twisting here and there, but always flowing towards the ocean of her true self. One moment she'd lean forward with an elbow on the table, her cheek in her hand and her wet eyes lasering into mine, and the next she'd lean back, cross a crocodile ankle over a knee and stretch her arms wide. I was no more than her punctuation: a question mark here and there, an occasional comma or full stop or paragraph break. I was a wholly passive listener, just catching the rain falling from her wintry sky, and asking myself only: *why me?* It's a question I asked myself many times. Both then and in the days and months to come.

Sex wasn't the only thing she talked about. She talked about her parents, her sisters, her friends, her ex-husband and her work. But the sex blots out the memory of everything else. I mean, how could it not? She'd grown up religious but had lapsed. A life-long Jerusalemite, married at twenty, divorced at twenty-four. After the divorce she started going around in low-cut jeans and T-shirts that showed off her midriff. She discovered the freedom of an exposed body, the breeze cool on her skin, the gazes and the compliments of men.

In truth, she confessed, polishing off another glass of wine, she'd discovered sex when she was still married. When her husband was away on duty with the army reserve, she had picked up a porn film from an automatic DVD machine. It was only that she'd been bored, and curious. But she was hooked right away. Before the end of her husband's reserve duty she'd rented ten movies and watched each of them a dozen times. She was addicted to masturbation. She never cheated on her husband except inside her head, where she cheated on him with everybody: the actors in the porn films, presenters on TV, footballers, ministers, waiters and chefs at work, passers-by she saw in the hotel or on the street. Every day, several times a day, whenever she could. If her husband was at home, then in the shower or another room. When he wasn't there, anywhere she could think of. The fantasies remained locked deep in her head and her husband, who was, like her, from a traditional background, knew nothing about her new discoveries and how much they excited her.

He'd been her first. She lost her virginity shortly before the wedding. When she discovered the orgasms and the fantasies, she tried to hint that she wanted more, but he wasn't interested. He simply didn't enjoy it as much as she did. The marriage died quickly, but not because of that. Because of unconnected things, some of which she told me about.

After the divorce the number of her lovers swiftly rose from one to eight. The sex was mostly disappointing, of course. Life is not fantasy. It's more complicated, it takes longer, the people are less attractive, less shameless. The other person doesn't behave as they do in the imagination, and neither do you. But in the lobby of the hotel where she worked she met Giora Guetta. He was wearing mirrored shades and had hair the colour of dark honey. She noticed his good looks, but the sunglasses were what snagged her attention. What gave him the confidence to show off like that? she asked herself. He gestured for her to come closer and when she did he took off his glasses and asked her out for a drink. She laughed: how brazen could you get? He was a security guard at the hotel: her first serious boyfriend since the divorce. Maybe the first serious man in her life. There was no need to keep anything from him. He loved what she loved, the porn and the fantasies and the games. But the moment it stopped being a secret, it stopped exciting her. The sex was wonderful, but it couldn't include the excitement of perpetual discovery. 'You're never happy. The grass is always greener. But I really loved him. He was a crazy guy, always surprising, always doing unexpected things.'

Shuli broke off – her voice had shrunk to a scarcely audible croak. Her lip trembled and her eyes filled once more with tears. She wiped them and her nose.

'What did he do?'

'He was looking for a job. He didn't know exactly

what – some kind of business, I think. He had plenty of ideas. Computers, maybe. He loved computers. The security guard thing was just temporary. One of those Ministry of Welfare jobs you get leaving the army.'

She fell silent. I stayed silent. I looked at her and I couldn't see in her any of the things she'd just told me. Her beauty had a cleanness to it. Coal-black shoulder-length hair, straight and dense, light mocha skin, a mouth naturally disposed to smile, and those big, black, deep eyes.

The place was filling up but everyone else there was quiet, wrapped up in themselves. Nobody bothered us. I wanted to stay and hear more, and not just because I was drowning in her eyes and gripped by her stories, but because the whole situation was so strange to me. For years I'd been continuously running, chasing time, fretting about lost seconds. The idea of a leisurely conversation lasting several hours in a café had never even crossed my mind. I'd forgotten that you could do such a thing. It just didn't have any room in my daily schedule. And now I was just letting the time pass without giving it a second thought. Without feeling that I was missing anything. Or almost. And time, for its part, hardly moved. Almost stood still, as if waiting for me to decide what to do with it, where I should take it from there. If a stray thought regarding time, or work, or Duchi, did pass through my head, I banished it immediately. The main thing here was not to take advantage.

'Tell me something else,' I said.

She was a chef in the King David Hotel, just up the road. It was hard work. An eight-hour shift on your feet, the only girl in a very masculine and physical environment. The other chefs in the hotel were mostly Arabs, with a sprinkling of Russians and two Israelis. She had no problem with that, but it wasn't easy to be part of their world. During peak hours there were five chefs in the kitchen working flat out. Tourism might have been hit by the bombs, but (touch wood) Jerusalem hadn't had a bomb for several weeks and the King David was pretty busy. She told me that she loved her work but wasn't sure how long she could last there. She had an evening shift she hadn't cancelled yet, though it wouldn't be a problem – they knew Giora. And then suddenly she wasn't so sure.

'Maybe it's better,' she said, 'to submerge yourself in work after a day like this.'

'With a bottle of wine in your head?'

'Right. But that's nothing new. Everyone drinks on shift.'

'A whole bottle?'

'Maybe not a whole bottle.'

She smiled slowly. I suddenly remembered: 'They never got back to us.'

'Who didn't?'

I took Giora's Palm out and showed her. 'OK,' she said. 'Maybe I'll try?'

She got a reply. 'Hello,' she said, in a sexy voice. 'This is Shuli.' I could hear a man's voice answering. She pulled a face which meant: what am I supposed to say now? I shrugged – just exactly what *should* she say?

'Who am I speaking to? Oh, hello: Binyamin. Listen, I'm Giora Guetta's girlfriend. You heard what happened to him?'

She listened for a few seconds.

'You don't know him? But he's got a meeting with you written in his diary. That's how I got this phone number. Sorry . . . hello? Hello?'

She took the phone from her ear and gave me a confused, rather drunken look.

'He doesn't have the faintest idea what I'm talking about.'

'We'll go there. We've got an address . . .'

'Now?'

'Whenever you say.'

'Tel Aviv would be too much for me right now,' Shuli said. 'Maybe tomorrow. Take me to work.'

I very much wanted to kiss her. But all I said was, 'Are you sure?' and she was.

# 16

*'Good morning, Svetlana, how is he? Keeping clean? Reactions?'*

*'His father said he opened his eyes for a moment yesterday. Apart from that, nothing. There's increased perspiration. And when you play him tapes of Amr Diab, his face looks calmer . . .'*

*'When you play what? What about nutrition? Infections? Pupils?'*

Not the torch, not the torch! Don't you dare, Svetlana . . .

*'The nutrition's going fine, Doctor. Up one point three kilos since he arrived. Excretion is textbook. No infection of the wounds. The massages are working.'*

*'Good. What day are we on? I think very soon we'll have a good idea which direction this is all heading.'*

The tiny apartment in Al-Amari was part of Grandfather Fahmi's and Grandmother Samira's house, which had been crudely subdivided into four flats. Over the years different branches of my uncles' and aunts' families lived in the various sections. There was a shower into which I now crammed myself, and a toilet bowl. Apart from the shower, there was a small room with a small sink and a small refrigerator on one side and a small bed, a small round table and a small TV on the other. Whoever didn't get the bed used the spare mattress that was propped up against the dirty yellow wall. The refrigerator contained milk, a few Al-Juneidi yogurts, a couple of eggs and some stale vegetables. Coffee, teabags, salt and a few pitas could be found on its top. A bare light bulb in the middle of the room supplied light during the day, since not enough sunlight came in through the crack in the wall above the sink or under the door.

I showered quickly and started tidying up, emptying the overflowing ashtrays, getting rid of the empty bottles and the paper wrappings, the rotten cucumber in the fridge, the debris on top of the TV and the round table. I made the bed, folded my clothes and gulped down a yogurt and only then noticed how hungry I was. I filled a pot and boiled some water with a potato and an egg. When they were cooked, I peeled them and cut them into a bowl, found a half-full tin of tuna in the fridge and added it. What a delicacy! Only then did I turn on the TV: music videos from Lebanon – just what I fancied.

*'Dr Hartom says you're getting better all the time. But they're still out there with their signs. Did you really do what they think you did, to the Croc? I used to like him when he was on TV, but not as much as I like you, Fahmi. I just don't believe them. I mean, they say your brother's a real terrorist, but you, I see you and I just don't believe you could have done that to the Croc.'*

The Croc? Where is he? We're on the beach, in his green car. I've an apple and a pomegranate for us to share.

Oh, man, I'm too hot. I'm burning up here . . .

'Is the bomb ready?'

'Almost.'

Bilahl came and ate the tuna salad I'd left him, talking on the phone in a low voice. He switched over to Al-Jazeera: the bombed building in Al-Birah, where Halil

Abu-Zeid had been killed. There were children searching for remains in the rubble. Bilahl watched it in silence, and left again. I rinsed my eyes with a dose of Shirin Abu-Akla, who was reporting, and when she finished I returned to the videos from Lebanon.

Lulu called from Murair. Father was sick, was worried about us. I told her to forget about Father's worrying and tell me how she was doing. What had she done today? How had school been? I hadn't seen her for months. She said she'd seen Rana.

I loved Rana. We grew up together. Because of her I was who I was. She was part of me. The only one. I missed her. But I had to leave her behind. Had to leave Murair behind. My sister, my father, my future. And now I was in a whole other place. Al-Amari. Bilahl, television.

I watched the dancers on TV and closed my eyes.

Bilahl wanted to carry out the attack as soon as possible, in revenge for Abu-Zeid's murder. He wanted them to know we could respond immediately. The shahid would refer to Abu-Zeid in the video to make it quite clear. To make them understand that their helicopters and missiles didn't scare us and wouldn't stop us. But Halil himself thought that it would be better to keep quiet for a few days, I said.

'Yes,' said Bilahl. 'But it's for him that it's important to do it quickly.'

I looked into his dark eyes and suddenly felt a strange surge of grief through my chest. I buried my face in my hands. I didn't mean to. My brother laid a hand on my heaving shoulders.

In the afternoon I went out into the camp to breathe some fresh air. Women with baskets on their heads. Green grass, yellow mustard and red poppies growing beside the dirt roads. I plucked a leaf from a big fig tree. Behind the mosque the camp's football team were practising on a pitch with a huge puddle in its centre circle. I sat beside several other bored guys and watched, the sound of ping-pong games from the club next door clicking in my head like a metronome. Al-Amari's football team had won the West Bank championship a few times but since I arrived at the camp, they hadn't been up to much. Maybe I was bringing them bad luck. I found a shekel in my pocket and bought two bananas from one of the stands. How pleasant to sit and eat a banana on a cloudless winter's day. Children were kicking a ball against the wall, as they did whenever I passed that spot. Life here doesn't change, I thought: only the slogans on the walls, and even they stay essentially the same. Any time now, my brother would be sending the kids with the green, black and red spray-cans out to praise the shahid Halil Abu-Zeid and to demand his revenge.

The *Istishadi* was a guy called Naji, whom Bilahl met in the mosque earlier that morning. Bilahl said his true intent was to go to God. He'd known Abu-Zeid in the mosque and wanted revenge immediately.

'But how well do you know this guy? How *long*?'

'I trust God. I try to sense the person. But I never know. How can one know what anyone's got on the inside? Naji looks good to me. A relaxed type. Strong nerves. But I might be wrong. I'm trying to find out about him and his family.'

'And if you're wrong?'

'If I'm wrong, that is the will of God.' Bilahl spoke with a businesslike assurance. He had taken Abu-Zeid's responsibilities upon himself. I didn't know whether or not he'd been given the role officially, or who he knew higher up in the organisation. 'In any case, he doesn't know my phone number or my real name. You'll show him how the explosive works. Apart from the two of us he won't see anyone or be allowed to call anyone. He'll come to the operations apartment, and from that moment on he'll be cut off from the world. On the last night he'll sleep here.'

I made tea. The flat was so cold I could see my breath steaming. Bilahl's mobile rang: the theme from *The A-Team*. 'Yes, Father . . .' I heard him say, and I imagined Father with his silver mane at home in Murair and heard in Bilahl's voice a reluctance to show disrespect. But Father and him . . . I remembered Father telling me, 'I have no authority over him – I haven't had for a while now. I've given up on him. But you . . . my heart aches for you, I know you're not a murderer. I know you, Fahmi, no one knows you as I do.' 'Of course I'm not a murderer,' I'd told him.

I put sugar in the tea and realised that Bilahl was now talking to someone else. The guy who'd checked Naji wasn't sure about him. There was some sort of criminal mess in his past. Bilahl called Naji. How can anybody know what anyone has inside them?

In the operations apartment, I removed the belt from its hiding place in a wall closet, unwrapped the blankets and old newspapers, and laid it on the table. Lifted it up and felt it. The tubes with the explosives were in order: nothing had evaporated. I took the ball-bearings and nails from one of the pockets, where they surrounded a sausage of RDX, and then pulled out the sausage to show Bilahl. 'We've got seven kilos of explosives and about ten kilos of iron here. This could create some damage.'

He nodded.

'Do you want to try it?' I said.

I didn't mean that he should think of himself as a candidate to be *Istishadi* himself. But I saw that that was what he thought. He shut up for a moment and looked up from the explosive, focusing on nothing.

'Let's see how Naji gets on with it,' he finally said.

Ali Jaafar Hussein's café, the only one in Al-Amari, was around the corner. I asked for a Coke and drank it slowly, sitting on one of the small stools outside. We were the only ones out there. A drizzly wind lashed our faces and the puddles soaked our shoes. After a few minutes Naji arrived and Bilahl and I exchanged a look. He was so young his cheeks were still plump and smooth and when he spoke he lowered his eyes like a young bride.

*'You're sweating again. What are you thinking about there?'*

I'm thinking: when will you stop jabbering at me?

*'Oh, Fahmi, did I tell you what a horrible night I had last night at home?'*

Did soldiers come and break your furniture, arrest your family, murder your mother? That kind of night, Svetlana?

The moment I put the belt on Naji I felt his body straining and his muscles tensing up. He bit his lips but didn't say anything. 'We've got to adjust the straps to your size. We need them tight so you can wear it under your shirt.' Naji was chubby and fair skinned. I tightened the straps. He touched my hand, a soft touch, to indicate that the straps were tight enough. I was close to him. I could smell him – the raindrops on his neck, the fear.

'This is the battery. You take it separately and connect it at the last minute. OK?'

He nodded.

'Because from the moment you connect it, there's an increased chance of an accident.' To demonstrate, I disconnected the explosive from the electric circuit and connected a light bulb instead. I showed him how to connect the battery and he managed it after a few attempts. There was sweat on his brow. Bilahl went out to smoke, and when he returned I gave him a doubtful look. You have to be cooler than a cucumber in order to do something like this: you need frozen blood. You need to be a little crazy. I couldn't understand why Naji had volunteered.

'After the battery, the safety catch. This nail prevents you from pushing the button. You pull it out like this.'

He did it.

'Now the button is free to push. Not too hard. It happens in the twinkling of an eye – the moment you push, you leave this life. You won't feel anything. Not the explosion, no pain, nothing except the certainty that you are with God at last.' Naji's breathing got heavier. He laid a hand on my shoulder.

'You will leave the life of suffering, the problems and the misery,' Bilahl said. 'A push of the button will send your soul to heaven, to God and to all the *shuhada*. You are going to God.' Naji pressed his forehead to my shoulder. I extended a hand and hugged him. I gave Bilahl a look and nodded my head slightly. The boy breathed into my neck. 'Push now,' I whispered. He pushed. The bulb lit up for half a second and then there was a loud fizz-crack and it went out. Naji jumped in panic.

'It's nothing,' I said casually. 'The bulb went, that's all.'

I went to get a new bulb. My hands were shaking so much I had to wait until they stopped. By the time I returned Naji had recovered. I changed the bulb and he tried again. This time he managed without my help. He took the belt off and laid it on the table. I went to the corner of the room and whispered in Bilahl's ear.

# 17

After I dropped Shuli off at the King David my headache started. Like needles stabbing my brain. I stopped and bought a bottle of water. Looking over the stallholder's shoulder, I asked for a Ta'ami chocolate bar, cigarettes and watermelon-flavoured chewing gum. I lit up a cigarette, though I don't smoke. (I did once, in the army, but it would take up too much of my time now.) It didn't stop the needles and made me feel nauseous. Two more puffs and I dumped the cigarette and the rest of the pack in a nearby bin. And the Ta'ami bar too, after a single bite. As I drove to my parents' house I sipped the water and chewed the gum so fiercely that I almost dislocated my jaw.

My mother brought me some pills and made us a schnitzel. We tend to eat in silence, my parents and I. The English teacher of thirty years, the former peanut butter importer and the directory assistance integrated-solutions provider.

'Shaar Hagai. That's a real escalation,' my father said after a while.

I nodded. Mother's eyes were aching. She asked whether Duchi was all right. Good question. I was thinking about Shuli, wondering how she was coping in the kitchen. I wanted to drive there and ask her.

'Duchi? She's OK.'

I ought to have called her, but I couldn't face the recriminations. The inevitable row. What for? Mother asked whether I'd had good meetings. Meetings? In Jerusalem, she meant. I told her they'd gone fine.

After the schnitzel, Danny Ronen's eyebrows on Channel 2. Mother discovered a stain on the sofa and began obsessively trying to clean it up while grousing in the general direction of her husband, though no one but herself was listening.

'The security forces,' Ronen told us, 'have conflicting evidence regarding the source of the terrorist cell that carried out the attack on the Jerusalem–Tel Aviv road, near Shaar Hagai. Initial evidence pointed to the village of Husan in the Bethlehem area, as reported yesterday. But today's findings contradict this. In a communication accepting responsibility by the Izz ad-Din al-Qassam Brigades, "sons" are mentioned, as opposed to the single marksman that had previously been assumed. Furthermore, posters in memory of the suicide bomber nineteen-year-old Shafiq Omar throughout the West Bank refer to Ramallah as the source of the No. 5 bus attack, and not Nablus as was initially assumed. The security forces are unsure whether the posters and the messages are reliable or intended to confuse.'

'Whatever the truth,' said Danny Ronen, 'the IDF Air Force carried out a "targeted assassination" this afternoon in the offices of the Islamic Charity Society in Al-Birah. As a result Halil Mahmoud Abu-Zeid, a senior Izz ad-Din al-Qassam Brigades member in Ramallah, thought to be responsible for the string of recent terrorist attacks – including Shaar Hagai, the Tel Aviv bus bombing, and the Sbarro restaurant on the Jaffa road in Jerusalem – was killed.'

'Yochanan?' I asked my father. 'Wasn't Sbarro the attack that the guy from the *last* targeted assassination was responsible for?'

'Yes. Him too. And the one from the targeted assassination before that.'

Judging by the targeted assassinations, the Sbarro attack was planned by five dozen different people, in Nablus, Ramallah, Hebron, Islamic Jihad, Al-Aqsa Martyrs' Brigade, Hamas. Everyone had a hand in it, and now they've all got a hand missing. If they're lucky, that is.

And on the TV the funerals processed. The sounds of bereavement. Funerals, eulogies. A race of red-eyed people.

'Finding whoever is responsible for this atrocity . . .'

'I don't understand, don't understand, don't understand.'

'He was a warm, kind person . . .'

'When I heard the news on TV, my heart stopped beating, as if something had hit me . . .'

'He will always bc with me, as he always was. He was the biggest influence on my life.'

We cut and zoomed in to the prettily crying eyes of an attractive female soldier, and the reporter summed it all up and returned us to the Jerusalem studio. Danny Ronen raised his eyebrows. Father asked whether he could change to a documentary he'd read about.

Duchi sounded businesslike. She asked me whether this was it. Whether I'd left home for good. If so, she would like to know why, and when I intended to take my stuff.

'Is that what you want to happen?'

'Am I the one who left and didn't make contact for twenty-four hours?'

'No, I am. But I'm still asking: is this what you want to happen?'

'I don't know. I don't think so. But whether I do or not, I think it would be more sensible if we talked about it like grown-ups, no? After four years.'

'I'm sorry . . . I have a headache. Yes, you're right. What are you up to?'

'Watching Channel Two. Where are you?'

'Jerusalem. Mom and Dad.'

Silence. I felt she was trying to assess the import of this. At least, she probably thought, I was in a familiar place and not evading the question or making excuses. But I knew her: that wouldn't be much comfort to her. The reflex towards catastrophic scenarios is intrinsic to the way Duchi's brain works – her mother's legacy. It came with a lifetime warranty – customer service and periodic software upgrades guaranteed even from beyond the grave.

'Send my regards.'

'They send theirs too.'

I imagined her on the other end, formulating her apocalyptic scenarios, holding back the tears. But instead I heard a chuckle.

'What did you say?'

'Nothing. Bibi's here.'

Bibi hates me; she told Duchi ages ago to get rid of me. Duchi told me that herself.

'Ah. I guess you're gossiping about me.'

'You'd be surprised, your name hasn't actually come up yet.'

I could picture Bibi, both thumbs up and suppressing her laughter at this.

'I'm sure that when it does, my ears'll be burning with the flattery.'

'OK.'

'What OK? That's it?'

'Do you have anything else to say? When you're coming

back, perhaps, or when you're going away?' I was taken aback by her confidence. She wasn't formulating disaster scenarios. She'd caught me on the back foot.

'I was in the Shaar Hagai attack yesterday. The back windscreen was shattered. And my mobile.'

'Croc. Call me when you have something serious to say and when you make up your mind what you want to do with yourself. You know where I am. I need to hang up now. When you decide, come back home and we'll talk about everything like adults.'

'OK.' I hung up and imagined the awful Bibi bursting into applause.

Had I imagined it all? Duchi hadn't even registered what I'd said. I ran my thumb over the unscratched phone display, then stepped outside and touched the Polo's gleaming rear windscreen, feeling momentarily insane. But I hadn't imagined the newspapers, had I? Or Humi, once a chubby soldier, into Zohar Argov. I started to walk, my legs unconsciously leading me down the old familiar route towards the kiosk by the park. It was closed, but nothing had changed in the twenty years since we were kids. The wooden kiosk was plastered with a new generation of Likud or Settler stickers. A Jew Never Expels A Jew. Hebron For Ever! Bibi: Strong Leader For A Strong People. And behind it, the little park of climbing frames and slides, where I smoked my first cigarette and coughed through my first joint, had my first kiss, touched my first breast. I crossed it and walked out on to the street on the other side and stood opposite Muku's house. He still lives in the flat he grew up in. When his father died he bought his mother a smaller flat and stayed on with his own family. I could see light inside, hear the kids. And then there Muku was, momentarily, moving through the frame of the window, gesturing to someone out of view. I called him. I moved my phone a little distance from my ear and heard the mobile ringing in the flat, the kids becoming quiet. After half a dozen rings an answering machine came on. I hung up without leaving a message.

The last time we talked was September 11th. The day of the catastrophe; the day of the embarrassment. How many phone calls had I made that day to explain to people why they shouldn't bother? What a mess Duchi's mother arranged for us, both in her life and after! If they'd asked me to do the inscription on her tomb it would have gone:

Leah Neeman
A Total Mess

Do I remember the conversation with Muku on that day? It's hard to unpick it from the rest. There were so many conversations that day it now seems like one long hallucination, like one endless red fog of humiliation. Mind you, we did have a world-class excuse. I suppose more embarrassing things have happened in the history of weddings. But never tell an embarrassed man it could have been more embarrassing. And with Muku, who's been married for years and already has three children and an apartment in Rehavia and a job in the Supreme Court, there was a different dimension to the humiliation. I felt that he'd been waiting for me to join the real, bourgeois world and, on the very brink of it, I had failed again. Thirty-two years old, and I couldn't manage to get married. That was the unspoken accusation behind our talk, and one of the worst memories of that day in general. After the phone calls I went to the place where the wedding was supposed to happen, to wait for the guests I hadn't got through to. Duchi refused to come with me.

I sat on our bench. How many hours had Muku and Danny Lam and I spent in this park, playing marbles, tag, football, cards, puffs? Coming of age in a park. They did it before us and they're already doing it after us. Danny Lam was killed the same day I almost died. I always felt it was a game of chance, either him or me, that I won in the end. Or lost, depending on how you look at life. I wondered how his parents were doing, and his sister, pretty Rachel Lam. His girlfriend Orit, who flew to New York a month after he died, in the middle of her national service, never to be heard of again.

An unfamiliar beeping in my pocket: Giora Guetta's PalmPilot. Its blue internal light illuminated my hands in the dark.

A diary reminder, entered by Giora: *S. – end of shift.*

So I got up from the bench and drove to the hotel.

Why did I do it? I'd already fulfilled my mission. I'd delivered the message that Guetta had asked me to, or almost. Anyone would have done that. Anyone would have gone to the funeral. And OK, I stayed with the bereaved girl a couple of hours and listened to her when she needed to get a few things off her chest in a café. Up to that point it all sounds pretty reasonable. So why did I do it? You know why I did it. But it wasn't planned. It wasn't *predatory*. It just happened. And that moment in my childhood park in Rehavia when the PalmPilot beeped and I got up and drove to the hotel was the moment it happened. At the same time, it couldn't have been more natural. The Palm beeped. I got up from the bench, I got into the car, I drove, and I arrived at the entrance to the hotel just as she was coming out.

They were surprised to see her in the kitchen – so she told me, because I asked her to tell me everything in detail – but she said she'd rather work. The head chef, Alon, had taken her aside and asked her whether she was sure. It was going to be a busy night. She wept briefly in his arms and said she was sure. For the first hour she worked in silence, and her silence infected Alon and the other three chefs working with her, Issam, Osama and Alex, and the waiters coming in and out with the orders, and the head waiter Yatzpan (real name Mahmoud, but he looked just like a fatter version of Yatzpan, the comedian), who came on to her on a daily basis, and the drinks guy, Natzer, though he never said anything anyway. The orders, fed into the restaurant tills by the waiters, flowed relentlessly from the two printers in the kitchen, and Alon read the print-outs and divided the salads, the roasts, the fish and the desserts between the chefs and took the orders coming in from room service, and Shuli, in her round-buttoned tunic and tall toque, concentrated on her work and thought about nothing whatsoever.

Garrulous Issam – curly haired, balding, ever smiling – began talking to Osama in Arabic, which was usually Shuli's cue to call over and ask what they were muttering about so secretly, or have a go at Osama for his maddeningly squeaky voice – 'like listening to a whistle'. But tonight she just cut the bagel, stuck it in the toaster, laid out the salmon, took the sheet of lasagna, red sauce on top, Parmesan, ten minutes in the top oven, checked the heat with a knife, pizza bases from the tall stack, tomato sauce, handful of mozzarella, handful of Parmesan, onion and green pepper, seven minutes on high and on to the wooden trays ready to go . . . she sank into the sensations and the smells. The slippery mozzarella, the translucent flesh of the fish, the dough's comforting elasticity; the salmon's fresh scent, the basil's sharpness, the onion coaxing the tears out of you. 'Alex: fruit salad and apple pie! Issam: ravioli, fries! Shuli: Artichoke Carpaccio!' Artichoke slices on a plate, olive oil and lemon from the big jugs filled by Alon, crushed peppercorns, salty Bulgarian cheese, dried plum tomatoes and rocket to decorate, and down on the aluminium surface for Alon, who was doing the announcing today. 'Artichoke, who asked for it?' She pointed to the bowl of rocket. 'More rocket!' She knows the menu by heart, has done for six months, and here comes another order from Alon and she's on it automatically, hand here, fingers there, grabbing, spreading, crumbling, kneading, chopping, deep-frying . . .

Despite the wine she'd drunk and the grief that weighed her hands down, she managed for a couple of hours. Then Alon told her to take a coffee and sit in the lobby for a few minutes: her silence was worrying him. She took a bottle of beer instead. As soon as she took her first swig she started crying uncontrollably. Deep sobs that hurt her ribs and shook her whole body. She felt hands on her shoulder and turned to see Marwan, a beautiful nineteen-year-old kid from Beit-Hanina with the eyes of a cartoon deer. Shuli was a quarter in love with Marwan but apart from a few meaningful glances (and her fantasies at home) there was nothing between them. Now his kindness made her feel nauseous and her weeping intensified. She shouted at him to get off her, and the alarmed Marwan recoiled and returned to work. Guests watched the sobbing cook. Alon was called from the kitchen. Did she want to go home? With her face in her hands, she said she didn't. What did she want to do, then? She said she didn't know. Did she want coffee? She responded with a long swig of the Heineken and another flurry of tears. And then she got up, washed her face in the bathroom and returned to work, back into her automatic mode. Her feet hurt, she hadn't slept much the previous night, her back bothered her, but she went on. One of her friends among the waitresses told her to go home. The plates piled up. Alon roared for Yusuf to bring coasters. Giora is dead Giora is dead Giora is dead, she thought in a loop. Giora, Marwan, Croc, Giora, Marwan, Croc. The Arabs were quietly humming an Arab song. 'Alex, bring lettuce!' Alex was flashing his silver tooth . . .

'Croc?' I said. 'You were thinking of me?'

We were driving from King David Street down towards the German Colony.

'Yeah,' she said. 'I thought of the Croc. Among other things.'

I didn't say a word. We took a left at the train station towards Arnona and Armon Hanaziv, and headed on past the Ramat Rachel Kibbutz. She took us to a spot where we could sit and look over the Judaean desert, and when I said wasn't it dangerous she just laughed.

'What was the message he wanted you to give me?'

A second passed before I realised what she was talking about.

'I don't know,' I said. 'He didn't get to say it. He was thinking. But I'm pretty sure he wanted to let you know that he loved you. Something like that.'

She looked at me.

'His look had that kind of meaning. It wasn't a "tell her to feed the cats" kind of look,' I said, staring at the gearstick. 'And I can understand him.'

'He didn't have any cats. He couldn't stand them.'

'I can understand him on that one too.'

She smiled. So I wiped her smile with a kiss. Her lips were soft as feathers, as deep and salty as the sea.

# 18

'We're human beings, not angels,' Bilahl said brusquely. Surprisingly, he wasn't angry with Naji. He had been in the room when the bulb blew too. 'Anyone can change his mind. It's natural. He said he didn't feel ready. Maybe in the future . . .'

'You think he's an informer?'

'Relax. He gave me the name of someone to stand in for him. Mahmoud Salam al-Mahmuzi: dedicated to the Holy Cause. Twenty-three years old and from Al-Amari. This camp needs a hero.'

'He's coming here?'

'Later. First we need to take a look at him at the operations apartment. See if he's got the right stuff. Then – your lesson, a video, a haircut, and, God willing, we could be on our way by noon tomorrow.'

*'. . . yes, Mama. Yes, Mama. Yes. Tomorrow. Mama, I can't talk in here . . . yes. Not now . . .'*

One tube for piss. Another for air.

*'No, I'm at work, Mama. It's not dangerous, he's not . . . no, that's crazy, he's fine. He can't do anything at all . . .* Stoi! Ostav'te menya v pokoe! *Leave me alone!'*

Oh, play me a song, Svet. Give me a massage, Svet . . .

*'God, what a pain she is! So: how are we doing? My mother's worried you're going to do something to me ha h . . . oh, have we done a poo?'*

Oh, Svet, just please, please, shut up. And here comes your phone again, and I can't do anything at all . . .

We passed Ali's café, where silver-haired men were playing backgammon or cards and drinking glasses of tea. Some younger, bored-looking guys. Bilahl nodded to them. As for me – in Al-Amari, all my friends are on TV. Rita Khouri off *The Weakest Link* on Lebanese TV, George Khourdahi off *Who Wants to Be a Millionaire?* on MBC, *Noah's Ark*'s Tommy Musari on Channel 2, Ihab Abu-Nasif, who hosts *The Mission* on Al-Manar – and beautiful Shirin Abu-Akla from the news on Al-Jazeera. Occasionally I might get a phone call from Rami, or from Natzer in Jerusalem, but Natzer just made me think how dead and gone my childhood was, and I'd let him go to voicemail . . . I grew up with him and Titi and limping Rami in Murair: marbles, donkeys, football, and later, messing about with girls, a little bit of school, football. A plastic bullet shattered Rami's knee when he was eight, during the first intifada. Titi works at the Majdal Bani Fadel checkpoint: he's got an old Peugeot van he sells cold drinks from. Every morning he fills a box with crushed ice and a few dozen cans from his Uncle Faez's store, and drives a quarter of an hour down to the checkpoint. But Natzer left the village. He works in the King David in Jerusalem, and lives in Beit-Hanina. I don't know exactly what he's doing, but the money's good. Pretty girls and so on. He once shaved his beard off because of a Jewish girl. Even when we were kids he'd make friends with the soldiers. Natzer likes the things that life on the other side has to offer him. He kept himself well away from Bilahl's wars and when he calls I let him go to voicemail.

*'Mama, I told you, I can't talk at work! I'm not shouting. I am not shouting. OK. OK, I'll come with you tomorrow morning. How dare . . . listen, someone's coming now, I can't talk . . .'*

A crescent moon spilled a little silver over the yellow-lit camp, over the one-storey shacks, the jungle of antennae on the tin roofs, the narrow dirt alleys and the few asphalt roads, the scattering of battered old cars and tired tractors and the dome of the mosque. From time to time we passed people on their way home. Children were playing football in the yellow street light and I watched Bilahl, who was once a pretty good footballer, follow them instinctively with his gaze.

Mahmuzi had grown up in Al-Amari. After high school he'd worked in Israel in agriculture and construction, until all his routes upwards were blocked. He came back and started studying at the Hebron Polytechnic but quit. In the past four years he had become completely dedicated to his prayer. He'd talked to Islamic Jihad members in Ramallah, but was told they weren't recruiting. He had just happened to talk to Naji that morning.

One sister. A traditional family, but the parents separated when he was seven or eight. They were angry kids, used to throw blocks at the mosque windows. He was still living with his mother, and still angry. His father had remarried and lived in Nablus. His sister was studying law in Amman.

'What depresses you?' I asked.

'I'm not depressed by anything,' he said.

'Did you bid farewell to your loved ones?'

'I didn't bid farewell to anyone.'

I explained about the belt, as I had with Naji. He had

good hands and a cool head. Afterwards Bilahl talked to him quietly and at length. As we were leaving, Mahmuzi knelt down in the corner on the prayer mat Bilahl had given him and bowed his back. When he straightened up his eyes were closed and a rapid, low mumble was issuing from his mouth along with clouds of his breath, visible in the cold air.

Bilahl told him not to leave the apartment and not to speak to anyone.

*'Tell me what am I going to do with this mother? She's driving me nuts!'*

At last! Oh, Svet. I need your fingers . . .

*'What are you thinking about? You're sweating again. There's a storm outside and here you are sweating. This'll make you feel better. Yes?'*

Yes . . .

There are eleven gates to heaven and rivers of many colours flow through it – white rivers of milk, golden rivers of honey, and crimson rivers of wines which never intoxicate. There are orchards of date palms and apple trees whose trunks and branches are made of gold. Jojoba and frankincense grow freely, and vines and flowers. Breath in heaven smells of ambergris. Light never fails. And there will be seventy-two beautiful virgins, dressed in white . . .

All of us die and it doesn't really matter how many years you've lived before death comes, ten or a hundred: you'll either be with God or you won't.

Bilahl didn't tell Mahmuzi but when we returned from the operations apartment to our own, I asked him where the next attack was going to be.

Jerusalem.

# 19

After four days of rain and fog it dawned so crisp and clear you could feel the air tickling the back of your larynx when you breathed it in. The sky was a very pale blue – as cold and clear as the eye of a Siamese cat.

Shuli lived in the German Colony, in a flat in one of the tall buildings at the end of Hazfira Street, where the tennis courts are. A nice neighbourhood: trees and little parks, the buildings clad in creepers, birds buzzing about. When I dropped her off that night I asked her whether she fancied a game, and she'd laughed and said, 'One day.'

'How about tomorrow morning? Are you working tomorrow?'

'I've got a night shift,' she said, touching my unshaven cheek with her palm and opening her door. It was her father's flat: Davidi Vaknin had been delighted to have Shuli back home after her divorce. Not only to help her through it but also because his daughter and her ex-husband had drifted away from religion in their four years of marriage and he nursed hopes of coaxing her back to God. And also because he was lonely. Shuli's mother had succumbed to a long disease a few months after the wedding, her sister was off backpacking round India.

'Night shift – which means I'm not working in the morning.'

So that morning I parked the Polo near her house and we walked along Hazfira Street towards Emek Refaim Street. I held her hand for a while, but she didn't seem comfortable with it. Her hands were cold, she claimed. She needed to put her gloves on.

'Don't worry,' she reassured me. 'You'll see. Tonight.'

'I'm not worried,' I said, and she lowered her eyes and smiled a smile that was half embarrassment and half a promise. I did know that she had just lost her boyfriend, that everything had just been thrown upside down, and everything like that, but it seemed to me somehow that she was the sort of person who would always be like this: heightened, impulsive, very alive. A wave of warmth broke from my heart and flooded upwards to my throat, and for a few seconds I actually seemed to be unable to breathe. I could feel my heart beating faster, desperately trying to get some oxygen into my blood.

We went to the post office. In order to get her chef's certificate she needed a year's experience in a recognised restaurant, references from qualified chefs (Alon had been happy to oblige) and to pass exams in theory and practice at the Tadmor Hotel in Herzliya. She sent off the forms she had to send off. In a bakery she bought a loaf of bread for her dad; in a stationer's she bought a notebook for herself. She had decided to write to Giora every day. I asked whether she was planning on telling him everything.

'I never hid a thing from him in the four months we were together.'

'And what about him?'

'Well, who knows? Every night when we went to bed we'd tell each other everything that had happened to us that day. I'd say, "Tell me something else", and I'd keep saying, "Something else" until he'd told me the lot. And then I'd tell him everything back.' She fell silent for a moment. 'Did you hear from the guy who met Giora in Tel Aviv?'

'Binyamin? The guy from the PalmPilot? We said we were going to go and find him in Tel Aviv.'

'Yeah, we said that, didn't we? But maybe tomorrow?'

I wasn't in any hurry. Tonight I was going to see. 'OK,' I said.

'Now I need an Ice Europa,' she decided. There wasn't any debate. She said it, we did it.

The place was pretty full. The security guard searched us with his metal wand on the off-chance we were packing any landmines, his big steel lollipop emitting its somehow disappointed little cheeps. Shuli ordered a croissant and an Ice Europa. I went for an egg sandwich and a cappuccino. I overruled her attempts to pay ('I owe you,' she said) and steered us towards a round table for two not far from the entrance and sat down facing the street. She sat opposite and stared at me until I said, 'What?'

'Why did you choose this table?'

'I don't know. It was free.'

She looked around and her gaze took in the other free tables.

'You want to move?'

'No. It's just that this is our old table. How did you choose this table out of all of them? And you talked to him a minute before he died. It's like . . .' She blinked back the tears that were never far from her surface. 'Don't listen to me, I'm talking crap,' she said. 'It's funny, I always sat facing the street, and he always sat opposite me. So now I can see what he used to see. All the people here.'

I stared at her and said, 'There's one thing he could see that you can't,' and the memory of the night before flashed like a bullet train through my mind: the drive to the edge of the desert, her smile, our kiss, and what happened after; her long neck, her dark silky skin, the dark down on her forearms, and how, when I kissed my way down to her breasts, she'd held her breath for what seemed like a minute until my lips grazed her nipple and she breathed out. How she'd unbuttoned and pulled down her jeans and how I bent over to her ankle and bit the little crocodile crawling up it, and how I travelled with little butterfly kisses over her knee, her thigh, navel, ribcage, breasts, collarbone, throat, jaw, all the way to the mouth that was patiently waiting for me. How my finger found one of the cotton flowers embroidered on her underwear, began to circle it, wandered with the help of another finger under the stretched elastic where her wonderful skin was softest of all. I touched the soft fluff, the hollow in the tendons of her thigh, and then slipped inside her, and she was kissing my ear by now and whispering to go on and my other hand was everywhere, and she came with her head pressed deeply into the space between my jaw and shoulder, my left hand bracing her bucking shoulder. Then she was sucking in air, almost sobbing, and my wet fingers were resting on her silver thigh, and, mixed with the smells of sex and coconut air-freshener, a very faint tang of gun oil from Humi's rifle – Humi, who only two days before had been sitting where Shuli was now catching her breath. She'd wanted to go home straight after. It was totally fine with me.

'What are you thinking about?'

The bullet train disappeared. I looked up, caught red handed, and saw that she knew what I was thinking about.

'Don't embarrass me,' she said, but she was smiling.

'Well. "We'll see tonight" . . .'

My phone intervened. Gili from work. I told her I was still in Jerusalem, and she told me that I was going to have some explaining to do to Jimmy. I said I'd explain everything. Shuli said, 'Nike and Nokia. That's who you are.'

'And who are you?'

'I cook for the Nikes and Nokias. Actually, I'm not sure. I never see them. I arrive when they're still asleep, along with the vegetables from the market and the bread from the Angel bakery, in the dark in winter. I come in the rear entrance, with the tahini from Nablus and the pitas from the Old City.'

The sandwich was as good as it always was. Sliced hard-boiled egg with tomato and mayo on brown bread. I always add lots of salt and pepper. Waste of time.

'D'you want anything else?'

'I don't know. I want to go to Giora's grave. To be with him a little bit on my own. And then maybe we'll go again to the shiva?'

I reached over to touch her hand. I was prepared to do whatever she said. It wasn't exactly because I'd fallen in love. I mean, something had happened, I'm not denying it. Something started growing there. But as much as anything else I was amazed by what had happened to time. It seemed to have stopped. I wasn't chasing after it, I wasn't running. Jerusalem was somewhere else. I looked at the people eating in the Café Europa: who were they? How come they had all this time? Didn't they need to work? A beautiful black-eyed girl smiled at me from the other side of the table and excused herself to go to the Ladies.

Only when she'd gone did I hear the music: 'Bab al-Wad'. *First star's light above Beit Mahsir*. Some people were moving their lips to the lyrics. I turned away and looked outside at the electric pale blue. Jerusalem itself seemed to be sitting under the sky like a growth of mould. It looked coated in fear. 'Gabi told the security guard to get the guy out of the restaurant. The security guard says,

"My shift doesn't start for ten minutes."' A group of guys at the next table. 'So Gabi says, "OK. You leave it a minute, then," leaves through the back door and runs a mile. So the guy pushes the button but he had a problem with the detonator . . .' The listeners burst out laughing. I looked over the red bar stools, the red and black tables; I smelled the coffee and the tuna; I opened a newspaper and I read that Private Humi Glazer, aged nineteen, had been laid to rest yesterday in the military cemetery in Petach-Tikva. Maybe I ought to visit his family too . . . I ate the little chocolate cube you got with your coffee, and then I ate Shuli's cube too. I wanted more coffee but didn't have enough energy to go and get it. Though I shouldn't overdo it with the caffeine: everything starts to feel as if it's taking place at some weird distance away from me. I got so worried I looked into it once: the caffeine increases neuronal activity, which fools the pituitary gland into releasing hormones that tell the adrenal gland to get pumping. And then the pupils widen, the trachea dilates, blood vessels shrink, blood pressure rises, the liver releases sugar into your blood to boost energy, the muscles tighten and, oddly enough, your hands cool down.

'Why are you looking at your hands like that?'

'What? No reason.'

'Let's change places. I want to see the street.'

I rose and waited for her to move past me and when she sat down I touched her on her shoulder – a small but intimate gesture. I moved to the other side of the table. She said – or so I remember – she said:

'I was thinking, Croc. I was sitting in the toilet and I was thinking that life really does go on. Life stays in this world. It doesn't disappear. Giora's gone, and you come and sit down at the same table, and life goes on. We're still breathing. He was a good man, did you see that at all?'

'Yeah. Yeah, I think I could.'

'He was a good man, and it is terrible. It hurts very, very much. I saw him every day. I touched him and talked to him. He had such a pretty voice.' Her voice, pretty too, was higher than usual and trembling; a little strangulated. 'But I was sitting there thinking that you just cannot stop this life. It's like water finding its way over rocks and concrete and tarmac into the earth. You can't stop it.' She fell silent and I don't think I said anything. Her eyes were fixed on some spot on the tabletop; possibly her fingers were stroking her Ice Europa cup. 'Whatever,' she said. 'I mean, it was a nice kind of thing to think. Maybe the nicest thought I've had in a while.' And she smiled, with her mouth closed, more with one corner than the other, a hopeful, sad, wise sort of smile, and it seemed like the air trembled between us.

# 20

*'The last thing in the world I need is those people with their Croc signs knowing I take care of you. Is it really true about what you did to him, Fahmi? I'd never have believed it in a million years. You look . . .'*

O country, O my country, O country of our fathers, I will sacrifice for you eternally, with determination and with fiery vengeance, made strong by my people's desire for our homeland. I climbed the mountains, I fought, I strove mightily and untied the chains of bondage . . .

*'You look so . . .'*

But the body won't move, and the eyes won't open.

*'. . . I don't know, good hearted. I can't imagine you hurting a fly, let alone the Croc.'*

The Croc? What *is* all this about the Croc?

*'You just don't have a murderer's eyes. I can tell. Maybe I should try and talk to them . . .'*

Where is the Croc? Not a bad guy. Five hundred shekels for a day's work . . .

*'But if they were here instead of me they'd have disconnected you. I could do it in a moment. The tube for your piss and the tube for your air, and then . . .'*

The Croc on *Noah's Ark* with Tommy Musari, and then

with me. With me, driving in his little green car along the beach, my apple in my lap . . .

The Al-Aqsa mosque was calling us to rise up against our exploiters. For you, my steadfast nation, together we will fight. Call with all your strength: *Allah Akbar, Allah Akbar!* We will revenge every mother's tear and every drop of blood, and for every shahid that dies another will rise. For you, my steadfast nation . . .

Mahmuzi woke early, read the Koran and prayed. Slept well. I wouldn't have managed to sleep at all on my last night.

Bilahl came, in Naji's Mazda. He wasn't going to give himself to the cause, but he was giving us his Mazda, for a day.

One more test for the explosive belt. Bilahl gave Mahmuzi some scented soap and sent him to scrub himself clean for his God. After he'd showered he put on the new clothes Bilahl had brought and we drove to Ramallah in the Mazda. Bilahl parked on a side street, gave Mahmuzi a twenty-shekel note and sent him to the hairdresser's. I got a hundred shekels to buy a videotape and rent a camera for the day.

One of the plastic lions in the square in Ramallah was missing its plastic head: above it a huge poster of Arafat told us *All you need is willpower*. I walked by the butcher's where the guy got murdered in a robbery – closed up now. There were lots of people on the streets: pretty women from the good Christian neighbourhoods come in for the markets, students on their way to the UNRWA College, seen-it-all old merchants lounging on chairs on the pavements like lizards, trying to soak up some sun.

'What's the occasion?' asked the grey-haired old guy in the camera shop, peering above his glasses. 'If I may ask.' The air smelled of mint, from his glass of tea.

'Of course you may, sir. Our friend is getting married. There he is, across the street at the hairdresser's, getting ready.' He explained how to use the camera, pushing a tape inside and shooting me as a test. Then I filmed him, framed against all the other framed portraits on his walls. I left my green ID card as a deposit and strolled over the road.

Mahmuzi was silent but the hairdresser wouldn't shut his mouth. He talked about the soldiers who'd come to his sister's house in Al-Birah the week before. They'd gone through the refrigerator and the cupboards and taken a whipped-cream cake. Ibtisam had made it for her daughter's birthday. They didn't break anything. But they stayed for hours, told her family where to sit, when to go to the bathroom. 'And the dogs ate the cake. Is that what you want?'

He was talking about Mahmuzi's hair. Clean shaven, with his hair wet and styled, Mahmuzi looked entirely Israeli.

'Everybody wants their beard off and a modern cut these days,' the hairdresser grumbled. 'What's the matter with them? I mean, I don't have a beard either but I think of myself as traditional. What's happening with the young . . .'

'How much?' said Mahmuzi.

When we got back to the Mazda, I saw that Bilahl was nervous. The driver he'd wanted to use had lost his nerve and disappeared after Abu-Zeid's assassination. He had to find a replacement, get an ID card and papers for him, and yellow plates for the Mazda. All the way back to Al-Amari, Mahmuzi looked out of the window in silence.

I hung both the flags – the green one with its quotation from the Koran, the white one with the drawing of Al-Aqsa, an assault rifle and the legend 'Izz ad-Din al-Qassam

Brigades will free the Holy Land'. Both the rifles we'd used in the Bab al-Wad attack were still in the apartment: I put one beside the prayer mat and made Mahmuzi hold the second, crouching down. Bilahl produced a rusty Kalashnikov and a few landmines that had been dug out of the earth over the years. None of them worked, but they looked good enough for the video. I hit Pause. Mahmuzi prayed, then got to his feet and tied a green ribbon around his head.

I released the Pause to record again and held up Bilahl's text in front of Mahmuzi with my free hand. He read:

'I, the living shahid Mahmoud Salam al-Mahmuzi, choose to die a holy death in the name of God, in the footsteps of the shahid Halil Mahmoud Abu-Zeid, a fighter in the name of God, a member of the Izz ad-Din al-Qassam Brigades. I will walk the path of the *shuhada* and revenge the death of the shahid Halil Abu-Zeid at the hands of the occupying army in order to free all the Islamic holy lands and to ascend to the great, the merciful, the compassionate God, to live for ever in his gardens and dwell beside the pools of heaven.'

He continued staring at the camera and I continued filming. Nobody said a word.

Svetlana, what the hell are you doing? I'm freezing here. Can we not get some . . . ah, *hot* water, that's just what I need, yeah . . . that's really not so bad . . .

*'You like the washing, don't you?'*

Not as much as *you* do, Svetlana.

*'You respond to the warm water, don't you? My hands on your body?'*

Not true, you little Jewish whore! Just shut up and tell me about the Croc. Where is he? And where's Mother? Where's Grandfather? Why is there nobody here? Why am I stuck here alone with you, Svetlana?

In this endless dream . . .

*'Now don't make faces. Don't get irritated. What did I say? Enough. Enough of this squirming, sweetheart . . .'*

The driver arrived. It was the woman from Shaar Hagai. Good looking. She was wearing a tight shirt and trousers and lipstick and shades and had her hair back in a ribbon: for the checkpoints. When I smiled at her Bilahl gave me a furious look and sent me inside. He talked to her quietly about the operation. All that remained was to dress Mahmuzi with the belt. I took out the bulb and the battery, connected the electric circuit and entered the safety-catch nail into place. 'One – connect battery. Two – pull out safety catch. Three – push the button.' He wore a shirt over the belt, and a sweater on top of the shirt. He washed his face, brushed his teeth, anointed himself with more perfume, and just before he left, put on a faded denim jacket. I wished him good luck. 'God willing, we'll meet again in heaven,' I said. Bilahl stood close to him and spoke with a quiet intensity.

'Give yourself to God. Free the holy lands of Islam. And when you are in heaven don't forget us. Help us to become *shuhada* as well. Speak well of us, that we might enter too. *Inshallah*, soon. This whole world is worth less than a fly's wing in comparison to being with God in heaven. There you will be the most glorious of kings. It is the will of God.'

Outside, the Mazda was already breathing clouds of white exhaust smoke into the cold air. Mahmuzi kissed his Koran, got into the back seat and closed the door. The Mazda pulled away, and that was all.

The driver dropped Mahmuzi about a kilometre before the Kalandia checkpoint and made it through without any trouble, smiling at the soldiers and flourishing her blue ID card. Usually it's enough. She drove two kilometres past the checkpoint and stopped shortly after the turning to Bir Naballah. Mahmuzi took a bypass route used by construction workers which the army hadn't figured out yet. To be safe he was carrying a fake work permit from the Hebrew University. She picked him up again and, on entering Jerusalem, bought a large bouquet of flowers which she laid on the dashboard. The sky was incredibly clear; perfect and pale. She drove on Route 1 until she saw the walls of the old city to her left, continued down towards the city centre, turned left into King David Street and drove to the end of it, and then on down the hill via the road adjoining the Bell Garden. She entered Emek Refaim Street.

Mahmuzi was quiet all the way, only peeking from time to time at his Koran and mumbling, 'Allah chose me.' She knew the Café Europa because she'd been there on a previous visit to Jerusalem. There was good coffee and always plenty of people. An older, bald man in a green shabby coat had made a pass at her. He'd asked what such a pretty girl was doing on her own in a place like that. Then he asked whether he could pay for her. She'd turned her back on him.

'Look to the right,' she said. 'That's the place. Quite full.'

As they went past, Mahmuzi turned his head. 'The security guard doesn't look too serious.'

'Good. If you're not sure, there are more places along the road.' Mahmuzi shook his head and she pulled up. Her stomach was aching with tension. She sighed. 'All these Arab houses. The thieves took everything. Without shame.' Later, when I learned about all of this, Bilahl told me that she was Halil's cousin. Mahmuzi connected the battery to the explosive belt.

'Take the bouquet. If you can, wait five minutes, until I'm far enough away. Good luck.'

He got out and she drove off, and in her mirror she saw him get closer to the target, a bouquet of yellow flowers in his hand, and it seemed to her as if he walked in without the security guard checking him. At one of the red lights on the way to Talpiot she looked in her mirror at the line of cars behind her and heard what could have been a faint explosion. She drove into the car park of a mall and went in to walk around. In the electronics shops there were radios and TV sets showing various channels. Although she couldn't hear what was being said, she stopped outside one and watched – she would be able to tell. A live interruption at that time of day would be enough. The solemn angle of Danny Ronen's eyebrows would be enough.

According to Channel 2's report later that evening, the guard (only lightly injured) would probably just have glanced at the bouquet and indicated with his eyes to Mahmuzi that he could go in. *Haaretz* described what the shahid would have seen: a lot of glass everywhere, those round red-and-black tables, a long wooden bar with round bar stools. He would have smelled the coffee and tuna. Perhaps, *Yediot Achronot* speculated, somebody (now dead) had spoken to him, and he would have smiled back and whispered in his heart, *Shut your fucking mouth, you're going to die.* He would have gone to the bar and waited in line and ordered something simple in pantomime, something easy to order, something fitting for his last drink on earth. Water, possibly, or a coffee. He would have sipped it and looked at his watch and pulled the safety-catch nail. And, perhaps, at the very end, he spat on the floor and looked up into the shocked face of the girl behind the bar (now dead) as she opened her mouth to protest. 'Don't . . .' she may have said, who knows, and that's when he would have pressed the button.

# 21

I don't know where I'd be today, or who, if we'd played tennis or gone to the centre of town, or if the day hadn't dawned so clear that Shuli had had the urge for an Ice Europa, or if such a thing as an Ice Europa had never been invented or if we'd left half an hour earlier or ten minutes later, or if – the biggest if of them all – she hadn't asked to change places. An infinity of ifs. We stand at a crossroads a hundred times a day and we have to make our choices or we can never progress, and our choices determine who we are. That's the way it is, and that's the way it was that cold, metallic morning. And yet I can't get rid of the feeling that, for the third time, it wasn't me but somebody else who was making the decisions.

Shuli returned from the toilet and said she had thought the nicest thought, and smiled her hopeful, closed-mouth smile, and then the air trembled.

It's impossible to differentiate between what I think are my memories and what I've constructed from newspapers, photos, TV footage and the accounts of other people who were there and whose memories may themselves have been constructed from newspapers, photos and TV footage. Maybe nothing of what I am going to relate now is really mine, or maybe it all is. In any case, what I think I remember is that the air trembled and there was darkness. As if we'd been teleported to a different place: water dripping from the ceiling, chunks of concrete and clods of earth, black-and-red tables flipped and shattered; puddles on the floor. A building-site smell, a scorched-meat smell, a tear-gas smell, and the smells of coffee, blood, gunpowder and flowers. I couldn't stop staring at a mobile phone, half spilled out of a woman's handbag, and I realised that was because it was ringing. It reeled my gaze in among the chaos of the shouting. If there was shouting. Wasn't there a sickening silence? Or both – first the silence, then the shouts, and then the crying. I didn't see Shuli at all. I don't remember anything of Shuli after what she said and her closed-mouth smile. I do remember a yellow flower – I don't have a clue how it got there but other people also mentioned seeing these flowers. They said there were three separate explosions, stark white lightning, and an intolerable feeling above all of being *trapped*. All that I seemed to have missed, like the kick to my head that needed a couple of stitches and left me with a bump and a permanent scar. I don't remember the kick but I do remember the foot that kicked me. I watched the foot fly towards me, wearing a heavy army boot. I didn't get it for a moment, and then I got it and I wanted to scream and maybe I did.

Someone was asking me whether I was all right. I opened my eyes but I couldn't seem to answer. I was hot, I felt as if my skin was speckled with little burning spots. A voice told the hand that was trying to lift me not to: 'Check that nothing's broken first.' The hand disappeared and came back as fingers gently examining my body. I was turned over and investigated further and I must have passed the test, because at last I was lifted up. 'Can you walk? We'd better get out of here.' I leaned on a shoulder and walked. Something was sticking to the heel of my shoe. I tried to clean it off with a piece of metal while I sat on the pavement waiting for an ambulance. I tried to clean the soles of my shoes and looked about me.

A body in a blue Adidas shirt was lying at an unnatural angle in the shattered glass and ash, its face burned, mouth wide open, eyes staring upwards, a ring on one of his fingers. People were shouting, 'Another piece over here,' and a look passed between me and a guy with scalp-locks who was covering up body parts. We both swallowed smiles. Why? I guess it must have been 'piece', meaning 'chick' in Hebrew slang. Somebody ordered me to cry and put a chocolate cube in my mouth. A tall girl in a Café Europa T-shirt was dazedly wandering around; another girl was refusing to get in an ambulance. Volunteers from ZAKA, religious types in fluorescent plastic vests, were collecting limbs and viscera and fragments of flesh in plastic bags so that the proper rites could be given over the bodies.

'Are you all right?' There was a hand on my shoulder. A bespectacled woman with short brown hair and a pleasant pale face. 'I'm Scclvia,' she said in a South American kind of accent. 'I'm from the mental health clinic in Emek Refaim. I heard the explosion and came down to help.'

'No, I'm fine,' I said, though I was shaking from fear. Sylvia moved off towards a fat and sweaty curly-haired man, one hand on his waist, the other touching a bleeding wound on his face. She laid a hesitant hand on his shoulder. 'Are you all right? I'm from the mental health clinic in Emek Refaim. I heard the explosion and came down to help.' The man looked at her in wonder. 'What's your name?'

'Avi.'

'Nice to meet you, Avi, I'm Seelvia. Do you remember what happened?' He looked at her. 'Do you want to tell me?' He continued looking at her, his T-shirt outlining his sizeable paunch – he looked to me like the football manager Shlomo Scharf.

'Avi, we're still in the event occurrence phase. If you open up now and share what happened, it will help later on.'

He continued looking at her for several more seconds.

'What do you mean, what happened?' he said eventually. 'Don't you see what happened?'

'Well, of course . . .'

'You're asking me what happened? You haven't noticed that some fucking stinking son of a bitch Arab with dreadlocks in his ass blew this whole fucking place sky high?'

'Yes, Avi. I just want you to try and share . . .'

'Share!' Now he was properly screaming, like Shlomo Scharf used to, and Sylvia retreated a step. 'Are you fucking joking? No, tell me seriously, are you all right or what? These fucking Arabs . . . fuck it! Fuck them all, now! What happened? She asks me if I remember what happened!' He was waving his hands around and you could see the deep cut above his cheekbone, and someone approached him and embraced or restrained him, and led him away from the psychologist. She didn't move for several seconds.

I came across Sylvia in hospital a few weeks later, when I came in for my group therapy meeting and my weekly visit to Shuli. It turned out that initially at least she'd had a little more success with her next patient, a teenage girl. But when Sylvia put her hand on the girl's shoulder to console her, she felt a sticky spatter of skin and flesh on the girl's shirt and she broke down. When I met her again she was still in recovery.

I remember the hospital clearly. My injury was superficial, but since it was a head wound they didn't want to take any risks. I had an ugly cut on my forehead and an uglier bump underneath it, and there was someone else's blood on my clothes. They stitched me up, gave me a blood transfusion (donated by someone who'd found the time to do so – unlike me) and sent me to the ward upstairs, where I fell asleep.

When I woke up, I sensed bodies in white moving near me, shadows in the light more than clear pictures. Cotton wool wiped my forehead and my mouth. I heard ringing from afar. My pillow was changed and I felt how heavy my head was, how full of pain. Very slowly the blurred image cleared up; the white body became a nurse, the colours around me became flowers and chocolates, sent by I don't know who. My phone chirruped its *A-Team* ringtone and the nurse told me it was prohibited to talk on a mobile in hospital. So I switched it off and as I put it back in my trousers, folded on the table beside the bed, my hand touched a shard of glass. I pulled it out: it was all that remained of the PalmPilot. Another victim of hostilities. Gone, and with it Giora Guetta's story.

'Where's Shuli?' I asked. My voice sounded crushed – what came out of my mouth was different from what I'd tried to say – but the nurse understood and promised to find out. Later she told me that Shuli was still in the emergency room, in what condition she didn't know. There were no visits to ER, she said, and in any case I wasn't allowed to get up yet.

Mom and Dad, Leah and Yochanan Enoch. Tears in Mom's eyes, horror and helplessness in Dad's. More chocolates and flowers. My brother in Maryland sent his regards: he'd tried to call, but the time difference made it difficult. He wanted to get on a plane and come. I said there was no need, no way. Grandmother had called too, asking whether I needed anything. My sister Dafdaf arrived, and then Duchi. It was strange to see her, but she looked so beautiful I couldn't help but shed a tear when I saw her. I rolled the tear around my tongue and returned her hug, smelling the old familiar smell, kissing the familiar soft neck. I kidded her: 'Duchki! What are *you* doing here?'

'Would you like me to leave?' She embraced my parents and my sister, went downstairs to bring coffee for everyone and returned with a nurse rolling a TV she'd sorted out for us, followed by Muku.

'It's bizarre, Croc. I was about to call you when I heard the explosion.'

'You heard the blast?'

'We heard it at home,' my father said.

'It sounded like somebody'd thrown a frog from the top of a building,' said Muku.

'A frog?' asked Dafdaf.

'A garbage frog,' said Muku. 'How're you doing, Dafna?' He kissed her on her cheek. Dafdaf is two years younger than me and Muku, but she's been in love with him since she was a kid. When she turned sixteen she lost her virginity to him. He told her he wouldn't do it before. I knew all the details, though she'd made him swear not to tell me a thing.

'I don't understand,' she said. 'What's a garbage frog?'

'I don't know if you have them in Hadera – these enormous green skip things.'

'Not Hadera, Muku. Pardes Hana.'

All of us were watching Dafdaf and Muku during this exchange: I suppose we were all thinking about their childhood love and imagining what might have happened if she'd stayed. Duchi caressed my face and hair with one hand, and held my hand with the other. It was pleasant. There was no need to talk, and no chance to anyway – my father shushed us as the news came on and we fell obediently silent.

'A few minutes before noon today,' Osnat Dekel said, her eyes shining with tears, 'a massive explosion shook the peaceful German Colony in Jerusalem. A suicide bomber entered the Café Europa in Emek Refaim Street during the busy lunch hour and blew himself up. Eighteen are reported killed and fifty-three injured. Danny Ronen brings us the details.'

When the number of victims was announced, you could hear a kind of rustle or murmur ripple through the ward. There were other TVs on, and all of them were tuned to Channel 2. Someone shouted, 'What?' Mom's quiet tears turned into outright crying and Dad enfolded her in a clumsy, confounded hug. Duchi pressed my hand and I could feel her trembling. Muku placed his hand on Dafdaf's shoulder. Danny Ronen started coming at us from all directions.

'Earlier today,' said Ronen, 'the Izz ad-Din al-Qassam Brigades, a military wing of Hamas, took responsibility for the devastating attack in Jerusalem. The bomber, they claim, was Mahmoud Salam al-Mahmuzi from the Al-Amari refugee camp. This afternoon a video of Mahmuzi was broadcast on Palestinian TV in which he claimed the attack was in revenge for the assassination of Halil Abu-Zeid in Al-Birah yesterday morning.' We heard a ragged chorus of protest or complaint from around the ward, as if everyone were watching an incompetently refereed football match. 'But military intelligence doubts Hamas's ability to organise a response so quickly. A senior source told me that it is possible Mahmuzi was not the bomber at all, or alternatively, that someone else appeared on the tape. The real bomber, it is thought, is likely to have been hiding out in Jerusalem for several days. An investigation is proceeding. Halil Abu-Zeid, you may remember, was the subject of a targeted assassination carried out by the air force in retaliation for the shooting at Shaar Hagai earlier this week.'

'Oh, what liars these Arabs are. It's just unbelievable,' Dad said, and at that moment the curtain separating us from the next bed was drawn back, and a woman's face appeared.

'Did you see that? Have they no shame? They're not human beings, they're animals! They shoot a video like that and expect us to buy it? I've said it a million times: get rid of them all, every last one of them! I don't want to see them and I don't want to hear them.'

All of us looked at the woman in surprise. She had a chubby reddish face, and a wild kind of quiff. 'Thanks,' said Dad, and drew the curtains back together.

Muku and Dafdaf left, then Mom and Dad. Duchi and I talked (complaints about the sons of bitches at work, especially the slippery Gvirzman) and gawped at the TV and ate. When she went to the toilet, I asked the nurse about Shuli. Still in intensive care. She had no idea what her condition was. Duchi returned and closed the curtains around us and turned on her phone, apologising about it – she had a court appearance the next day and needed to make a few calls. I watched her in admiration. Usually she had nausea and couldn't sleep the night before she was in court. While she listened to her messages she lifted her eyes to meet mine a couple of times. 'People are looking for you,' she said. 'What people?' 'I don't know. Different ones. Check your phone. Maybe there's something important.' 'But it's not allowed,' I said. She talked to Boaz about the next day's meeting. When she hung up, her phone rang. It was for me.

'Eitan?' A girl I didn't recognise.

'Yes.'

'Hi. I'm Yaara from the Rafi Reshef morning show on IDF Radio? How are you feeling?'

'All right.'

'Eitan, would you be willing to talk on tomorrow's show? To say a few words about the attack? You'll just tell us what happened? Like, Rafi will ask you questions and you answer?'

'Why?'

'To hear it from someone who was there? A victim's angle? People are fed up with politicians? It'll be very short? Five or six minutes?'

'Five or six?'

'Something like that?'

'Uh . . . OK.' I stared at Duchi, who was scrutinising me. We arranged a time and Duchi made a face.

She stayed till late. It was very quiet in the ward. She peeked outside the curtains, and then closed them. When she turned to me, her eyes were smiling.

'Did you ever play doctors and nurses?'

But when Duchi lowered her head beneath the sheet, I couldn't stop thinking of Shuli. She'd told me it would happen tonight, and it was happening, but not with her. She might not be alive at all, and no one wanted to tell me. She'd had a nice thought and she had given me that sad closed-mouth smile. Duchi was good, and I could feel a tear make its way down my temple. I came in silence. She wiped me and herself, gently kissed the tear, and the bump on my forehead, touched my unshaven cheek with her palm, and left.

# 22

'How did he behave? Very naturally, Tommy. More than you'd have imagined possible. When the driver came to take him he kissed the Koran and was very relaxed. That's the only word for it. He wasn't tense at all. Just like I'm speaking with you now. You wouldn't have detected anything unnatural in his behaviour.'

'What were the final words you said to him?'

'"God willing, we will meet in heaven. I ask God to lead me on the same path as yours."'

'What was his mood like?'

'He laughed. Like I say, Tommy, he talked completely normally, like a person going off for a weekend away. Not like someone who was going to blow himself up. He was very reasonable, very natural, relaxed, smiling.'

Tommy Musari rubbed his chin, as he always does, and turned to the camera with a severe look. '*Noahs' Ark*, with Fahmi Omar al-Sabich. Don't you go away during these messages!' The audience clapped and Tommy told me I was doing fine. I drank a glass of water that a pretty woman handed me and we were back on.

'Did the driver tell him anything on the way?'

'No, no. The only important thing he had to remember

was that the mission had to get past the checkpoints, and if he was picked up, to blow himself up immediately so that both of them would die. We might not reach our goal, but being blown up's better than being interrogated and tortured and betraying your brothers and friends.'

'Tortured?' Tommy Musari looked shocked. A collective intake of breath from the audience. 'Hm. What was he supposed to look like?'

'He shaved his beard, cut his hair in a Western style. Sideburns. He didn't know any Hebrew but I taught him a few words – good morning, good evening and so on. I hope he didn't mix them up and start saying good evening to everyone!' The audience laughed and Tommy gave me a grin.

*'Hey, Svetlana. How are you?'*

Lulu! Get me out of here, Lulu. If this is a dream, then please wake me up . . .

*'Hey, Lulu. Oh, great, more Amr Diab tapes!'*

*'You like him?'*

*'Well, we're listening to him all day long so what can I do? And Fahmi likes him, so I'm trying to get into it . . .'*

*'How is he?'*

*'Well, he's got a pretty fun life, being fed, being looked after, being massaged . . .'*

*'He hasn't opened his eyes? Talked? Moved?'*

Please, Lulu, wake me up and take me out of here. Take me to our place below the village. Take me someplace where I don't have to remember everything.

*'All of that, to an extent. But what else is new? How are you? How was it getting here today?'*

*'Ppffhh . . . same as always. Hours. I just thank God the lot with the signs don't know who I am. There were policemen down there just now.'*

*'But what they say about your brother, I mean, it can't be.*

*Did he hurt the . . . is he a murderer? I saw the Croc once on* Noah's Ark . . .'

Oh, *Noah's Ark.* Of course . . .

'Isn't it difficult to walk with the belt on you?'

'Very simple, actually, Tommy. When you believe in the cause and in your mission, it's easy to act naturally. You laugh and listen to the radio, you smoke cigarettes. If the belt weighed twenty-five or thirty kilos, as your defence minister Mofaz says after every attack, yeah, it might have been difficult to carry. But come on, Shaul Mofaz, does anybody take him seriously?' Tommy Musari made a 'what do you think?' face and the audience burst out laughing. 'Exactly. But with ten to fifteen kilos, it's fine.'

'Before he presses the button, he says "*Allah Hu Akbar*"?'

'No. It's too dangerous. Allah is *Akbar* without his having to say it. It's just a myth.'

'And how does he pay for the bus ride?'

'If the mission involves a bus I check the details – how much the fare is, if there's a discount for students or soldiers . . .'

'Is there a discount for Hamas soldiers?' The audience roared with laughter again. I joined in. Tommy was feeling good about himself.

'Tell me, if he sits on the bus and an old lady gets on, would he get up for her?' The audience were on the floor.

''Cos you gotta help the aged, right?'

*'It's boring in the village. Nothing happens. I'm fed up. When you get better maybe you could come back? I sit on my rock for hours, just looking down at the plain. And Father's sadder than I've ever seen him. He hardly speaks. You have to come back. For me.'*

I can see the beach but I can't reach it. Something is pulling me away.

*'Cousin Nizrin's getting married next month. To Mustafa. He's a chemistry teacher at the university. She'll have to move to Kalkilya. But he wants to go to study in Dubai. Are you interested in this at all?'*

Don't stop, Lulu, please. I love your voice so much.

*'Are you there, Fahmi? How come you never answer? You look so . . . well. Svetlana showed me the shrapnel on the X-ray. So tiny. If she hadn't shown me I wouldn't have noticed. The size of a spectacle screw. Just a speck on your forehead.'*

In the afternoon Mahmuzi's name was released, and the fact that he came from our camp. The army was already roaming the streets, and though it wasn't yet an official curfew, people stayed in their houses. I joined Bilahl for the night prayer – *Salat al-Asah* – and on the way back from the mosque we walked by Mahmuzi's house. It hadn't yet been destroyed. Soldiers had been posted outside, and a small crowd had gathered. Hamad, a cousin of ours who worked for a locksmith's in the camp, waved us over. 'I don't understand what they're thinking,' he said. 'They're going to beat the army? What's the point of it? It's asking for trouble. And now we're all going to suffer.' Neither of us said anything. 'My father's furious,' said Hamad. 'He said whoever set it up's a fucking son of a bitch. That it's impossible to live here because of them. He's fed up with all these wars.'

'In my eyes,' Bilahl said, quietly, 'he's a hero. He's given us pride.'

'Some pride . . .' Hamad sneaked a look at the soldiers. 'I can't remember when we had any pride. Tell me, Bilahl, how proud does it make you to have them barging into our houses and turfing us out in the middle of the night?'

The curfew was announced, so grocery stores would be open late, until it started. We bought stuff and made our way home quickly under a cloudy sky lit by flares. I made both of us tea from a single teabag while Danny Ronen told us the mission couldn't have been in revenge for Halil's death because there was no chance we could have got organised so fast. Bilahl snorted.

'This Danny Ronen, you look into his eyes, and you see how dumb he is.' The real bomber would've been in Jerusalem for weeks, Ronen declared. 'You dumb shit,' Bilahl jeered. 'Now we need to plan the real thing.'

With the two glasses in my hand, two fingers in each handle, I stopped where I stood. I raised my eyes and smiled. 'Are you joking?'

'The mother of all operations. Something no one's ever seen before in this country.'

Outside, the soldiers were announcing the curfew over loudspeakers. I pulled the mattress down and threw a sheet and a blanket on it. They'd carry on shouting at us for several minutes, but there was no need to. Suddenly I was too tired to do anything other than crash on to the mattress. Bilahl continued watching the TV in silence, lowering the volume to a minimum. Before I fell asleep I thought of our father, after Mother's death, crying without stopping and laying a hand on my shoulder, for my support, or possibly for his own.

# 23

I woke to moans of pain – whose, I didn't know because I was surrounded by a curtain. I hadn't slept much. Every time the bump on my forehead touched the pillow a wave of pain shot through me and I pictured the army boot kicking my head over and over. At some point I gave up and decided to visit Shuli in the emergency room. I had a vague idea that, Bruce Willis-like, I'd probably have to creep past some sleepy guard in order to reach her bed. But the emergency room is on high alert twenty-four hours a day: critical patients coming in, nurses and doctors and beds on wheels, the screams of the injured, the tears of the relatives. Even at 3.24 in the morning, when my ward was as silent as the grave. The nurse at the entrance looked at her clipboard and told me I couldn't come in. I looked at the board too. I asked how Shuli was doing and she told me 'stable'. I said, 'Good,' though I hadn't a clue what it meant.

'Maybe let me in anyway?'

'No,' she said, and answered the phone. I crawled back to my bed and I guess I must have fallen asleep for a while, before the moans of pain woke me up.

Breakfast arrived on a tray. The next course was a psychological counsellor.

He started gently with a 'How are you?' before moving to a full-on attack. What did I see? What did I hear? What did I do? What did I think? What did I feel? I was to tell him everything and he would write it down. We were going to reconstruct everything that happened to me on the day of the event. It was very important. Even the events before the trauma itself. They were important too.

I answered drowsily and then told him it was my right to know what had happened to Shuli. He agreed with me, then carried on.

'OK, Eitan. Your system has been thrown out of balance and is still extremely sensitive. Right now, however, there is a window of opportunity. Immediate therapy is critical for your recovery. Do you understand?'

'Recovery my ass. What are you talking about?'

'Your condition is highly labile and without therapy it is likely to deteriorate. I suggest a group of nine to twelve people, all like you, in your condition, victims of shock or people injured as a result of terrorist attacks. Some of them might even be victims of the same attack as you.' He wrote something in his notebook.

'You think I'm a shock victim?' I thought he looked more in shock than I did. I couldn't stop staring at the large beauty spot by his eye and had noticed that he couldn't hold my gaze.

'It's too early to say, Eitan, but it's best to take all the measures we can in order to diagnose and treat it, if this is indeed the condition.'

'So what happens in these meetings?'

'Everyone tells their stories. Group therapy is known to be very helpful in these situations. I recommend that you at least try a few meetings. The mentor's called Ilan. Look. Nobody's going to force you if you don't find it useful.' He bent closer, trying to establish an intimacy between us. Was there a touch of French in his accent?

'Being in such an incident causes damage, that's certain. But the damage is reversible. Without therapy, it will be much harder to turn the trauma around.' I frowned. 'Without therapy, I guarantee you will feel much worse in the long run. I guarantee it.'

We were interrupted by my phone and I apologised and answered. It was Yaara from IDF Radio, good morning and how was I doing? They were patching me through? Right after the next song I was on air? I explained to the counsellor that he'd have to wait a few minutes, and suddenly the deepest voice in the history of voices was tickling my ear, an all-business voice rumbling me fully awake.

'A devastating attack in Jerusalem. Eighteen killed and fifty-three injured. It seems not a day passes this week without news of another tragedy. Joining us from the Hadassah Ein-Kerem Hospital in Jerusalem is Eitan Enoch. Hello, Eitan.'

What should I say? Hello? Hey there? Hi, Rafi?

'Good morning, hello, hi,' I said, and regretted it immediately.

'Morning, yes, let's just explain to the listeners, Eitan. You were sitting in Café Europa on Emek Refaim Street during the attack yesterday.'

'Yes.'

Did he want me to say something else?

'Tell us about it.'

'Uh . . . we arrived there a little before noon.'

'"We" arrived?'

'Yes. I was with a friend.'

'OK . . .'

'We got our coffees and sat down. I had an egg-and-tomato sandwich.' I felt like an idiot. 'It was a very bright morning. She said I'd chosen the table where she always used to sit with her boyfriend. Giora. Uh, he was killed in the Tel Aviv attack at the start of the week.' The counsellor's eyes widened.

'What?'

'Yeah,' I said.

'Do you remember anything from the . . . explosion?'

'No. A foot hit my head. It was dark. I don't know how I got outside. There was a woman with a South American accent. A guy who looked a bit like Shlomo Scharf shouted at her. Maybe it *was* Shlomo Scharf.' What was I talking about?

'And your . . . friend?'

'What about her?'

'Yes. What about her?' asked the deep voice.

'Uh. I don't know. She's in the emergency room. No one tells me anything. At three a.m. someone told me she was stable.'

'Stable?'

'Yes.'

He went quiet for a few seconds. 'It must be very hard for you.'

'Yeah, well. It's just . . . When Shuli came back from the toilet she wanted to switch places. To sit where she always used to sit. We made the switch, and right after that it happened. I mean, if we hadn't traded places, maybe I'd be in a stable condition right now and she'd be talking to you. I don't know.' Why had I agreed to this interview? 'On the other hand, the guy in the Bab al-Wad attack . . . he was sitting next to me and he died too, so . . . I dunno.'

'Eitan Enoch. One of those injured in the bombing in Emek Refaim Street yesterday. And I think that with these two simple words – I dunno – he expresses better than any politician the feelings of all of us this week. And it's interesting you mentioned Bab al-Wad, because it's our next song. Eitan Enoch, in hospital in Jerusalem, we wish you a quick recovery. And may we only hear good news!'

At least he hadn't signed off with 'May everything pass on the other side', like that guy in the eighties used to. Whatever the hell *that* meant.

I hung up and the phone rang immediately, so I rejected the call and it rang again. I turned it off and lifted my gaze to the counsellor's beauty spot.

'How was it?' he asked. He was writing something in his notebook.

'I don't know. Pretty terrible, right?'

'Yeah . . . no! No, not at all. Not at all. Tell me, what you told him about Bab al-Wad . . . you were there too?'

'Yeah. Why? I was on the Little No. 5 in Tel Aviv too. Giora Guetta, Shuli's boyfriend, was there.'

At last the counsellor looked me straight in the eye. It was the same look of stunned disbelief that I'd seen on a number of faces outside the Café Europa.

'I'll go and check on her condition for you,' he said.

During the morning I gazed at the clouds outside. Around noon the air seemed to grow sourer and the counsellor returned. He said that Shuli was in a coma. She had been moved to intensive care on the eighth floor. It wasn't clear how long it would last, or even whether she would come out of it at all – a coma could last from two to four weeks, and after it the patient might wake up or deteriorate into a vegetative state or die. Mom and Dad arrived with good food in plastic containers and messages from all kinds of people. They'd been getting phone calls from abroad. Why hadn't I told them I was going to be on Rafi Reshef? Why hadn't I told them I was in Shaar Hagai? So I told them everything, and their faces were astonished, but I just wanted to go to sleep.

Experts came and tested me. My head seemed fine but you can never tell with a serious blow, especially if you've been unconscious. I would have to remain under supervision for several weeks, if not months. 'Unconscious?' I asked. 'Didn't you lose consciousness?' 'I don't know.' 'Do you remember everything that happened from the moment of the explosion until you arrived at hospital?' I tried to remember but I couldn't. Fingers explored my body, and then I was outside. 'No,' I said. 'So you lost consciousness.' I would receive follow-up tests every Wednesday, before my therapy.

'What therapy?'

'The talking group. Wednesdays at seven-thirty.'

They were like a hallucination, my two days in hospital. Visits and doctors. Phone calls and troubled sleep. Walking in corridors and devouring Twixes from a machine. Journalists sitting next to my bed and scribbling quickly in notebooks. Dear, kind Duchi. Jimmy, for ten minutes, running to the airport to catch the flight to Brussels. And I took the lift up to the top floor and saw Shuli. I couldn't stop the tears. I broke down and they had to take me back to my bed in a wheelchair. And of course, embarrassingly almost, there was adrenalin and a weird exultation and euphoria. I was alive. I felt tremendously alive. I had looked death in the eye and evaded it.

Only sometimes, especially at nights, a feeling seeped through my elation – the feeling that death was getting closer, that death's interest had been roused and it was looking for me, and that it would eventually, inevitably, find me.

The day after I was discharged I appeared on *Noah's Ark*. My memory of it is much fresher for the simple reason that I've watched the tape of the show a dozen times. Like a wound you're dying to scratch, from time to time I can't stop myself and I stick it on – and then regret it. It swamps me with memories.

The morning I came out, a girl who described herself as a researcher called me, then put me through to Tommy

Musari himself. I haven't had much time to watch TV in recent years but even I know who Tommy Musari is. Even I couldn't avoid his all-conquering smile and triumphantly gleaming glass eye after Friday night dinners at my parents' or Duchi's father's or (before September 11th) her mother's. Not one of the three living rooms that hosted family meals on Friday nights (when we couldn't duck them altogether) managed to avoid one or the other of Musari's shows over the years – *A Little Bit of Musari, Most Musari, The Nation's Musari*. Musari, I should say, happens to mean 'moral' in Hebrew: hence the endless terrible puns. But even I knew that the jewel in the crown was *Noah's Ark*. It seemed that everyone in Israel except me watched *Noah's Ark*, the show that brought together a left-wing widow and a right-wing widow, or a settler and a Tel Aviv resident, or an army dissenter and a general, a cynic and a patriot, a celebrity and a destitute woman. Everyone watched it, left and right, east and west, rich and poor, just like their adverts said they did. Duchi watched it. In Time's Arrow people discussed it over lunch. Talia Tenne said that the show was even popular in Egypt, Jordan and Lebanon. So when Tommy Musari himself invited me on to his show, I appreciated the importance of it. And I said no.

'Good evening and welcome to *Noah's Ark* with your host . . . Tommy Musari!!' I watched the intro on a monitor in the green room, as I waited to be called up to the stage. The audience was applauding almost hysterically. 'Good evening. Thank you. Thank you. Thanks. Enough . . . Enough!' Tommy quietened the cheering with tamping gestures. 'Tonight is a very special night on *Noah's Ark*. Tonight we have . . . a *croc* with us.' A murmur went through the audience – a *croc*? Tommy broke into a smile and his non-glass eye broke into a twinkle. 'No, not a real crocodile, but a young guy called Croc.' He switched his gaze to a different camera. 'We Israelis have had a pretty rough week. Three major, savage attacks.' He paused to raise the tension, and continued in a low voice. 'Are we going to break?' 'No,' chanted the audience. 'Are we going to give in?' 'No!' 'Or are we going to link hands until we're stronger than ever? Are we going to stay here because this is, simply, *our land*, and we have no other?' 'Yes!!' roared the audience, prompted by the cue cards somewhat superfluously held up by technicians.

'Hello, Eitan? Am I speaking to Eitan Enoch?' Tommy Musari had said when he called that morning, and for some reason I'd said, 'You can call me Croc. That's what everyone calls me.' 'Then that's what I'll call you too. Croc, I heard you on Rafi Reshef and I was moved to tears . . .' It was him all right: you couldn't mistake the famous Musari intonations. 'I understand you were an eyewitness to the attack in Shaar Hagai, and then you were in Café Europa at the time of the bombing?' 'Eyewitness? Well, the soldier I'd given a lift to got shot in the neck.' 'Two attacks in the same week – an amazing coincidence . . .' 'Three, as a matter of fact,' I told him. After all, it was Tommy Musari. He said it was simply unbelievable, supernatural. He said that someone was protecting me, that I'd been chosen to show we can stand up to them, that I was a symbol. I told him I didn't want to appear on TV. But then he hit me with all of his famous 'Moshe Dayan charm', as they called it. An intense bombardment. I resisted until I could no longer bear the headache he was giving me. I gave in.

'Now, the Croc is a very special guy. In a quite astonishing coincidence, he was involved in all three of this week's terrorist outrages. He lost friends and witnessed things that will stay with him for the rest of his life. He saw death, ladies and gentlemen, but you know what?

He stood up to it.' Applause: the audience were drinking Tommy in. 'He looked death in the eye and he said no thanks!' Tommy gestured to quell the applause. The camera cut to a close-up, his face growing solemn. 'So Croc is today an Israeli symbol. He is the man who experienced terrorism first hand and said *no, thanks*. Ladies and gentlemen, I am thrilled to introduce this brave man, the Crocodile of attacks, CrocAttack: Eitan Enoch!' The researcher gave me a gentle shove in the shoulder and I stumbled forward.

'Welcome, Croc.' Wide smile, arms spread in a wide wingspan, warm hug, shorter in reality. 'In a moment I'm going to ask you to tell us all about your ordeal, and where this name of yours comes from.' Laughs from the audience, a smile from me. 'But first, you know how it works on *Noah's Ark . . .*' The audience shouted, 'Two by two! Two by two!' 'Exactly. Two by two. Couples from both sides of the fence. And this evening we have a very special girl joining the Croc. Don't go away during these messages!'

After the show, people approached me on the street and said it was the most moving edition of *Noah's Ark* they'd ever seen. Kids shouted 'Hey, Croc!' at me from the windows of buses. Friends from the distant past and long-forgotten relatives called. Tommy Musari called twice: first, to thank me and say he didn't remember being so moved in his entire career, plus the viewing figures had been spectacular. 'Unbelievable response. We'll invite you again soon. We'll find a reason.' The second time he wanted to tell me that the president had called him to congratulate him on the show.

'Lieutenant Dikla Gadasi served for two and a half years in the territories and was discharged from the army last week. As a military police officer, Dikla prevented countless terrorists from penetrating the border. She saw, close up, the roots of hatred. Please welcome . . . Dikla Gadasi!' A thin, bespectacled Yemenite-looking girl entered and sat opposite me. Tommy exchanged a couple of sentences with her. She hated them. Hated their guts. She thought that any soldier serving over there *had* to hate their guts, in order to keep from slipping up. 'They're right under your nose, and sometimes the smell from down there isn't all that pleasant.' It got a laugh. 'You can't turn the other cheek. You can't get soft. Until you're a hundred, a thousand, a million and ten per cent certain that this person isn't going to hurt you or your people, you don't give him a thing. Doesn't matter how much he cries or whatever sob stories he pulls about his pregnant wife or his sick kid or the work he's missing. I'm really not interested at all.'

'Mmm . . . interesting. Noah's Ark: the two sides of the fence. On one hand, the soldier who protects us from terror, and on the other,' he gestured towards me, 'an innocent civilian, a victim of that terror. Croc, you saw the effects of terror with your own eyes. Do you agree with Dikla? Do you hate them?'

'Uh . . .' I thought for a moment. 'I . . . dunno, really. I try not to hate anyone. Even someone who wants to kill me. I just think we should stay strong no matter what. I suppose.' Mild applause. Had I actually said that? The bespectacled girl wasn't having any of it. 'I don't understand why you wouldn't hate someone who's trying to kill you. Especially them. You want to be over there in their shit, excuse me, for two and a half years and then you might understand what I'm talking about. All the bleeding hearts ought to actually go out there and see these disgusting places for themselves and then see if they support a Palestinian state.' Tommy rubbed his hands. 'Yeah, well, I'm not saying I don't hate someone who wants to kill me.' I'd started sweating. 'Uh . . . we shouldn't give in, sure. We must put pressure on them.' How had it come to this? I didn't know the first thing about politics. 'A text from Ran in Ramat Gan,' Tommy read from a piece of paper he'd been handed, 'says that we should look at ourselves. "The smell may not be pleasant because we make them live in a sty, they make the—" Hold on, Dikla, hold on, let me finish reading Ran's text: "It's our illegal occupation and soldiers like Dikla who are giving them reasons to kill us."' Tommy lifted his eyes from the note. 'Dikla, we know what you think about this, but I'm interested to hear your thoughts, Croc.' I swallowed half a pint of spit. 'Yes, I can understand him. We really can't keep pointing only at the other side.' Dikla started to say something and I tried to appease her. 'I can understand your anger, but sometimes their anger is understandable too.' 'I don't believe this – he's justifying terror! He was in three attacks and he justifies terror?' Contempt was coming off Dikla like musk. 'Justifying terror? You're crazy.' 'Let's not get carried away, Dikla, no one was justifying terror. I assume Croc is asking himself questions. After such a traumatic week in his life – in all of our lives – you can't stop asking yourself why. Why is it happening? Where is it coming from?' Tommy looked at me reassuringly. 'Right. That's what I meant,' I said with relief. We moved on to what had happened. I was pretty good at what had happened; I simply said what had happened. When they want your opinion, that's when you have to watch out – that's when you know you're in trouble.

Tommy turned to me. 'To sum up,' he said, 'what do you have to say to our people? Is there anything we should be doing? How do we respond to terrorism?' 'We need to be strong, not to be cowed,' I said, and I saw a glint of vindication behind Dikla's glasses. 'Everyone should get on with their lives. Get on buses. Drive on roads. Drink coffee! Because if we don't have a normal life, what do we have left? We have to remain human beings. That's the most important thing. That's the only thing, I suppose. Because what are we if we're not human beings? If we lose ourselves, then . . . well, we've lost.' A second of silence and then Tommy leaned over and shook my hand, and the audience exploded in a wave of aggressive-sounding applause. I was dripping sweat. People I didn't know shook my hand. My chest was frighteningly constricted. I went to the toilet and I don't want to describe what came out there. I had nausea. I didn't understand why I'd come or what I'd said. I went out to get some air and once outside I didn't see any point in going back so I went home, and kept sweating and trembling and checking over my shoulder the whole time to make sure I was on my own, the audience's violent and hysterical applause ringing in my ears all night long.

# 24

Why no music, Svet? Play me one of my tapes . . .

*'Good, movement of the eyes . . . Dr Hartom will be happy to hear . . .'*

My brain must be stuck.

*'And now it's time for your wash . . .'*

A never-ending dream, and always the same.

*'Oh, Fahmi, you wouldn't believe it. You know the guys with the signs? One of them got in here last night. Security managed to pick him up just in time. Took three of them to get him out, screaming about the Croc . . .'*

Yeah, the Croc . . . in his little green car, and me with my apple . . .

The first time I saw him, watching *Noah's Ark* from under my blanket in the darkened room, lit only by the blue of the TV and the two orange bars of the heater – long before we met, before we drove in the car together – I liked the Croc. What had happened to him really was an amazing coincidence, as Tommy Musari said.

'We have to take this Croc out.'

'What?'

'An "Israeli symbol". The "man who said no, thanks". What a bunch of fucking morons.'

'Look at them,' I said. 'They're already terrified. They're shaking in their shoes. They can't talk about anything but us.' In my heart, I thought: *my brother is never satisfied.*

'This Croc has to die,' Bilahl said again.

'I'd kill that dark girl without thinking twice.'

'No, the Croc. He's the one we want.'

The noise of the bulldozers had become a constant background hum. Children went out to throw stones at them: from time to time you'd hear the shots and shouts. One day a tank crew accidentally shot another patrol. In a fury they destroyed the house next door, because it had obstructed the tank crew's field of vision. In the operations apartment, Bilahl and his friends came and went according to the curfew and in the evening sat and smoked and talked (Jews, Americans, humiliations, asymmetrical warfare, jihad, armaments, Jenin, Gaza, Hebron . . .) until my brain hurt. At night they slept on the sesame matting with their guns; during the day they went to the mosque or college or into town – always remembering to pray. When they relaxed the curfew and I finally went out, I saw that the camp was covered with fresh graffiti about Halil and posters of Mahmuzi taken from the video I had shot.

Strange days. A feeling of great power, of triumph, mixed with the continual humiliation of an army lurching clumsily around our camp doing what it pleased. And, out of nowhere, a terrible yearning for Father and Lulu and, like a sharp pain underlying everything, for Rana: her smell, her skin.

From our window we saw two columns of soldiers in helmets and bulletproof vests creeping behind an armoured personnel carrier. On their backs military packs, on their shoulders straps to support the rifles they held in both hands. Right hand on the trigger guard, thumb caressing the safety catch, forefinger squeezing the trigger to its locking point. Left hand on the stock, under the plastic shield. A brief command, a few movements of the fingers, and so much would cease to exist. When they took off their helmets, their faces – their eyes, their haircuts and goatee beards – fascinated me.

'Look at them all,' said Bilahl, 'shivering with fear.'

Sometimes the window frames would begin to shudder, then the floor would start, then you'd feel it in your body, and only then would you hear it: a bulldozer approaching. They used one to destroy Mahmuzi's family's house and to widen a few roads that an armoured personnel carrier couldn't get through. I wondered what Grandfather Fahmi would have said. First they threw him out of his village. Then he lived for eight years in a tent. Then, very slowly, he built himself a temporary home out of nothing. Some sheets of tin and a little dried mud; later, breeze blocks, mortar, cement for floors. Building his temporary home very slowly as the years pass, and his neighbours building their temporary homes very slowly. A whole neighbourhood being built, very slowly. A refugee camp turning into a town. And then the makers of refugees come, the displacers themselves, and the width of the roads in the camp is not to their taste. They flatten fences and walls, flip cars over, knock down poles that took ingenuity and sweat to find and erect – the poles that carry the wires which bring us electricity and telephone calls – so that an armoured personnel carrier can go where it pleases.

Air stale from the curfew, overturned cars like turtles on their backs, the clattering of rifle butts on iron doors . . .

Low-flying fighter jets scratched white trails in the sky. Helicopters rattled overhead. Soldiers broke into houses and slept on beds with mud-caked boots. They emptied closets, shattered windows, stank up toilets, tore posters from children's walls, hammered holes in dividing walls to scurry from house to house. They dropped clementine peels, sweet wrappers, chewed gum, used tissues behind them as they patrolled, like a wake of contempt. They destroyed all the equipment in the camp's clinic and looted the medicines. They shot a woman who was hanging up her washing. They shot a kid who had painted his face green and was playing the fool in front of them. A yellowish cloud of dust raised by their boots hung over the camp. I thought: let the Croc come and see this cloud.

I wanted a soldier to come into the flat and overturn things, break our furniture, mock and threaten me. I imagined head-butting his nose, the sound the breaking bone would make, his scream, the smears of blood on my forehead. As I pictured him on the floor, crying in pain and pleading for his life, my jaw would tighten and I'd find my mouth full of saliva and realise I was actually drooling for vengeance.

They wouldn't let her have a glass of water. A dirt ramp went up one week and came down the next, and no one knows why it went up or why it came down or who gave the order.

Who's here? Who's touching my face? Stroking my hair? Talk to me. Please, say something.

I can smell that it's you . . . Say your name.

I'm sorry I left. I'm sorry I didn't come back. I'm sorry. I'm sorry.

* * *

Bilahl got away right under their noses and went to Gaza, and she came to me from Murair. I don't know how, through the cat's cradle of patrols and jeeps and bulldozers in the middle of the curfew, but she did. Bilahl never liked her. Bilahl thought she was . . . well, you can guess what Bilahl thought. I touched her hair, and she didn't stop me. My heart was jumping into my throat. I couldn't stop touching her hair. I smelled it. I was entranced by her hair; how it was separate from her, not quite her, but also her. Not her but hers. I stroked it for several minutes and we didn't look at each other or speak. She lowered her head, hugged her knees to her. Eventually she got up and looked at me.

'Why didn't you come?'

I thought, *Why am I denying myself what I want? What she wants? Bilahl is in Gaza . . .* How easy it is to justify the things you really want! Rana stood in front of me and I leaned back on the sofa and looked back at her.

It was as I dreamed it. Through that winter I liked to get really close to the electric heater. I'd let the glowing bars heat my trousers or my sweater to burning point and then I'd press my clothes against my skin to feel the almost unbearable heat die down into a pleasant afterglow. I moved closer to the heater and, when the trousers began to burn my skin, I peeled them off quickly and pulled her on to the sofa.

Who's here? Who's touching my face?

Say something, Rana!

Please, Rana!

The curfew was relaxed for a couple of hours for Halil Abu-Zeid's funeral in Ramallah. The walls on the way there were almost invisible beneath new posters and graffiti. A huge crowd was marching and milling around with yellow Fatah flags and green Hamas flags: 'To Jerusalem we march, a million *shuhada,*' they were chanting. I tried to get close enough to kiss the body, but the pushing and shoving were too much to struggle against. Soldiers of the resistance covered their faces with keffiyehs to avoid being photographed by the army helicopter circling low above us. A fighter jet shot past, shaking the houses. Someone fired into the air, but the Jewish troops kept their distance. If only they'd dare, I heard people say.

On the brink of the grave, watching the earth and sand being shovelled on to the coffin, stood the driver, Halil's cousin, her lips moving unceasingly, unthinkingly, her head shaking from left to right, again and again, grief stricken, heartbroken, mad with rage.

Bilahl had returned from Gaza with money and approval for an operation, the 'mother of all operations', and we walked back from the funeral together. At the entrance to the camp we ran up against a new checkpoint and a young soldier stopped us. I saw the look in Bilahl's eyes and whispered, 'Don't be stupid,' but he wasn't listening. 'You know who I am? How dare you ask me for ID? *You're* telling *me* whether or not I can go home. *You're* telling *me* when I'm allowed to walk around? You're doing me a favour by relaxing your curfew for two hours?' The soldier didn't have a clue what he was saying. '*Shu?*' he said, his eyes giving away his fear. He glanced over his shoulder and shouted, probably to someone who could speak Arabic, but I explained in Hebrew that we just wanted to go through. I smiled, and Bilahl looked at me with a scorn I'd never seen before. The soldier returned our ID cards. '*Ahalan Wasahalan,*' he said, which was probably all the Arabic he had. Be welcome. We walked on without talking and after a few paces I ducked down to pick up a wrapped sweet from the dust – almost certainly dropped by the soldiers. I unwrapped it, and put it in my mouth. Sour-sweet, tasty, soft centred. Bilahl watched me and spat furiously.

Maybe I should have said something to my brother, who hated even a Jewish sweet. Maybe if I'd stood up to my big brother and said something I could have knocked a little sense into his proud head.

# 25

I visited the support group every Wednesday for the next thirteen weeks. At 7.30 every Wednesday I would go to the room on the fourth floor of the Hadassah Ein-Kerem Hospital, four floors below where Shuli lay in a coma.

Wednesday became the day that held me together. The other days of the week were like a rollercoaster that had skipped the rails, with no direction or control; time distended like stretched gum. Some days sank slowly into a swamp of zombified routine, brushing teeth, sitting in front of the computer, Channel 2, takeaways, arguments with Duchi ('Who the hell is this Shuli you were talking about on Rafi Reshef?') and wondering where the time had gone . . . The rest of the time, frankly, I was just a confused insomnia-dazed mess. Wednesdays were my bulwark against it all, something solid and stable at the week's midpoint. Wednesdays were a point of orientation, a reminder that something had changed, a focus for the rest of the week. They stopped me escaping to the past of Before, stopped my attempts to block out the present of After. They took me back to Jerusalem and nailed me to the cross of reality. They stilled time.

Every Wednesday at 2 p.m. I would drop everything

else and take a Little No. 5 to Tel Aviv's central station. From there, a No. 405 to the central station in Jerusalem and then a No. 27 to Hadassah Ein-Kerem. It was Ilan the group leader's suggestion – Duchi wanted me to take the Polo – and I was happy to give it a shot. But the first time I set foot on the minibus I threw up. People were very nice about it: some of them recognised me as the Croc. I threw up again. Duchi argued for the Polo again. But Ilan convinced her, and she convinced me, and after that first time I didn't throw up. More than that. As the nausea subsided, I began to enjoy it.

My days at the hospital began with a Twix from the machine on the ground level and a visit to Shuli. Then a check-up with the doctor, who measured the gradual reduction of the bump on my forehead, told bad jokes – 'I gotta take your head for a test, can you manage without it for a couple of hours?' – and gave me my medication. After the group had finished, around 9.30, I'd take the No. 27 back to the station, have an egg sandwich in the Café Europa there (Ilan's idea – to have what I'd had on the day of the bombing) or some falafel (my idea) and then No. 480 to the Tel Aviv North train station, where Duchi would be waiting to pick me up because, as she put it, 'Enough is enough!'

Ilan was losing his hair and wore it long at the back. Not quite long enough for a ponytail, thank God, just a balding man's compensatory mullet. He also had a goatee, and was rather short and chubby. There was no denying the fact that Ilan was extremely ugly, and I'm not just saying that because of what happened later. His impressive blue eyes stood out, but only in the way the Taj Mahal stands out from the squalor and cow shit of Agra.

Maybe the Taj Mahal's on my mind because of Naama, the prettiest girl in the group, who'd been to India a number of times. I found it hard to take my eyes off her at the first meeting. Fortunately she talked a lot – she talked all the time – and it got on my nerves after a while, but at first I just wanted her to keep talking, so I could keep looking at her. She'd been in an attack in Jerusalem five years earlier. Her two best friends had been killed right next to her. Since then she hadn't travelled on buses, didn't sit in cafés or restaurants and kept away from the city centre. When she walked down the street she avoided bus stops and other places which she'd marked down on a map. Every time there was an attack in Jerusalem she added its location to her map. She had a theory she repeated every week, which explained in almost credible scientific detail why it was her destiny to die in an attack. She'd become accustomed to living with the fear. Her radar was permanently on: every five minutes she was compulsively checking out what was behind her.

'But where's the logic?' I asked her in my first meeting. 'They never bomb the same place twice. They know the security will be tighter and so on.' It reminded me of the argument with Duchi the day after the Little No. 5 attack. But Naama wasn't Duchi and didn't yell back, only dropped her charming long lashes over her eyes and hung her head. 'Let's listen to our friends' stories, Croc, and not interrupt,' Ilan said. 'You should recognise that logic is not always what determines our lives. There are other forces in action.' I swallowed, pulled my head back into my shell and apologised.

'They bombed the No. 18 twice in two weeks,' said Naama.

'You've got a point,' I said.

Uzi Bracha was a welder who was called out to fix a broken traffic light one morning. He went up on the cherry picker to weld the pole. He hadn't been told that it had been broken in an attack. Or that there would be pieces of skin and what he was sure was an eye still on it. Uzi Bracha went home that day and called a locksmith who installed eight locks on his door. After that he went to a gun shop on the Jaffa Road and bought a pistol. He came home and sat with his pistol cocked on the armrest of his chair opposite a door that was locked eight times over. I liked Uzi. He didn't speak much and looked genuinely frightened: I liked the sincerity of his fear.

I told them about Giora Guetta, Humi and Shuli, still lying in a coma above our heads. I described the shattered rear window, the boot hitting my head. I said, 'I don't think I'm a shock victim.' They asked me, 'Do you check over your shoulder sometimes?' Sometimes. 'Does your heart suddenly accelerate?' Nought to sixty in five seconds. 'Do you get nauseous?' All the time. 'Does the sound of an ambulance make you break out in a cold sweat?' So that's what a cold sweat is. 'Do you cry?' No, but my eyes can suddenly fill with tears. 'The theme tune to the news?' Yeah, that'll do it. 'Classic shock victim,' Uzi concluded. 'Allow me to make the diagnoses, eh, Uzi?' said Ilan. 'Look, Croc, the danger of damage to the body is signalled by the body's own alarm system – fear. Fear is a crucial biological defence mechanism. It's healthy.'

Yulia cried constantly. At first I hated it but after a few meetings it became a background hum. She'd been in Café Europa. My sister-in-arms! Yulia remembered all the faces, including mine and Shuli's. She'd been brought to the emergency room in what Ilan called a dissociative state and suffering from severe sleep problems. Daniela, or Dani as she insisted we call her, was with her sister and her sister's two-year-old daughter at a wedding in Bet-Shemesh. Her sister and niece were both killed. Dani was severely injured but managed to drag herself out of the rubble. She was in hospital for three months, and it took her much longer than that to learn to walk again.

But her physical condition didn't interest her. Dani couldn't stop trying to reconstruct what had happened to her sister and niece. Where exactly had they been when the bomber blew himself up? How exactly were they killed? The explosion itself or the collapsing building? She was tormented by guilt about surviving. Did she limp past her sister and the baby, ignoring their moans of pain? 'A little child, always talking, babbling away . . .' 'The worst thing,' pretty Naama added, 'is that a child doesn't know, can't understand. That's what's so unnatural. I mean, an adult knows the risks, knows there are terrorist attacks, that there's the possibility he'll be next, but what did she know? Though at least she went with her mother and not alone – I mean, imagine if . . .' She liked to talk, Naama. And there was the guy who'd had seventeen different operations; the girl who'd stopped eating; the guy with a huge burn on his forehead and hearing in only one ear; and an older woman who arrived every week with a different son, daughter, granddaughter or grandson and who never, we noticed, ran so low on relatives that she ever had to bring the same one twice.

Every week for two hours I immersed myself in this world. I listened to intimate confessions and cried along with my fellow therapees, and they cried along with me. Memories came back to me with force and clarity, though somewhat mixed up with each other. Ilan said that I was 'concurrently experiencing three different phases of post-trauma': the *Event Phase* for the Café Europa attack, the *Immediate Reaction Phase* for Shaar Hagai and the *Early Reaction Phase* for the Little No. 5. He said there weren't many cases like mine. Like everyone else, Ilan had seen me on *Noah's Ark*, something which I felt bothered him, though he never said anything. Maybe my status as a famous survivor didn't sit well with my being a newcomer to the group. But all the others were fascinated. I felt that they were proud of me, that I somehow represented them. They liked to walk with me in the hospital corridors, where strangers would recognise me and shake my hand and offer condolences. Once I was walking with Dani when a member of the Knesset visiting the injured stopped us and shook our hands. He stank of aftershave and told a lousy joke about a member of Hamas arriving at the gates of heaven and getting the good news and the bad news.

The way the group therapy worked was you had to repeat your story every session to try to bring a little more to the surface. You'd keep telling it and you'd reach a new perspective, that was the idea. We heard the same stories again and again, and we were happy to. From time to time Ilan would interrupt us and ask a question which everyone would answer briefly.

'What does an explosion sound like?'

'A little "puck",' said Noa.

'A big "boom",' said Dani.

'"Vooomm", like in Lebanon, like a mine,' said bearded Uri, or Roy – I always mixed them up.

'Nothing,' Roy said, or Uri. 'Just pain in the ears. And the air moving. I felt it and I lifted my head.'

'The sound of blood hitting a wall.'

'Handclaps, or fireworks,' said Yulia of the Café Europa.

I said: 'Shattering glass, and a humming silence like you get in an elevator . . .'

'What are we talking about?' said Uzi Bracha. 'Why do we need to sit here and tell each other what an explosion sounds like?'

No one answered. Ilan said, 'Did I tell you about the mice?' Without waiting for a reply, since he knew he already had, he went on:

'They were testing the reactions of laboratory mice to electric shocks. One mouse which had been given an electric shock was released from its cage into a safer environment. It learned its lesson and never returned to the place where it was hurt. A second mouse was given the same shock but in a closed environment. It became ill, lost its hair and developed an ulcer. Now, two mice in a closed cage were given shocks but did not become sick. Because they had each other. They were stuck, like the second mouse, in a dangerous place without an escape route but they were not alone. This is what we are doing here. Every one of us is stuck in a place he can't escape from at this stage. But we have each other.'

'And we're not losing our hair,' I said. Ilan gave me a sour look and didn't respond. We all sat quietly, listening to Yulia's crying.

'A trouble shared is a trouble halved?' said Dani.

'Well, sort of,' he replied, stroking his goatee.

Every Wednesday I also took the lift up to the ward on the eighth floor to sit with Shuli. I came to know her for longer, and better, in a coma than I'd known her awake. Her face was unchanged and still beautiful, except that her eyes had lost all their depth. There were tubes connected to her mouth and arm, tubes disappearing under the sheet into the heart of her. The machines fed her, made her blood flow, breathed for her. The one thing they couldn't give her was sleep.

As the weeks passed I learned to recognise Shuli's mood by subtle changes to the air in the room. One time, when I was sitting alone next to her telling her something, she blinked, and I felt it was for me.

On her birthday I brought her flowers. 'Happy birthday,' I said. There were other flowers and presents beside the bed. 'In this country, every birthday you celebrate is an achievement,' I said. 'And a marriage? Something to be proud of even if it didn't last. And a kid – you've really got it made. You've created a dynasty. I read in the paper that we're making a lot of babies here. You know, relatively.' She didn't blink. I would describe the view to her, the best view in the hospital, looking down over wooded hills and valleys, and when I was there on my own, I would raise the bottom of the sheet and touch the crocodile on her ankle. It was my secret sign to her – our sign. One warmer evening I arrived to find the windows open and a battered-looking pigeon fluttering around the room, like a synapse firing in a brain. It saw me and took off. Maybe *that's* a sign, I thought. Or maybe it's just a pigeon.

Her boss came often – Alon, the chef from the King David, sometimes accompanied by other chefs from the hotel. He told me she had talent. He'd known Guetta too: 'a lovely guy'. Shuli's father and sister came every day, always depressed, crying, and praying for a miracle. I heard Shuli's father tell Alon that it was insensitive to bring Arabs along, and rather than reply Alon and Osama left the room. 'I should have said something. I got plenty of things I could've said,' he told me in the corridor. 'I'm not a fucking lefty but come on. A little respect for human beings.' Shuli's bed became a meeting point. I followed the soap opera of her aunt's health, advised the aunt's partner on the telecoms market and recommended a travel agent to him, and, in return, was recommended an accountant. Guetta's father always asked me about what Giora had been up to in Tel Aviv on the morning of his death, and I always replied that I was sorry but I didn't know. He asked me to write something for a commemorative booklet and I promised to think about it. I even brought Duchi once, after our 'Who the hell is this Shuli?' argument.

And all the time the thing that connected us lay there above us all, silent, lonely, machine-bound, lifeless yet alive, waiting for something to change. And then something did change.

The thing I enjoyed most about those Wednesdays was the journey home. An intercity bus ride at night has a charm of its own. It's uninterrupted thinking time. The whole day seems to sink through you and dissolve in the blood. People talk, but not so much and not so loudly – out of deference to the darkness, perhaps; the steady hum of the engine and the rhythm of the passing lights, the lights of the villages off in the night, the bluish light of the bus's interior. On my night rides I laid my forehead against the window and let myself breathe deeply and relax. It was on the bus, quietly, that I really examined myself. That was where the memories returned. It was on the night buses that carried me back from Jerusalem to Tel Aviv that I began to accept myself as I was, and began to think about who I was going to be.

# 26

*'You know something, Fahmi? I think you may be the perfect man. You never shout at me, never disappear, never turn up smelling of vodka and cigarettes and other women. Even Mama would like you. Let's see . . . physiotherapy in an hour, then a wash. Massage first. You had a busy day yesterday. Both Lulu and Rana. Very cute, Fahmi. Still not talking to you, but I saw her kissing your forehead.'*

Bilahl believed that he could carry out what everybody else only talked about: the mother of all operations. After his visit to Gaza his confidence had gone through the roof. It was *power* he was feeling.

He wanted to talk to me about his ideas.

Ben-Gurion International Airport. Since the Fatah operation in the seventies no one had managed to get near it. The passenger lounge was a good target. An aircraft was a possibility, either in the air or on the ground. Huge impact. Great damage to the economy. The feeling that their escape routes had been blocked off, that running to Mummy in America was not so easy. The feeling that they were locked up in here with us.

Second option, Eilat airport. A little far but the impact

would still be considerable. A small airport but relatively light security. Near the city centre and the hotels. Less guarded. Several options to get there: from the southern part of the West Bank; from the Gaza strip via Egypt, along the border or from Sinai; through Saudi Arabia or Aqaba, in a commando boat. Eilat was vulnerable.

I said, 'It's not a coincidence that Eilat's hardly been targeted yet: it's not Palestine.'

'New York and Munich aren't Palestine either.'

'Right. But you're talking about the mother of all . . .'

Third option, a big hotel in Jerusalem. 'Like the Jewish operation against the British in the King David. They drove a car in with two hundred and fifty kilos of explosives. This is what I'm talking about. Something that will go down in the history books.'

Fourth option: a symbol. David's Tower.

'Oh, come on: David's Tower?'

Fifth option: the Knesset. 'Get people with weapons inside with the caterers or cleaners, in trucks through the back gate. You get someone to work there for a few months.'

'It's not easy,' I said.

'I didn't say it was easy.' He looked up with irritation. 'We will keep thinking. I'm happy to hear more ideas. Anyway, you're to start working on the explosives. Start gathering quantities. Slowly.'

*'How are the muscles responding, Doctor?'*

*'Well, you know. He's not moving them like us. You should be giving him more massages every day, here, and here, like this . . .'*

*'I know – I've already increased the number of deep massages. He gets more than anyone, longer than anyone . . .'*

*'And always check underneath, because that's how he usually lies . . .'*

*'I do. I'm determined that he won't get any pressure sores. I've been working on reducing these inflammations, too. Here, help me turn him over, Doctor . . .'*

*'I'm impressed, Svetlana . . .'*

*'Careful with the tubes now . . . One for air, and another for urine. He's lucky we treat him so well. Nobody else gets such personal treatment, Doctor.'*

Outside, the armoured personnel carriers rolled by, leading columns of soldiers like ducks leading trails of their young. We'd grown used to them and, as in the zoo when the animals get to know each other, we feared them less. Kids were already throwing stones at them, almost affectionately, as it were.

I poured Coke into a couple of tall Coca-Cola glasses I got free with a box of six bottles and Bilahl lifted his glass dubiously, the drink sizzling with a thousand tiny explosions beneath his lips. I didn't like his attitude. I didn't know what they'd told him in Gaza but I'd seen the money they'd given him. Two thousand in cash. Two grand, and even a glass of Coke was somehow impure and decadent. We should have enjoyed it more, should have realised that the tap could have been turned off any time. But it's easy to say that in hindsight.

I drank Coke and ate sunflower seeds and watched *Who Wants to Be a Millionaire?* and *The Weakest Link* and *The Mission*. A contestant on *The Mission* managed to reach the Golden Question, giving himself a chance to double the five million Lebanese lira he'd already won.

The Golden Question was this:

'Last week members of the Izz ad-Din al-Qassam Brigades carried out an attack on a bus on the road between Jaffa and Jerusalem. In what year did Palestinian freedom fighters carry out similar attacks against Jewish buses on the same road?'

'1978,' said the contestant, and my smile disappeared. Up in heaven I guess Grandfather Fahmi's did too. Ihab the host stared at the contestant for a few seconds before telling him he'd just blown five million lira. He recounted the real story of the Beit-Machsir fighters. When Bilahl came back I told him and he switched the set off and snapped that I needed less TV and more mosque in my life. I said nothing. I just looked levelly at my brother and leaned back on the sofa, where Rana and I had done something he never had.

# 27

I tried to return to my previous life, and to two things in particular – Duchi and Time's Arrow. Duchi was sweet, considerate and kind, or tried to be. Time's Arrow also welcomed me back with open arms. They equipped themselves with plenty of patience and understanding and were obviously giving me as much time as I needed. Jimmy said he was sure I'd organised everything to get out of the Brussels trip. *Little by little* was the phrase I kept hearing – at work, on Wednesdays in therapy and beside Shuli's bed – *little by little*.

It wasn't easy. In retrospect, it was impossible. For a start, in my previous life I used to sleep. In this one I didn't. I would wake long before dawn, exhausted by my own dreams and, hating the silence, wander through the rooms or sit in front of the television's fuzzy, comforting light. In order to pass the time I started smoking, which made me grumpy and nauseous. Duchi tried to talk to me but I pushed her away, telling her to go back to bed because she couldn't understand. Several times I called Uzi Bracha, who was always awake in the small hours, but it didn't help. After a few weeks the doctor suggested some sleeping pills called Zopiclon, which sometimes worked and sometimes didn't but always left me apathetic and addled. Sleepless nights led to bad days, and vice versa. It was a vicious circle. I had a permanent headache, my nerves were frazzled, my thoughts were racing and my body was running on empty.

But now I was also . . . *CrocAttack*! Magnet of attention, symbol of resistance, vessel for other people's ideas. New forces were taking control of my life and I couldn't, or perhaps didn't want to, avoid them. Here came the offers and the pressures, the strangers and the advisers . . . every day I was approached by people I'd never talked to who knew what I needed, or who needed to know what I thought. Could I lend them my voice, my support, my opinion? It didn't matter to them that, in most cases, I had no opinion.

I got a call from *Left and Right* on IDF Radio, a kind of sub-*Noah's Ark*, with people from the left and the right shouting at each other. 'Eitan Enoch, what do you think about the decision to impose a curfew on the territories for the duration of the holiday season?' 'Mr Enoch, as someone who has personally experienced the intifada, could you please explain to my dear friend sitting in her air-conditioned studio in Tel Aviv the reality of terror?' 'Eitan Enoch, what do you think about a unilateral withdrawal?' 'About the planned construction of a Separation Barrier?' 'About the transfer of Jewish settlers?' 'About the two-state solution?' They called two or three times a week and I don't know why they bothered because I never had any answers. On the curfew, I said it was very hard to live like that and we should find ways to relax it. On terror attacks, I said we had to put an end to them and fight with all our might. On the wall, I said we should cause as little damage as possible. On unilateral withdrawal, I said only on the condition that security could be guaranteed. I said words which added up to sentences which grew into paragraphs but I wasn't really saying anything whatsoever. I talked like a politician and said nothing at all and it seemed to go down fine with them, because they kept calling.

After a particularly pointless conversation on *Left and Right* one day, I received a phone call from Benzi Dikstein, spokesperson for the Communities Committee. I asked what the Communities Committee was. He said, 'Exactly! That's exactly our problem: no one's heard of us. We're a group of lobbyists who represent a few communities in Greater Israel opposed to the dismantling of settlements and the transfer of Jews.'

'Ah, settlers.'

'We prefer "inhabitants",' said Benzi. 'Eitan, as someone well known, someone who's experienced a lot and knows the reality intimately, we think you would be a tremendous asset to our cause.' I burst out laughing. 'Me?' 'But you were speaking against non-voluntary transfer on IDF Radio only a couple of minutes ago. By the way, do you know where the name Enoch comes from?' 'Uh . . . no. I keep meaning to go to the Diaspora Museum and check it out.' 'Well, it's a corruption of Chanoch, the father of Methuselah, and they never managed to kill him either. Or not for a long time, anyway . . .' He gave a couple of barks that must have been some kind of laughter.

One day Shmulik Kraus called. 'Oh my God,' I yelled to Duchi, 'Shmulik Kraus!' Duchi came running and then stopped. 'It won't be him,' she said, 'it'll be that lefty.' I put my ear back to the phone. '. . . not Shmulik Kraus the singer, of course, I'm Shmulik Kraus from Stop the Occupation.' 'Oh,' I said.

'We really liked the things you said this morning,' he continued, slipping from single into plural, 'against this ridiculous curfew that our genius defence minister gave the residents of the West Bank for a holiday present, not the Jewish ones, of course' (I couldn't remember what I'd said, but I may possibly have called Mofaz a clown), 'and we wanted to ask whether you would like to be one of the speakers in our demonstration this Saturday night in Rabin Square?'

I kept having conversations like this. Calls from the right, the left, the non-aligned, the Society against Violence in the Family, and one time – after I accidentally stepped in some dog shit on Ibn-Givriol Street while talking on my mobile to the radio and had broken off to curse dog-owners who didn't clean up their dogs' mess – from the Society for a Clean Tel Aviv, who turned out to be pro transfer of dogs.

'Sue the National Insurance,' I was told, 'and you'll get one hell of a pension.' A lawyer volunteered himself on a no-win, no-fee basis. A special committee of the Defence Ministry – three legal experts who debate lawsuits from alleged victims of terrorist attacks – approve or deny your compensation. My lawyer told me that my fame would guarantee compensation because I was a media darling and they wouldn't dare not pay. I went to meetings, discussed tactics, cut out articles from newspapers. They threw my claim out. My lawyer, head in his hands, said it was unbelievable how heartless they could be. 'This country's falling to bits!' he said, and blamed my fame. Then he asked for a $2,000 fee. Duchi called me an idiot, having warned me early on not to get into it. Someone else had suggested that the Hostile Actions Casualties Organisation would be more sympathetic. So I tried. They weren't.

And what else? The General Security Services came to say hi, though it took me about half an hour to figure out what they wanted. I'd been in three consecutive attacks and got away without a scratch. Wasn't that a little suspicious? Did I have, or had I ever had, Arab friends?

Friends from the territories? Did I feel empathy for the suffering of the Palestinian people? Did I support their struggle? I told them that they were a national disgrace and that they should pick on the perpetrators not the victims and then burst out crying. Eventually they got off my back. Or I think so, anyway.

A private association helping victims of terror called One Family asked me to come and speak to other victims once a week. They thought that after *Noah's Ark* and all the articles and the radio I might lift a few spirits. So I went a couple of times but quite a few of the audience blamed me for shamelessly exploiting terrorist attacks which had killed and injured others. I'd escaped without a scratch and was now trying to cash in and promote myself. I showed them the bump on my forehead and said I wasn't making any money: 'I wish I was!' I told the hecklers that I hadn't asked anyone to write about me. It didn't matter: I was arguing with people who'd been injured or lost their family and friends. They were looking for a target for their anger and I would do. So I removed the target from their sights, though I was criticised for that too. I was told that I'd only stopped going because the media weren't there and I was only interested in the media. One of the things I learned during those months is that sometimes you can't win. And you can't even say that you can't win, because then they say that you've a nerve to complain while others have lost limbs or are traumatised for life, so I ought to just shut up.

I tried to shut up.

But there I was on the cover of *People*: 'Eitan Enoch – The Escape Artist'. *Maariv* published a profile of me. You could see me in another newspaper answering a questionnaire about things like my favourite colour and my favourite song of the year (grey; 'Nine' by the Nomad

Saddlers). In *The City* I read that I had been '**Spotted**: the man who said "No, thanks!" to terror, **CrocAttack**, on his own in hip boho eatery **Bar BaraBush**, ordering a hamburger called "The Cannibal Is Hungry Tonight".'

Of all my new friends, the real and the fake, the temporary and the permanent, the two I liked the most were policemen. Inspector Avi 'Almaz' Yahalom headed the investigation into the attack on the Little No. 5; Zion Ferrer investigated the Café Europa attack. Almaz's team consisted of himself and a policewoman called Ricky. Zion's team consisted of Zion. It's not that they don't investigate terror attacks, but as soon as it becomes clear that the motive was political most of the work reverts to the General Security Services. The police work on the criminal aspects of the attack: stolen vehicles, thefts that might tie in, life or property insurance swindles, victim identifications, and occasionally they turn up things the GSS can use.

Almaz and Zion Ferrer contacted me as they did every eyewitness (the inspector who investigated Shaar Hagai contacted me too but I'm not going to waste precious seconds of our lives on him because he's a stupid arrogant fatso who thought it a good idea to put the GSS on to me) and I made an appointment to see Zion in Jerusalem on one of my Wednesdays. It was one of the first warm days after the winter, with the sun very clear and unsoftened by the haze you get in the Tel Aviv sky. Ferrer had sunglasses on a cord around his neck and two sweat-circles darkening the armpits of his pale blue policeman's shirt. He met me at the gate to the facility, as he called it, on the Bethlehem Road and led me to a trailer among the eucalyptus trees where he showed me the CCTV footage of the Café Europa, in which, it turned out, I was starring. I sat in the trailer smoking a cigarette and hating it, and watched a black-and-white silent film about me. There I was, on my own, drinking coffee, my eyes staring off at some random point in space, and then focused on something closer, something specific ('I think you're checking out the talent,' said Ferrer), picking my nose, wiping it with a paper napkin, looking at my watch. Then Shuli arrived and we exchanged a couple of words, changed places. Now I'm sitting with my back to the camera and Shuli is properly visible. Shuli, in the last seconds before everything changes, smiling, flirting, stroking her Ice Europa cup with her index finger. She leans forward and starts talking to me. I could remember it, almost word for word, I could read certain words formed by her lips. She'd had a thought, maybe the nicest thought she'd had in a while. And then she gave her half-sad smile and the air trembled, only this time I could see it trembling. Zion stopped the tape there, rewound, froze the frame and showed me the terrorist. His name was Mahmuzi. Freeze-framed, his image shivered slightly, as if in anticipation of the blast. I felt none of the hatred I expected to. On-screen, paused, I was juddering too: horizontal spikes of pixels shooting in and out of me, as if I were shaking apart, and suddenly that *was* me again and I was shaking, I was falling apart and pouring with sweat, a pulse thudding in my temples so loudly I seemed to have gone deaf. A wave of nausea broke over me and I vomited noisily. I tried to get up, to walk, but I was too weak. 'Get me out of here,' I tried to say. 'GET . . . OUT!' A hand tried to support me and I passed out. They found me a bed in Hadassah, but after an hour or so I got up and went to my therapy group, and not only did I start pulling myself together again at that meeting but I felt stronger than ever before. Crazily invulnerable.

Almaz, the investigator from Tel Aviv, invited me to a meeting in a café in Yehuda Maccabi Street. He wasn't wearing a policeman's uniform. He didn't show films. It was a pleasant conversation. He was of Egyptian origin, lived in Bublik Street in the north of Tel Aviv, married to an Irish woman he'd met on a flight. After the small talk we discussed the attack. I told him everything I knew, about Guetta and his life in Jerusalem. I told him that Shuli and Guetta's parents had no idea what he was doing in Tel Aviv that morning, and that Shuli and I had decided to find out about it. He said that being in a certain city without telling your parents or girlfriend was not a criminal offence. Maybe, I said, but it was still interesting, and I wanted to do it so that I would have an answer for Shuli when she woke up. He said, 'Sure, go for it.' I told him about the PalmPilot and he smiled and said he could arrest me for theft.

'Come on. I'll give what's left of it back to the family. I've got the best intentions.'

'That's what everyone says,' he said. 'But the law says you don't.'

The gamblers saw me on *Noah's Ark* too and they wanted a piece. The gamblers – or 'Itzik', to give my caller his name – lived in Netanya and operated an illegal casino on the second floor of a 'normal pub' (his description) in the city's industrial zone. I refused his invitation to come and drink 'whatever I fancied' on the house. Among other activities in the casino he was operating a numbers racket, betting on football matches and terrorist attacks.

I have to confess here that I had myself once placed a few shekels on an Attack Pool. Bar had organised one at work – where the next attack would be and how many would be killed. I said Jerusalem and four. It was three but I won the pot – thirty-five shekels. Then Bar told me he had friends in Holon who gambled professionally on attacks. I gave him a hundred-shekel note to place on Jerusalem. Two weeks later I got two hundred back. So when Itzik called me, it wasn't the idea of gambling on attacks which surprised me so much as his proposition to me.

'I want to employ you as an expert,' he explained. 'Tell me where the next attack's gonna be and I can rig the odds according to what you say.'

'What?' I was in the street. I had to stop and sit on a bench. 'Why am I an expert?'

'You think I didn't see *Noah's Ark*? I'll give you a thousand dollars a month. Retainer. Whatever happens, attacks yes or no, whatever, you get a thousand a month. Just tell me where the next attack's going to be.'

'Tell me, Itzik, do you . . .'

'OK, listen. Don't tell me where the attack's going to be, just tell me where *you're* going to be.'

'Itzik . . . I'm sorry. I can't. I never leave Tel Aviv anyway.'

'Two thousand dollars. Two grand a month for scratching your balls. How bad can that be?'

'It's not bad at all.' It really wasn't. 'But I just happened to be in several attacks in a single week. It was just a coincidence. Doesn't mean a thing. A few weeks have passed since then and nothing's happened anywhere I've been to.'

'There haven't *been* any attacks since then,' said Itzik.

Invitations to movie premieres, a psychologist wanting to try out a radical new therapy, Shlomo Yarkoni's widow, the army looking for an inspirational/motivational speech, flower shops wanting me to advertise them, Shlomo Yarkoni's girlfriend, an offer to be a judge in a children's talent show . . .

And Humi's parents came to visit. His mother had a tale of terrible woe to tell me. Humi's brother had been killed at the age of ten by one of those exploding soft-drinks bottles they ended up having to recall. *Tempo*, the drink was called. The PLO should have used it. They were now divorced. Five months ago Humi's grandfather on his father's side had died of prostate cancer. Four months ago his grandmother on his mother's side succumbed to Alzheimer's. And now Humi.

She said: 'You think it's a normal day and it just isn't. It turns your life upside down. There are so many things I have to talk to him about. You, your life is nice and safe and warm and pleasant and you've got your family and friends. There are no tragedies in your life.' I mumbled something about getting on with life and she didn't like it. She said, 'You're wrong. You're so wrong. You can't get on with life. Not after losing a child. The grieving never ends.'

'Etti, stop it, stop it, please. It's not his fault.'

'I didn't say it was his fault, but how can he sit there and tell me about getting on with life?' Etti replied, tears falling now. The ex-husband rolled his eyes at me. There was a radioactive tension between the two of them. Maybe they needed it. Because when she lowered her head, a look of complete despair overtook his face too.

# 28

Al-Amari was becoming unbearable. The curfew was lifted and then reimposed, and every night the Israelis staged raids, shouldering their way into houses, breaking furniture and confiscating property, yelling and hitting people. They would lead all the men outside and hold them in plastic cuffs and cloth blindfolds for several hours before detaining a random few. They were pushing money at anyone who might talk, and in Ramallah there were plenty of dogs who would. Twice they battered at our door in the middle of the night and marched me down to the mosque, where I was made to kneel for hours, blindfolded and in pain. Not wanting to risk getting picked up, Bilahl slept on the roof, which was a much greater risk in itself. Under these circumstances the mother of all operations wasn't getting anywhere. The money from Gaza was trickling away and I tried to help Jalahl out with little electrical jobs, but he didn't have enough work for himself. I sat at home and watched TV, but there's a limit to the number of times you can watch *The Weakest Link*.

One day, many weeks after the last attack, water ceased to flow from the taps. The hot days had come as hot days always do; too soon. Within an hour there were no bottles in the grocery stores. I was thirsty, and being thirsty made me think about Mother, and thinking about Mother made me think of Lulu. I missed her intensely. I hadn't seen her for months. I called home and she answered. She was all right; Father was all right but sad. Everything was the same as ever. But her voice was different, I thought, more serious, the voice of a thirteen-year-old girl putting her childhood behind her. It made me frantic to see her.

'Lulu, I'm coming to visit you.'

'Really? Really really? When?'

'Right now,' I said.

When I was a kid, Grandfather Fahmi would ride from Al-Amari to visit us in Murair. It would take him an hour. Today, in a car, it takes three hours if you're lucky. Twenty kilometres as the crow flies. Where else in the world does it take longer to get from place to place as the years go by?

I chucked a few clothes into a holdall and left. The camp glowed yellow in the bright morning light. Every building was still wallpapered with posters and graffiti about Mahmuzi and Halil; huge chunks of concrete lay scattered about the streets. At an army post on the way out of the camp a soldier in sunglasses waved me over. He checked my green ID card, opened the bag, took everything out, turned it inside out and then shook it. He frisked me roughly. 'Where you going?' he asked in Hebrew. 'Murair.' 'Where is it?'

I pointed in roughly the right direction. 'Don't point, say where it is.' I didn't know what to say. 'It's over there, beyond Ramallah.' I had to explain why I was travelling. He demanded I show him a *Tasrich* – a permit to move freely around the West Bank – and I showed him the permit Jalahl had managed to get hold of from the electricity company in Ramallah. Then I got detailed instructions, what I could do and what I couldn't. I nodded. I turned left towards Ramallah and walked along the main road that cuts through the city north to Nablus, until the checkpoint was out of sight. Then I stopped and waited until I managed to get a lift. Five minutes later we were at the Beitin checkpoint.

'It'll be an hour at least,' said the driver. I got out of the car and strolled towards the pedestrian gate. A soldier blocked my way.

'What do you think you're doing? Get back in your car.'

'I don't have a car.'

'You lying to me? Aren't you ashamed? I just saw you get out of that car there.' I could tell he enjoyed peering down at me through his sunglasses. 'You think I'm an idiot?'

'It's not my car, I was hitching a lift.'

'Do you think I'm an idiot?'

'No, no,' I said. He frisked me and went through my bag and let me past to the queue for the pedestrian gate. A friend of my aunt's was there, carrying two chickens in a basket. I talked to her as we stood in line, and to an elegantly dressed bearded guy who turned out to be a good friend of Bilahl's from the Al-Birah mosque. After we'd waited for almost an hour, the pedestrian gate was closed down. 'That's the instruction from command headquarters,' a soldier told us, and you could see from his face that he hadn't a clue why they'd closed it either. Only cars with special permits were being allowed through.

I went back to the queue of the cars and saw that the guy who'd given me a lift had given up and turned back. So I tried offering drivers money to let me go with them. One was apprehensive, a second looked suspiciously at my holdall, a third asked me what we would tell the soldiers. I showed him my permit: 'We'll say we work together.' His name was Muhamed Mahmoud Zakat, on his way to Nablus to buy supplies for his stationery shop.

I sat on a rock beside Zakat's rusty sky-blue Subaru and called Bilahl, who wasn't happy. He wanted to work. But it had been weeks, and it was clear we weren't going to be doing anything for a while. 'Come on. How long is it since *you* saw Lulu?' 'How long are you going to be?' he asked, as if I were headed to the other side of Earth. At this rate I was going to be six months. 'A day or two, maybe longer. Oh, man, these soldiers. They're driving me crazy already, and we're not even past Beitin.'

I keyed in Rana's number but didn't dial it. I wasn't sure I had the right to call her. In front of us were cars, chickens, people milling around or sitting on luggage. Behind us the same. You could hardly say the queue was moving at all. Zakat was chain-smoking behind the wheel. He offered me one, which I refused.

'They won't let you through,' he said.

'Why not?'

'Well, when was the last time they did something you wanted them to?'

'Good question,' I said, and pressed Dial. She didn't pick up.

*'Oh, you bad boy, Fahmi . . . what's going on with you down there? Who are you thinking about? Here now . . .'*

Svet? I'm so hot . . .

If I'm dreaming, this dream is never-ending.

An ant zigzagged between my feet towards the checkpoint: but would they let it through without interrogating it? When it overtakes the Subaru, I decided, I'll call again. The ant was the fastest thing on the road, and it was soon forging ahead of the Subaru.

Rana answered: 'You weren't supposed to call.'

I wanted to tell her how much I'd missed her, her voice. 'I'm coming to Murair.'

She swallowed and said nothing for a while. 'When?'

'I'm at the Beitin checkpoint.'

'Oh. So you might not make it at all.'

'Did I say I was going to make it?' I got a reluctant laugh from her.

After growing up together, after spending seemingly every minute in each other's company, after all the times we used to sleep together in our secret hide below the village, after all the times we planned our wedding, I left the village without saying a single word. Bilahl said she wasn't a good Muslim, was too advanced. Rana said he'd never had sex and was scared of women. Young as she was, she looked down on him, which was difficult for me. He was my older brother and deserved her respect. But he also deserved her contempt.

I left, I missed her, I dreamed of her, I never called her and then she appeared. She didn't ask why I'd vanished or say how she had found me in the middle of a curfew. Was she there at all or was she an apparition in the night? She took her clothes off standing up while I lay on the sofa. We didn't stop or sleep all night until I dozed off some time after dawn, and when I woke she was gone and there was only the numb sweetness in my body to remind me. Ever since, I'd been imagining her mouth – like hot ice cream . . . Another ant was hurrying to join its sister in front of the Subaru. Muhamed put the car in gear and rolled about a metre and then turned the engine off.

'How long are you coming for?'

'I don't know. A couple of days, maybe more.'

'I'm happy.'

I thought about our place, below the village. Quietly I

had said, 'I love you.' When she finally replied, I could hear a twist in her mouth. 'Yes, but not as much as the jihad.'

*'Maybe I'm wrong, Dr Hartom, but I think he's been responding more over the last couple of days. For instance . . .'*

*'Oh . . . I see what you mean. Has this been happening a lot recently? Don't laugh, Svetlana, it's a natural bodily function.'*

Oh, why did you have to do that, Svet? With that old bitch Hartom . . .

*'Yes, Doctor. It's happened several times. His girlfriend was here a few days ago . . .'*

*'That's not always the reason, you know. Sometimes just . . . anyway, good. Pupils, please.'*

Aaaaiii!! The light in my eyes . . . the sun . . . the little green car . . . the Croc . . .

*'Good. But in terms of movement and cognition he's more or less in the same place, I understand.'*

*'More or less. Except for the . . .'*

*'Yes, Svetlana.'*

Muhamed gestured at me to get into the car. We had managed to reach the first checkpoint. The bag was peered through again, another body-search, X-ray machines, ID cards, permits . . . go to that caravan and wait for half an hour while we check something. Maybe the plan was to bore us to death. It used to take my grandfather an hour on horseback! I wanted to reach up to the soldier's arrogant face and crush it between my hands. Brother, there was no need for sophisticated operations with a fool like this – just take his fool's head between your hands and squeeze.

We made it through and Muhamed took the road east, through Beitin and Ein-Yabrud towards Nablus. I used to drive this road a lot, and it was in a worse state than ever.

There was a new barrier on the way – unmanned that day – three giant concrete cubes and barbed wire. 'Fucking Arabs suk asses HOORAY the settlers!' was written on one of the cubes in Hebrew. There was a constant traffic of jeeps on the road: one of them stopped us and checked the bag again and searched the car. They made me take off my trousers. Yet still, it was a beautiful road. I missed these hills. Grandfather Fahmi always talked about Beit-Machsir and the hills of Jerusalem but there's nowhere like Murair. This is where I grew up, in the dirt and the scrub, surrounded by the bone-dry hills.

Muhamed dropped me off where the road was nearest to Murair and I started walking along the narrow road, its asphalt cracked and crushed by heavy military vehicles. In the middle of the way there was a dirt mound. I climbed up and pissed on it. But this was the best part of the journey – the seven kilometres between the road and Murair, the easternmost village on the ridge that overlooks the Jordan and, on clear days, the distant mountains of Edom and Amman. No cars moved in either direction. I was alone with the hills and the eastern landscape, which revealed itself slowly, bit by bit, the higher I rose and the more I strained my legs; the valley to my left, the valley ahead, the yellow glare of the desert, without even one Jewish settlement to ruin the landscape and the mood. At last I saw the small old ochre houses of Murair on the hill, the tall column of the mosque, the small blue tractors of the farmers. It had taken four hours. It seemed to me satisfying, exciting, to arrive like this, after a fatiguing journey. And then I answered myself in Bilahl's voice: Don't be so craven. So pathetically positive. A humiliating four-hour trip instead of half an hour, and you think it's satisfying? You still think the glass is half full? 'One of these days,' my brother once said, 'you're actually going to tell me that the occupation was necessary and did us good.'

I was parched when I arrived, and there, in Murair of all places, I finally satisfied my thirst, drinking water and tea with my father and Aunt Lily. And there was my dear little sister Lulu, with her smile and the stories she'd saved up to tell her older brother – but only when we were alone, near the big cave at the edge of the village, on the ledge of the cliff that fell to the valley below. By the time Lulu and I returned from our walk, Bilahl had already been arrested.

# 29

Time's Arrow – *Every Second Counts*. But when I returned to work it just somehow didn't any more. Jimmy called me into his office for a welcome-back pep-talk. 'How you doing, CrocAttack?' 'OK.' 'You look tired.' 'Yes, a little . . . it's OK.' A silence. 'So! Back with us again!' 'Yes.' 'Good. Get back into things at your own pace, but not a too-slow pace, if you know what I mean.' 'Yeah. How was the Brussels trip?' 'It didn't work out in the end. They put us back to next week when we were already in the departure lounge. Time-wasters. But you'll be joining us, right?'

'Sure I will,' I said, disappointed. There didn't seem to be much more to say, so I got up to go.

'Oh, and, uh, by the way, Croc . . .' I looked back at Jimmy, who was blinking and running his hand over his lustrous head. 'You will be happy to know that I contributed my part in removing the . . . problem that . . . uh . . .' He blinked again. As I said, Jimmy had started out in the Time Management Unit of the air force. He'd helped coordinate the bombing of the nuclear plant in Iraq and various air force raids on Lebanon, and he was still occasionally called up for one-day reserve duty. Then the day after, you'd read in the paper that the air force had carried out a targeted assassination. I think he was trying to tell me that he was on duty when they assassinated that guy in Ramallah, the commander of the terrorist group. But Hamas said that the Café Europa bombing had been carried out in revenge for the assassination. So thanks, Jimmy, for your contribution.

Work was no different from the rest of the country in that I was the object of plenty of attention. There were 463 emails in my inbox to deal with or delete, long chats in the corridors, longer phone calls, endless retellings of my synopsis of what had happened. I told Jimmy I was willing to go to Brussels only if I could be back home by Wednesday. We went to Belgium, then to France, with the desperate Yoash, but the nights in Europe were no better than those in Israel. I did my best to work. I wrote a presentation about an accelerating world, about pre-worn jeans and superfast toasters and about fast talk, blah blah blah. (People generally talk at 150 words per minute but the human ear can decipher 600 wpm. All Time's Arrow's answering messages run at around 450 wpm, which people like – they hate slow and option-infested messages.) I used to make a presentation in an hour; two tops. Now it took me a day and a half – including seven cigarette breaks, three cold-water face-washes, an hour's rest with closed eyes on the sofa in the fun room and quite a lot of directionless wandering between rooms. Bar sent me some new numerologies: Croc = attack yesterday. Croc = sole explosion in mall. And the one he shouldn't have sent me: Croc = huge attack coming.

One day Jimmy phoned me from the meeting room. 'Come over here a moment, Croc,' he boomed, his voice simultaneously audible in receiver and corridor, 'I want you to meet Roy.' When I entered, Jimmy gestured towards a guy wearing a skirt: 'Roy Abramov, a young talented designer, the new star from Bezalel College of Design. He did the poster for Israel's Jubilee, if you remember.' I didn't. 'Roy, this is Croc, from Sales. Croc . . . Attack!' He shot the word 'attack' out explosively, as he'd already done a couple of times since I'd come back. No one had ever been scared, or laughed. To be fair to Jimmy, you had to say he was persistent. Also present were a couple of guys from Marketing, Noga and Jeremiah (or 'The Prophet Jeremiah' to me).

'So we've been thinking about a new company logo. Roy, show the Croc the options.' The stare I gave Jimmy slipped over his oiled head like water: I hated these balls-aching marketing discussions. There was this one time when the telecoms giant Bezeq had asked us to come up with a number for their new directory enquiries service. The number was supposed to somehow get across the message that the new service would be quicker and cheaper than the old 144. 'Let's do 77 – half the time, half the money,' said Jimmy. 'Brilliant,' said the product manager from Bezeq, and everyone agreed. But then someone pointed out that 77 was *not* half of 144. 'Half of 144 is 73.5.' Foreheads were wrinkled, biros were chewed, low whistles were whistled. A problem. 735 now became the leading contender, but it somehow just didn't sound right. Jimmy called Talia Tenne to canvass opinion. Talia said, 'Tell me, are you all out of your minds? Half of 144 is 72!' Eventually they decided on 122. The service still isn't operational.

The designer had a number of mock-ups of our new logo. 'The arrow is movement, movement of time, the arrow of time,' he said, glancing at Jimmy, who nodded with satisfaction. 'The circle,' which he made with his hands, 'is like harnessing the arrow, it is the company, the organisation, the order behind things. We have a conflict here, going forward . . .' '*Running* forward!' thundered Jimmy. 'OK . . . running forward, together with order, discipline, responsibility. The circle is also identified with a clock, of course . . . That's the basic principle. You can play variations on the arrows, the colours, the shapes and the directions.'

For this they pay thousands of dollars. For some star from Bezalel to waft in in a skirt and state the blindingly obvious. 'I want the logo to be a globally identifiable design meme,' said Jimmy, 'like the Nike Swoosh, like Intel, Microsoft, Apple.'

'Why?' I asked. 'Every human being on Earth is a sales target for them. We're not like that.'

'We're the twenty-first-century Fed-Ex,' Jimmy intoned.

'The arrow turns left,' said The Prophet Jeremiah. 'We might have a problem with the political connotations.'

'Well, it can always turn right,' said the designer, demonstrating. Noga pounced on a design with an arrow pointing upwards, but it was green on a red background.

'No. Too like the Delek logo . . .'

'If anything, the Palestinian flag.'

'So, blue and white?'

'Don't want to be identified with Israel too much.'

'Red and blue?'

'Not too American?'

'Red and white?'

'God, no, Hapoel Tel Aviv.'

'Red is hot,' said Roy. 'And green is young. Maybe stay with it after all?' His eyebrows went up and stayed up throughout the ensuing silence.

'Maybe we'll call Talia Tenne,' Jimmy said.

But Time's Arrow had bigger problems. The situation was to blame, and the business plan, and the management method, and the unplanned investments, and the Indians in the call centres. When problems start, it's easy to find reasons. We weren't selling the product to enough customers, and those who were buying weren't paying enough. When the representative of the Venture Capital Fund told us in a meeting that the Fund believed in the company, and would back it whatever happened, we knew for sure that the shit had hit the fan and the investors were losing patience.

The first round of dismissals came about two months after I returned. Jimmy called me into his office and stared at the sea through the window. 'You're staying, Croc, but I'll be frank. Since the attacks, your productivity has gone down the drain, your motivation is on the rocks. Every second doesn't count for you any more: you arrive later and leave earlier, and what you do in between . . . it's not the Croc I used to know three, four months ago, or even two years ago. But . . .' He turned from the window and sat down. 'I understand. You've been through a very difficult experience. Plus there's this fame stuff. Time's Arrow can't afford newspaper headlines saying that the CrocAttack was fired. But I'm asking you: pull yourself together, because nothing is safe any more.' You don't say, I thought. 'For a start,' he said, flapping a bitter hand at the view of the glittering Mediterranean, the beaches, the city, the three helicopters heading low above the shoreline, south towards Gaza, 'say goodbye to all of this, because we're moving to Rosh Haayin.'

'What?'

'Don't tell anyone yet.'

Ron and Ronen were stunned. Three minutes later Talia Tenne burst through the cloudy glass door and asked with shining eyes whether the rumour was true. 'We don't know anything about rumours,' said Ronen. She looked at him furiously, sat on an empty chair between the three of us, and stared us out using her pretty eyes until we cracked. 'I'll kill you if it leaves this room,' I said. 'Obviously.' She smiled her sweetest smile. Ten minutes later Bar sent the numerologies: 'Rosh Haayin = bad for Time's Arrow' or 'Rosh Haayin = international future for Time's Arrow', whatever we chose.

Jimmy was right. I wasn't doing my job very well. I couldn't care about another sales presentation, another meeting summary, another two-day trip to Europe with non-stop work on the plane: flying, landing, taxi, identical hotel room, identical meeting room, identical dinner, identical porn, identical breakfast. Since the euro had come in I couldn't tell the difference between the countries: everybody spoke English with the same accent. After sleepless nights, it was a real effort to clear the fog and think logically. My work hours were still long but I worked much less. I frittered away time in the smoking corner, I fell asleep on the sofa, I found myself on Ynet, porn sites, gunning down Danish drug dealers on gaming sites, I spent a third of my day making coffee on the espresso machine or compulsively scoffing pretzels and biscuits while chatting to whoever was in the kitchen. I wasn't really interested in the Austrian telecoms company that wanted to improve its directory enquiries service, or in saving half a second per call in Spain or in real-time solutions, server efficiency, long, wide and flat databases, probability-based algorithms, voice recognition upgrades, interfacing, sockets, schmockets, websphere voice response, killer apps, blah blah blah blah *blahhhh*. Time's Arrow continued to streak into the future, but I wasn't on it any more.

We moved to a modern building in the business park in Rosh Haayin, an ugly little town twenty kilometres east of Tel Aviv. Duchi and I bought a clapped-out Peugeot 206 for twenty thousand shekels – Duchi continued driving the Time's Arrow Polo and I drove the Peugeot though she was only driving to Ramat Gan and I had to get to Rosh Haayin. She was a lawyer halfway through a lucrative trial and I was just a failing salesman in a start-up company. I drove every morning ('against the traffic, against the traffic!' crowed Jimmy with such delight that he almost sold us on the virtues of not working in the centre of Tel Aviv) to our offices on the second floor of a three-storey building populated by start-up companies in various degrees of trouble.

Lunch consisted of hummus, stuffed vegetables or pasta served 'à la mode Rosh Haayin', which, Talia Tenne assured us, would one day soon be nationally renowned. Instead of espresso bars and sushi, street food, beans and rice and stews from Shabazi and Shimson Absolino's; instead of the Mediterranean, the arid hills of Samaria. The guards at the entrance to the Dizengoff Centre were replaced by a razor-wire fence and the quasi-military park security; the sounds of the city with the calls of the muezzin, or, in the evenings, shooting from the direction of the territories. A single melancholy table-football table replaced the fun room and our designer kitchen became a nook with a microwave, a fridge and a kettle. Economy waffles stood in for organic brownies from the bakery. Cheap veneered MDF replaced clouded-glass doors and silvery steel tables. Colour disappeared from the walls and from people's faces. Ronen and others left. Eight workers were dismissed, including Shoko from IT Support and Noga from Marketing.

The last time I'd thought about Giora had been beside Shuli's bed, when his father had asked again what he'd been doing in Tel Aviv on the morning of his death.

The PalmPilot, which I'd been going to start solving this mystery with, had perished in Café Europa. If the Palm doesn't exist, I thought, neither does Giora: there was nothing to be done. But when I tried to connect my computer to the network in Rosh Haayin there was a problem with Outlook. I reinstalled the program, and when I did that, it asked which user I would like to choose. Two options: Croc or Guetta.

And then it hit me – the day after the first attack, before heading out to Jerusalem, I'd synchronised Giora's Palm to my computer. The aluminium and silicon bowels of my computer contained all the details of his life.

Croc or Guetta?

I sat in front of the screen with my mouse in my hand, and thought about the options. Choose my name and continue with my life or choose Guetta, the stranger with honey-coloured hair and mirrored shades who, by exchanging a couple of words with me, had sent me to Jerusalem, to Shaar Hagai and Café Europa, to a funeral, to the bedside of a girl I was half in love with. Deep inside, I felt that somehow this was a sign that Shuli would wake from her coma. Didn't this little coincidence *compel* me to try to find the answer for her as a present on her return to life? That was why – along with nosiness, voyeurism, a sense of adventure, and other reasons which all helped to obscure the fact that perhaps it really didn't matter any more – I chose Guetta. Click. There he was.

# 30

Omar Sharif came from the village of Beita al-Fauka near Nablus. Nineteen years old, with long-lashed eyes and a floppy fringe as dark and lustrous as Tom Cruise's. He volunteered, and Bilahl was impressed. The one time he came to our place, during the curfew, I remember him gazing through the bars on the window and showing us a dog in the street. 'Look,' he said – an Israeli soldier was trying his best to stroke it.

Bilahl recruited a handful of others along with him. He went to Qibya and Rantis, the two villages closest to Ben Gurion airport, and met people who wanted to help. He went to Gaza again. When he returned he was already beginning to think in terms of a combined attack: one unit would proceed on foot from either Qibya or Rantis and attack the hangars and planes on the ground with Qassam missiles; a second unit would drive a booby-trapped car through the new terminal, which was under construction and (according to recently updated aerial photographs Bilahl had come across) not very well guarded; a third unit would consist of two *Istishadin* travelling on two separate buses – one from Jerusalem, the other from the Raanana Junction. The logistics were overwhelming, the number of people involved unprecedented, the risk very high. It's easy now to point out Bilahl's mistake, but it was understandable. For an operation of that scope you had to build hierarchies of command and responsibility, and so, when Omar Sharif made such a good impression and said he would recruit other people, Bilahl gave him his phone number.

*'. . . one of them in prison for the next four hundred years! And the other lying there like a cucumber!'*

*'Stop it, Father. We didn't come here to weep.'*

Why didn't you come on your own, Lulu? You should have left him at home with his tears . . .

*'Please try not to shout like that near him, sir. Try to say only positive things.'*

*'What did the nurse say to me, Lulu?'*

*'She said to say positive things.'*

*'How can I say positive things when my child is a murderer? He's going to kill me – he'll give me a heart attack! Two sons I had, and he was the good one. He promised to go to the—'*

*'He will go, Father, you'll see. Now, let's have some music.'*

Yes, Lulu. *'Amarein'*. The two moons . . .

On Channel 2 Danny Ronen referred to a warning the GSS had received concerning a major operation aimed at the heart of Israel. Every time he mentioned it, Bilahl became more convinced that we had a leak. We tried suspending all communications; we tried disinformation . . . but the reason Omar Sharif was picked up had nothing to do with the 'warning'. A routine patrol rounded up all the men from his village (in plastic handcuffs and cloth blindfolds) and he was one of the ones detained. No particular reason. Maybe the soldiers liked his long lashes, or maybe it was recorded somewhere that he'd been in Al-Amari. They have ways to retrieve information like that. They also have ways to locate a mobile phone. They found Bilahl's number in Omar Sharif's mobile, called it, located the mast the signal had been sent to and dispatched dozens of soldiers in jeeps, armoured personnel carriers and on foot to scour the area in circular sweeps, turning every stone, entering each home. After an hour, the soldiers disappeared as if nothing had happened, everyone returned home, and things went back to normal, except for Bilahl Naji al-Sabich, apprehended on a mattress on the roof of his apartment.

*'What have I done to deserve this? How did I bring such a monster up?'*

*'Father, stop! You promised. It's not helping anybody, standing here and crying. Let him listen to the music. I know he likes it. I can tell.'*

Yes I do, Lulu. Yes I do . . .

Murair had hardly changed since I was a child. There were no new buildings because there was no money. The village was getting drier, there was no work locally and any outside jobs were too far away for people to commute daily, at least in the current conditions. The few who worked in agriculture became fewer because of the lack of water and restrictions on movement. Anyone who could moved to the big cities, as I had. The others were waiting. So the frozen village was like a museum of my childhood, like travelling to the past. Lulu was like a mirror into the past too. When she talked to me I saw that her new experiences – her discoveries of hidden corners at the edge of the village, her need to be alone with her thoughts and the hills – were simply my old ones . . . After we'd drunk tea with Father and Aunt Lily, Lulu and I went for a walk in the village. I said hello to familiar faces and noticed how they'd aged. We visited Mother's grave in the rocky, sandy cemetery where Sabres cacti grew and that plant with the meaty triangular leaves which I always loved to make crescent-shaped cuts in with my fingernails.

After weeks of planning operations or sprawling in front of TV, it was pleasant to hear about the real world. There isn't really a normal life in Palestine, but there are places where private life is a little less distorted by history, where friends, family, work, school predominate. Lulu talked to me about her friends from the neighbouring villages, about walks to caves near by, about a guy from Duma who rode around on a horse and took her for rides along the ridges. 'How old is this kid?' 'Sixteen.' I tried to look at her through the eyes of a sixteen-year-old boy, but managed to see only my little sister with her straight brown hair and little girl's smile.

'Lulu, I don't know if you should ride around on a horse with a sixteen-year-old guy.'

She laughed. 'Nothing happens. My friends ride with him too.'

It sounded slightly weird coming from her. I said, 'What do you mean, "nothing happens"? How do you know something *could* happen at all?'

'You think I'm still ten? All my friends have already been kissed.'

'What? Lulu, stop meeting the cheeky bastard. What's his name? I'm going to talk to him.'

'Relax. It wasn't with him.'

'It? What's "it"?'

She led us on an expedition to the place she went to to be alone. 'You should feel special,' she said. 'I don't bring anyone down here.' I told her I always felt special with her. It was true. If I ever turned into a teacher, or the imam, or her horse, she was always on the same wavelength. She was talking about her friends; I said, 'But why didn't you do your homework today, Miss Sabich?'

'I did in all my other classes, master teacher. Fahmi?'

'Goddammit, soldier! What did you call me?'

'I mean Lieutenant, sir!'

'Goddam right, soldier!'

'Sir, yes, sir!' It was idiotic, but it made us laugh.

'I was visiting Mother's grave once,' she said, 'and I sneezed on it, and I just couldn't stop laughing.' She started again with her contagious laughter, like a water sprinkler, like a machine gun. She couldn't breathe. I laughed too, like a horse; huge, liberating laughter which set her off again – we couldn't stop. We laughed, in fits and starts, not knowing why, all the way to her secret place.

'Now I know that you're my sister,' I said.

'Why?'

'Because this is my place.'

'Yours? It's mine!'

'Are you sure it wasn't me who showed it to you?' She was sure. It was mine and Rana's place: a little plateau behind the Sneina family's house, halfway down the slope descending from the edge of the village. There's kind of a small clearing, and smooth rocks you can sit on or lie on in complete solitude. If you're not a member of the Sneina family, it takes almost ten minutes to get there from the road, which makes it even more private. I hadn't been there for years. I might even have found a pack of my old condoms if I'd looked for it, but I wasn't going to with Lulu around. We sat next to each other, brother and sister, and we didn't say a word for a long time. Rana was in my head and in my ears, our conversation that morning, our latest meeting. 'What are you thinking about?' my sister asked. 'Nothing.' She gave me an inquisitive look. 'This place reminds me . . . Do you know how long it is since I was here?' 'Was it really your spot?' 'Really.' She smiled. 'I'm glad. It's a good place, right?' 'The best,' I replied. 'I wish I had a place like this to run away to where I live now.'

When we returned Father was in a state. Someone had called and hung up, and then called again and said nothing. My mobile had rung too, he said, several times. I ran to the holdall and fished it out. I had voice messages. Two of them said nothing. The third was a short message: 'Bilahl has been arrested. They're calling all the numbers on his phone. Turn off your phone and get rid of it. Call in a few days if you can. Be careful.'

I turned off the phone. Lulu saw the fear in my eyes. I steered her out on to the terrace, trying to appear calm in front of her and Father.

'Take the phone,' I said. 'Hide it in our hiding place, and don't turn it on. You mustn't turn it on, OK?' She nodded.

'What's happened?'

I looked at her, my little sister. How much I loved the little girl in front of me! 'Nothing,' I said, ignoring her sceptical look: I had to leave immediately. How long had I been here? Two hours? Three? The soldiers might already be on their way. If they had Bilahl's phone, it would only be logical to send troops to Murair. I didn't know anything – not how or where Bilahl had been caught nor what he'd told them, nor whether they realised who he was, what he'd done, what he was planning, who was connected to him – and when you don't know you have to assume the worst. Bilahl had been arrested and I was in real danger. I had to disappear. I didn't have a clue where to go.

Lulu was standing watching me as I was thinking all this. I took her face in my hands and said, 'I have to go. I'm sorry, I was planning on staying a few days. But I have to go now.' 'Because nothing has happened?' 'That's right.' 'Can I come with you?' I actually laughed. 'What do you think?' She shrugged, disappointed. 'Soon I'll come for longer, I promise,' I said and kissed both her cheeks. 'You be a good girl, OK? And watch out for that guy from Duma with the horse.'

*Lucky*, I was thinking as I left, with the holdall slung over my shoulder, no phone, no way of contacting the world, not knowing where I was heading or where I would sleep, *you're so very, very lucky*. Why had I made the decision, on the spur of the moment, on this day of all days, to call Lulu? Someone up above had taken me out of Al-Amari today. Grandfather Fahmi was protecting me, I was sure of it. And he would keep watching over me. And then I told myself in Bilahl's voice, for the second time that day: stop looking at the full half of the glass, little brother. Pull yourself together. Be careful.

# 31

Shuli died on a Wednesday, thirteen weeks after the attack. I'd come to Jerusalem for my thirteenth and last group therapy meeting. The doctors were unsurprised. The machines, they said, could maintain a certain amount of body function, but they couldn't make the brain live. 'What about the ones who stay in comas for years?' I asked. I was in shock. I seemed to be sitting on the floor. 'The ones who wake up after seventeen years and ask for a Pepsi?' 'That's a different story,' they said, and didn't elaborate.

The night before I hadn't been able to sleep and the morning had passed slowly and foggily. When I stepped on to the Little No. 5 I felt a hideous breaking wave of nausea and stumbled off and threw up on the pavement. For a long time I sat on a bench and sipped water with a head full of noise and then I took a taxi to Jerusalem. The air was heavy and not easy to breathe. The machine didn't have Twixes. On the top floor, Shuli's bed was not in its place. I asked the nurse what had happened, but I already knew that she was going to say what I'd been imagining for months. The nurse said, 'Shuli? I'm sorry. She passed away.' I went down on my knees and cried without stopping, until doctors came, and then I felt hands on my shoulders. They were the hands of Alon, the chef from the King David Hotel. He walked me to a bench outside the hospital and we sat there for a long time, silent, smelling the pine trees, looking at the Jerusalem hills. I didn't say a word in group therapy either, and no one tried to make me. The next Wednesday I didn't bother to come at all. I only came back to Jerusalem for the funeral. The Mountain of Rest cemetery, where we'd first met on a stormy day three months earlier. I felt as alone as I'd ever felt in my life. It was a bright spring day, and between her grave and Guetta's there were two rows of fresh graves, marking the weeks that had passed, the unostentatious, steady labour of death. I didn't make it more than halfway through the ceremony before running out of the cemetery, carrying in my ribcage a leaden mass of grief which would make breathing an effort for weeks afterwards.

In the mirror: a man aged thirty-three and a third, beginning to recede. Some grey hairs. A small paunch, scarcely there, really, actually not a paunch but a temporary bulging of the stomach. Hairs in the ears and nose. Red eyes with heavy lids.

'What are you looking at?' Duchi's voice from behind me. I shifted my eyeline to an angle where I could see her in the mirror. She was standing in the doorway in a white robe, her wet hair darkened almost to black. Her eyes were smirking. 'At this handsome man?' She came and hugged me from behind. 'Not so handsome,' I said. 'You're still cute,' she said, and nuzzled her soft cheek against my back. 'You think so?' I frowned my eyebrows down and gave myself a glance in three-quarter profile. It looked a bit better that way. 'Obviously unbearable sometimes,' she said, 'but I still remember the cute Croc, and I know he'll be back.'

Duchi tried so hard to be good to me. She was patient

and solicitous and accepted the sleepless nights and the jumpiness and lack of concentration they left in their wake. We hardly argued. It was so strange, so unsettling, that I had this weird feeling something was missing. I asked her whether she'd taken anything out of the flat, changed the furniture around or something. But it was the arguments. In bed one night, when I asked her why it hadn't been like this before, why she was suddenly so nice, she gave me her profound look and let out a brief bark of hollow laughter.

'Dimwit. You really think I've changed?'

'You haven't?'

'Of course not. It's you.'

'Me?'

'You've stopped arguing about every petty thing, and looking for reasons to fight because you're under pressure all the time . . .'

'OK, OK, I get it.'

'Like, now there are other things.' She didn't conceal the expression on her face. 'You're . . . difficult. You can be cruel and self-centred and you don't sleep, and I still don't see how the cigarettes can be helping.' I looked at her. 'OK, not cruel,' she said. Some seconds elapsed. 'Maybe a little,' she said.

Since September 11th the word 'wedding' had resurfaced only once. Duchi's brother Voovi had mentioned it during a dinner at ours. It sort of fell out of his mouth like a fledgling falling out of a nest, just toppled off his tongue on to the floor, where it collapsed.

But I couldn't bring myself to abandon the Guetta investigation. I recruited Bar to help. I call it an investigation because I have no other word for it, but it was hardly that – Inspector Almaz had in fact classified it as 'a case not worth investigating'.

The first thing you notice when you meet Bar is his loose posture. He's a loose guy: thin, not so tall, always wearing a shabby baseball cap, a size too big, on his shaven head. He has small ears and these incredibly bright blue eyes. He wears a permanent five o'clock shadow to compensate for the premature baldness. The timing was good for him. Work bored him and even the numerology was starting to pall. He'd served in military intelligence, I don't know in exactly what capacity, but I trusted him. And besides (I discovered later) he's a big Hercule Poirot fan.

He transferred the contents of Guetta's Palm to his computer and started scanning it. After about an hour he sent me an email with these details:

- On the morning of his death Guetta had a meeting at eight: BMW. Coffee Bean, Yehuda Maccabi Street. A mobile phone number.
- In Guetta's address book under B, Binyamin Warshawski is listed next to the same mobile phone number listed for the meeting above. Almost certainly, the 'BMW' mentioned in the note about the meeting is Warshawski's name.
- That number is disconnected. The phone company says the number is not in use. Under pressure from this investigator, the customer service representative told me it was a withheld number, but admitted that it was cancelled by the customer. The date of cancellation was a few days after the meeting.
- The phone book lists three Binyamin Warshawskis. One on his own, two with a partner. One lives in Tel Mond, two in Tel Aviv.
- Giora Guetta's nickname was 'Gigu'.
- Two days after his death, Guetta was supposed to collect a new credit card from his bank in Jerusalem.

- In numerology, Giora Guetta from Jerusalem = a very dark and complicated affair = a meeting in Tel Aviv. I swear this is true: the sum is 845 for all three sentences.

The guy's a genius, I thought. All this after an hour's work. I made an investigation team appointment in ten minutes' time at the falafel stall downstairs.

'Not bad for an hour,' I said in admiration.

'Yeah, but it's easy. When you're scanning soft material, you find ninety per cent of the good stuff quickly. The problem is finding the remaining ten per cent.'

'Soft material?'

'Soft material's the stuff you don't expect to be searched or examined. Normal citizens, like you and me, accumulate stuff and lists and diaries without worrying about security. The opposite of coded or classified material you get in organisations.'

We bought falafels and fruit shakes from the next stand, and sat on wicker chairs on the pavement. Hamelacha Street in the Rosh Haayin Business Park is not one of Israel's most glamorous locations. 'OK,' I said, going over a print-out of Bar's email, 'Binyamin *is* the guy's name. Shuli called the number, and he answered and said he was Binyamin. She asked him about Guetta and he hung up.'

'You remember the date?' asked Bar.

I certainly did. 'A couple of days after Shaar Hagai.'

'That fits. Maybe he got scared of Shuli's call. But it's only a guess.'

'What about these B. Warshawskis?'

'Well, it would make sense if it was one of the Tel Avivis,' said Bar. 'But it could be the Tel Mond one. Or maybe our Binyamin's unlisted. Better do it carefully, if he cancelled his number. I'll finish scanning the PalmPilot first. There's a lot more in there.'

I took a bite from my falafel. Not too bad. Bar sounded as if he knew what he was doing. 'Carry on, then,' I said. 'Send me a message, when you've got something to send.'

The spring and early summer had already begun to hammer the coast of Israel with heat. Those little gauntlet-runs from the air-con in the car to the air-con in the office to the air-con at home got more and more debilitating as the days passed, especially since one of the air-conditioners was in a ten-year-old car. Cold showers extended in length. We were all attached to our water bottles like drips. Hummus was off the menu. And public interest in the Croc waned. The phone rang infrequently now: a charity night here, a tribute there, a local newspaper from Rosh Haayin which'd discovered the thrilling fact that I was now earning my corn in their beautiful municipality, a local newspaper from Jerusalem (the local newspapers are blind to their subjects' lack of civic affection) and, very occasionally, someone from the past, someone whose existence I'd forgotten, a voice that took me way back into the long ago.

It was shortly after Shuli's death, during those exhausted, surreal, stifling days when looking for Guetta was apparently the only thing holding me together. I was still waking up well before dawn. I'd leave the flat and wander through parks and streets to meet my comrades in insomnia, sit on a bench and exchange a few words with them. So I was half asleep and driving to Tel Aviv in the crappy Peugeot at the end of the working day, with the sea in front of me and the Ramat Hasharon Tennis Centre on my left, when the phone rang. 'Crocos?' said a voice, and the crappy Peugeot suddenly metamorphosed itself into a time machine, taking me back, east, up to the hills above Rosh Haayin and farther, up to the cliff above the valley, up to the village. I could taste something bilious in my mouth, felt a burning in my throat and eyes. Gadi. Lieutenant Gadi Gidon. In short, Gadgid. How many years since I'd heard this voice? 'Gadi.' 'Who else?' 'Years,' I said. The time machine landed in the watchtower at the entrance to the village, opened its doors and turfed me out.

Gadgid is leading a platoon of soldiers on a routine patrol inside the village. A wide road winds from the entrance of the village to the top of the hill. Along its sides a few houses cluster sparsely, but the heart of the village is higher up, at the end of the road. There the alleys are narrower, and the houses crowded together. I'm in the watchtower at the entrance to the village. I watch the file of soldiers getting smaller as they make their way up the road, then disappearing at the top of the hill. Gadgid is walking point – tall, confident, tight black curls on his head, an impressive nose. When all the soldiers have disappeared from sight, I look around at the arid winter landscape. I sit down with my back to the wall and drink from my water bottle. 1988: curfew; intifada; morning; silence.

We met at Bar BaraBush. 'Crocos! My God, you're a star!' Gadgid still held himself very straight and tall, but his formerly distinctive nose had disappeared somewhat into a fatter face, and the curls had gone. He had glasses. 'You've become an intellectual, Gadi?' I ordered my Cannibal and he got the beers in. I always liked Gadgid in the army because, like me, he didn't take it too seriously. We became friends in Balata, where we watched Israel v. Colombia on a tiny black-and-white TV hooked up to a generator. Valderrama's free kick through our joke of a wall, Yoram Arbel's now-classic commentary, 1–0 – and once again we weren't going to the World Cup. Gadgid made me laugh the whole game, and I swear on my life that he said, 'That's no way to build a wall' ten seconds before Arbel did.

'You know,' I said, 'when you called, the moment I heard your voice saying "Crocos", it was like I was there. Like I was touching the dirt, smelling the smell.'

'The tear-gas smell, huh?' He smiled. 'That son of a bitch would have got what he deserved even without your contribution.'

I sit down and drink, and fall asleep. And the next thing I know is . . . I don't know . . . shouts? My backside inexplicably getting warm? The whispering sound of flames? A stone landing next to me? A shot? I don't know. I remember watching the soldiers disappearing over the top of the hill. I sit, I drink, and then . . . I look down and see that the tower is on fire. And twenty-five feet below there are . . . I don't know how many, five, ten, a dozen of them. They see me and shout and start to throw stones. I whip my head back in. I can hear flames, shouts, the stones hitting. There's a terrible smell of burning plastic and wood. I glance down again – a stone flies past my head. And they start to climb. It is utterly terrifying. I scramble over to the radio and call Gadgid with no code words, no military terminology or radio lingo. I scream, 'Gadgid, come and save me!' and he replies, 'We see. On our way.' I curl up in the corner, my head buried in my hands. I'm starting to hyperventilate, and I don't want this, no, no, no, no, no, and there's a shot and another and the shots are coming thick and fast now and yelling and the sound of blows. And my head deep, deep, deep between my knees in the corner.

I was drinking vodka and passion fruit, trying to get a grip of the elusive seeds with my tongue and keeping an eye on the big tits of the girl on the other side of the bar. A ring of smoke sidled out of Gadgid's mouth.

'So tell me again. How did you manage to let them burn the tower like that?'

'I don't have a clue.'

Fifteen years later, I still don't have a clue and I never will have. But I do know this: the same day my close friend from Jerusalem, Danny Lam, was driving a jeep on a patrol in the central section of Lebanon's security zone. At 11 a.m., when I was sitting in the burning tower waiting for my end, his jeep arrived at a puddle that may possibly have been deeper than it looked, and stopped in front of it. I've relived this moment many times: me, on my own, in a burning watchtower in a West Bank village. Danny Lam and his friends, in a jeep in Lebanon, on the edge of a big puddle. And up above, God choosing which button to hit.

'God, Crocos, what a fuck-up! A whole regiment had to come in after us to restore order, no?'

'Yeah . . . I'd almost blanked it out, and suddenly you turn up from the past. Where did you come from?' I said.

It was late and he'd already drunk several pints. He told me his war stories and the history of his life since, his marriage, his success as a chemistry student at the Haifa Technion, his divorce, and his work at the Weizmann Institute in Rehovot alongside attractive twenty-something researchers from the former Soviet Union.

After we said goodbye I got into the car and started driving, but I didn't go home, I drove just to drive, to think. I drove slowly in no particular direction, down near the beach, around squares and roundabouts, slowly, directionless, drowned in memories. I drove like that for a long time, thought about what I'd done and not done and tried to put work and Duchi and home and all that on the other side of the balance. What could I have done? Who could have guessed that Gadgid would call all of a sudden?

# 32

I met Dayek after about an hour of fast walking. He stood in the middle of the path, looked at me with his big brown eyes, and batted his long grey eyelashes. His grey hair was soft to the touch, although he was so thin his ribcage was visible. We had a donkey when we were children, and it was thanks to him I'd come to know all the paths around Murair, which, give or take a few dirt ramps, haven't changed since the days of the prophets. I knew what it was like, riding on the back of a donkey, the pain that grows in your back, and in your spread legs, until you have to move both of them to one side for a while. I remembered the feeling of the boy discovering the big world outside of his village, with the assistance of his first mode of transport. There were a few bicycles around, and now there are more, but a donkey was a luxury when we were kids.

When I left the village, I could have turned in any direction – east, down the cliffs, to the Jordan Valley. North, to the villages on the ridge and farther on to Nablus. Back south, towards Ramallah. All of these options I knew well, but I had no idea which to choose. I turned north, on the assumption that if Bilahl had been caught in Ramallah, it was best to get as far away from there as possible. The donkey accepted my choice humbly. We called the donkey we had in my childhood Nasech, because he was fat. This one had thin legs, and his backbone was protruding and quite painful to my backside. So I called him Dayek, meaning narrow.

In the first village we went through, we stopped in the grocery store and I bought water, pita bread and cheese, and a kilo of carrots for Dayek, who devoured them hungrily. I don't know why I went for carrots – donkeys are happy with grass or hay, or can even make a meal of bushes and the bark of trees. But I decided to give him a treat. I ended up staying with Dayek a whole week, and I'm convinced that by the end of the week his weight had gone up by several kilos. At any rate, the bones on his back and ribs weren't sticking out so much. His fur had thickened and looked healthier. I was proud of myself – at least I had made one Palestinian donkey happy.

Dayek had a crooked tooth in the front of his mouth, which gave him character: when he exposed his teeth, the crooked one gave the impression that he was smiling. I smiled back at him and patted his nose, between the ears and eyes. We headed up to the hills. For hours we didn't see a living thing besides a few birds and a couple of wandering goats; we heard only the sound of the cicadas. We stopped near a cave with a flat area of dirt in front of it. It was starting to get dark and I decided to sleep there. I took out the food and water I had left. 'The hills of Palestine,' I told Dayek, 'are the most beautiful place on Earth. You should realise how lucky you are to be able to spend your life here.' I put another carrot in his mouth and he chewed it loudly.

Though the days were getting warmer, the nights in the hills were still very cold. Without a blanket I was facing a hard night. But I was also exhausted after a day of travelling, riding a donkey, the excitement of meeting my sister and anxiety about my brother's and my own destinies. I fell deeply asleep on the cave floor for several hours. The chill woke me long before dawn, even before I heard the muezzins calling from the mosques. Dayek was up and ready for another day on the paths. I descended to a village and, still with help of the dark, took a blanket and a long shirt from a clothes line in a backyard. 'Support the struggle,' I whispered in the direction of the house, 'I'm sure you'll understand.' By luck there was a small café there that served hummus and *ful* to the labourers on their way to work. I ate well and took pita bread and *labbaneh* with me for the rest of the day. In the grocery I stocked up on water and food for Dayek.

We went on like that during the day, through villages, between the hills, eating, talking. In the middle of the day I heard a muezzin calling for the second prayer, and felt he was talking to me: 'Come to pray, come to success, Allah is the greatest.' I went to the mosque and prayed, and at the end of the prayer, I added a personal prayer for Bilahl and Lulu. Although I wasn't a believer like Bilahl, I liked being in the mosque.

The second night I slept much longer and more comfortably under the blanket. I discovered an old coffee kettle, built a fire and made myself tea with sage and other plants that I collected from the hill around me. I started to feel like Izz ad-Din al-Qassam himself. True, I lit the fire with a lighter rather than sticks or flints, and true, we had the villages for our food, but the feeling of being alone in nature was very powerful. It took hold of me, and got stronger every day, and especially every night that I spent outside, on my own, with only a donkey for company, and a half-moon for light.

But worry about what had happened was gnawing away at me. The next morning I met a shepherd who didn't have a mobile phone himself but directed me to a grocery in the next village. There I called Halil's cousin, the driver. She was the only person I could think of. She was surprised to hear from me, asked whether I was OK, told me not to say anything. She was afraid. She asked whether she could call me back in an hour. I got the number from the guy in the store after I'd promised to pay him for receiving a call.

We ate. I didn't ask where I was. It wasn't important. A beard was beginning to sketch itself in and my hair was wild. While it was still dark that morning I'd supplied myself with a T-shirt and underwear from the clothes line of some sleeping villagers. On an old tractor I found a baseball cap, with a green plastic net and an adjustable plastic strap at the back. On the front there was white padding and a drawing of a cement mixer with 'Israbright Cement Factories Ltd' in Hebrew lettering around it. The shade was green and made from the same padded material. I fell in love with the hat immediately. God knew how much I needed it, how merciless the sun could be.

An hour later she told me what she knew. They'd caught Omar Sharif, she said, who had Bilahl's number. Bilahl was picked up that same day, she didn't know where or how. I told her where I was, more or less. I needed to hide well away from the expected places – Al-Amari, Murair, friends, family. She managed a quiet laugh. 'Like a cowboy,' she said. 'Let me try to arrange something. I'll call this number the same time tomorrow.'

Oh, your fingers, Svetlana . . . so deep in my back, in my muscles . . . mmm . . . Where was I? In the mountains . . .

What they managed to arrange for me was: a flat in Kafr Qasim. With the blue-card Palestinians, the Israeli citizens. There was a free room in a flat that belonged to one of the supporters of the movement in Gaza. He was renting the flat to a family from the village, just a normal family from Kafr Qasim, who didn't even know about the Gazan landlord. One room in the flat was rented separately, which saved money for the family. I could stay there for a while, until things cleared up, or the situation eased. 'How long?' 'For the time being you will be there.' 'What sort of family is it? I have to live with a family? An Israeli family? To eat with them?' 'I don't have the exact details, but you don't have many choices, if you don't want to keep wandering the hills of Nablus on your donkey.' I was silent. 'What will I tell them? Where am I supposed to have come from?' She laughed. 'You think you're the only one there? That they wouldn't recognise the look, the accent? There are plenty of people from the West Bank living in those places.' 'How will I get there?' She was a little impatient. 'Try to get there on your own. It's safer. Get there, and start getting organised. Slowly.' She gave me the address. 'What about work?' 'We'll see . . . I'll ask. But look for work by yourself. The room will be free, by the way. It's a pretty good deal, Fahmi.'

'I know.'

My real journey began there: a week on the road on donkey-back, without a map. Navigating according to hunches and from rough directions given by people, picked up from the roads I crossed, the villages I entered. My beard thickened. My body got thinner and stronger from the effort of riding on a donkey's back for a week.

We didn't come across one soldier during the whole time. I realised this when at last we saw a lone soldier from a distance, on a road, waiting to hitch a ride, and suddenly appreciated what a nice week it had been. I got used to eating little. Every morning I bought a few pitas, some cheese, a little olive oil and *zaatar*, and a bag of carrots, two or three of which I would eat myself, feeding Dayek the rest over the course of the day. When we passed a heap of hay or a field, I stopped and got off Dayek.

I looked into his big brown eyes and couldn't say no to them. I let him enjoy the plenty, and he ate unstoppably, with huge circular motions of the jaw that showed his smiling tooth and the pinkish insides of his grey lips.

We rode in the hills and the valleys and on paths through terraces of olive trees. Every day I prayed the morning prayer and the night prayer: I might enter a mosque if I heard a muezzin call at a convenient time. I washed only when I came across a tap. We crossed black roads that led to settlements perched on ridges, the neat red-tile roofs shining over the green lawns, and dirt roads or worn-out asphalt bleached almost white leading to hillsides cluttered with dense construction, a mosque tower above and always the field below with its single haggard cow. We spent one night near Asira al-Qibliya, and the next in an arid valley, not having encountered a living soul the whole day. Near Deir Istiya we picked up another blanket and a pair of trousers from a clothes line. I wanted to take things from the settlements we passed on our way, Itamar and then Yitzhar, the industrial zone of Barkan, but I didn't want to risk getting too close and being shot by a settler.

I was alone with my thoughts – I could talk to Dayek up to a point but there wasn't much else to do but think, about daily survival issues – food, path-finding, physical pain, places to sleep. I imagined Mother drinking tea with me near the fire, praising it, saying she was happy to see me make something other than bombs. I was sorry that I'd had to flee the village after only a couple of hours with Lulu, and barely having seen Father at all. And I hadn't even seen Rana. Couldn't I have just stopped by to explain, to say goodbye, to kiss her? She would have been wondering, perhaps offended. Who knew when I would see her again? And I was worried about a future in a room in Kafr Qasim, with an unknown family who would have to be told some story or other. What would

I talk to them about? How would I make a living? What about papers? What would happen to Dayek?

As Dayek and I started to descend from the hills of Samaria towards the lowlands, I knew we were getting closer. Roads crossed our path more frequently and more of the cars on them bore yellow number plates. Villages were becoming small towns; the land was becoming harder worked. Tall copses of eucalyptus trees replaced olives and scrub and I grew more cautious, making diversions through obscure valleys and asking goatherds or workers we met for directions to Arab villages. So we travelled from Deir Istiya to Karawat Bani Hasan, from there to Biddya, then to Mascha and from there to Az-Zawiya, where we arrived around noon. There we waited out a long afternoon. I wanted to leave after dark because I had to bypass a Jewish town on the way, Rosh Haayin. According to workers I asked, I had two hours of riding left to Kafr Qasim.

While we waited, Dayek and I prepared ourselves for the next stage of our lives. I found a field on the outskirts of the village, tethered Dayek to a fence with a long rope, and left him to gorge himself on the grass and alfalfa. I walked into the barber's in the village and asked for a shave and a very short cut. It was the first time I'd seen myself for over a week, and I couldn't help but laugh at the beard, the dusty tangle of hair. After an hour I came out of the barber's a new man, wearing a buttoned shirt I'd stolen early that morning in Biddya. I wondered whether Dayek would recognise this neat young man in the fresh shirt with the smooth face and cropped hair, smelling of aftershave, but the moment I climbed on his back he knew it was me. At dusk we set off on the last leg of our journey, making a wide semicircle around the industrial park of Rosh Haayin: and a couple of hours later I was standing under street lights, on a paved street of well-maintained houses, in front of my new home in the village of Kafr Qasim.

# 33

In the nights, memories and theories and Guetta and Shuli ricocheted around the walls of my skull, crashing into each other. In the mornings I'd spend long minutes under the shower trying to chase the fog from my brain. I was slow to see it, but I think now that Bar was trying to keep me going with the Guetta investigation. First thing I did on the drive to work was call him; he would also be driving to work from Tel Aviv. Sometimes I'd see him mid-conversation, revving impatiently at a zebra crossing with an Every Second Counts sticker above his petrol cap, or pelting down the fast lane to Rosh Haayin, both of us talking into our hands-frees about Guetta, about Binyamin Warshawski and his wife Dvora, or Tamer Sarsur and his brother Amin. But I'm getting ahead of myself. At work we kept up a steady back and forth of emails on the subject: Internet search results, falafel lunch meetings . . . Shuli's death had almost stopped me. But Bar had such energy he drew me along in his slipstream.

When I wasn't working on Guetta, I contributed to Time's Arrow by putting some serious hours into computer gaming. I engaged Ron, who'd announced he was leaving the company, in various forms of combat. When Ron wasn't available, I fought myself. Bar and I often went straight from work to Bar BaraBush, where we'd continue discussing the case and other stuff. It was easy for Bar, who had a huge network of friends but lived on his own, and who could get away with not working at Time's Arrow because his manager, Ron, didn't care any more. For me it was a little harder. Duchi thought I was having an affair, and when she realised I was with Bar, accused me of having an affair with him (Talia Tenne also asked more than once whether something was going on between us). Plus I had the problem that I was working closely with the managing director of our company.

I had to fly to Croatia, to a company named Connect, which wanted an ultra-fast search engine for their databases. The trip's goal was ostensibly to get a dialogue under way between our technical people and theirs. But Jimmy wanted me there to sell them our voice recognition system: 'To flog them something under the table, Croc, without them even noticing, OK?'

I don't know how I managed to forget. Maybe because my partner for the trip was Amit from R&D, who I'd never travelled with before. When I went with Jimmy or on my own, he used to drive me crazy for a whole week beforehand. When I travelled with Yoash Green, we prepared for our meetings together. But with Croatia it sort of slipped through the net: a small, uninteresting customer, lots of technical stuff and Amit, with whom I had no regular contact. When Amit rolled his little suitcase into my room and asked whether I was ready, I lifted my eyes from the carnage on my screen and said: 'What for? Where are you off to?'

The morning after my meeting with Gadgid, after my sleepless night of driving in circles, thinking in circles, Jimmy called me into his office. He stood by the window, as if gazing out at the Mediterranean and the Tel Aviv skyline as he used to, though all he could see through this window was the rest of the business park, a field or two with a skinny donkey cropping brown grass and the sun-beaten hills vanishing into a grey heat haze over Samaria. 'Franklin Roosevelt once said,' Jimmy declared, '"Lost ground can be reclaimed – lost time never."' Oh, right, I thought, it's one of *those* speeches. He turned and stared at me. I wilted into a chair. 'These days, we expect a lot from life. We want to work in an interesting, fulfilling, well-rewarded job; to be in a meaningful intimate relationship; to keep abreast of politics, to read books, listen to music, watch movies, visit exhibitions, watch sport, *play* sport, explore our spirituality, our sexuality; to have a wide and various circle of acquaintance, to dance, cultivate a garden, cook, keep fit, raise our families.' He walked around his desk and sat in front of me, then bent towards me and, to my amazement, took both my hands in his. 'To travel, at least once a year, to somewhere you've never been, to stay in touch with friends from all periods of your life, from all around the world, to continually make new ones. It's a hell of a list, Croc. And when I ask myself "Which of these things am I trying to achieve?" the answer is "all of them". Are you?' I nodded distractedly. All night and all morning, the memories Gadgid had summoned had been jabbing and taunting me, refusing to let me alone. God's finger poised above his buttons, me in the watchtower and Danny Lam in his jeep in Lebanon, inching forward into the puddle . . .

'With a list like that, is it any wonder you don't have any time?' asked Jimmy Rafael. No, Jimmy, it wasn't. 'No. You can't manage everything. That's crystal clear. Croc, I'm not going to tell you what to do with your life. But I'm going to be frank. The company is not in such brilliant shape right now. In a month or two – and I'm asking you to keep this between the two of us – we're going to have another round of dismissals, and I want you to be part of it. Your recent contribution has been pretty average. We've talked about it already, and I was hoping that after two, three, four months you'd get over it. I don't have much patience in general, but for you I had.' I nodded, deeply embarrassed. 'But *you are not getting over it*. It's not just forgetting flights, although that was the straw that broke my back. If I could, I'd fire you today. But, as you know, it's a problem. You're a national fucking hero. Wouldn't be very good for the company's profile. The heartless bastards. They went and fired a victim of terror, the CrocAttack himself. Now, I've talked to the investors. Most of our clients are foreign and couldn't give a damn about your arse but our investors are Israelis. So they've approved a special budget to keep you, for now. But I can't leave you in your position. You're moving to QA. Talia Tenne will be moved up the ladder and replace you in Sales. Guy will replace Talia as QA manager, and you'll . . .

Two shots. A blow. I don't dare raise my eyes. I tense myself to receive a bullet. In Lebanon, Danny's jeep moves very slowly forward into the puddle and detonates a roadside explosive device. Danny is killed instantly, as are his commander and the two other soldiers in the jeep. The driver is somersaulted through the air and slammed into some scrub – the impact breaks his pelvis. But he makes it . . . And meanwhile me, in the tower, lifting my head only when I finally understand that the shouts I'm hearing are 'Crocos! Crocos! Are you there?'

. . . Croc, are you with me?'

I started. 'Sure,' I said. 'Guy will manage the QA and I'm going to be working with him.' Some fraction of my brain had been processing Jimmy's words. 'Right,' he said, with severity. He didn't like me as he used to when I was his twin, when we used to sit together in departure lounges, working our phones and making appointments until the very last call before boarding, waiting until our names, variously accented, would echo over the state-of-the-art public address systems of European airports.

'I do understand,' I told Jimmy. 'I . . . I'm sorry I disappointed you. But I couldn't have behaved any differently.' Jimmy extended his hand. 'Look,' he said, 'what I just said, that I would have fired you . . .' 'It's OK,' I said. 'No, no, listen. You know me. It was in the heat of the moment. I'm happy you're staying. And if you return to form, you can go back to what you were, yeah?' I nodded. 'Your salary will go down from twenty-five a month to fifteen.'

I nodded and went without fuss.

It was my fault that Danny Lam died. We were together in basic training, which was a stroke of luck: we were mobilised on the same day. (Muku was younger than us and joined up three months later.) We volunteered for the same unit, were sent to the same base, ended up in the same platoon, two childhood friends from Jerusalem. It was crappy at basic training, but at least we had each other. At the end of it they asked who wanted to volunteer for the reconnaissance unit. I raised my hand. Danny didn't. I persuaded him to accompany me to the tests. I pleaded with him: I said that as a friend it was his duty to support me in the tests. So he came. And passed. I failed. I stayed in the regular unit and was posted to the West Bank. He was in the reconnaissance unit and got sent to Lebanon. He died. I didn't. But I am convinced God meant to select my button. There was some mistake there.

And it was also because of me that Gadgid killed a

seventeen-year-old Palestinian. When they saw the flames climbing up the watchtower the patrol came running back down the hill. Gadgid saw the kids climbing on the tower and stopped, drew a bead and fired. Plastic bullets. One shot cracked the knee of a sixteen-year-old, who also broke his collarbone when he fell. A second shot hit another guy in the neck. The son of a bitch deserved it, said my comrades. For several hours afterwards we all stood around the tower, unable to sit down, the adrenalin burning in everyone's blood, telling stories that over time would become legends to be repeated hundreds of times, for decades – like the ones Gadgid told me in Bar BaraBush. And Danny Lam was blown to pieces and since then, perhaps, he's been watching over me.

I went back to Bar BaraBush the next evening, on my own. It has a long bar and walls the colour of claret wine. The bar is designed in an L shape, with a long wing and a short one (try the excellent chicken wings, by the way: Bar calls them 'Vings'). The short wing is where I usually sit. Why am I telling you all this? Because Bar BaraBush isn't one of those bars with the plasma screen permanently showing MTV or some fashion channel, just a small TV which they put on the short wing after terrorist attacks – with the volume off, since there are always subtitles giving the important information and no one wants to stop listening to music in a bar. There's a limit to everything.

That evening someone said that there'd been an attack and Noam the barman brought the TV out: an attack on some steakhouse in Tel Aviv. I was sitting in my usual spot and the two barmen and a few others who'd come in from the tables on the street crowded round the little screen. Cigarette smoke, Underworld hammering over the speakers, Danny Ronen mutely manipulating his eyebrows. The subtitle 'Attack in Tel Aviv restaurant' was replaced by: 'Two killed, eight injured'. You could almost hear the collective sigh of relief of millions all round the country, and alongside it a faint scintilla of disappointment. 'What a half-arsed attack,' I sneered in a voice loud enough to be heard above the music. As the leading authority in the room in matters of terrorist attacks – as the CrocAttack – my verdict was final. Everybody returned to their private conversations, the little TV made its way back to where it lived beneath the bar, and my phone went.

'Tel Aviv, Croc, Tel Aviv! Nice work.'

It was Itzik, the Attack Pool guy.

'You going anywhere soon, Croc? We'd be very grateful for . . .'

I hung up.

# 34

I'd been anxious about coming to Kafr Qasim but within a few weeks it was as if I'd never known any other life. Al-Amari faded into memory. Bilahl and Rana and Lulu and Father seemed to me almost like characters in another play. Of course I missed them and worried about them, and thought a lot about Mother and Grandfather – when you're alone, you live with the people close to you inside your head – but they seemed to belong to the past.

My room was almost as big as the whole of our flat in the camp. The floor tiles were level, the walls white, the bed was more comfortable and much, much bigger. I was addicted to the reliably hot and muscular jet of the shower. I loved the big kitchen, the new kettle, the fridge (a whole shelf of which was mine), the colossal TV with its perfect picture and sound, the stereo, on which Amr Diab sounded better than ever. And I liked the family. The father, Razal, owned a pharmacy in the centre of the village, on the main road. His wife Wasime was an English teacher in a local school. She was pregnant. Their first son was a six-year-old boy called Atta who gave me a poster of Zidane when I told him that he was my favourite player. But after a month I was too busy with my worries and my work to pay much attention to the comfort and the kindness around me.

I sold Dayek the day after we arrived. That first night I found a place for him in a building under construction, left him some grass and carrots and wished his smiling face goodnight. The next day I walked him by foot out of the village. I asked some of the workers I met whether they knew anyone who wanted a donkey, and they sent me to their bosses, who passed me on to their friends, who made phone calls, and found a buyer in a packing-house a few kilometres away. I almost couldn't believe it when I received four new hundred-shekel notes: in the West Bank you wouldn't have got half of that for a donkey. But when I turned my back on Dayek, my fellow-traveller, my only friend during a long and lonely week, a wave of pain broke over me. Another separation.

It was late afternoon by the time I got back, but it had been the most profitable day of my life. When Razal opened the door to me, pretty much the first thing he said was, 'Have you heard about the attack?' My stomach, and probably my face, fell. Halil's cousin had told me that they wouldn't know anything about me. It took me a moment to realise that he was talking about a new attack – and that was a surprise too. There hadn't been an operation for a while and I'd come to think that if we couldn't arrange one, no one else could.

'What?' I asked him eventually.

'An attack,' he said. 'In Tel Aviv.'

Danny Ronen's face looked fatter. Either it was the widescreen TV or he'd put on quite a bit of weight. A shooting attack. Two killed. Not serious. Who were these clowns who made it all the way to Tel Aviv and then only managed to kill two? In a restaurant? I almost asked Razal and Wasime, but stopped myself in time.

'Only two killed,' said Wasime.

'Lucky,' said Razal.

'Will there be a curfew now?' I asked.

They looked completely at a loss.

'I mean in the West Bank,' I said, in a sneeze of nervous laughter.

'Probably,' said Razal. He was going to say something else, but didn't. I'd told them I was from Ein Rafa near Abu-Gosh and that I'd come here on the bus. Maybe they knew I was lying. My looks and accent weren't things I could disguise and I'm a pretty unconvincing actor. But at least I was trying to pretend, and that in itself might have been good enough for them.

Next day it was *Noah's Ark*, which I hadn't seen for a while, and I asked Razal and Wasime whether I could watch TV. 'Only if you're watching *Noah's Ark*,' they said, 'because that's what's on in this house.'

But as we waited for Tommy Musari on the turquoise sofa that was so soft it threatened to engulf us whole, we were amazed to hear that the programme had been cancelled. Instead, said the presenter, with deep solemnity, Channel 2 would screen a special programme to commemorate last night's attack. Wasime emitted a scream. 'A special commemorative programme?' Razal growled. 'Attack? What attack?' said Wasime. 'That shooting? They call that an attack?' I looked from husband to wife. I was too surprised to speak. The programme started, and within a few seconds the mystery was solved. Max Caspi from the show *Mad Max* had been in the restaurant at the time of the shooting. So they had to have him do something, didn't they? Even if only two people had been killed. Instead of *Noah's Ark*, Max Caspi and friends in the restaurant. You could see why the shahid had only got two – the camera showed the broken window through which he'd fired. What an amateur! Why hadn't he taken a small shotgun, shot the security guard and then sprayed inside with an Uzi?

Max, with his thick black-framed glasses and thicker black hair, which everyone knows is a wig, was raging at the camera.

'This piece of shit came from Tulkarm to scare us. But we will not be scared!'

Max's friends clapped their hands.

'Not of him, not of any of the other pieces of shit sitting in their caves in Tulkarm and Jenin and Nablus and Hebron and Gaza planning their next outrage!'

Max stood there in his wig, jabbing his finger at all the pieces of shit who were planning operations against him. How utterly terrifying. I wanted to laugh. Then he and his singer friends started performing tragic ballads in the restaurant, and the camera pulled focus from the shattered window to the candles sitting on top of their piano and I just got too fucking angry to bear it a moment longer. If they'd just keep going a little longer, I thought, maybe I'd get a lift into Tel Aviv and finish the job off properly. I got up and went to my room.

During those first days I'd walk around the village, or down the main road to the football pitch, where I'd watch Hapoel Kafr Qasim train or play matches. I didn't see much of Razal or Wasime or Atta: I preferred to eat in my room, either something I'd brought or meals that I prepared in the kitchen when the family were finished there. Because I had so much time on my hands I usually responded to the muezzin's calls and went to pray in the mosque, which was where I befriended a couple of guys who taught me the rules of the game in Kafr Qasim. They explained to me that there were two main types of Palestinians in Kafr Qasim. The 'IRs' – Illegal Residents – were ordinary people like them and me, who the Border Police were trying to catch and expel (they told me to watch out for checkpoints or random searches). And there were also the 'collaborators' – drug dealers and mafiosi who lived in villas and did whatever they liked with impunity. The locals didn't think much of either type. There were plenty of Kafr Qasimis willing to inform the Israeli authorities about us, but also plenty who liked the Israelis even less than they liked us. I was told that forty years earlier the Jews had slaughtered fifty villagers for no reason at all and successfully covered it up.

My friends at the mosque introduced me to Sa'id, who came to the first and fourth prayers every day and managed a packing plant for Shimshon, a company exporting fruit and vegetables. Every day his packing-houses received tons of tomatoes and watermelons from the south, mangoes, bananas and avocados from the Sea of Galilee and the Golan Heights, citrus fruits from the Sharon, parsley and basil from the West Bank and much more. 'We sort everything out according to the orders, store what needs to be stored, deliver what needs to be delivered to the airport and ports. It's hard work,' he warned me. 'And the worst of it is that you'll never want to look at a fruit or a vegetable again.'

'I'll give it a go,' was my answer – as if I had a choice.

The packing-houses were some way outside the village, in the fields spread out east towards the brown hills, but still in Israeli territory. It was where I'd sold Dayek (I met the buyer, and my old friend was doing fine). But Sa'id hadn't been kidding. My body was not prepared for the shock of the work. I'd done physical jobs before, but this was relentless. One after the other the trucks came in, packed with crates of carrots, cucumbers, potatoes, radishes, bananas and tomatoes, and the smell of it was terrible, especially the tomatoes. At home, a few fruits in a bowl give out a pleasant scent. In huge warehouses piled to the roof with it, the smell almost made you pass out. And besides, it was summer, and summer in Kafr

Qasim was very different from summer up in the mountains. The heat was a nightmare, and carrying boxes of fruit in it was a double nightmare. It was my job to shift the boxes from the trucks coming into the deck to the forklifts. Two handlers worked on each truck that came in, one on the truck, the other on the deck. Eight in the morning to five in the evening, sometimes longer, with almost no breaks.

I was just a single ant in a huge anthill. The forklift drivers ferried the boxes to the storage rooms; other teams loaded the produce from there into huge containers for the cargo ships, or into smaller containers destined for the airport; others operated forklifts in the cold-storage rooms – they were sick most of the time because of the cold and therefore made better money. I made enough. In Al-Amari I could have lived very comfortably on my wages. But even in Kafr Qasim it was good enough. And if the work was hard, it gave me a reason to wake up in the morning at least, a daily routine. It developed my muscles and I made a few friends, like Majed Hashem from Kalkilya, a blond, bright-eyed guy with arms like a gorilla after years at the warehouse, and Ibrahim Hasuna from Bani Naim near Hebron. Ibrahim was short and skinny but also very strong. He had a black moustache and hair, sang Lior Narkis songs all day – Jewish crap:

> Oh, sweet soul, the only one who knows me –
> With you, I'm the whole world,
> With you, I'm the whole universe,
> Without you, I'm half a person . . .

Majed and Ibrahim weren't close friends. Unlike the guys from the mosque, they weren't religious and knew nothing about politics (girls and football: that was what they talked about) and I hardly saw them outside of work.

But I enjoyed our days together in the packing-house – the condescension of the locals and our constant fear of the Border Police forged a bond between us.

Rana, I can smell that it's you . . . I can feel your fingers on my face.

Say your name.

I'm sorry I left. I'm sorry I didn't come back. I'm sorry. But please say something . . .

*'Sorry, Dr Hartom, I'll be right there . . .!'*

*Svet?* Is that you, or Rana?

If I'm dreaming, this dream is never-ending . . .

With the peak of the summer behind us, the air began to move and suddenly it hit you that air wasn't just a suffocating blanket but something you could actually breathe. Of course, I was missing home, and Lulu and Rana, and even places like Ali's café in Al-Amari. But after two months of working in the packing-house life had settled into a routine. I grew used to the village, the people, the job, and never saw any Jews. Maybe that was why everybody seemed so relaxed. Who knows how long I would have continued in this comfortable routine if my back hadn't gone?

I'd had a few little warning twinges, but I'd just ascribed them to the new stresses on my muscles. And then one afternoon, it was like my whole body had suddenly seized up. I couldn't move. Even sitting on a chair, doing nothing more than breathe, waves of pain were shooting through me. I couldn't even answer the floor manager when he asked me what had happened. Was it my back? I nodded. He told me to lie down on the floor and raise my knees to my stomach. I wasn't the first worker it had happened to, he said, and I wouldn't be the last. I lay there for a few minutes with my back on the cool floor and sipped slowly from a glass of water he'd brought. Gradually I began to feel better. I managed to get up and walk slowly. Breathing became easier and the pain faded away. I signalled to the floor manager that I was able to carry on and slowly but successfully made it through to the end of the day. In the small hours of the night I was woken by an overwhelming pain.

I didn't know what to do – who I could call, where I could go in the middle of the night. I lay there drowning in my suffering, waiting for the time to pass until dawn.

# 35

'Are you completely crazy, Croc?' She looked a little crazy herself – red eyed, mad haired. I was hardly looking my best myself. I'd had one too many, as they say. I'd had two too many. Even I could smell the stink of the cigarette smoke I'd been marinaded in for hours.

'What?'

'Didn't you hear there was an attack?'

'Oh, a half-arsed one, come on.'

'Half-arsed? Two people have been killed, you fool! You call that half-arsed?'

'You think that's *not* half-arsed?' I just wanted to sit down, drink a glass of water, get rid of my stinking wrinkled clothes and go to sleep.

'Where *were* you? Don't you understand I was worried about you? You don't come home and you don't call. Just like last night. You don't even call to wish me good luck for the trial . . .'

'Yeah, sorry, I . . .'

'There's an attack in a restaurant, people are killed and I . . .' Duchi gave in to great high-pitched sobs, spasms of furious tears that shook her shoulders. I stood there, looking on. 'Where were you?'

'In Bar BaraBush. Where else? That's where I always am. You don't think I'm the kind of loser that goes to those steakhouses, do you? I actually find it a bit insulting that you think I'd be there.' She ignored my attempt at humour.

'What were you doing in Bar BaraBush? Why the hell do you go there every evening? With this *Bar* . . .'

'Not every evening. And I wasn't with Bar, I was on my own. And the night before I was with Gadgid, a guy who was in the army with me . . . Look, Duchki, I don't understand. Haven't you realised yet that the attacks *can't hurt me*? They can't touch me—'

'*You* don't understand. They're following you! And eventually they'll get you! I was just so completely sure you were there today.' Her rage was diminishing to relief. 'You're always eating steak.'

Things will be all right, and if they aren't, that's all right too. Or things will not be all right, and if they are, that's not all right either. Me v. Duchi.

'OK,' I said in a softer voice. 'Let's just go to sleep.'

'No, I'm furious. Who is this "Gadgid" person? Why are you up until four in the morning with him? And the rest of the time with Bar. What do you talk about? What's so . . . where are you going? Croc, Croc, don't . . . oh, how brave! Turning your back. Too tough for you, is it, to have to listen to this?'

'I need to piss, what do you want?' I muttered, heading for the bathroom, but she was still talking and I don't think she heard me. Lawyers, I consoled myself, make speeches as a form of keep-fit. '. . . blah blah blah, is that what you're talking about in Bar BaraBush? You were supposed to be too old now for getting shit-faced in bars. What happened to that?'

'I don't know,' I said, mid-piss. 'I really did think I was getting older.'

I was still drunk. I felt nauseous. I announced that I was going to sleep. She was angry but could hardly stop me. I got undressed and passed out, basically. Every three or four nights, the accumulated exhaustion would hit me and I would sleep like a dead man, and when I woke up she had already gone.

She called in the afternoon to say she was sorry. Well, me too. Bibi had invited her out, she said, so if I wasn't planning to go home then she'd go over to her place. I told her not to go. I would come home.

'Can we watch *Noah's Ark* together?'

'Of course,' I said. 'Let's do it.' I gave her a kiss down the receiver.

I left work early and went to the supermarket to buy stuff for a dinner of appeasement: wine, pasta, a few leeks, mascarpone cheese (for a recipe from the first *Naked Chef* book which I planned to cook), ingredients for a salad, strawberry-cheesecake Häagen-Dazs and Swiss chocolate with pistachio nuts. I was in a reasonably good frame of mind as I queued, full of good intentions and refreshed by a night's sleep and an easy day at work. But the line wouldn't move forward. The girl at the till was slow and the guy in front of me kept changing his mind and scuttling off to get new items. A quiet fury was rising within me like blood pressure. And then suddenly, out of the background noise of honks and engine noise, there came the unmistakable sound of an explosion.

What happened afterwards was relayed to me by Almaz. Apparently I shouted 'Enough!!' several times. I was instantly drenched in sweat (my underpants confirmed Almaz's story). My eyes looked 'distant and hazy'. I picked the bottle of wine up and shattered it on the floor then grabbed the guy in front of me by his shirt-front and shook him violently, babbling something about the dinner and crying uncontrollably. Then I seem to have started throwing my tomatoes, one after the other, at the wall. Not ripe enough to splat against the wall, they had bounced back like rubber balls. Then, according to various other witnesses, I ran out on to the street, pausing only to shove the security guard in the chest, still crying and yelling an unintelligible stream of something. I flopped down on a park bench, occasionally shouting, 'Enough already!' while my phone rang and rang until I took it out of my pocket, screamed, 'ENOUGH!', threw it on the pavement, stomped on it, found a rock and crushed it into fragments of plastic and glass. All this because of a misfiring exhaust.

It was lucky that the policemen took me to Almaz's station, and luckier still that Almaz saw me there. Duchi picked me up. She took me home and helped me undress and shower. I couldn't speak; I couldn't even tell her I'd been planning to cook her a meal. She nursed me quietly, with eyes newly red or still red from the night before. Then she talked on the phone and I understood that it was Voovi she was talking to, and that her father had left his third wife and moved into his son's place.

We sat down in front of the television. Here's something that'll ease my mind, I thought. I was wrong. *Noah's Ark* had been cancelled. Instead they showed a laughable programme with the laughable Max Caspi about last night's half-arsed attack. Why? Because Caspi had been in the steakhouse at the time of the attack. He was a regular there. 'What a clown,' I said. 'What a pathetic clown! There's an attack on his favourite restaurant so he suddenly discovers we're at war and it's time to make a TV show about it?'

'Come on. There were two people killed,' Duchi said.

'In Jerusalem there were nineteen killed. But they shot his fucking steak and now he's had a revelation!'

'Don't shout,' she said in a low voice.

'I *will* shout! It's a disgrace. What about Afula, Netanya, Hadera? Nahariya? Haifa? Nothing. Jerusalem? Nothing. You want some ice cream?'

I looked for the Häagen-Dazs, but of course it had never made it home, and all the freezer held was a strange grey icy residue of something or other. Max Caspi was sitting in his stupid steakhouse talking about getting on with our everyday lives and beating the terror. 'Fuck that!' I howled. 'What everyday fucking life? We've already lost! We lost a long time ago. There isn't anyone left in this place apart from security guards!'

'Croc, can you calm down?'

I sat back on the sofa. Max Caspi threatened the terrorists, his wig shaking. 'I'm sure they're quaking in their fucking boots,' I said. 'They're watching Max Caspi and saying, "Allah preserve us, we'd better stop with the bombs now that Mad Max Caspi's on to us."'

'I called the Warshawski in Tel Mond,' said Bar. We were outside the falafel stall. Bar's black baseball cap hung loosely on his bald head. The straw from his juice waggled in the corner of his mouth as he spoke. 'He claimed he hadn't stepped on Tel Aviv soil for thirty-one years, and never would until the day he died. Though you should remember that he might have been lying.'

'And what about the Tel Aviv Warshawskis?'

'One's a professor of "nuclear medicine" at Ichilov. He lives with his wife in the King David Tower. The second one lives in Ramat Aviv. Retired from the university. Published a book about Churchill.'

'Churchill?'

'Yes, don't know why. He's a widower, lives on his own.'

'So what's the link to Guetta?'

'No idea. Unless Guetta was doing research on Churchill, or had an interest in "nuclear medicine".'

'"Nuclear medicine"? Maybe Guetta had some disease he didn't want to tell anyone about . . .'

'I doubt it. Why meet him in a café and not the hospital? As far as I can tell so far, no one knew about him having any disease.'

'So it's a dead end. Our case is dead.'

'Not at all. Did I tell you I spoke to Guetta's friend? Haim? He was in the army with him. He was listed in Guetta's address book, and I had a hunch he might be interesting. He said Guetta was a killer, in Gaza.'

'A murderer?'

'In the army, Croc. He was in the Border Police. They called him "The Killer". He scratched two "X"s on his barrel during the intifada, possibly three. There's an argument about the third one, with some other killer in his company.'

'I remember. There were quite a few Border Police at the funeral.'

'Yeah. Haim and Guetta did their service together. They were in Gaza for a couple of years and saw some terrible stuff, he claims.'

'So that helps us how, exactly?'

Bar adjusted his baseball hat so it shaded his eyes and stood up. 'Come on, Croc. Stick with it. Poirot always knew that *everything* was a clue.'

When we returned to the office, he emailed me. 'Binyamin Warshawski = suspect of investigation = the murder suspect = this is a suspicious historian.'

My new role in Time's Arrow was to test the voice recognition system's capacities. On older telephone switchboards, operators wasted an average of forty seconds on each call: the welcome greeting, the request for name and town, the computer search, reading the number, and then a farewell to the customer. The new system saved time by replacing the operators at the beginning (greeting, request for name and town) and end (reading the requested number, farewell) with the software. In this way the operator's contribution to the call was shortened to twenty-something seconds.

But lots of companies do this, and Time's Arrow needed to find an edge over them. Hence the voice recognition system we'd developed. Our goal: the whole call handled by the software. But voice recognition is extremely complex. People talk different languages, or dialects; they speak in different accents and make mistakes in their pronunciation; there's the problem of background noise. So, in order to adapt the product to our various customers, we were 'teaching' the software to recognise the languages and the local accents. My role in QA was to conduct a long series of tests of the system's success in recognising languages and accents. So for a French client I would get a Frenchman to try the system out, then test it with my own voice, then find a North African French speaker, a West African one, and so on. It was a pretty easy job. All I needed to do was conduct some tests and fill in some forms. And, as Jimmy had mentioned, the company wasn't doing too well, so I was hardly snowed under. I was working on software we'd developed for the Belgians: tests in French, Flemish and all the relevant accents.

One day, while drowsily scrolling around an Internet map of Africa to see where the Belgian Congo was, my phone rang.

'I think I have found something of immense value.'

'Who am I speaking to, if I may ask?' I said, suddenly excited.

'It's Bar, you imbecile.'

A falafel-stall meeting was convened. Bar had indeed found something: in Guetta's Palm's Notes sub-folder he had discovered a single encrypted file. When he tried to open it, he was asked to enter a password. He tried 'Shuli'. It worked. The note said:

> Tamer Sarsur. America Fruit and Veg, Be'eri.
> Physiotherapy. Don't mix with the brother.

So we decided to drive over after work and, having walked the length of Be'eri Street, came across a greengrocer's on the corner of Weizmann Street which was indeed called 'America Fruit and Veg'. We entered and bought cherries, tomatoes, grapes, and asked the guy who was serving to cut a watermelon in two for us. We observed him intently: an Arab. What it meant, we hadn't a clue.

Duchi was surprised to see the cornucopia of fruit that had suddenly taken over the fridge.

'But I was in the supermarket just yesterday,' she protested.

I shrugged. 'I just felt like it, Dooch.'

We never got round to eating the fruit in any case. Several weeks later I found the grapes and cherries in the fridge, rotten and stinking. The half of watermelon met its end in a violent collision with the road.

# 36

The doctor told me that if I didn't want to ruin my back for ever, I could no longer work in such a strenuous job. After four days off I returned to the packing-house and talked to Sa'id. He agreed to train me as a forklift driver but couldn't promise work. And so it was. Except for a single day when I covered a sick driver and suffered every minute through inexperience, the packing-house never called me again. I went back to asking around for work – in the mosque, guys I'd met at the packing-house, even Razal and Wasime. One evening my friend Ibrahim from the packing-house called me at the house.

'Fahmi, I'm in hospital.'

'*Ahalan* Ibrahim – what's the matter?'

'My wife's in here with a burst appendix. She needs an operation.'

'Oh. When is it?' I wasn't sure why he was telling me this.

'Tomorrow morning. Listen, do you want to replace her at work, until she recovers? It'll be ten days, maybe two weeks. She's a cleaner.'

'Where?'

'In a park in Rosh Haayin.'

For the Jews. Cleaning for the Jews. It didn't sound that attractive.

'Going to work for the Jews?' I heard Bilahl sneer. 'For this we worked so hard? So you can clean their offices like a miserable servant?'

'I'm not anybody's servant. I'm stronger than them. I'm just taking their money, that's all.'

'Hello?' Ibrahim was saying.

'That's how they rule us: they make us dependent on their money.'

'Easy for you to say, but how do you want me to live?'

'Live on faith. Study Islam and go to the mosque, and Allah will help you. How do you think I've lived all my life?'

'And where are you now, Bilahl? Are you dead? Is Allah helping you now, brother?'

'Fahmi? Hello?'

'Just give me a second . . . Let me think about it.'

'What do you need to think about?' Ibrahim was right. I didn't know anything about cleaning and I didn't like Jews, but it was better than sitting at home and feeling sorry for myself. And I needed the money.

'Do you have to lift heavy stuff?'

'A mop is heavy stuff?'

'What about papers? I don't have a blue ID.'

'They never check. You just have to be out of the park before eight. Look, Fahmi, my wife hasn't got an ID either, so make up your mind. I need to get back to her.'

Oh, your smell, Rana. Is that you? Oh, I love your smell . . .

*'Good morning, sweetheart. How was your weekend? Did you have guests?'*

Oh, Svetlana . . . I thought it was . . .

*'Oh, look! Your nostrils twitched! It's this perfume, I knew it.*

*I hope you don't mind, I asked your girlfriend what perfume she was wearing. You like it, don't you? You like my smell now? I just wanted to cheer you up. It's funny, I spent the weekend waiting for work . . .'*

Dear Svet. Don't you get a chance to talk at home?

*'Another thing about you in the paper. You and the Croc. And your brother. I just refuse to believe it. I shrug it off now. OK, gonna flip you now . . .'*

The Croc . . . with his red eyes and green car. Not a bad guy, really. I can see him on the beach, but I can't seem to reach . . . or am I getting closer?

*'Are you smiling because of the massage, Fahmi? Or something else? Are you smiling? You don't know how I've been looking forward to seeing you . . . la la . . .!'*

I waited near the mosque after the first prayer and boarded a minibus full of construction workers. After a brief ride to the business park we passed through its gates without being checked. Inside, there was a one-way road lined with office buildings and warehouses. The minibus let the noisy builders off in front of an unfinished building and I was left alone. The driver asked whether I was Zahara's replacement and parked the minibus outside a building near the entrance to the park which housed several restaurants.

'OK, here's the schedule,' my new boss said. 'First, this restaurant.' He fished out a bundle of keys and signalled for me to follow him. 'Opens at eleven. You've got two to three hours to get it done.' He showed me cleaning materials, explained what needed cleaning. 'At eleven the owner, Shimshon Almozlino, will be here, so you've got to be done by then. At eleven,' he continued, pointing to a falafel stall at the edge of the complex, 'you come here from Shimshon's, OK? Quick clean, half an hour.' Bilahl was right, I was thinking. What the hell was I doing here?

Was I really going to clean toilets and falafel stalls for the Jews? There was something terribly wrong about this. 'After the falafel you can take a break, but be careful,' he said, waving a hand at a big new building of tan stone: the orange Orange offices. 'There are armed guards in the Orange building who keep an eye out for Arabs. They've already arrested some.' He measured me with a long look. 'And the Border Police sometimes do the rounds looking for IRs. I don't care who you are. To me, you're just Zahara's temporary replacement, but I suggest you be careful.'

I said nothing. We walked on to another new office building. 'Three o'clock you come here. You'll need this to get in.' He handed me a keycard and after a brief exchange with the guard we went on in and up to the third floor, where a second card opened the offices of a high-tech company. Then another building, another keycard, another identical high-tech company's office. Five until seven: two more hours of Jews. 'Have you got everything?' he asked. 'Because you look like you're in shock.' 'No, no, I'm fine. I've got it.' 'When you finish here, you wait for me downstairs at seven-thirty, OK? Even a few minutes earlier. From eight there's a guard at the entrance to the park who checks IDs, so we want to leave before that, yes?' I nodded. 'What time do you wait for me downstairs?' 'Seven-thirty.' He scrutinised me. 'You look in shock, kid.' 'Not in shock,' I replied. One more mention of shock and I'd bury him under the foundations of one of these half-built offices, among all his Jewish pals. 'Beware of the Orange guards,' he said. 'And look out for the Rosh Haayin private security patrols when it gets dark. And the Border Police. Any questions?' We'd arrived back at our starting point.

'How much do I get?'

'Two hundred shekels a day, cash, when I drop you off

at Kafr Qasim at night. Any problems, I'm Samir.' He turned and beeped his minibus locks open with his key-fob. 'Good luck.'

*'They're not standing outside any more, at least. I think they wouldn't put up with it after the guy got in . . .*

*'All right, we're finished now. Let's turn you over . . . careful of the tubes . . .'*

One tube for piss, one tube for air . . .

*'Back in two hours, sweetheart . . .'*

I thought I wouldn't last a day but I made it through the whole two weeks until Zahara recovered and reclaimed her job. It wasn't hard work, because there were breaks during the day. My back gave me a few worrying little spasms on the first day and then I never heard from it again. Not having any expenses, I managed to save a little money: I'd grab an illicit breakfast from the restaurant's refrigerator, and was given a falafel from the stall for lunch. The lunch breaks I usually spent napping on the site where the builders from Kafr Qasim worked. There was a room with plywood on the floor, covered in blankets, which the workers – Palestinians and a few Romanians – didn't mind me using.

The easiest work was in the never very messy offices of the high-tech companies: I vacuumed the carpets, cleaned the kitchenette, washed a few dishes, bagged the garbage and replaced the bin liners. It was all meant to take four hours. I did it in two. The girls were pretty, and smiled at me; there were always cookies and pretzels to steal from the kitchenette; the toilets were new. Every evening after the last place was empty, I put the cleaning things back in their place and went into the small toilet for a long, satisfying, symbolic crap.

So once again I had a routine. The morning trip, the

restaurants, the nap, the high-tech offices, the mop, the Hoover, the farewell message of my concluding shit. I returned to the village at seven-thirty, received my two hundred shekels, used twenty of them to buy *shawarma* and Coke on the main road and pocketed the rest. Sometimes I'd sit in the *shawarma* place with the builders who rode back with me, and sometimes I met friends. But most evenings I went home. I couldn't stand the locals looking down at us. The glances that said we were contemptible refugees. As if those complacent white-haired old fatsos with their beads, backgammon, blue ID cards and stinking tobacco were doing us a favour by not calling the Border Police. Fuck them, with their Israeli friends who hate them and mean them every bit as much harm as they do us. My people? No: fuck 'em.

From the Israelis' most dangerous enemy to the least of their servants. It was a humiliating comedown, but I kept at it. I told myself that I wasn't working for the Jews but for Samir, that Israeli money was going into Palestinian pockets, and to remind myself that I wasn't a traitor to my people I would commit petty crimes: I took food and drink from the kitchens and pens from the desks. Reparations on a tiny scale. Once I saw a hand-held computer on a desk and fitted it into the palm of my hand, pushed the buttons, caressed the orange plastic. I almost took it.

But always there was Bilahl in my head, sneering at my insistence on seeing the glass as half full. I held the glass up and examined it. Which was it? Half full or half empty? It was both, dear brother. I worked for them, but I never forgot who they were. I didn't pretend not to see the looks the security guards gave us whenever we talked Arabic among ourselves or simply clustered together at lunch. How could Bilahl say I was bowing my head to them, or not doing enough for the cause? What was *he* doing? There were likeable people in the offices, but I made it a principle not to like them, not to cross the line.

Only once did I cross it. I was in the office I cleaned last. It was evening and most of the workers had gone home. Except for the humming of the computers and music from one of the more distant rooms, it was completely quiet. I ate a few biscuits and drank a cup of coffee in the kitchenette, and then headed out to bag the garbage and replace the bin liners. I was clearing the used coffee cups from the desks when I saw the orange gadget again. I picked it up from its cradle and fiddled with its buttons.

'You can have it,' said a voice from behind me.

I spun round in alarm. 'What?'

'You can have it.'

Just an ordinary Israeli guy with a big Israeli nose and heavy-lidded eyes, who I'd seen in the office a couple of times. But as he stood in front of me and spoke, and I connected his voice to his face, I suddenly realised I'd seen him before. I dredged up rusty Hebrew from the depths of my brain.

'I can have it?'

'Yeah. I noticed you looking at it. It's not working. But you can have it if you want.'

I looked at the little orange device. Was he doing this to humiliate me? I put it in my pocket and kept looking at him.

'What?' he said. 'I need to get back to my desk. Do you mind?'

I moved aside and he flopped, rather wearily, into his chair. For a moment I stayed where I was, examining his face.

'What?' he said again. 'The Palm is yours. What now?'

I knew what it was now. *Noah's Ark*. I wanted to ask

him about it. But he was just some arrogant, self-satisfied Israeli. Why bother?

'Nothing. Thanks,' I said, and beat a retreat, his eyes crawling all over the back of my neck. I kept thinking about him on the way home and the rest of that evening. His *Noah's Ark* had been a few months ago. He'd had some weird name, which Tommy Musari kept repeating. And his partner in the couple ('Two by two! Two by two!') had been some imbecile girl from the army . . . I put his Palm on my shelf and tried to recall how the show had gone. First time I'd ever seen someone who'd been on *Noah's Ark*. Pity he was such a son of a bitch, but what else would you expect from a Jew?

Yeah. What else?

*'Well, Svetlana?'*

*'Well, Dr Hartom . . . there's nothing much to say. He's been the same for weeks.'*

*'Well. We're getting near the point where we can make a pretty accurate prognosis . . .'*

*'But there's still a chance he'll come out of it?'*

*'There's always a chance.'*

*'But what kind of . . .? What percentage?'*

*'Svetlana, please. I'm relying on you to keep me informed of any changes whatsoever. Anything at all.'*

*'Yes, Doctor.'*

# 37

'What day does Elvis come?'

Elvis was our cleaner.

'Tuesdays, remember?' Duchi said. 'Obviously Tuesdays. You used to know that sort . . .'

'Where's he from?'

'What? Somewhere in the south of the city, maybe?' she said. 'Down where all the foreign workers live?'

'I mean which country?'

'Ah. I don't know. Is it Ghana?'

'Ghana . . . What bit of Africa's that?'

'I don't know, Croc.'

'Near to the Congo?'

'Congo's in the middle somewhere. I don't know.'

'Well, who were Ghana a colony of?'

'I don't know! Why are you asking me all these questions? Is this something to do with cleaning the flat?'

'No,' I said, a little absent-mindedly perhaps, a little inattentive, 'it's for work. I need someone who speaks French and Flemish in an African accent.'

This was what lit the fuse of our final row. It irritated her that I was thinking about work and not about home. Duchi used to hope that we could go back to how it had been before. But we never did, and for months we were on the verge, on the verge . . . and then came the attacks. She understood the gravity of what had happened to me; she gave me time and tried to help (she *did* help); she accepted the weekly trips to Jerusalem, the sleepless nights, the nervousness, the ruined concentration, the demotion, the drop in salary; she tolerated Bar BaraBush, the long silences, my generally vile behaviour towards her, the evenings with Bar, and the obsession with a comatose girl in Jerusalem . . . she tolerated all this because she thought it wasn't 'the real Croc'. She tried not to judge. It was Uri, of all people – the therapist who used to tell her to get rid of me – who had told her to be patient.

She contacted Ilan, who told her that I'd erected a defensive wall around myself which I was in denial about. Everyone close to me, especially her – he said – ought to give me as much warmth, understanding and positive reinforcement as they could. It was crucial to try to reproduce the conditions of my previous life, as far as it was possible. So she'd tried, though there were days when she'd had enough and hated my guts. And hating me made her feel guilty. Being absorbed in her work made her feel guiltier. With every passing day she hated herself and me more. She said that she had never been unhappier. I didn't care about her, or anything at all! Not once – *not once* – since September 11th had we talked about the wedding or our relationship.

'You don't pay attention to me, you never ask me about my life, you don't care how I feel, don't do anything for the house, and I have *lost hope*, Croc,' she said. 'I have lost hope that things are ever going to change.'

'What about all that fruit I bought the other day?' I went to the fridge, took out the half of watermelon and held it out like an exhibit in court. 'What's this?' She just carried on crying, as she had throughout her speech.

'What the fuck is this if not something for the house?' She couldn't answer. She shook her head.

'What?' I screamed. 'I can't hear you!' I swivelled and threw the half-watermelon out of the open window. 'Huh?' Faintly, we heard the splatter of the watermelon three floors below.

She said, 'I'm sorry, Croc. I'm so sorry. But I can't. I'm going out of my mind!' She was hardly able to speak, sucking in deep wet gulps of air. She said that she had really tried but she no longer believed things were going to change. I couldn't function as part of a couple right now. I couldn't deal with the responsibility and effort of a relationship.

'Maybe a shock will help. You know. The shock of splitting up, it might help you . . . come back. And . . . and if that happens maybe we could see, but I just can't be around you any more, Croc.'

I was surprised. Almost impressed. She once told me she'd never left any of her boyfriends, even the ones she'd wanted to. She was always too sorry for the other person to be able to go. But I didn't remind her.

'Is there someone else?'

'Of course not!'

'Is it Ilan?'

'Oh God, no, no way. There's nobody else, Croc, I swear. It's got nothing to do with anybody else. Weren't you listening to what I was just saying?'

I couldn't believe what I was hearing. *Ilan*. 'Goddammit. That fucking mullet! *And* he's going bald. And fat – I mean, you're always telling me I look three months pregnant – he's in his second trimester! And that ridiculous goatee! I thought you couldn't stand facial hair. Bibi put you up to this, didn't she? Fucking Bibi—'

'Croc, stop it! Please, stop it! There's nothing going on with Ilan or with anyone else! Why can't you stick to the point?'

She burst out sobbing again and I stood and watched. I'm sure there was contempt on my face at that moment. That fat, bald, softly spoken snake: I couldn't believe it. How low could you stoop? But I didn't say anything. She lifted her face to the ceiling. It was all bent out of shape from crying.

'Say something,' she said. 'What are you thinking?'

'Something,' I said. 'Nothing.' A dozen things were going through my head but what I remember above all is the feeling of enormous relief.

In the end, it turned out that Elvis was a lot of help. He's a Nigerian, so he didn't know Flemish or French, but he had a Congolese friend called Clinton who spoke both. The Belgians had given me a list of names and Clinton came into Time's Arrow one day and read them out for several hours. He was delighted with the five hundred shekels he got in cash and found us a Chinese guy and a Vietnamese girl from his neighbourhood in South Tel Aviv, and once they were done I only had one accent left to test. I'd left it to the end because I thought it'd be pretty easy to find an Arabic speaker in Kafr Qasim. Maybe even someone from the park itself.

'Didn't work out too well the last time you were hanging out with Arabs,' Guy smirked at our weekly meeting. Guy's a hard-line religious nationalist. 'Check whoever it is with seven eyes. ID, everything, I don't have to tell *you*, do I?'

Duchi moved out the day after the row with the help of Voovi and her father, who took me aside to tell me how sorry he was. He couldn't understand what was going on with his daughter lately. Ilan didn't dare show his face, luckily for him.

Bar decided it would be a good idea to turn the flat

into the Guetta investigation headquarters (they were surely missing us in Bar BaraBush) and we spent hours on the sofa, with the TV on mute and the air-con thundering away, going over possible leads.

Tamer Sarsur. America Fruit and Veg, Be'eri.
Physiotherapy. Don't mix with the brother.

We hadn't made any progress with the greengrocer's, so we decided to focus on 'physiotherapy'. It took us a whole evening, on the Internet, going through reference books and the Yellow Pages, checking all the physiotherapists around Be'eri Street and Yehuda Maccabi Street, where the meeting between Warshawski and Guetta took place. The next day Bar called every name on our list and asked whether the name Giora Guetta meant anything to them. One said it sounded familiar, but he couldn't find it in the client records. It was only when Bar returned to America Fruit and Veg that it hit him. So obvious that he actually slapped himself on the forehead. Right in front of him, crowned with its helipad, was the colossal glass cliff of the Ichilov Hospital. It had to have a physiotherapy department.

He neatened himself up, straightened his baseball cap, and wandered the hospital corridors until he found the physiotherapy department on the ground floor of the main building. The department had a reception desk and, farther down the corridor, a waiting room. It was a little after 9.30 in the morning – in a minute he would have to return to his car and drive to work. He couldn't see the physiotherapists from the waiting room, and besides, he didn't know what he was looking for. Another dead end. A physiotherapist's head appeared and called: 'Mor Shimon.' No one answered. Two minutes later the physiotherapist's head returned: 'Mor Shimon!'

'Sorry, I was miles away,' Bar said. 'That's me.'

Three years earlier he'd twisted his knee on a skiing trip and had been in physiotherapy for several months: pretending he'd had a relapse would be easy enough, he thought.

'No it's not,' said the physiotherapist, 'I know who Mor Shimon is.'

Humiliated, Bar shuffled off, exaggerating his old limp. But when he passed reception, with its list of physiotherapists on the wall, one of the names caught his attention. Tomer Sarsur. No, he wasn't in today, the receptionist told him. He'd be back tomorrow morning.

We went early. It was my first visit to a hospital since the last time in Hadassah and memories of Shuli were trying to shove their way into my mind. Bar led the way to the physiotherapy department, where we were surprised to encounter the Arabic guy from America Fruit and Veg in a nurse's uniform.

'*Ahalan* – America Fruit and Veg! What're you doing here?' said Bar.

'That's Amin,' Tomer Sarsur said. On his chest was a tag with his name, and in smaller letters below, 'Physiotherapy'. 'I'm his brother. I work here.'

'It's amazing . . .!'

'Yeah,' he said, 'why don't you ask me for a kilo of tomatoes so we can get it over with? Then go and ask Amin for a back rub. It was funny the first thousand times.'

'No, no, it's just amazing how similar you look. Are you twins?'

'No, we're not. Are you here for physiotherapy? Which one of you? What's the therapist's name?'

There was an embarrassing pause. Bar was the first to come to his senses. 'Listen, do you know a guy called Giora Guetta?'

'Guetta? Has he been treated here?'

'Uh . . . we don't know.'

'Never heard of him. Why should I know him? Who are you, anyway?'

'Just friends of his. We had an idea that you might know him.'

He studied us curiously. 'Sorry I can't help. Now, excuse me but I'm going to work.' He turned and walked away. I stuck my hands in my trouser pockets, and Bar passed an anxious hand over his ginger stubble. If that was Tomer Sarsur, then who was Tamer? We crossed the street to America Fruit and Veg.

Not quite twins but close enough: the same nose, long-lashed black eyes, the same lopsided smile. Amin was in a good mood. It was a hot, quiet morning without many customers and he was happy to talk. Tomer, he explained, was actually Tamer: he'd changed his name to the Israeli to spare his patients the anxiety of dealing with his Arabic name. Everyone thought they were twins, and confused them when they were out together, or when Tamer covered for Amin in the store so he could visit their sick mother. She was dead now, Amin said, but when she'd been ill he'd spent a lot of time with her. Maybe he was compensating for Tamer, who had cut all contact with the family back in Kafr Qasim. The brothers had been living together in a flat on Weizmann Street for four years. But no, he said, he'd never heard of Giora Guetta – and he looked as if he was telling the truth.

We'd found Tamer Sarsur, and we understood 'don't mix with the brother', but we hadn't found Warshawski, and couldn't see what connected him and Sarsur. We were stuck. I suggested that we involve Almaz but Bar claimed he would just laugh at our little investigation. So the days began to pass with nothing much happening and Bar stopped coming over in the evenings and it hit me as if for the first time that I was on my own. I wondered where Duchi was and what she was up to. I missed her. One morning I received a cheque from Itzik for five thousand shekels, with a cheery note thanking me for my help: I stuffed it in the back of a drawer and found the wedding ring I'd never given her and sat staring at the wall of the flat for a long time, remembering the way she would laugh and call me an idiot whenever I did something funny. I came to see how much I still loved her; how much I'd lost. I called Muku, but he was busy. Gadgid didn't have time either. I went to Bar BaraBush and had a Cannibal but there were too many pretty girls there, and it depressed me to be alone with a hamburger. I called Uzi Bracha, my fellow laboratory mouse from therapy, who told me that Naama – beautiful but unshutuppable Naama – had asked about me. She'd broken up with her boyfriend, the mountain climber. So I called her, but the conversation just reminded me of her miserable state of mind, and my own, and everyone's in that group. It was too depressing. We both said we ought to meet up, but I didn't call again and neither did she.

And then one evening at work (I'd started staying longer again, because there was nothing to do at home and pretty much everyone else had already left for the day) Bar called in a state of high excitement and told me he had something I might like to look at.

A standard Hotmail screen. 'Well – Hotmail. So what?'

'Look whose it is,' said Bar, and I followed his finger to the corner of the screen: gioraguetta@hotmail.com.

'How the hell?'

Bar smiled with satisfaction. 'Just luck. I had a bit of time, so I started messing about with it. Actually, I'm an idiot – I tried weeks ago, but with one "t" instead of two. I was trying a few combinations of his name and password today and . . . what do you think it was?'

'Shuli?'

'What else?'

'How come we didn't think of this earlier?'

'That's exactly what I said.'

I sat down next to him, shaking my head. We may have been a pair of idiots but Bar was also a bit of a genius. 'Well?' I asked eventually. My heart was racing. 'Anything interesting there?'

'Emails from Binyamin Warshawski. One before the attack, setting the details of the meeting. The other the morning after, asking Giora where he's gone and why he's not answering the phone. It says he's beginning to worry and tells him to get in touch urgently. Says he hopes Giora's not planning on disappearing with the money.'

'Disappearing with the money?' I stared at Bar.

'That's all. Nothing interesting in the other emails. Even these two don't tell us that much . . .' He removed his cap and scratched his dome. 'But at least we know who Binyamin Warshawski is now.' He showed me the details at the foot of the email:

> Prof. Binyamin-Moshe Warshawski
> Nuclear Medicine Department
> Tel Aviv Sourasky Medical Centre

And below that, the address, phone number, fax number.

'What's the Tel Aviv Sourasky Medical Centre?'

'Wake up, Croc,' he said. 'It's *Ichilov*.'

# 38

I fixed his PalmPilot in half an hour. The contacts were a little flimsy, and the batteries dead. That was all. All he'd needed to do was pop into an electrician's. But he was delighted when I gave it to him the next day. He played around with the buttons for a few seconds and said, 'Hey, man, you're a genius!'

I shrugged. 'I just' (I mimed the word I was missing in Hebrew. Fiddled around) 'with the contacts a bit.'

'The contacts? Really? I tried them myself and nothing happened.'

'You should have just given it to an electrician. He'd fix it for you, no problem.'

I had to go back to work, so I left him to play with his new toy. But as I walked away I heard him calling me back: 'Hey, wait a minute!' I came back and he glanced up from his computer screen and handed over the Palm. 'Take it, it's yours.'

'What do you mean? It's working now.'

'Exactly,' he said, 'I gave it to you. Well done for fixing it, but it's still yours.'

On the one hand I thought, I don't need favours from a Jew who treats me like I scarcely exist and if I manage to close an electric circuit suddenly thinks I'm a genius. That side of me wanted to chuck the thing at the wall. My calmer side knew that the wall was made of plywood and nothing was going to happen even if I did throw it. It was the second side that spoke.

'You were on *Noah's Ark*.'

'What?'

'You were on *Noah's Ark*, right?'

He looked at me and frowned. 'You watched it?'

'Of course I watched it, what do you think? You had a strange name . . . You were on with that stupid soldier girl.'

'How'd you remember that? It's been six months!'

'How could I forget? You were very much sweating.'

'You know something? You're the first person ever to mention that to me. Yeah, I was. But listen, how come . . . I mean: do you people actually watch *Noah's Ark*?'

Samir had said not to speak to anyone. Not to talk to the Jews. It was better like that.

'Tell me what your name is.'

'Croc,' he said, somewhat surprised.

'The Croc. Right. The Croc of the Attacks! How could I forget? Musari said it about a thousand times. CrocAttack. *Timsach*, in Arabic.'

He laughed. 'I'm amazed. I didn't know you people watched that stuff.' I said I needed to work, took the Palm and said thank you. In the kitchenette I washed dishes, threw away the garbage and wiped the surfaces. Then I started vacuuming the carpets. The next time I passed Croc's room, he called me in again.

'What's your name?'

'Fahmi.'

'Fahmi,' he repeated. He kept staring at me from under his low lids. His eyes were red. 'Do you happen to know French?' I smiled. What was he on about? Of course I didn't know French. He asked me a few questions about where I lived and what I did and so on. 'OK, then: do you want to make five hundred shekels for one day's work?'

'What work?'

'Here in the office. You just have to say a few things that I'll tell you to say. To test our system. Sit down.'

I looked at my watch and saw the time was twelve minutes past seven. Time for a shit. I could feel the sweet pressure building in my bowels. You weren't supposed to sit down, but I did, keeping a wary eye on the door.

'The system we're developing here is supposed to understand people's voices on the phone. I'm testing to see if it can recognise different accents and I need an Arab. It's for a Belgian client: they've got Arabs there, and Africans, and Chinese and Vietnamese, and I've done them already. I've only got the Arabic left to do.'

I was silent. It was a lot of money, but . . .

'Come on, it's nothing. You come here for a few hours, I tell you what to say, we record you, test the system, and that's it: three to four hours, five hundred shekels.'

'When?'

'Whenever you want.'

This was a Wednesday evening. Zahara had almost completely recovered from her operation and was supposed to return after the weekend, when I would be out of a job again. We decided on Sunday morning.

*'We were at Bilahl's trial, Fahmi. Me and Father . . .'*

Lulu? What about Bilahl?

*'Just a little room. We sat on blue plastic chairs. Bilahl was in a brown prison uniform, but he couldn't stop smiling. He looked very well. Clean. He was playing with a little length of black thread and reading a small Koran. He said that because Allah was protecting him, he was made of steel. He showed total*

*contempt for the soldiers in court. I'd never seen him in such a good mood. Father's mobile phone rang and the judge got really angry. But he said he was ashamed of you, Fahmi . . .'*

Ashamed of me?

*'. . . because of what happened with the Croc. He said you were never really faithful to the cause . . .'*

I couldn't shake the feeling that Grandfather Fahmi was somehow guiding my life from heaven. Bilahl hated it when I said that: he said that only Allah was guiding everything. But meeting the Croc made me wonder just who it was who was controlling my destiny. I remembered how Bilahl had said that we needed to kill the Croc because he'd been turned into a symbol for the Jews. He would have said that Allah had placed the Croc in my hands for just that reason. Our poor father would have said that Allah had introduced us so that I could see he was a human being like myself.

Thursday was my last day as a cleaner in the business park. On Friday, the day when everything converged, I woke with a powerful urge to pray. When the first call came I washed my face, hands and legs and went to the mosque, where I stayed longer than usual. I repeated the *Surat al-Fatcha* dozens or even hundreds of times, and the tears poured down my face. I missed Lulu, Father and Murair; I missed Rana; I missed Bilahl and Al-Amari; I missed Titi, Natzer and limping Rami; I missed Halil Abu-Zeid and I missed my mother . . . and yet I felt strong. When you live on your own for months, you learn to live within yourself.

As soon as I got back home I called Halil's cousin, who was pleased to hear from me. They'd been meaning to contact me some time anyway. Now that there was contact with Bilahl again, the big operation was back on.

'What did you say?'

She couldn't believe I didn't know. Bilahl had been in contact from his jail. He had confessed to planning the attacks, and would probably get multiple life sentences.

I was unable to breathe for a moment. Air jammed in my throat.

'What do you mean, confessed? He told them everything?'

'I don't know exactly what he said. You can call him, but be careful. They've given him this line just so they can monitor his calls.' She gave me the number and asked how I was doing. I told her about the Croc.

'The fool who couldn't die. Well, you must take care of him.'

'It's not that simple. I'm on my own here. Where am I going to find a weapon? Where can I escape to?'

'You've done more complicated things than this, Fahmi.'

I was still having trouble getting air into my lungs. The sense of convergence I'd had in the mosque that morning; the feeling that Allah, or Grandfather, was guiding things from above; Bilahl suddenly only a phone call away; and all of this happening when I still had my appointment with the Croc to come . . . It all felt connected.

I called the number and asked for Bilahl. Two minutes later I heard his 'Hello?', and it was like something floating up from the depths of my memory.

'Bilahl.'

'Fahmi?'

We were silent for a long time. Strange, to have to think very carefully about every word you spoke to your brother.

'How are you?' he asked. 'How's the village?'

'Good. Comfortable. There's work . . . a little bit in the packing-house. You know, bits and pieces here and there.'

'Good. And you're praying? Continuing to fulfil the six commandments?'

'Yes.' He was playing with fire. I understood what he

meant at once. There are only five main commandments in Islam. The sixth commandment was: to continue with our operations.

'Very important,' he said. 'All the commandments, all the time. Make use of every opportunity to be a good Muslim and fulfil all six. Every opportunity.'

'Yes.'

He meant the Croc. It was as if he knew that an opportunity had presented itself, even if he didn't know its details. He was my brother. He could sense it in my voice, in the fact of my making the call. He could sense an internal conflict, and he was demanding that I keep going.

'What about you?'

'All-powerful Allah will decide. When he wants me, I will be there. Let us hope it will be soon.'

It was a short conversation but it carried a lot of weight with me. My brother's power over me was always stronger than I was willing to admit to myself. Even over the phone, from a prison, in code, he was telling me something clearer than the sun: God had placed an opportunity in my hands. He had walked me through the mountains, on donkeys, broken my back with boxes of apples, he had burst an appendix and broken a computer and with infinite care brought me to the right place at the right time because he had a mission for me: to kill the Croc.

And yet, and yet . . . I squirmed restlessly in my chair. I was sorry that I'd ever met the Croc; but I was sure that God had sent him to me. I should never have told anyone that I'd met him, but Bilahl had sensed something without my even saying anything. It was destined; it was random. One minute I wished I was somebody else; the next I felt that I had been chosen by a higher power to complete a mission I had started.

At last the thought came to me, like a balm: it didn't matter. Whatever was fated to happen would happen.

*'There was a female soldier there in a grey uniform with her hair scraped tightly back, blushing and looking insecure. She had glasses with purple plastic frames and three stripes on her shoulder. A soldier shouted, "All rise for the judge!" and everyone stood up. Except for Bilahl, Fahmi! He said: "This is an illegal court whose authority I do not accept. It is illegal just as your occupation is illegal." The soldier girl in the grey uniform and the purple glasses and tight hair read the indictment. She talked about the attack on Jerusalem. How Halil Abu-Zeid had planned it before they killed him, how Safi Bari had made the bomb . . .'*

Safi? Well, that's not . . . what about me?

*'Both of whom are now dead anyway. She talked about how he'd carried out the Shaar Hagai attack with Safi as well. Then she gave a long speech about everything that had happened in Al-Amari. Meetings in secret flats, details of the planning, the bomb-making, recruiting the bomber. But your name never came up. Father was overjoyed. He said he knew you'd never deal with . . .'*

Bilahl. My brother. My big brother . . .

*'. . . every Jew killed in the attacks was an intentional murder. Bilahl would get a life sentence for every person killed. It's going to be something like four hundred years, the sentence. But he's happy. He says that Allah . . .'*

Wasime knocked on my door and invited me for dinner. We made tedious small talk about pharmacies, the economy and little Atta's behaviour – the boy was cranky, crying, throwing his food around the table and smearing his own face yellow and brown with egg and Egozan. When we'd finished and Atta had calmed down sufficiently to be put to bed, we had coffee in the living room and watched *Noah's Ark*. I was thinking about Al-Amari, and the first time I ever saw the Croc. Tommy was on good form. One couple consisted of the cover girl of a new men's magazine called *Passion* and a brilliant student from a rabbinical college in Jerusalem. The model kept saying that she thought the guy was sexy. He wouldn't look at her. Again and again the close-ups showed him averting his eyes. 'Almost!' Tommy said every time. 'But *not quite . . .*' and the audience laughed and clapped their delighted little hands.

*'Goodnight, Fahmi . . .'*

Don't go, Lulu . . . Tell me more about Bilahl. Where is he? Does he have friends with him in jail? What . . .

*'I wish I could understand your language. It sounds so pretty . . .'*

*'It's Arabic, Svetlana. It* is *beautiful. See you. Keep taking good care of him, yeah?'*

*'Yeah, I will. Goodnight, Lulu. Goodnight . . . I . . .'*

*'Svet?'*

*'No, don't worry. I'm sorry. Don't mind me. I'll keep taking care of him.'*

Oh, Svetlana.

The lights are blinding, and baking, and sweat is pouring from my forehead and armpits.

'Fahmi Omar Al-Sabich?' Tommy asks.

'Yes. Good evening.'

'Good evening! So, after three major attacks, Fahmi, you decide it's time to finish off the Croc, the great CrocAttack, the symbol of our survival, is that right?'

'That's correct, Tommy.'

'I'm sure you know what happens next . . .' he says and the audience scream. 'Two by two! Two by two!' Among the audience I can see Bilahl, Abu-Zeid, Rana and

Grandfather Fahmi. They're all giving me encouraging smiles and making victory Vs with their fingers.

'That's right: two by two! So now, let's meet Fahmi's partner on *Noah's Ark* this evening . . . ladies and gentlemen, please give a warm *Noah's Ark* welcome to – who else? – the Croc!'

The audience go wild and I go white. I hadn't been expecting this. My downpour of sweat is becoming a monsoon. The Croc bounds on to the stage, waving to the audience and the cameras, clasps my hand in both of his and sits down.

'So, Croc,' says Tommy Musari, 'tell us what your first thought was when you heard about Fahmi's exciting new plan . . .'

# 39

Friday was the beginning of the end of the summer. The wind had gained a little strength, and clouds were cooling some odd corners of the sky. The first days of the end of the summer are the best days of the year. They're the farthest point in time from the next summer.

Bar bought a large bouquet in the lobby of Ichilov and described nuclear medicine to me on our way to the department. 'It's basically mapping of the body. Huge cameras that photograph the inside of the body.'

'X-rays,' I said.

'Not X-rays. It's similar but a lot more top-end. In X-rays you can only see the bones, but nuclear mapping lets you see everything.'

'What's nuclear about it?' I was picturing the blood flowing, white blood cells, muscles being stretched and relaxed, fat, microbes, lungs dirty from nicotine.

'The nuclear cameras can decipher radiation emitted by the body,' continued Bar. We'd arrived at a quieter part of the hospital. 'They inject this radioactive fluid, a really low isotope, whatever, into the blood and the . . .'

'Can I help you?' asked a brown-haired nurse.

'Ah, yes, we're looking for Professor Binyamin-Moshe Warshawski.'

'Can I ask what it concerns?'

'Yes. He recently treated our mother, so we just wanted to give him these flowers and ask him a couple of brief questions about the diagnosis.' I don't know how Bar comes up with this stuff sometimes.

'And your mother's name?'

'Enoch,' Bar said. I kept my head down in a women's magazine, whose cover promised me twenty-five tips for a perfect sex life on page 31. I flicked through to page 31.

'Sorry, sir. There doesn't appear to be any Enoch in the system.'

'Look, is he here? We just need to ask him one small thing.'

'I'm afraid that's impossible. The professor's extremely busy this morning.'

'Tell him it's related to Giora Guetta,' Bar said, deciding to deploy the one weapon we had in our armoury.

He came out immediately. He looked old. Later, we would learn that he was only sixty-one, but our first impression of him was of a man in his mid-seventies. White hair, white beard, a high-blood-pressure colour to him, a wide mouth and large tombstone-like teeth. His eyes were clear and intelligent, but there had been fear in his first glance towards us. It was the fear which had made him seem old. Weak handshake. He took us to the cafeteria and ordered coffee for us and tea for himself.

'Who are you?' he said. Professors of nuclear medicine tend not to watch *Noah's Ark*.

'We're investigating the death of Giora Guetta,' said Bar.

'Guetta . . . he was killed in a terrorist attack, wasn't he?'

Warshawski's hands were both palm down on the table, like he was braced against a shock. His voice was weak and defeated-sounding.

'Yes he was. But a short time before the bombing he met a Professor Binyamin-Moshe Warshawski in a café in Yehuda Maccabi Street.'

'How do you know that?'

'Let's just say that we know,' said Bar. 'And we know that money was involved.'

Warshawski raised his eyes and looked at us in turn.

'Who are you?' he said. 'What do you want?'

'Why did you meet Guetta?' asked Bar, with a persistence that reminded me of Duchi.

Warshawski didn't answer for a while.

'Who are you, and what do you want?' he repeated. And we could have told him the truth: that we were trying to find out about Guetta as a gesture to his girlfriend, who had since died. He looked like a basically decent man to me. I thought he'd give us the answer and we could put the whole story behind us. But Bar suddenly stood up, scribbling his phone number on a piece of paper:

'We'll be back, Professor,' he said. 'If you remember why you met Guetta on the morning of his death, give us a call.'

'What was all that about?' I asked Bar, trying to catch him up. 'What are we hiding?'

'We've got plenty of time,' he replied. 'And other leads to check. We don't have to reveal everything, do we?' Bar stopped next to a bin and threw the bouquet into it. 'Listen, Croc, if he realises that he's dealing with a couple of nerds playing at being detectives because they're bored, he won't tell us anything.'

'I'm not playing at detectives because I'm bored,' I said, but Bar was already striding ahead of me into the Sarsur grocery.

We asked Amin whether he knew Warshawski, and he did: he and his wife Dvora were regular customers. They lived near the store, in King David Street. But when we asked him whether his brother had any dealings with the professor, Amin clammed up. It was Friday and there were a million customers to deal with, and he was suddenly too busy to talk.

'Interesting,' said Bar, and we went back to the hospital to look for Tamer. But he wasn't at work, and his next shift wasn't before the middle of next week. Another dead end, in my opinion. It infuriated Bar whenever I said that – and I said it pretty often.

'No, man – we're almost there. Stick with it. All we've got to do is connect Warshawski and Tamer, and then we'll get the link to Guetta.'

'Yeah, but how are we going to do that?'

'We're a couple of bored nerds playing at detectives. We'll find a way.'

On Sunday morning I recorded the Arab guy who had replaced this rather cute cleaner we had at Time's Arrow, a kid with a wispy moustache and a startled look. I wouldn't have given him a second thought except he'd fixed my PalmPilot. After lying dead on my desk for almost a year, my Palm was reborn after a couple of hours in the hands of Fahmi the Cleaner from Kafr Qasim – who'd have thought? I can't even remember how it came about. Once upon a time, he told me, he'd been an electrician. Then he asked whether I was the Croc from *Noah's Ark*. Weird to think of Arabs watching it. Anyway, the Belgians had asked for a North African Arab and I suppose if I'd searched hard enough I could probably have found a

Moroccan or a Tunisian, but what the hell, I thought, let's see what our software can do with a Palestinian accent.

He was a little nervous when he showed up on Sunday, so I told him not to worry – no one was going to bite him. He told me he wasn't worried, just a little sick in the stomach. I wanted to say something like 'Too much hummus, eh?' but I managed to stop myself. There's a limit.

I think I used the hummus joke later that day, because it turned out that Fahmi was an all-right kid. He did Palestinian, Egyptian, Jordanian and Lebanese accents, which he'd picked up off the TV. He didn't know a North African accent, but the system got along fine with him. He had a funny 'Hello', which he kind of mooed while lowering his head: 'Hellooooo.' I started to imitate him and he laughed and said that at least he didn't keep a broken PalmPilot on his desk for a whole year. At lunch I asked him whether he wanted to let me buy him a falafel and a Coke. The falafel was OK, he said, but not as good as in his village.

'You ever tried the falafel in Tel Aviv?'

'I've never been to Tel Aviv . . .' he said, and we were interrupted by Bar's arrival. I introduced him to Fahmi and he inexplicably shot me a look as if he wanted to kill me. Maybe he was angry because I was lunching with an Arab. Or just annoyed that I'd forgotten him: it used to drive Talia Tenne nuts when people ordered food without telling her. But he took me aside and told me I was an idiot.

'Don't you get it? He's from Kafr Qasim!'

'Yes, so?'

'The Sarsurs are from Kafr Qasim.'

'So?'

Bar shook his head at me and then his anger dissolved into laughter. 'Oh, man. You're the true heir to Poirot, aren't you? Fucking . . . Hushash the fucking Detective is nothing next to the CrocDetective. It never crossed your mind to ask him about the Sarsur brothers?'

'Well, what could he find out?'

'I don't know, Hushash, but we need to try. Don't you think?'

Fahmi and I continued working through the afternoon. Once I'd filled out the test forms, we drank coffee and chatted for an hour in the dining area. His Hebrew wasn't bad and improved as he loosened up: I liked him. He told me about his grandfather, and how he used to ride a white horse through the hills of Samaria. So I told him about Duchi's grandfather, who was in the patrol that bumped into Izz ad-Din al-Qassam himself in 1935.

'You know who Izz ad-Din al-Qassam was, right?' I asked.

'Oh, yes.'

'God,' I said, 'it used to be like cowboys and Indians around here,' which made him laugh.

It was Sunday evening in a deserted Bar BaraBush: Fahmi, Bar and me at the bar. Fahmi was running his finger down an almost empty pint glass of beer and telling us more about his grandfather, also named Fahmi.

'You know where Beit Machsir is?' Neither of us did. 'These days the Jews call it Beit-Meir. Above Bab al-Wad,' he said.

'Yeah. We know all about Bab al-Wad,' I said.

'He was a teacher who got involved with operations against the British during the thirties. With the Jews he was actually OK, but he hated the British. Because the whole thing was their fault. He killed three British soldiers. But they caught him and put him in the prison in Acre.'

A couple of girls came in who were so good looking they stopped the conversation. One of them approached Noam behind the bar and asked for a couple of Orgasms. Three heads turned towards her: she was already waiting for us with a smile. Short brown bob, apple cheeks, sweet little pout, a total babe. Torture. She flicked her attention back to Noam, already busily fulfilling her needs, and Fahmi sighed and continued. 'They sentenced him to be hanged. He sat in the prison in Acre and waited for the end. He had to wear these red overalls you wore if you were to be hanged. One day they told him his last day had come. They led him from his cell to the gallows and asked him if he had a last wish. What do you think he asked for?'

'What was it?'

Fahmi pointed to his nearly empty glass.

'His last wish was a beer. The first time in his life. We Muslims aren't allowed alcohol, you know? So he says: one time, I will try it. They bring him a glass of beer, just like this, and he starts drinking.' Fahmi broke off and concentrated on his own beer. He seemed to be following a train of thought somewhere else. Bar and I drank quietly.

'Well?' said Noam, from behind the bar. 'What happened after the beer? Did they hang him?'

'No, they didn't,' Fahmi said, coming back to us. 'In the middle of his beer, a miracle happened. An Englishman rode up on a horse and told him he was free to go. They let him finish the beer, made him take off his red overalls and set him free.'

'You serious?' asked Bar.

'Totally serious.'

'Why?' I asked.

'He never knew till the day he died. No one explained, not then, not ever. He thought it was probably a mistake. They'd mixed him up with someone else. But he never knew who or why.'

Bar and I chuckled, and Noam too, his pointed sideburns seeming to smile more widely as he laughed.

'Maybe it was the beer,' I said.

'That's what he always said. So after that he drank beer all the time. Everyone in our family does. And he also stopped hating the British. He never got into any trouble again for the rest of his life.'

'Thanks to the beer, huh?'

'Thanks to the beer. If someone is angry, he needs beer. That way there are no problems. I'm going to take a piss.'

'Complete and total horseshit,' Bar said when he was gone.

'Well, maybe . . . he sounded kind of honest to me.'

'Yeah, well. I just hope he's not going to bullshit us about Tamer Sarsur.'

Tamer Sarsur. I'd almost forgotten why Fahmi was sitting with us in Bar BaraBush. It had been Bar's idea to invite him to Tel Aviv. Fahmi had been nervous initially, worrying about the Jews' attitude. I told him that he'd be with us, and that I'd take him back to Kafr Qasim afterwards, which seemed to do the trick. And after his first ever beer in Tel Aviv he relaxed and started telling his grandfather stories.

When Fahmi came back from the Gents, Bar started in on Sarsur. Did he know a Tamer Sarsur in his village?

'Sarsur? There are many Sarsurs in Kafr Qasim. It's a big family there. But I don't know a Tamer.'

'Or Amin?'

He frowned and thought. 'No, sorry. Why?'

'Tamer and Amin are brothers. They live in Tel Aviv, in Weizmann Street. Amin runs a fruit-and-veg place. Tamer's a nurse in Ichilov. The hospital. We need to find out about him.'

'Well, what do you want to know?'

There was a silence. Bar looked at me. I said, 'Come on, tell him. What harm can it do?' So he briefly detailed the story of Guetta and the attack, Shuli and the Palm

(Bar asked Fahmi whether he knew what a PalmPilot was, which made us laugh) and Warshawski and Tamer and Amin.

'We're trying to understand the connection between Tamer, Warshawski and Guetta. You could ask around in Kafr Qasim. Ask about Tamer. Maybe you'll find something, maybe you won't. That's all. I'm not saying you will. I'm just saying it's worth trying. You don't have to. Maybe the two of us could come over and sniff around one day.'

'Are you crazy?' That was me.

'But why are you doing this?' Fahmi asked bewilderedly.

'I promised Shuli I'd find out what Guetta was doing in Tel Aviv that day.'

Fahmi stared at me. 'But this Shuli is dead.'

'It happened after we got going. Her death wasn't in the plan. But we started this thing and we want to finish it.'

He drained the dregs of his beer. 'Don't go to Kafr Qasim. You won't get anything. You know Arabic?' We shook our heads. 'So what are you going to do, walk into the mosque and ask about Tamer Sarsur in Hebrew?'

There was nothing to say to that.

'OK. I will ask. I'll try. *Yalla,*' he said, getting up and pulling out the notes he'd earned that day in Time's Arrow, 'are you taking me home?'

'Put them away, I'm paying,' I said, and pulled out my wallet.

# 40

During the whole long day I spent with the Croc, I told myself time and time again: he's your target. Get close, but don't get attached. Create opportunities, not obstacles.

The work had been easy and the money was good, but he paid for me everywhere. He paid for lunch, for my hamburger in the evening, for my beer, like I was a refugee who needed feeding, like a charity case who has to say thank you very much for every shekel spent on him. I got annoyed and started telling them stories about Grandfather that I just pulled straight out of my arse.

Tel Aviv, I had to admit, was full of beautiful women. The bar, they said, was empty because it was Sunday. I ought to come again at the weekend and then I'd see. And I thought that the next time I'd be there the place would be full of pretty girls, and maybe I could send some of the beautiful women of Tel Aviv to hell along with the Croc.

But I didn't want to die. I wasn't a shahid. I didn't have that fearlessness, that certainty of will. And how would I do it, if not as a shahid? I'd killed the enemy before, but only from a distance: I'd made plans, made bombs, opened fire from the ridge above the road. I was a follower of instructions. I followed my brother, and my grandfather, and my conscience – I was not a man with a knife in a crowded bar. I tried to tell them that on the phone but they just thought I needed strengthening in my belief in the cause, and started lecturing me about Allah and the Holy Land. It didn't do any good. And that evening in Tel Aviv only worsened my fears: the security guards, the suspicion and the staring, the unbearable feeling of being totally alone, as if I were a dead man already, a spectre spurned by the living.

*'No, Dr Hartom. He just isn't responding any more. It's like he's sinking farther away from me. I give him his massages and I shine the torch in his eyes, and I talk to him, but there's no response. There's nothing, Dr Hartom!'*

*'All right, Svetlana.'*

*'There's no defecation, Doctor. Isn't there something . . .?'*

*'It isn't surprising. Not after this length of time. We did think it was going to go either way. Mmm. Pupils aren't . . . OK: we're going to . . .'*

The next day I started my search for Tamer Sarsur. I had nothing else to do.

Sa'id from the mosque told me that there were plenty of Sarsurs in the village, but most of them prayed in the other mosque. He didn't know any names. So I started asking people coming out of prayers at the other mosque. They were very hostile and impatient – this is the last thing I need, I thought, just as they're beginning to get used to me: someone reporting me to the Border Police. One of them directed me towards an old guy in a keffiyeh.

'Yes, I'm a Sarsur. But you won't find many of them in the mosque.' He laughed, showing tobacco-yellowed teeth. His voice had been dried to a whispering wheeze. 'Farther away from the mosque you look, the better your chances. Get as far from the mosque as you possibly can. Then start looking.'

I went home to call Croc and tell him I'd tried and got nowhere. But as I was hunting out the number he'd written down, I came across Ibrahim Hasuna's. I called him, and discovered that Zahara had already told him I was hanging out with the Jews. I put him straight on that. But he didn't know Tamer either. I tried Majed, my other friend from the packing-house. He *thought* he remembered Tamer. 'But I've not seen him in a long time.' A wild-goose chase. I wandered into the kitchen, where Wasime was having dinner with the boy, and quietly made myself a cup of tea.

'How are you doing?' she said. 'You seem to have been pretty busy lately.'

'Yes, thanks be to God.'

'Where's Daddy?' said Atta, staring at me with his big brown eyes. The lower half of his face was covered in egg crumbs and cottage cheese and Egozan.

'He'll be back soon. Oh, someone brought you a parcel today! Said he was your friend. Asked to put it in your room himself. Eat your bread, Atta.'

'What? Who?'

'Weren't you expecting something?'

I went to check and found a brown cardboard box by my bed. I opened it up cautiously. Scraps of cloth and screwed-up balls of paper with something solid at the centre. Very slowly I exposed it, something smooth and round as an apple and green as olive oil, with the letters 'IDF' stencilled on it. I stared at it in horror: *a hand grenade*. They were mad. Where did they get it from? Who brought it here, and how did he get into the village? Oh, God Almighty. How did you operate it? My phone went off and I almost had a heart attack. It was Halil's cousin.

'You got it?'

'Yes, right this moment. Are you crazy? How did you get it here? Who brought it?'

'That's not for you to worry about. You should be thinking about how you deploy it.'

This was a real problem. I didn't want to die. I didn't want to be a shahid. And I didn't want to spend the rest of my life in prison. But I was too afraid to say this on the phone. I said nothing.

'Is there a problem?'

'Yes, I'm . . .' I didn't know what to say at all.

'You don't want to do it, now? Do you realise how dangerous . . . I convinced people that you can, and want to, carry out this operation. I organised the—' At that moment there was a knock on the door and I covered the parcel with my sheet. It was Wasime.

'Fahmi? Is everything all right?'

'Yes, yes, yeah, it's fine, I'll come in a second,' I said. 'Just looking at my parcel!'

I got back on the phone in a whisper: 'Hello?'

There was a silence, which Halil's cousin finally broke. 'So what are you saying?'

'I don't know. Listen. I never said I wanted to carry out this operation. I mean, I do want to. I have an opportunity. But . . . I don't want to die, or to get caught.'

'So put your trust in Allah and he will guide you. Think of a way. Allah loves you. You will succeed.' She hung up, and I sat on the bed for a while before making my way back to the kitchen.

Atta was almost asleep. Wasime's face was a little flushed with embarrassment, I think, at disturbing me. 'It was OK, just a parcel from my brother.' She smiled and caressed her big belly. She was pretty, just like her name said she was, and I thought she was one of those women made prettier by pregnancy. 'Tell me, Wasime. Do you maybe know a guy from the village called Tamer Sarsur?'

'Sure, why?'

'Really?'

'Of course. He's the brother of one of my best friends. Works in a hospital in Tel Aviv. When their mother was very sick he hardly ever came to see her. Even at the end. He comes back to see his friends from time to time. Amin – that's his brother – used to visit their mother pretty much every weekend. Lovely guy. You know them?'

'Me? No. Someone from work in Rosh Haayin asked me something about him. I knew there were quite a few Sarsurs in the village, so . . .' I petered out and sipped my tea. It was cold.

'I can ask his sister for you,' Wasime said. 'I see her almost every day. We can get in touch through Amin. They live together. What does your friend want, exactly?' Atta was pulling at her hand and she took him to his room before I had to answer.

I'd almost lost hope of finding someone who knew Tamer Sarsur, but still, this wasn't any help. If I talked to Wasime's friend or Amin, I'd have to explain why, and I couldn't see that working. And then Wasime came back into the kitchen.

'You know what you should do?' she said. 'You know the Ramoon restaurant? On the main road? Go there. Tamer's friends are there most nights. The manager's a friend of his. Avi. It's the only place he goes when he comes here. Go talk to them.'

*'He's not responding. I want to do some neurological tests, talk to the intensivists, and then we'll make a decision. No visits for the moment.'*

*'But do you think . . .'*

*'I think I'm going to do a few tests, Svetlana.'*

*'Yes, Dr Hartom.'*

*'. . . Phew, what a bitch, did you hear her? Fahmi? Don't go, Fahmi. You hear me? Don't leave me now.'*

I went to the Ramoon – the Pomegranate – the next day. I ate slowly, enjoying the meal. I missed the food in Ramallah, but this was close: fresh salads, better steak than that bar in Tel Aviv had, and good coffee, which I eked out with tiny sips. I heard one of the waiters call the name Avi. It was late, I was the last customer and he was sitting with three other guys, talking and laughing, and getting louder as the evening went on. I finished a second coffee, still uncertain how I could bring Tamer Sarsur up. The waiter, in white shirt and black trousers, came over with that suspicious look the locals reserved for West Bankers. I could smell arrack on his breath. 'Everything OK, sir?' 'Yes, thanks very much. I'd like the bill now.' I gave him a big note and when he returned with the change, left an almost ridiculously large tip. I saw his eyes take it in and seized the moment.

'Tell me, do you know Tamer Sarsur?'

The waiter's head came up quickly.

'Tamer? Of course! What have you got to do with him? Hey,' he called over to his friends, 'this guy knows Tamer Sarsur! Thank you, sir,' he added, counting the notes.

'Who knows Tamer Sarsur?' thundered one of the voices, and the waiter gestured at me. It was Avi.

'Where do you know him from?'

'From Tel Aviv. I don't really . . .'

'Did he send you here?' asked someone else.

'Not really. It's just I met him a while ago in Tel Aviv . . . He told me about this restaurant so I thought I'd give it a try, that's all.' They didn't answer. They were all looking at me now. I didn't know where to take the conversation, exactly. 'You all know him?'

Avi laughed. 'Of course we know him. Since we were

this high. You see him at the hospital in his nurse's outfit?'

'Yeah,' I said. 'And very nice he looks in it too.' Everyone laughed.

'And you saw Amin's fruit-and-veg place?'

'Sure. Everyone gets them mixed up. At the hospital they ask for vegetables, and at the grocery they ask for a massage.' They laughed at this too and I was momentarily grateful to Croc for giving me the line. Avi sent the waiter over with the bottle of arrack and a glass. I could hear one of them say something like 'I wonder if the old dear can tell the difference?' Someone else said, 'Or maybe they're both doing her, and she doesn't know!' This caused a long outburst of laughter. I smiled, not quite getting it. It was the kind of laughter that feeds on itself, that goes on too long – the laughter of men in groups. Eventually Avi, with tears in his eyes, asked me whether I had seen the old lady.

'The old lady? No, I didn't see her. What old lady?'

'The old Jew Tamer is fucking. Didn't he tell you?'

The waiter said, 'He never stopped talking about her, till we told him to go to the old people's home and try it on there.'

A guy with shoulder-length hair and a moustache said: 'We told him, "Always check afterwards to see she's still alive."'

Once they'd finally calmed down, Avi explained. Tamer had said he was fucking a Jewish woman in Tel Aviv. He was very proud of it. Avi impersonated Tamer's boasting and the others pretended to be themselves being impressed. But then it turned out she was fifty-four to his twenty-five, and the restaurant had never let him live it down. He'd never mentioned her again. I laughed along with them. It was the laughter of arrack, of the brotherhood of men, of the end of the day, and it was also, for me, the laughter of relief and release, of knowing my future. Because there was one little detail in what they'd said that I realised was the thing the Croc and his bald friend were looking for; the thing that gave me a reason to meet them again in Bar BaraBush.

# 41

'Nailed it!' said Bar.

Whether he'd suddenly figured something out, or heard something I hadn't caught, was difficult to tell. Two days earlier Fahmi had called to say that he'd got something for us. He wanted to meet in Bar BaraBush, where you could watch beautiful women ordering up Orgasms. I told him Thursday was the best night and picked him up at the entrance to his village. But they were having a South American night and the noise was unbelievable. The place was packed and the acoustics were terrible. A killer combination. You had to stick your ear into someone's mouth in order to hear anything, and Bar was closer to Fahmi, who talked so very gently, with such a soft accent. He'd found out that Tamer was fucking some woman here in Tel Aviv. 'Fifty-four years old!' he'd said, and laughed, and Bar and I raised our eyebrows. And then he must have said something I hadn't caught, because Bar spread his hands wide and said, 'Nailed it!'

I'd been in such a fug, so preoccupied with Guetta, so out of it, that I hadn't noticed what was going on in Time's Arrow. That Thursday morning I finished the Belgian project and passed everything on to Guy. We went over it together and I asked him what was up next.

'Next? I don't know,' Guy said. 'There aren't that many projects on at the moment.'

'Really?'

'Is this news to you?'

It was news to me. At lunch I ordered Thai (TukTuk) and ate with Talia Tenne, who had dyed her hair as red as her finger- and toenails.

'Well! To what do I owe this honour?' she said.

'Today you're going to explain to me what is going on in this company.'

'Happy to,' she said, but there wasn't that much to tell. They just weren't selling the system any more. The Indians were killing the market. The downsizing and the move to Rosh Haayin had stabilised things for a few months, but the investors were feeling the pressure again.

'Jimmy's really stressed recently,' said Talia. 'He screamed at Yoni Bronco yesterday because Yoni might have lost us the Scandinavian thing. And the Belgians aren't happy any more. They might even ditch the system. It's going round that they got an offer from another Israeli company. Check your emails, Croc – there's a company meeting this afternoon.' In the striplights of the dining nook I could see the first wrinkles in Talia Tenne's palely freckled white skin. 'It's not like the good old days, Croc. Haven't you noticed?'

But I hadn't. I hadn't been aware of the shouting or the failures or Jimmy's moods. I didn't even have the faintest clue who the hell Yoni Bronco was. All I'd actually noticed was that the Thai food wasn't bad at all.

At the company meeting I saw a Jimmy stripped of his old enthusiasm, his customary sharpness. He talked about the usual things, but he didn't seem to believe in what he was saying. The great Rafraf – the brains behind the air force's Time Management Unit, Time's Arrow's King of Time, Mr Every Second Counts – looked like a man who'd been stopped dead in his tracks.

'Do you know the Hofstadter law?' he asked us, but there was no answer, because nobody did. 'The Hofstadter law says: everything takes longer than you expect it to take, even if you take into account the Hofstadter law!' He looked around the room. No one's expression changed. 'And what does that mean? It means things take longer than we planned. It means we need patience. And that includes somebody like me, who memorises the Hofstadter law every morning while doing my press-ups and simultaneously watching the morning news on Channel Two – even I lose my patience!' Jimmy's voice climbed alarmingly in volume and assertiveness, as if someone had accidentally turned his amp up to the max.

'Look,' he resumed in a calmer voice. 'No one has any time any more. Sixty per cent of Europeans said in a recent poll that they didn't have enough time. And the Venture Capital Fund investing in us – Venture Capital Fund, ridiculously long name, by the way, must take at least a second and a half to say it, way too much – they don't have enough time either. They're losing patience. They gave us money for twelve months and after twelve months they want to see results. They want to see what I promised them – the twenty-first-century Fed-Ex.'

Jimmy sipped from a glass of water. Talia Tenne's eyes asked *See what I meant?* and my eyes replied *Yes, I do*.

'Why are we forever running from one place to another? Because we exist in a state of terror: the terror of time, the terror of time ending, the terror of death. Because we're afraid of time, we look for solace in the patterns we create in it, in the circle of an hour, in days, in the illusory beginnings and endings of events without any. We try to escape it – in sleep, in dreams, in drink, in meditation, in mystical beliefs – or we work like crazy to try and create the illusion that we are in fact in control of it.'

I can't remember everything he said. Only fragments of ideas and occasional sentences. He talked about Chronos, the Greek god of time. About Native American tribes that don't have words for 'late' or 'wait' or even 'time'; about time's arrow, a river flowing in one direction only, from past to future, a series of events that cannot be reconstructed; about Stephen Hawking and the ten dimensions. We sat there in a state of shock. We were asking ourselves: what does he want, this man? What is he going through?

After the meeting we crowded into the kitchenette to drink coffee.

'To think we used to swallow all his bullshit about time,' Bar said. 'We actually used to get *motivated* by some of that crap!'

I didn't say anything. But I wanted to say: don't you see that it's not Jimmy who's changed, it's us? It's *us*. *We've* changed.

At the end of the day I called Fahmi and picked him up on the way to Tel Aviv. He had one of those little leather pouches on a belt that backpackers like to strap round their waists, which he dangled over his thigh. We didn't talk much on the way: he seemed a little stressed. It was nothing, he said. He just wanted to get to the bar.

The place was heaving, but I managed to find us some seats at the corner of the bar. Fahmi was happy with the spot. Bar arrived and started telling us about the Maccabi game and explaining the finer points of basketball to Fahmi and then Dafdaf called and wouldn't get off the phone. She'd had a major row with her husband and wanted to know what I would do – as if I had a clue!

Me, who hadn't managed to get married; who hadn't even managed to not get married. It felt as if she was trying to tell me something but I wasn't sure what it was exactly, and they turned up the volume of the salsa music so I had to hang up. It was nearing midnight by the time we finally broached the subject of Tamer Sarsur, and Bar spread his hands and shouted out. I leaned over and yelled in his ear.

'What do you mean, "Nailed it"?'

'What?'

'You said, "Nailed it"!'

'Didn't you hear what he said?'

I shook my head. 'Let's get out of here! I can't stand this! Can't hear!'

'What?' shouted Bar.

I pointed outside. 'Out of here!'

Fahmi looked taken aback. 'Out? Why?'

I put my mouth to his ear. 'I can't hear anything! Let's get out of here!'

'No! Stay longer! I want to look at the girls!'

'Come back later! Talk outside! Then come back!'

I struggled through the crush towards the exit. At the doorway I turned around and saw Fahmi reluctantly trailing after Bar, his pouch slung over his shoulder, as if he were a child dragging its heels. I walked out: it was like getting out of a vacuum cleaner. It felt like the first air I'd breathed in two hours.

'Goddam, that was noisy!'

We decided to walk down to the beach in front of the Hilton, where we found three sunloungers. We lay on them and listened to the sound of the waves whispering. There was no one else around on the beach; from time to time a pleasant shiver ran through me to remind me that summer was finally loosening its grip. I eased my lounger back, as if I were moon-bathing, and lit a cigarette.

'All right,' I said, 'can someone tell me what is going on?'

'It's very simple,' said Bar. 'Tamer fucked the professor's wife.'

'What? How do you know?'

'It's what Tamer's friends told Fahmi. That he was fucking "some doctor's wife" in Tel Aviv.'

'But he's a hundred years old. You saw how old he is. She's . . . what?'

'Fifty-four, according to them,' said Fahmi.

'So Tamer was screwing Warshawski's wife. What's the link to Guetta? How exactly does this mean "nailed it"?'

'You'll have to ask Warshawski,' Bar said.

'Me? Why me?'

'Who else? This is all to do with you, Croc. Not me.'

'You don't have to ask him at all. It's obvious.' This was Fahmi. He was lying on the middle lounger, and both of us turned our heads towards him. 'Warshawski paid Guetta to kill Tamer.'

'What?'

'You said there was money involved. You said there was a secret meeting. You said nobody was talking. I'll bet you that's what it is.'

'But Guetta was just a kid, just out of the army.'

'Exactly.'

'Well, where did he meet Guetta? How did he come across him?'

'How do I know?'

We didn't say anything for a couple of minutes. Eventually I said, 'I don't think so, Fahmi. Things don't work like that in this country. To murder a cheating wife – it doesn't make sense. We're not some . . . not some African . . .'

'Don't forget, he's only an Arab.'

'So what?'

'An Arab's life isn't worth anything. The doctor would have killed plenty of Arabs in 1948, so what would one more be to him? Not a problem. He was fucking his Jewish wife. A good enough reason to kill an Arab.'

We fell silent again. Now I didn't know what to say. Fahmi was fiddling in his leather pouch again: he'd been doing it all night.

'What you got in there, Fahmi?'

He pulled his hand back out. 'Nothing. It's, uh . . .'

'You want to know what I'm thinking?' Bar said. Even at midnight under a nearly full moon, he was still wearing his shabby baseball cap. Now he shifted it slightly to one side. I waited, staring up at the stars, listening to the unhurried waves.

'I'm thinking that what Fahmi said sounds pretty reasonable.'

I stared at the stars some more, absorbing this.

'So what does that mean? What should we do?'

'Not "we", Croc. This is all about you. I'm done now. If you ask me, you should go to Ichilov and have a little chat with the professor.'

'And then what?'

'And then you'll see.'

We stayed on the beach a while longer, saying little. I was thinking about Jimmy, trying to remember exactly what he'd said in his surreal speech and feeling a little sorry for him, when Fahmi broke into my daydreams. Didn't we want to get back to the bar? I said I didn't feel like it: the noise there was killing me. Bar didn't fancy it either, so I asked Fahmi if he wanted a lift home.

He was silent all the way to Kafr Qasim. I had thought that over the course of the day we'd spent together we'd become, if not close, then kind of friends. Yet there were no signs of it that evening. It was as if he'd come because he was obliged to, as if it were a continuation of the work he'd done for Time's Arrow. But it wasn't work: we hadn't paid for the information he'd dug up, and he hadn't asked for payment. I mean, until that evening, the whole Guetta thing had seemed like something between friends. I couldn't understand what had happened. It was difficult to understand why he'd bothered coming to Tel Aviv at all, if he was going to be so withdrawn and distant, if he wasn't, in fact, our friend. Whatever, I thought: I'm not going to bring it up. We rolled in silence up to the entrance to Kafr Qasim and I slowed to a halt to let him out, and Fahmi dug his hand once again into his little leather pouch – and that's the last thing I remember.

# 42

*'Hello, sweetheart. Let's see how you're doing . . . oh, hardly anything. Less work for me! But not so good for your body,* lyubimyi moi.

*'Your big day today. The medical committee, Fahmi. Everyone's going to be here this morning. Your sister, your sweet girlfriend with the perfume, your father. Good luck, sweetheart.*

'Ya polyubila tebya s'pervogo zglyada, *Fahmi. At first sight, Fahmi.*

*'The committee are talking to the intensivists and the neurologists. Then Dr Hartom will present her conclusions to the supervising consultant.'*

I don't know exactly what that means.

*'Fahmi, can you hear me? You have to wake up now. Be a good boy. Wake up. Fahmi.* Ya lyubya tibya, *Fahmi.'*

The Al-Aqsa mosque is calling me. Rise up for your nation against those who exploit us. For you, my steadfast nation, together we will fight. Call with all your strength: *Allah Akbar, Allah Akbar!* We will revenge every drop of blood, every tear shed by a mother for the children taken from her. And for every shahid that dies another will rise. Soon you will attain eternal happiness with the prophets. With all your heart yearn to see the face of death. Strike like champions. At last the time has come . . .

*'Please carry on, Dr Hartom.'*

*'Thank you, Dr Baram. Well, the patient was injured in a car. Its door was open and he was probably getting out. But he was still at least mostly inside. The exact location of the explosion has a very precise impact on the type of injuries we get in this context. A closed car is a particularly lethal space.'*

*'Yes, of course, the collapse inwards occasioned by the vacuum. The implosion in addition to the explosion. It's a wonder he's still alive at all. Amazing that no limbs were amputated.'*

*'Exactly. That's why I mention the opened door. Almost certainly he was hesitating, and threw the grenade away from the car at the last moment before detonation. Forensic evidence located the exact point of the explosion two metres away from the vehicle. There was another passenger, but he doesn't remember the . . .'*

*'Hold on, don't tell me this is the case of that what's-his-name, the Croc . . .?'*

*'Exactly. This is the case.'*

*'Extraordinary. So, what have we here?'*

*'A small fragment of shrapnel in the frontal lobe. You can see the point of entry here.'*

*'Mmm. I wouldn't have even noticed if you hadn't pointed it out.'*

*'It supports the theory that he might have regretted his actions. Apart from the trauma to the forehead, his injuries were light. Minor shrapnel wounds here, here, here and here. The other passenger suffered only shock and a few minor flesh wounds from the shrapnel.'*

*'And cerebral function, Doctor?'*

*'I might have determined brain death at any point over the last few weeks, but he responded to touch, music, smells, voices of relatives.'*

*'Mmm . . . What kind of responses?'*

*'Perspiration. Dilation of the pupils. Sexual arousal. Facial expressions and certain sounds . . .'*

I had so many chances – in the bar, on the beach, during the drive. Perhaps I drank too much. Or perhaps it was too little. I was trying to drink enough not to be afraid. But I ruined everything. I couldn't do it. He was silent the whole way and then we reached the entrance to the village and . . . what happened?

*'Mmm . . . very interesting. And you're saying that in the last forty-eight hours there has been a regression?'*

We sat near the sea, me and the Croc and the Croc's bald friend. The sky was full of stars: half as bright as daylight. Now the skies are grey and the rain is wild. The muezzins are calling me to the mosque but I am not worthy to go. I played with the ring of the apple. The beer played its music in my head. Why don't they play Amr Diab any more? Where is Lulu? Where is Rana? Not a good Muslim woman. But such a sweet Muslim woman. Leave me, brother, leave me, Father, leave me. I'm going now . . .

The Croc stopped at the entrance to the village. I toyed with the ring. I opened the door. This was the moment. There was no heroic option. Either way.

Now are you satisfied, Bilahl?

Lulu? Is that you? Where are you, Lulu?

*'I'm fourteen today, Fahmi. Wish me a happy birthday. And say goodbye now. They told us to say goodbye. If you can hear me . . .'*

Our secret place, overlooking the Jordan Valley. The winter will come and rain will fall, but it won't bother us. The air will still be the same air of my childhood. There will be no army. There'll be no dirt ramp. Life will be normal, Lulu. You will grow up and go to university. Father will be proud of you. Bilahl will be released. I will forget Kafr Qasim. I will forget the Croc and Tel Aviv. I will try to forget the soldiers in sunglasses with their hands in their pockets watching me strip and then stuffing my socks into the crack between the ceiling and the wall, to block the leak there, saying, 'Look! Now you've actually done something for your people. Now the rain won't leak on to those who come after you.'

I can smell you, Lulu. I can . . . oh! I can feel your tears on my face, Lulu.

Before I left home, I looked at the grenade for a long time, maybe half an hour. I looked at it and thought: our land, our people, the *shuhada*, the pictures in Al-Manar, the mosque. I closed my eyes. I opened them and it was still there. I picked up the smooth green apple and laid it in a pouch I found in the closet in my room. I called Rana. The phone rang three times. She answered. I didn't speak. She asked who was there, twice. I said 'I love you', silently, in my heart, and hung up and walked to the village entrance, my throat dry as sand. That was where he picked me up. That was where we returned after midnight.

*'Svetlana, could you hurry, please? Tell Mr Sabich that it's time to . . . are you all right? Svetlana? Come on. Be professional, please.'*

*'I'm fine, Dr Hartom. I apologise. I'll be fine. Mr Sabich, if you could please . . . Yes, I know, I understand. Oh, my God. You're going to be with God now, Fahmi . . .'*

So what is going through your head when you are sitting in a green Polo on a clear night, a hand grenade inside an imitation leather pouch on your lap? Your finger in its ring, like the wedding ring you never had, like the wedding ring he never had, bringing you together in holy matrimony, you and the grenade – the pomegranate, the apple of knowledge. What is going through your head? Beer is bubbling through it, and all the pretty girls of Tel Aviv are dancing through it demanding orgasms, the waves are whispering through it, and all the people who told you what to do, where to go, what to believe in, who to hate, who to be. Grandfather Fahmi, who taught you what a hero was and wanted you to be fierce, and Mother, who taught you that sometimes there is no reason for things, and Bilahl, who taught you hatred, and wanted you to believe, and Rana, who taught you tenderness and how to be vulnerable, and Father, who taught you patience and wanted you in Bir Zeit, and Lulu, who taught you happiness, and only wanted to be near you . . . What would be left of you after you took away what everyone told you you were? Who were you, eventually, when you were only you, when the donkey carried you back into yourself? And who were you *not*, eventually, because your past was stronger than you were and came to you, demanding to be paid? And who do you want to be now, with the ring around your finger and the Croc by your side in his little green car? Do you even care? Is it important for you? You wanted your life to have a purpose. But will it matter at all, to anyone or anything, if you take your finger out of the ring, open the door and climb out of the car and go back to Wasime's house, and in the morning set off back home to the camp or to Murair to find work, to eat, to sleep, wait, grow older, marry, live quietly? Though you'll have to spend days and nights in front of the TV with your ears filled with the sound of destruction, your eyes with the disgrace of blood, your nose with the smell of decay, your tongue with the taste of fire? Does it matter if you build a bomb? Rot in the ground? Start university? Go to Australia? Hold the grenade to your chest or throw it away? Does it matter?

I'm running out of the village now and Dayek is there and time is passing at the pace of generations. Lulu, my love, Rana, my love. Time is passing in milliseconds. I am floating in the sea, and the beach – the beach is gone.

# 43

Warshawski looked even older than he had the first time I saw him. This time it was only him and me, in a small café in a side street. 'Not in the hospital,' he'd insisted. Under his sparse white hair his scalp was pinkly visible. His beard was well trimmed but his eyes were full of defeat and – it took me a few minutes to comprehend this – full of fear. Professor Binyamin-Moshe Warshawski feared me. On the phone I'd told him that I knew all about Tamer and his wife and about Guetta and the money.

'Do you want money?' he'd asked.

'I want to meet, and to hear the whole story.'

'And after you hear the whole story?'

'Then I'll decide what to do.'

I ordered hot chocolate, he ordered tea. Outside the café window it was clear but cool. My hearing was almost back to normal. After several weeks of constant pain, the discomfort from the wounds to my calf, my thigh and my lower arm was beginning to subside. I spent a couple of weeks with Mother and Father, and when I came back to Tel Aviv, Dafdaf came and stayed in the flat along with my brother, who flew over from Maryland to be with me. Between them they dealt with every phone call or text or email from *Noah's Ark* and *Left and Right* and all the rest of them. They said no to everything for me. Including Duchi.

'Are you going to go to the police?'

I gave Warshawski my coldest stare. You could see the fear crawling all over him.

'I don't know. I want to hear the whole story.'

'Who are you? Who are you acting for?'

If I wanted to know anything, I had to maintain his fear. I couldn't say who I really was: it was the card I had to keep hidden.

'We are whoever we are, and we work for whoever we work for. I can't tell you who it is but let me give you some friendly advice: don't mess with us. It won't be worth your while.'

He asked for a cigarette. I raised my eyebrows in surprise but lit up for both of us. His hands were trembling. 'I'm not supposed to smoke,' he said. I waited.

'I discovered my wife was having an affair. There were signs. Her skin had a glow to it. Dvora always said I had the eyesight of a hawk. I also have an extremely good memory.' He exhaled smoke, with eyes lowered, the cigarette vibrating in his jolting fingers. 'What's the point?' he said. 'What is the point of this? You won't understand.'

'So you realised your wife was having an affair.'

'It was just . . . forget it, young man. My marriage was over before that. It was just the last straw. It hurt. This country . . .' There was something very unsettling about Warshawski. I was beginning to wonder if it hadn't been a mistake to come here without Bar. I felt out of my depth.

'Tell me what happened with Dvora,' I said.

'One day I came home in the middle of the day. I never do, though I live near the hospital. It was a time when I was . . . I was tired. As I was arriving at our building,

I saw him leaving. Dvora was at home. She was wearing a robe. She works at the shop at the Tel Aviv Museum. She doesn't come back home just like that in the middle of a working day and put on a robe. She said she didn't feel well, but I'm not a fool.' Warshawski rubbed his eyes under his glasses. 'I didn't say anything. I turned around and walked out on her there and then. I saw him four or five days later in a hospital corridor. He was wearing a nurse's uniform. I didn't recognise him at first, but my memory got there in the end. The label on his chest said "Tomer". All I could find out from the hospital was he was called Tomer and worked part time in physiotherapy. But something was niggling me. He was familiar from somewhere.' Warshawski looked at me, enjoying his own sleuthing. 'His brother's greengrocer's. America Fruit and Veg.'

'What did Dvora tell you?'

'Listen, you won't understand. I told you, young man. You don't want to hear the story of my life. It would take me a week. It would . . .' He was groping for words. 'Our marriage was already finished. It had happened before. If I hadn't bumped into him in the hospital corridor, I wouldn't even have . . .'

'OK. I understand,' I said, though I didn't entirely. 'Let's not get into it. Go on.'

'So I went to the greengrocer's and it all fell into place. I told Amin there was a nurse in the hospital who looked a lot like him. He says it's his brother. "Tamer." "Tamer? Not Tomer?" "He calls himself Tomer in the hospital so there won't be any problems, you understand?" I did. I got out of there and walked a few steps down the street before I flopped down on a bench. I wanted to throw up. I was ashamed. I was, I was . . .' Warshawski raised his head and looked at me but I merely stared back at him. 'This country . . . Listen, I don't know your opinions. In the hospital I don't dare say anything. There is a witch-hunt against anyone who dares to say that this country is falling into the abyss. That we need a strong leader, someone who knows how to get things done. Have you ever read *Grey Wolf*, the biography of Kemal Atatürk?' I shook my head. 'Do you know who he is?'

'The, uh, the Turk.'

'Read it, young man. The subtitle is "An Intimate Study of a Dictator". I'll tell you something else.' He leaned forward and lowered his voice. 'Read *Mein Kampf*. If you want, I have recordings of Hitler's speeches I can lend you.' I looked around me uncomfortably, but the café was almost empty. 'I don't need anyone to tell me about Hitler, but only a blind man could fail to see that what's going on here is another Weimar. The humiliation, the shame, the betrayal of the people by weak governments, the left-wing control of the media, people escaping into sex, hedonism, anything, the *fear* . . .' He fished another cigarette out of my pack.

'Are you sure those cigarettes are good for you?'

He laughed. 'I'm sure they're not. Cheeky boy.'

I didn't want to hear any of this. The fear seemed to be transferring itself from him to me. I could see it leaving his body, could feel it settling in mine.

'I thought about going to Amin's store at night and burning it down. I thought about the ways I could hurt Tamer himself. Poisonous rats were scurrying round my head, gnawing at me, making their plans. Don't get me wrong. I have no problem with them. I have no problem with them selling me fruit and vegetables, as Amin does. But I remember one attack, in Jerusalem. I sat in front of the TV and I wanted someone to . . . You sit in front of the TV and you can't understand this impotence. Screw what the world thinks. Screw everything. The Arabs are making fools of us. We must teach them a lesson.'

Warshawski was finding his voice. He wasn't hesitant any more – his confession had begun to evolve into a speech.

He had still been a baby when his family emigrated from Poland to Israel at the end of the Second World War. He didn't remember Europe but he remembered his childhood in Israel very clearly: Independence Day celebrations, the constant Arab attacks on Hadera. His father and mother were both in the Jewish underground, the IZL, during its heyday. In the quieter early sixties he was a radio operator in the army, serving at Zrifin Base. To see the first settlers celebrating Passover night in Hebron and then, months later, in the second settlement at Sebsastia had made him burst with pride. The nuclear medicine came naturally: a mother who wanted her son to be a doctor, a son too obedient or meek to oppose her. The degree, the apprenticeship, the wife, the kids. 'Kids?' I said. He nodded, and didn't elaborate. He was a riddle. He had a straightforward, regular, respectable side, but he was detached from it. His real self seemed to be with *Mein Kampf* and the teaching of lessons to others.

He ordered another cup of tea from the waitress, and took another cigarette without asking. His fingers were still shaking – not fear, but an old man's palsy. I reminded myself of the email Bar had sent me that morning: 'Binyamin-Moshe Warshawski = the Arab did her'. It didn't seem funny any more.

'And Giora Guetta?'

'I met him in Jerusalem. I went to teach a course in Hadassah. They'd installed a new system, a wonderful machine. Our department in Ichilov had already been using the same system for a year – we were the first to get it. So I was the leading expert in the country. It's a Positron Emission Tomography system – it combines positron tomography with a particle accelerator. We were one of the first in the world to use it. A unique system, very complex – it gives a complete map of the body, its pathologies, its . . . never mind.' He laughed, seeing the look on my face. 'I had to travel to Jerusalem for three days, and I preferred to stay in the King David. Better than driving back and forth every day in that traffic. Guetta worked there as a security guard. I didn't notice him the first day: you never notice the faces of security guards. But on my second morning, we got talking in the lobby. He was getting something from the drinks machine and he'd come up a shekel short, so I gave him one. It was a particularly warm day, at the end of the summer. Nearly a year ago, now. Guetta said, "I owe you one" and I waved my hand and said, "Come on, you don't owe me a thing. Drink. Enjoy." And then that evening I was thinking about it. Jerusalem always depresses me. And I'd been thinking about Dvora and this kid . . .' He was remembering it. 'When I came back from Hadassah the next day, I asked him if he'd like to join me for coffee in the lobby after his shift. He gave me a look. I had to tell him I wasn't like that. "But," I said, "I might have a job offer for you."'

Warshawski took off his glasses and cleaned them with his shirt cuffs, coughing. I took a sip from my second hot chocolate. I felt pressure in my chest. I saw Guetta, beside me on the Little No. 5, showing me his Palm. I remembered Shuli's hands clasped around her cup in the café near Montefiore's wagon.

'Are you all right, young man?' said Warshawski. I ordered a glass of water while he waited for me.

'Giora Guetta. He told me he had just left the army. The security-guard job was one of those Defence Ministry "preferred jobs", where they give you a grant for six months. He was thinking what to do next, after he got the grant. He wanted to open a business, or be a computer programmer. I was interested in what he did in the army.

Border Police. In Gaza. It sounded interesting. And then he told me they called him "The Killer". That he'd engraved three Xs on his rifle barrel. He spent two years in Gaza. He saw a lot of disgusting stuff. He said, "If all those lefties could spend just one week in Gaza they'd change their minds by the third day." It wasn't only that the opportunity arose. It was more than that. I hadn't come to Jerusalem and met this great kid by chance. You understand?' I nodded weakly. 'I said I had an offer for him that he would like a lot. A lot of money, but it would have to be a secret. We would meet to arrange it in Tel Aviv. "Don't worry," I said, "it's not anything you haven't done before." Ha ha ha, et cetera. "But in return for your secrecy, and in return for this conversation, I am writing you a cheque for a thousand shekels. It doesn't matter if you take the job or not. You can disappear if you want to. But you should know: there's a lot more money." Then I took his phone number and his email.'

I told Warshawski not to leave and went to the toilet. I stood and watched my stream flow down the smooth white wall and I thought about myself, how I was in a café on a weekday morning with a Hitler-reading Polish Jew who had hired a young guy to murder his wife's lover, and I was here because the young guy's girlfriend, with whom I'd fallen in love – a love that had somehow led to her death – had asked me to find out what her boyfriend was doing on the morning of his death by suicide bomber on the minibus on which I'd happened to be travelling. Adultery, murder, terrorist attacks: nothing surprising about it. It happened all the time. The surprising thing, I saw, was me. It was so strange that there should be somebody who linked these people. Even stranger that it should be me: that it was me at this moment in this café toilet.

'We met,' Warshawski continued with a certain relish

when I returned, 'in Tel Aviv at the Coffee Bean in Yehuda Maccabi Street – as you know very well, young man. I told him everything he needed to know about Tamer and offered him thirty thousand shekels, with ten thousand as down payment. He didn't even ask for time to think. It was like that. I gave him Tamer's details and he entered them into his little electronic notebook. We agreed on the time. We shook hands. I was scared. But Guetta was perfect. You know? Young but experienced. Enthusiastic but reliable. Not involved in the criminal world. He didn't look like a killer should. He was really up for it. He had already killed and thirty thousand shekels was a fortune for him. He said there was no problem getting hold of a gun. An impressive kid. Confident. Handsome. Knew what he wanted. A real Jew.'

Now that I knew what Guetta had been doing, what did I feel? Nothing. I looked at the Polish professor, and felt nothing at all. How much time had Bar and I spent on this 'investigation'? And now it was solved and so what? I asked for the bill and insisted on paying. They brought our coats and we went out into the chill. 'In fact, I'd changed my mind even before I heard that Guetta had been killed,' Warshawski insisted to me as we walked down the boulevard. 'I tried to call him but the line was dead. I left a message. I wrote him an email. When I read in the newspaper that the Arabs had killed him, I felt responsible. I was ashamed. But my first thought was that I'd made a terrible mistake. Like in Jerusalem, when I thought I had to do it. Sometimes life gives you these clues. You think you see a pattern, you understand? Afterwards I thought about him. Another young life lost, because of this damned country. This defeatist country.'

I was thinking about what I was going to do now. Where did I take this from here? Warshawski was on automatic, letting everything out, and I didn't stop him.

'Dvora and I are still together, somehow. She confessed to it one evening. I pretended that I didn't know. I'd already forgiven her in my heart. She hurt me. I hated her, but I'd had my revenge – without her knowing.' It was as if a weight had been lifted from his heart. He couldn't stop talking. 'I didn't tell her anything. A day or two after the bombing I got a phone call from Guetta's girlfriend; wanting to know what he had been doing in Tel Aviv. I turned the phone off and put it out with the garbage. The next day I changed my number.'

'Listen,' I said, almost apologetically. 'I've got to make a move.'

'What are you going to do?'

'I don't know,' I said. I turned and walked away down King David Boulevard. I walked all the way home. A weekday afternoon. Guy had said he would call me if he needed help at Time's Arrow. I didn't get a call. I went into the bedroom at home and fetched my cheque out of the drawer: the way things were going I might have to cash it. I sat on the sofa and didn't know what to do. I didn't have the energy to do anything about Warshawski. I thought about telling Almaz everything, but gave up on the idea. What was the difference? Guetta was dead. The phone rang, but I didn't answer. What good would it do anyone if Warshawski lost his job or went to jail now? I honestly didn't care any longer. I had done my bit. I looked around at the vacant white walls. I breathed deeply; closed my eyes. Unconsciously, I ran my finger over the scar on my forehead. I thought about Shuli. The moment we switched places and we touched, how she wanted to look out on to the street, her smile. Then I was thinking about Duchi and a dull general pain set in. The phone rang again and I answered it. It was my brother.

We picked Dafdaf up from work in his hire car and sped up to Jerusalem.

We met Mother at the entrance.

The doctors said it was a relatively minor heart attack.

Father lay in pyjamas on his hospital bed. He was pale, and there was a breathing tube in his nose. He looked at me. I held his cold hand and burst out crying. I couldn't stop. I had to go out into the corridor. In the corridor I saw a nurse sitting on a bench crying too. A Russian girl. She looked up at me as if to ask me to stop, or as if to offer me consolation, or ask it for herself, but I couldn't stop. We couldn't stop crying.

Special thanks to the Ucross Foundation, Wyoming, USA